Last
Lap

DR. C. THOMAS SOMMA

TRINITY PRESS

Last Lap
A blind runner's choice for oblivion

Outskirts Press, Inc.
http://www.outskirtspress.com

ISBN: 979-8-218-97414-5

TRINITY PRESS

PRINTED IN THE UNITED STATES OF AMERICA

Table of Contents

LAST LAP PROLOGUE

Danny was born a loser. At birth born with club feet, and confined to wear thick boots to turn his feet inward, gave him the gait of a ruptured duck. His awkward waddling invited the scorn of both genders of his classmates and isolated him from everyone except the all too eager bullies.

While these traumas at school were bad enough, he was often bullied on the walk home by his classmates. One day they picked him up and threw him head first into a barrel of raw meat outside a butcher shop. This was so reminiscent of a trip his aunt told him he to visit animals, which he thought was at the zoo, but was instead at a Butcher shop. It was such a traumatic experience that I wrote this about it.

THE BUTCHER SHOP

It was on the day the black snow fell that Danny was to learn that things had to die. He sat with his legs swinging off the side of the metal bed thumbing through a tattered book of farm animals given in a time of tinsel and colored lights. As he turned each page tracing each word with his index finger, he mouthed carefully the names as he had been taught. "Bun-ney, Raa-bitt,", then turning the page again, "chick...", forgetting the rest, he remembered the other name. "Hen", he said confidently. He was practicing because this was the day his aunt Maria said she would take him to see real animals, not just those in picture books.

"Danny," his mother called from downstairs, "aren't you ready yet? Your Aunt will be here any minute. And when you get back, it's back to your room for you, understand? I'll teach you to never play near that shed again. You hear me?"

Danny didn't respond, but walked to his third story bedroom window. Wiping the mist from the inside with his tiny palm, he looked out through the grey streaked glass speckled with melting flakes. He saw the water collect, run and drip from the clothes-lines that connected the long line of three story brownstones that lined his block, with the large textile factory in back. Snow from an earlier time sponged the soot from the discharge of its galvanized chimneys.

He looked toward the garbage shanty, the reason he was confined to his room. It was there he had found real animals to play with. He would lay pieces of bread crust near the sewer opening and then watch for the bad things, as his mother called them, to appear. Though he couldn't find them in his picture book, they looked a little like the rabbits, so he called them the big bunnies. His mother always said that, "Danny, if they bite you, you will die." They wouldn't bite him; he was their friend. "Oh sure, well your Uncle Salvator got bit by one and he died. You want to end up like him?"

"What is die," he thought, what is die?" He remembered the last time he saw Uncle Sal was when he had his face and lips painted all funny red and was sleeping in a box in the room where the big people cried. They made him kiss him good-bye, and that was the only time he didn't want to.

"Danny, you hurry up and get down here right now." It was Aunt Maria; his favorite aunt. "We've got to hurry before the weather gets worse, so hurry or I'm leaving without you.", she called. He sprang from the cot, grabbed his hand-me down coat, and at the bedroom door dipped his two fingers into the holy water urn, hung beneath the icon of the crucified Christ looking imploringly upward through glazed ceramic eyes. Danny made the sign of the cross, as he did each time he left his room, sure that only good things would happen to him when he did. He ran past the room which was always kept locked, then nearly tripped down the stairs in the oversized hand me down coat.

His Aunt Maria always reminded him of the clowns on cereal boxes. She was pear shaped like the Little Abner Schmoos in his toy box, and always painted like the last time he saw Uncle Sal. He usually first noticed her ankles which were twice as large as her arms, and draped with stockings that only went halfway up her leg. He loved and trusted her and spent more time with her than even with his own mother who worked evening shifts at the factory in back. Weekly, he would go with her to Lombardi's where any confection was his for just the price of a wishful glance. He stood on his toes to receive the perfunctory peck on the forehead from his mother and the admonition to be good then walked with his aunt out into the dead grey day. Armed with shopping bags and a purse, she pulled him by his hand up the steps of the bus. She allowed him to drop the coins into the still, much to the annoyance of those still waiting to board. He found a seat by the window and his aunt fell in beside him nearly filling both seats herself. He wished he had remembered to take his picture book with him. After a short ride, they alighted from the bus; the brakes signed a release and hissed hydrocarbons in their face as it strained on past them. Strange he thought, he didn't see any zoo or farm; they were still in the city.

She grabbed his hand and nearly lifting him off the ground pulled him across the street, avoiding the on-coming autos. They stopped in front of a store whose steam clouded windows concealed what went on inside, and at first he smelled it then saw the tiny black flecks of snow that drifted from the sky just in front the place. "What that?", he said pointing in circles around him, at the strange black flakes that fell. "Snow?" he said looking to her for the answer he knew she would have.

"No Danny, it's not snow. It's from them burning, " she hesitated, "well... things."

"Things?"

"Yes, just things. Well, now you'll finally get to see some real live animals," she said, "won't that be nice?" Danny, now somewhat apprehensive, hesitantly nodded his head, as she pulled open the door and they were greeted by a bell that hung overhead. It was the smell of the place that first upset him. It was the same smell he remembered whenever he played near the place where

the bad things lived. He looked at the bone white floor set in quarter sized octagonal squares, strewn with brown and white feathers of different sizes. There were birds here, he thought as the fear gave way to expectation. He stooped and picked up a tiny feather in his hand. Grinning, he proudly showed it to his aunt. She smiled, and then led him around the room to see all the animals in the cages which he had just noticed. He pulled free and ran to a cage with two chickens in it. Placing both hands on it, he said "Hen?" He grinned and looked to his aunt for verification.

"Very good, Danny. That's right. Now don't get too close and keep your hands off the cages," she warned.

"Bunnies", he squealed running to the other side of the room. "Come here, come here, bunny," he said putting his hands on their cage. But in a single hop they leapt to the back of the cage, eyeing him sideways through wide baleful pink eyes, sensing him with their twitching noses. He was upset at how different they looked from his picture book, in which they always appeared so happy and almost seemed to smile. But that was on the farm and this was a different place, where the air was damp and smelled like a wet coat.

He saw two swinging doors and before his aunt could finish her "Danny, no!" he shoved his way through and ran into two rigid leather covered limbs. His eyes slowly crept up the brown leather apron painted in blood and feathers, to the grinning, stubble-faced man, with the loose hanging flesh where an arm should have been, a vision worse than anything he knew hid under his bed. Fear glued him to this apparition from hell, he was soon swept off his feet by the behemoth's one good arm and held close to its green toothed mouth that clinched a smoldering black Italian stogie in its side.

"Well, aren't you the big boy, now? Are you here to see how we make the food?" The man wheezed through tobacco saturated breath. "Come, come now, let's have a look."

By now his aunt had pushed through the doors, apologized and tried to retrieve Danny from the towering man. "But Maria, some day he may want to be a butcher, a fine profession that will make

his mother proud. People always gotta eat, you know. Ain't that right, young man?", Mr. Datelli said giving his captive a knowing wink.

Danny was too shocked at what he saw to have even heard the thing that held him captive. First there was the smell, the smell of boiled flesh in the simmering cauldrons where the headless chickens were dipped, then were tossed on a table where a young apprentice scraped feathers from the limp carcasses with a black rasp. This sickening scraping sound mixed with that of a floor drain sucking blood and body fluids as if through a bent straw. Another was shoveling the severed heads of his precious hens into a small oven. Twisting in the coals he saw what looked like a blackened piece of fur that twisted and turned on its own as if still sheltering some tiny animal soul squirming to get out. Now he knew what things made the black snow.

"Come Danny boy, now I'll show you how we fix the rabbits." He carried him through the thick steam toward the back of the room. Neither his tears nor the thick steam were enough to mercifully blind him to what he would now see.

"Please Mr. Datelli, I don't think he's old enough to...," his aunt entreated. Danny turned to his aunt, but she no longer followed him and had abandoned him to this place more terrible than the dreams he had when his mother worked nights.

Mr. Datelli ignored her and brought the boy to within three feet of the hooks. Danny fought desperately to get loose, but could not move from the tight muscled arm that pressed him against the wet and bloody apron. There, impaled through their necks upon metal hooks, were three rabbits each sharing the different stages of dying. The large brown one had already been stripped of a mottled fur that dangled in clots from beneath its skinned legs. The other two, one white and the other a spotted black, still silently kicked with legs that tried to lift them from the thick barb that pierced their fur throats and pulsed the warm red life from their bodies that saturated and matted their fur in a crimson glaze. Both looked at Danny through leadened eyes and began frantically pawing the air as he grew near as if reaching to him for help.

It first began as a choke, then a shrill cry as Danny screamed, pulled his arms free, and then reached out to the twitching bleeding images before him. Mr. Datelli backed him away and lost his grip as Danny fell to the floor and slipped in the fluids and excrement that covered the tile floor. He crawled, stood, slipped again and then stood and ran from the thing under the bed, the shadow on the stairs, the night creaks in the attic, the red thing that burned all the bad people in hell, through the swinging doors, past the cages of the damned and out through the front door. He ran up the street, ignoring his aunt's call mingled with the bell that clanged over the door. He ran and didn't stop until he was sure he was where the black snow did not fall.

His aunt, after she had caught up with him, dampened a hankie with her saliva and tried to wipe his face and clothes clean. He fussed and tried to pull away, and then she led him, wordlessly to the bus stop.

They sat in silence on the bus all the way home. Danny idly poking and smearing the black flakes into his coat with his finger one by one, as if trying to erase a memory. His hands were still sticky with the brown red liquid that smelled like old pennies and had caused him to slip.

They entered the quiet house. His mother had already gone to work and his brother was still at school. She walked with him up to his bedroom and sat next to him on the bed.

"Danny listen to me," she said sitting him on her lap. "I'm sorry for what you saw today. I didn't mean for you to see everything you saw. I thought it would be nice for you to see real animals like those that live on farms, honest, but I didn't mean for you to go back there." Danny stared in silence at the holy water urn that was supposed to make only good things happen.

"Listen Danny, although it's not my place, I think it's time you learned about things. Your mother should have...".

"Things", he said looking down and thinking about the burning twisted thing that tried to crawl out of the furnace, but only made black snow.

"Yes, Danny. We all have to end sometime, sort of like those flakes on the window there." He looked in the direction of the now darkening window. "First they are there and then they melt and are gone. We all have to go sometime."

"Where go?"

"Well, to God, that's where we all go, to God. When we are good we go to God. That's why you must learn to be a better boy, and listen to your mother. She's trying very hard to raise you and your brother all alone, but we all have to go sometime."

"Like bunnies on hook?", he said blinking back the tears that were now starting to rim his eyes.

"Of course not, they are killed for food so we can eat, that's all, they don't feel anything."

"Legs move.", he whispered.

"Well yes, sometimes they kick, but it's nothing they feel. You see it's, well, it's sort of a death twitch, a good-bye."

"They want off hook. It hurts them. They want off hook!"

"No, I said they don't feel anything, they are dead, believe

me when I say they are dead. Listen and look at me Danny," she said shaking him, "We all have to die, Danny, it's time you grew up and learned that we all have to die."

He refused to look up as his aunt left the house. He turned and watched the ice flakes slide in rivulets down the dark window. Then the realization hit him. He thought he had heard the word before, but never understood its meaning until now.

So that is die, he thought. That is Die. Die is the bunny on the hook with no fur. Die is their good-bye kick. Die is the man on the cross that always looks up, die is the picture book of St. Stephen with the arrows in his chest, die is St. Catherine on the wheel with sharp points, die is St. Joan with the fire at her throat, and die is Uncle Sal in the room where the big people cried. And, and die is ...die is... his eyes suddenly widened for now he understood.

He jumped from the bed and ran down the dark hall toward the room which was always kept locked. He pulled and jerked on the glass handle until it came lose in his hands and pushed it open on hinges that squealed resistance. He ran headlong into the dark room almost knocking the marble lamp from the night stand, past the bed that was never turned down nor slept in anymore, and to the dresser cluttered with letters, crystal carved perfume bottles hinting of lilac and rose, and scattered lipsticks in shades of stale blood his mother no longer used. From behind the oriental jewelry box smelling of sachet and teak, sent from a faraway place, he found the framed picture. They had told him the man in the brown uniform wasn't coming home again because he was in a better place, but some day he would see him again. He was never sure what they meant, but now he knew. He wasn't going to come back. He wasn't ever going to come back because he now knew what the ribbon draped on the frame meant. It was the same color as the terrible smelling snow that came from behind the butcher shop. "That is die, daddy, ...that is die."

He returned to his room and sat on the bed, his tears tracking down his face like snowflakes on a city window. He sat quietly on the bed, his heart in rhythm with the steady pounding of the cast iron radiator, coughing up steam from the boiler in the cellar. His room had grown dark. He stood and walked to the window. The lights, now on from the factory out back, lent a pristine dignity to the melting flakes that surrendered their shape and ran in vein like trails down to the windows edge. He now could remember the last time with his Dad, during the season of tinsel and lights, and that it was he who had given him the picture book of farm animals. Sitting on his lap, on their last night together, Daddy showed him all the animals in the book. He said we should trust and protect all the animals, for they always knew what was in our hearts, and they could always tell who were their friends. Dad then taught him how to say all the names in the book, and promised that when he returned, he would take him to see the real ones that lived on the farm. Then the next morning he went away and Danny never saw him again. He was left with only a picture book.

It was too dark for him to see the garbage shanty, or the bad things, but he knew they were there and that they liked to come out at night. It was wet and dark out there, but he still had time to warn them. Yes, he would warn them of the terrible man in the wet apron with one arm who would come for them all one day. He would not forget to tell them of the boiling pot, and the hooks, the terrible hooks, and of the oven that would turn them all into black snow. His aunt had lied to him about going to the zoo, just as the nuns had lied about what they did to those saints and to the man on the cross hanging above the holy water. His mother had lied to him about Uncle Sal and she even lied to him about his father. They didn't go upstairs to heaven, no, they were all turned into the black snow. And he even bet that she had lied about the bad things too. He would prove that she was wrong. He would pack some cookies for himself and some stale bread for his friends, a flashlight, a few of his favorite toys, and of course his picture book of animals. He would leave this place and go hide behind the shanty with his real friends. There he would wait for daddy to come find him, just like he promised. He would go and wait there with the bad things. He knew he could trust them; daddy had said so. They wouldn't bite him; he was their friend.

CHRISTMAS IN NEWARK

Since we were Catholics, by tradition we were not allowed to celebrate Christmas if some relative died during the year. This expresses it well:

It's almost Christmas and no one has died this year. That means we can decorate and get presents and celebrate the day. But hurry for uncle has taken ill.

Let's drag out the old paper and wire tree. City children don't know of scented pine and real twigs. Don't all trees smell like moth balls?

See it's already decorated and lit. How bright the lights shine? Perhaps just a little too bright.

Let's sing carols! But not so loud because uncle grows weaker.

Let's wrap presents! I've got a vase I made out of a fruit jar for mom and dad. I made a paper train for sis that I know she'll like. I've got a picture book of animals for brother, which he gave me last Christmas. I hope they can't guess what they are getting. Sure I believe in Santa, but maybe he needs just a little help.

I heard them talk about a priest. Why should a priest be here on Christmas Eve? Maybe he's here to help us build the manger. Tomorrow is Jesus's birthday. I'm really glad he was born on

Christmas. Good night Jesus, and hurry Santa.

But when morning came there were tears instead of tinsel, black instead of rainbow. The tree was gone and without those colored lights an old picture book can't look new, a paper train doesn't really go, and a pretty vase is only a painted jar.

"Now I lay me down to sleep,
I pray the Lord my soul to keep.
Please God, if you really can hear,
don't let anyone die next year."

MOTHER DEAREST

His mother bordered on bi polar mood swings, that went to obsessive control to outright brutality. She was the only figure in the household, neglected by a husband who claimed to bowl every night until the wee hours of morning. She took her vengeance for him out on Danny.

Danny grew thin and malnourished with lunches packed with salami and butter on white bread. During school breaks at St. Antonius, when everyone could buy chocolate milk and cookies, he could only watch.

Always weak and frail, dinners at home were particularly traumatic because his mother would hit him with a wooden spoon if he failed to eat or didn't eat fast enough.

He and his sister used to bath together, and one day he asked how come she was different down there? She told him she once was, but she cut it off because she was bad, and now she was nice and clean down there. From then on Danny always slept on his side with a protective hand between his legs.

She would never allow him to even talk to girls, and caught him talking to two twins up the street, grabbing him by the hand, calling them whores, she dragged him home.

He was so afraid of his mother, that when home from school he would just lock himself in the bathroom until his father would come home late at the night.

Was he always destined to a life of fear? No, one day he discovered its antidote, and quite by accident. His mother had a bad habit of unscrewing fuses to turn the entire house into blackness, or even worse, to let out blood curdling screams.

One day she was chasing him up the stairs swinging a wooden spoon, Danny ran into the closet, and found an old sword from an uncle who fought in the Spanish American War. He grabbed it, pointed it at her, and warned if she dared come any further he would run it right through her. She stopped, and crying ran back down the stairs.

This was now the most defining moment of his entire life. He realized that both fear and hate could not coexist in the same person at the same time. And hate was just so much more desirable.

BORROWED SHIELDS

He embraced it as a mantle of amour and started training with weights, and went after all bullies as a champion of all underdogs and joined the Virginia Beach Auxiliary Police. He was involved in the labor day riot of 1989, but here is an account where I was assigned to guard a grave all night long. Gives you an idea of what he encountered as a volunteer. He wrote this in his early days as a police officer in Newark, N.J. where a young girl, Camellia eventually died at the hands of her adopted parents. He had made several calls to her house, but social services always at that time sided with the parents. Then one night he received a call from a fellow officer, who gave him the terrible news. She had no one in her life to grieve her, but he paid tribute to her by attending her autopsy and wrote this eulogy.

You can't understand,
Why your frail body, so naked and blue?
Shamefully dresses the coroner's altar.
Why the gowned man wields such a sharp knife,
While assistants stand by
With suction and saw

DR. C. THOMAS SOMMA

Why must they photo
The bruises and burns
Placed by adopted parents.
Just what is it
They still hope to learn?

Like robots they probe,
Measure and dictate.
In infinite detail
They speculate, as to why
Your small four-year-old body,
Became just one more case.

Wasn't it enough
You never shared
A real parent's love
Your gift to them betrayed.
While others turned away
With blind leaden eyes?
How did the canon of the law
Sanction their deed,
As bishops with the inquisition,
A dogma sanctified in blood.

Descending now,
The whine of the hungry bone saw,
Whose anxious cold bite,
Finalizes the desecration,
Forcing the final stigmata.
While heedless to all,

LAST LAP

The plea of your silent scream,
Soundless as vespers
Mimed by a nun.

Yet that man standing there,
The one with the badge,
A shield far too small,
To defend and protect you.
He couldn't intervene then,
They won't let him now.

But Just enough time
To whisper a eulogy
To what once was a child,
Reduced now to relics,
Bottled and tagged.
Gone is the chalice,
To just evidence.

GREEKFEST RIOTS
LABOR DAY 1989

Summer came early that and so did the trouble. By mid-March 1989 the weather had turned unusually warm at the Virginia Beach oceanfront. A time when the dealers, prostitutes, vagrants, drifters, addicts, mental cases and fortune seekers descended upon the city.

The migration always centered on the beachfront where the deadly network and connections could be easily made. The city of Virginia Beach would see its population swell four times normal and its crime rate climb by ten. Area residents would no longer walk at night and only cautiously venture out by day. The 911 line would ring continuously, and the cases would be prioritized and stacked by the dispatchers at the central communications center. They alone had to make the distinction from what may only be a barking dog or a psychotic intruder. They did this in order to ration out to the 10 to 15 police officers that covered any of the shifts that were assigned the second precinct at the beachfront.

The city did have an additional reserve, in its 60 auxiliary police, non-paid volunteers who contributed over 30,000 hours a year in the defense of their city. Regardless of why they did this type of work since they accepted and encountered the same dangers. The city trained, armed and depended on these dedicated unpaid volunteers in order to back-up the regular officers and to team up with the summer walking beats at the oceanfront.

They would face their first summer marked by the worse racial riot in the city's history. In full uniform, as fully sworn police powers wearing their badges, their borrowed shields, bearing the seal of the city and their number for as long as they wished to remained with the force. How soon would Danny be indoctrinated with violence, police brutality, and bound by the code of silence.

This was his first encounter with the real criminal mind and its seeming lack of consciousness. It is a story of a summer that would challenge and change him. A summer when every cop became a target...a summer when a city burned, and was brought to its knees.

What motivated him? Best expressed in these Bible verses:

"....For he will deliver you from the snare of the fowler
and from the deadly pestilence;
he will cover you with his pinions,
and under his wings you will find refuge;
his faithfulness is a shield and buckler.
You will not fear the terror of the night,
nor the arrow that flies by day,
nor the pestilence that stalks in darkness,
nor the destruction that wastes at noonday.
A thousand may fall at your side,
ten thousand at your right hand;
but it will not come near you...
For he will give his angels charge of you

to guard you in all your ways."
-Psalms 91: 3-7, 11
"As a fine soldier of Christ Jesus take your part in suffering evil"
- 2 Timothy 2:3

"Who is it that ever serves as a soldier at his own expense?"
- 1st Corinthians 9:7

"Is it not one father that all of us have? Is it not one God that has created us? Why is it then that we deal so treacherously with one another"?
- Malachi 2:10

"The Lord said whom shall I send, who will go for us?"
"I said I will go, Send me."
-Isaiah 6:8

They would face their first summer marked by the worse racial riot in the city's history. In full uniform, as fully sworn police powers wearing their badges, their borrowed shields, bearing the seal of the city and their number for as long as they wished to remained with the force. How soon would Danny be indoctrinated with violence, police brutality, and bound by the code of silence.

This was his first encounter with the real criminal mind and its seeming lack of consciousness. It is a story of a summer that would challenge and change him. A summer when every cop became a target...a summer when a city burned, and was brought to its knees.

1989 ALL OVER AGAIN

The violence we are witnessing today of police brutality against black citizens are reminisce of the Greekfest riots in Virginia Beach, Labor Day weekend in 1989. I was present all three days of those riots as an Auxiliary Officer with the VBPD, and would like to lend my perspective as to what happened when the black fraternities came to the oceanfront, as they did every year, but were always confined to Croatan Beach and were peaceful.

The incident started on a Friday night, when youths threw bricks through several windows on Atlantic Ave. at 17th street inciting the riot. But these youths were white locals, and not the black fraternity subjects but never noted in the paper.

We grabbed our riot gear and headed to 37th street and marched south behind an armored vehicle. But the time we headed south Atlantic Ave. was in shambles. Storefronts smashed and mass looting. Some injured from both sides, but what transpired on the send night, when the Governor called out the National Guard. was far worse.

Those blacks, both male and female still on the street, were beaten with clubs by our State Troopers. I was witness to this as the national Guardsmen just stood by shaking their heads in disbelief.

But it got worse. Aside from our own police force, units from all of the other police localities were called in to help. They then systematically marched up the Boardwalk, and entered the motels lining it, and dragged and beat with clubs all they could find, Both male and female.

I was witness to all this and the bought two T-shirts sold at muster before the nights of the riots. One showed a white officer with dark sun glasses and a baton in his hand, with the words, "It's a White Thing and we will make you understand." I reference to the Blacks comments that "it's a Black thing so you can't understand."

The second shirt was far worse. It showed a caricature of a black with big lips holding a brick in one hand and a pistol in the other, with the words, "No looters and no Shooters." With a red circle across his chest indicating he will be shot.

The city praised the efforts of our police, but why against an unarmed population, as we see today again throughout our country. Sure there are looters and opportunists taking advantage of the Floyd murder, and many police officers being injured all across this country. So when will it end? When all lives matter, and in the words of Rodney King nearly beaten to death by white officers with side handle batons, "Why can't we all just get Along?"

POLICE SIRENS

Police sirens have a language all their own. There is the constant wail, like a hungry baby's frantic search for their mother's nipple. Then there is the yelp sound, like a dog crippled and rebounding off the front bumper of a speeding car. And finally the hi-low alternating sound that to me always seemed to implore, "help me, help me." The wail is used in straight pursuit, when no other cars are in between. The yelp is to move vehicles that get in the way. The hi-low is used when going through intersections, in the hope that you won't get broad-sided. It seems to call, "let me, let me, let me through and let me live another day." Three different sounds, three different calls, yet each holding the promise of desperation and pain.

FIRST NIGHT OUT

After graduating from the academy, Danny had to ride with a field training officer for 40 hours until he could be released to ride alone. It was a cold November night and he had been assigned the gruff FTO Dickerson. After doing the required vehicle check, and responding by radio that their unit was 10-8, available, they left the parking lot at the 2nd Precinct and headed to a south zone. Dickerson warned that we always patrol with the windows down to hear problems we don't see. Unfortunately, I had not brought my coat since I had my safety vest and felt I wouldn't need it. I was wrong.

No sooner had we arrived at our zone when a call came out of a violence up all the way up to the North end of the beachfront. Dispatcher reported of someone smashing the windows out of cars with a dumbbell in his hand and she called for all available units to respond. Since we were lean that night, and other units tied up, we took the call and we responded code one, lights and siren all the way up Atlantic Avenue. I remember the sensation, part excitement, yet a fear that some other unit would respond and we would be called off. I wanted this just to see how I would respond to this violent person.

LAST LAP

We arrived and excited saw one white male 6 feet naked from the waist up. He raised his hands and began to approach. With my side handle baton, I shouted HALT, and told him to drop to his knees. Grinning a toothless smile, he complied and in going behind him I noticed he had a large buck knife stuck down his pants. I handcuffed him when another unit showed up and he was placed in our back seat.

I interviewed neighbors and found out that he had probably been on drugs because another neighbor tried to stop him and hit him square in the face with a rake which had no effect. That explained his toothless grin.

On transport to the 2nd precinct he just babbled nonsense. When we excited he we brought him before the magistrate to book him. To my surprise my FTO told me to take the handcuffs off because this guy, Werner, had calmed down. I looked warily at Dickerson, but felt I'd better comply. The magistrate started to ask him some questions, but Werner just stared saying nothing. Then he began some rapid forced deep breathing and with his free hand smashed the Plexiglas shield. I immediately grabbed him and replaced the handcuffs.

Officers from the entire second precinct heard the commotion and threw him to the ground kicking and beating him bloody. I tried to intervene, but was pushed back. They trussed him up with chains and straps, his hands behind his back and tied to his legs. Some continued to kick him. One said legs toss his stupid ass in the jail, but I said, more determined than usual, that he needed medical help because of his teeth having been knocked out. A Sargent was notified and he agreed. My FTO held a finger up to his lips and shaking his head said, "Not a word of these other injuries he deserved from us." Thus I was to learn the Code of Silence that night,

25

but not for the last time.

When the ambulance came and he was being strapped to a gurney, he looked at each of our name tags and called out our names, and said" I will get even with all of you fuckers someday", then looking at me said" But not you Somma."

Months later at his trial where he was only convicted of disturbing the peace, destruction of property, and Threatening bodily harm. He was released upon his own recognizance and posted bond. He saw and approached me apologizing for the incident, and shook my hand. I smiled and commented on how his new teeth looked. While my FTO muttered under his breathe, "Asshole."

Werner left and I turned to Dickerson, "Well maybe he will help us someday, you never know."

Well guess what? We responded with shots fired at the north end and was one of several units on the scene. Me and Dickerson were ducked behind a vehicle that was slowly going in the direction of where the shots were fired. Then from the other side of the street, a door opened, and there was Werner shaking his head and pointing to the opposite side of the street with our backs exposed to it. So he prevented us from getting shot in the back. The shooter was indeed in that house and finally talked into submission. A close call as I nodded my thanks to Werner, while Dickerson ignored us both.

We Don't eat DONUTS

Always facing scrutiny from the regular officers who felt we were just pretend cops and risking their jobs and raises, since we worked for free. One Sargent commented on us Auxiliaries during muster one shift. "All you Auxiliaries are good for just two things. Eating donuts and siting around with your thumbs up your ass."

I raised my hand and said, "Sargent you are only half right. We don't eat Donuts."

GRAVE GUARD

Danny wrote this true encounter to lend an idea as to the diversity of the work of a volunteer police officer and the power of the imagination on a long dark night guarding a grave. He changed the location and the race of the individual which was him, for obvious reasons.

"Spirits sublimate giving form to dark secrets long buried in red, echoing a hollow lament to the consciousness of the living. Vapor memories distill into shapes longing to tell, to remind and to be remembered, to touch a soul, share a tiny tendril of time, and to once more live again, if only for a moment, in the memory of the living. This the hope of the dead.

The late October sun dipped beneath the tree line of the purple forest. The waves of Cheatam Lake lapped the wooded shoreline, propelled by the late October wind from across the bay. A biting wind shook the trees around the site, flapping the yellow crime scene markers, sounding like birds scared from their roost. A green tarpaulin covered the blackened remains of the corpse. A solitary figure in blue sat in silent vigil over the grave site.

In the distance Craig heard the sound of a four wheel grinding a noisy path through the woods. "Bout time my relief got here," he thought to himself.

"What've we got?" Carter asked swinging his lanky legs out of the four wheeler.

"Haven't you heard? It was in the morning paper or don't your kind know how to read," Craig mocked sucking the last drag off of a short cigarette and crushing it with his boot.

Carter ignored his partner's last remark since he knew this form of banter marked his acceptance as the only black officer on the all-white force in Brewster Township. He found it a welcome change from the stoic formalism that had initially greeted him.

Craig approached the four wheeler, "Some camper's dog dug up a body here. The mutt had been lost for days, then the owners finally found him here on top of this grave site. He'd been clawed to death. Maybe a bear, or maybe who knows what."

"So why don't they just dig it up and move the damn thing, why the hell do we have to guard it?" Carter mouthed holding his Zippo to a cigarette and walking to the perimeter of the yellow ribbon.

"Ain't quite that simple. Ya see that thing," pointing to the green tarpaulin, "is old...maybe real old. They're waiting for some forensic expert from DC to come down and examine it before it gets moved. Seems as though they suspect foul play, even if it was a long time ago. And since the paper blabbed it to the whole world this morning, they're afraid we'll be getting some noisy on-lookers or maybe whoever did it wanting to come back and trash the evidence."

"I'm gonna take a look, since I have to spend the next shift with whoever it is, I think I'd just better get acquainted."

"Help yourself. Do I need to make any introductions?" Craig laughed the hollow laugh that numbs the fear of truth. "I've been told that there's not a hell of a lot left though. Leave it to a camper's mutt to find them bones." Carter sucked the last drag off his cigarette and tossed it to the ground. He pulled his collar up around his neck and then cautiously ducked under the yellow tape and approached the green tarpaulin which seemed to swell at the center. Carter took one last look at Craig and then lifted the tarpaulin. He felt the same chill at the back of his neck that he felt as a kid watching those old horror movies. It took a while for his eyes to adjust to the fading light, then slowly he recognized a human form. There were some blackened bones, shattered maybe by the dog, and some rotted cloth dangling like willow spiders from parts of a yellow lichen covered rib cage. Oddly no grubs or worms, so this had to be an old corpse. Though he tried to avoid it with his eyes, he was magnetically drawn to the human skull that looked at him with wide empty sockets and a jaw locked in a permanent imploring grimace of pain.

"The skull's too small to be an adult. This was just a kid, maybe early teens at most. Take a look Craig!"

"No thanks", he replied with his back to Carter. "I think I'll just pass on that idea, if it's all the same with you."

Carter ignored his partner and continued his examination. Then he noticed something odd, half-buried above the pelvic bone forming a cross with what once was a spine. "Craig come here and take a look at this! There's a chain near the region of the waist." This did get Craig's attention as he walked toward the site.

"I'll be damned. Looks to me like someone chained it to something out here and then did him or her in."

"Or left it for the animals to get", Carter said dropping the tarpaulin over the remains and ducking back under the yellow barrier.

"Well it don't matter much to me or it anymore cause I'm hungrier than a bitch wolf and I'm outta here. Your relief will be by at three am." Climbing into the four wheeler, Craig quipped, "Well it's getting colder than a well digger's ass. You have fun and don't ya freeze off anything ya might be needing. At least you'll have some company to keep you warm." Craig laughed pointing to the now darkened site, as he started the vehicle.

Carter didn't hear the last comment, still staring at the site and thinking about the rusted broken chain, he wondered what it all meant.

Shifting into first gear, Carter mocked, "Oh, and I don't think you should worry any about them bears in these here parts. I hear they don't like dark meat!" Craig roared his usual hollow laugh and drove off. Carter watched the malevolent red eyes of the tail lights grow dim as they retreated into the dusty darkness.

Typical cop banter he thought. Using humor to shield the fear, since both emotions cannot exist in someone simultaneously, and fear is the only emotion no cop will accept. But Carter was afraid. Not so much of any real danger from intruders or animals, which he knew he could handle. And not really from the person who perpetrated this horror on this poor youth, because he was sure that monster was long dead. But maybe just from knowing he had to face the long silent hours ahead, with nothing to distract him from those demons in his mind, that occasionally visited his sleep. And there was something else: an uneasiness that he couldn't describe but felt now and that caused him to dread the hours that lay ahead. Something like Jesus must have felt that night at Gethsemane, lonely and abandoned, and yet somehow still knowing the worst was yet to come.

Carter sat on a flattened rock and leaned his back up against a decaying stump. Might as well get comfortable since it's going to be a long lonely night, he thought to himself. Barely able to make out any of the surrounding land due to the now nearly blackened sky, he looked for a moon that would not reveal itself this night since it had waned to a sickle wide crescent the night before. One-by-one the stars of the ancient constellations began to appear like tiny fireflies trapped on black tarpaper, shedding their flickering waning signal across the eons of empty space. He searched for Orion and Taurus the bull, favorites that he had learned about as a kid. They would be easier to find atop this dark forest than from the ghetto rooftop of his childhood home in Newark. There the lights of the airport, and the blinking neon Ballantine beer sign crowded out all but the brightest from those polluted skies.

Carter hated the South. He ended up here after being discharged from the Navy at his last duty station in Norfolk. He never returned home due to the race riots which decimated his home in Newark and left him without a family to return to. His parents and kin had scattered to other areas, no better than the three-storied house they had been assigned by the housing authority. He stayed in the Navy, because he would be less of a burden on his parents. He remembered the back of his house where an old factory stood. There were clothes and a power lines, but no trees. Tonight he was surrounded by trees and he could hear their wail in the rising wind and smell their vapid dankness. No, he could never return to what once was his home despite his feelings for the South.

He migrated to this small North Carolina Township after being discharged and answering an ad in the local paper he read in a diner. In his first few months on the force he was met with

silent reserve by his fellow officers, as he was the first black officer that had ever been hired at Brewster. On calls they began to appreciate his ability to diffuse potentially hostile situations with his calm dignity and sense of humor. He knew he had been accepted when they began to chide him about his race, since they now felt comfortable enough to even mention these differences. So now Carter could give it right back to them. He would often go drinking and hit the weight room with the blue-bigots, as he liked to call them, especially Craig who had been his first and longest standing partner.

He knew this area had once been a slave plantation and that the forest surrounded the tobacco fields of a Master Brewster before the Civil War. He smiled at that oxymoron, a "Civil" War. Now this was the far perimeter of a camp ground frequented by all races oblivious to the evils that may have been perpetrated by the great white Master who had given the township its name. He wondered what life would have been like back in those days as he lit another cigarette; the flame of the Zippo lighter flickering rapidly in the biting wind. He coughed and studied the glowing ember and thought that he too was as much a slave as his ancestors, if only to the tobacco product that Brewster once grew here.

He pulled up his collar again, feeling the dropping temperature as the wind bit at his ear lobes. He would save his last cigarettes for later and then clicked off his radio in order to save the batteries and laid it on the ground next to him. He searched the sky one last time for Orion the hunter, but noticed those tiny fireflies were blinking out one-by-one. They had become veiled by a thickening mist which drifted in from the lake cloaking him and the forest in a silent shroud.

He knew he needed to save his Kel-Lite for when he really might need it. After seeing it's reassuring beam one last time he clicked it off. He figured he might as well catch a few nods to make the time pass. It didn't matter since no one would see him, no one except maybe just her, he thought as he strained his eyes toward the black area of the tarpaulin with its ever flapping yellow perimeter. Her? Now why did he say her, he mused? Suddenly a chill, this time not caused by the night wind, passed up his spine as he slowly unsnapped his holster, removed his 9mm and placed it on a stump close to his side. With his hand still on it, he took a deep breath and closed his eyes.

At 11:00 pm he heard it before he saw it. His eyes groped the dark as his limbs, now stiff from the cold and the position in which he had been sleeping, would not respond. His pistol arm had fallen asleep. This numb limb knocked his gun from its resting place and it was swallowed up by the decayed wet leaves of the forest floor. He struggled to get up, but his feet slid out from under him greased by snail slime and moist leaves. He toppled over onto his side groping to no avail for the security of his 9mm and his radio. Blackness, and then the one emotion that was not allowed, engulfed him as the night's mist. He realized he must now lie very still and wait for whatever was out there to make the first move. He didn't have to wait long.

Carter struggled again to sit up and lean his back against the security of another tree stump. Always protect your back, then you only have to contend with what is in front of you...basic academy training. As the blood flow reentered his arm, and the numbness gave way to a tingling sensation, he very quietly patted the wet ground around him in search of his weapon. His eyes tried to adjust to the darkness in search of what was in front of him, out there, now silent, watching and waiting, deciding when to make a move on this blind, confused and helplessly disarmed victim.

He felt for and slowly pulled his Kel-Lite from the O ring on his duty belt and clicked it on. The dim beam reflected off the stalking nightmare: a formless rage venting through wide scaly eyes and a gaping abyss lined with ivory brown spikes and frothed in saliva. On his back, Carter screamed and began to back pedal with legs and arms up the hill behind him sliding on the slick carpeted forest floor. He was oblivious to the rocks and twigs that tore into his neck and back and insensitive to the hundreds of black mandibles and eyeless white larval grubs, those silent stewards of death, that sought the sweet red fluid of his oozing wounds. A fallen log stopped his backward retreat and then he knew the end had come as he began to slide back down the hill closer and closer into the maw of the mighty beast. Does the jawed prey continue to resist till the end, or does it just succumb to the inevitable law of hunter and hunted? There were no thoughts of prayer or repentance; no flashing of his life before his eyes; no long white tunnel with his dearly deceased waiting to receive him; just the tetany of his bleeding body and the piercing sound of this dying officer's baleful primal scream.

Sharp spike-like claws raked his rib cage from left to right throwing him on his side. He tried to crawl, waiting for the jaws to descend and clamp on his limp body. Carter could smell its fetid breath and feel the vapid heat of its body...then it's enraged charge had stopped. Had the bear lost the scent of his prey in the dark? Carter lay very still hoping against all hope that this was just a nightmare from which he would soon wake. Hope dissolved as a morning mist when he heard the beast growling above him. Carter twisted to his side and looked above him to confront what was to come. But the bear, caught in the beam of the lost Kel-Lite, was standing tall on his hind legs distracted by something behind his helpless prey. He rocked from side to side sniffing the air, and then returning to all fours, backed away. He gave a brief disinterested glance at Carter then turned, exiting the beam of the light, and sauntered back and was enveloped by the blackness of the forest.

Carter lay there gasping for air, not believing what had just happened. His survival instincts told him to find his weapon as soon as possible, so he painfully crawled on bloodied knees toward his Kel-Lite. With his Kel-Lite in hand, he found his 9mm, cocked it and instinctively pushed the safety to off. He leaned back against another stump as his mind cleared and his eyes adjusted to the light of the flashlight. He did a quick survey of his body with the light and noticed that his side and legs were bleeding badly, but his armored vest had protected his vital organs from the worst of those claws. He quickly tried to brush off the insects that were nursing at his wounds. He wanted to call for help, but his radio was nowhere to be found.

Something had frightened the bear and he needed to know what it was. His light was now growing dim and he banged it a few times with his braised hand, wincing until the light grew a little brighter. The light beam probed the dark and caught the late autumn dance of mayflies and gnats. Then in the vicinity of the tarpaulin, he saw her. A waif-like black girl, no more than maybe twelve or thirteen, dressed in a long soiled linen dress that covered her from neck to toe. Her hair was pulled back, braided on top, and in her right hand she was holding what looked like a tattered doll wearing a calico scarf. Her other hand rested gently on her swollen abdomen.

Carter, though dazed, said, "Hi there! You lost? What're you doing out here so late?" She gave no response, but a questioning look. "What's your name?", he asked.

She still didn't answer but just stared at him with wide vacant eyes, and began a slow sympathetic smile.

"You're not hurt are you? Well I know I am," Carter exhaled, feeling with his hand the broken ribs jabbing into his right side.

"Too shy to talk? Well, that's okay, just come with me. I'll take care of you and see that you get back to your folks in one piece." She slowly shook her head from side to side and gave him a soft smile, then held out the doll for him to take. He didn't understand the gesture.

Still holding her in his light, he limped toward her, and then froze when the beam reflected off a chain wrapped and locked just above her swollen abdomen. It was then that he knew.

She slowly rocked back and forth stroking the dormant child within her abdomen, still extending her right hand with the tattered toy. Her dark eyes revealed to him a tragic story of long ago. He now knew and would forever be her voice, her witness, her epitaph. Carter now became the last witness of her short and tragic existence, the last conscious link to two innocent lives ended too soon. She now gave proof that she and the life growing within her did at one time exist. Her blue knight in tattered armor would now always remember her. And through him, her and her child would achieve immortality in the tale he would tell. She smiled just as his light failed once more.

He impatiently pounded it against the ground until the beam came back on, but when he pointed it again, she was gone. He probed the perimeter of the crime scene, but the beam no longer reflected the image of the tiny slave girl that knew the things of the forest and had saved his life.

Falling to one knee he sat down and fumbled for a cigarette. Then he thought of Master Brewster, his tobacco plantation and of the way he tried to bury his shame in these woods that kept their silence until this night. He tossed the lit weed into the dark, collapsed and then mercifully lost consciousness.

Carter awoke days later in a clean hospital bed to Craig's familiar taunting, "Hey black boy, don't you know there's a law against feeding the bears?"

Carter's eyes fluttered and then focused on the tall image of his partner. "You were damn lucky boy, damn lucky. When the dispatcher doing a routine check couldn't raise you about midnight, she sounded a signal 13 and we all came out. We found you sleeping against a tree and plain torn all to hell. You're gonna get docked for that snooze time don't ya know," Craig grinned. "Biggest damn bear I ever seen was no more than ten, maybe fifteen feet away just a sittin' and a grinnin' at your ass. Not sure why he didn't just finish you off. I guess he just didn't like black meat." Craig howled at this and Carter knew that he had not been damaged too bad or Craig would've been a lot more somber. "You're one damn lucky blackassed Yankee at that. You've got that dispatcher to thank for saving your life." Carter smiled because he knew better. "And by the way, what was all that gibberish about some black girl you where spouting about on the way to the hospital? You been holdin out on me boy?"

"What day is it?", Carter coughed reaching for his water glass with a gauzed hand leashed to a clear vinyl intravenous line.

"Wednesday. You been out for two days so now don't ya think it's time you get your sorry ass back to work? I'm tired of carrying your shift for you. If you don't hurry back, I hear they may transfer you to animal control."

Even Carter had to laugh at that remark, his scored ribcage reminding him of that night.

"Well I gotta hit the streets. Everyone sends their best, and by the way, that guy from DC said the body dates back over a hundred years or more when the area was still a plantation. The bones were of a female, a young one at that. They could tell by the pelvic bones or something. Seems as though our town's namesake had a bad habit of knocking up the local help and then chaining them in the woods for bear food. Nice guy, huh?"

"Yes I know," Carter responded.

Craig didn't hear Carter's last remark and went on, "Seems as though our local paper is denying it, but I read it in the Washington Post. It's even supposed to be on the national news tonight. That oughtta give our old town council something to celebrate next Brewster Day." He laughed and shook his head. "Almost makes you want to quit smoking, don't it now? Well almost. Also seems as though one of your Yankee organizations up north is going to erect a monument or something near where she was found. I don't know why they have to keep stirring up past shit. What difference does it matter now? Why can't they just let us forget it all. What's done is done?"

Carter's mind grabbing at the phantom images of that night said "Because those who forget the past, are condemned to re-live it."

"And who might have said that?

"George..."

"Governor George Wallace?", interrupted Craig.

"No, Santayana, the philosopher, You idiot."

"Well I knew it was one of them George's", Craig grinned and then got up to leave. "Oh, by the way I almost forgot, this here is for you," as he handed Carter a paper bag.

"What is it?" Carter asked clutching the bag with his only good hand.

"Well I thought you were a little too old for this stuff, but I always did have my doubts about you boy. But when we found you, sleeping with a bear just a short charge away, your 9mm in one hand and this here thing was in the other."

Carter reached into the bag and pulled out an old decayed gingham doll wearing a calico scarf, careful to hold back the tears he knew would come, until his partner was well out of sight.

THE TRUE STORY OF MY NEAR KNIFING

JANUARY 23, 1993

Raoul Horton was an escapee from the Eastern State Mental Institution near Williamsburg, Virginia. He was on heavy meds but had none with him. He took a place on the second floor of the Econo- Lodge on 31st and Atlantic Ave. The Wednesday before the incident, he had taken a 9mm firearm and blew off the hinges and the door of the room he was staying in. The Manager, instead of calling the Police, told him he would overlook it if he repaired the door. So to my benefit, he pawned his 9mm and had the door repaired. If he had that weapon when he left the balcony I wouldn't be writing this now.

It was sunny morning, and normally a quiet shift in the 226 zone. We got a call of a person on the balcony screaming and jabbing a knife in the air. I was driving and exited my car and told the guy to please keep calm and I'll be right up.

Officer Biltown never left his vehicle, and worse never warned me that Raoul had actually left the balcony and was running down the stairs then turning the corner toward me. I drew out my side handled baton and yelled for him to STOP. He stopped a mere 8 feet in front of me, but kept the knife raised and jabbing it at me. I just kept up a running conversation with him, as I drew out my 9mm switched it to my right hand replacing it with the baton. I pointed my 9mm at him, but realized I could never shoot because my line of fire was facing the motel office where there were a bunch of people in there screaming at what was happening. They were the ones who dialed 911.

Eventually I angled him away from the office to obtain a clear shot, still keeping up a calm running conversation with him. When all of sudden, he screamed lifted up his arm, and then threw down the knife to the ground. I immediately took him down single handed and handcuffed him while Biltown still just sat in his car.

When I got up and looked around there were at least 13 squad cars with officers pointing their pistols at Raoul. Someone in the office had called for a Signal 13, Officer in Danger.

He was transported back to the station and I was asked to press charges, but refused. He had been off his meds and needed medical help and not criminal prosecution. He was transported back to Eastern State Mental Institution.

The aftermath was both interesting and troubling. While I was praised for my effort to control the situation and not shoot by the regular officers, since according to our handbook, we allowed the use of deadly force if an armed assailant gets within 20 feet of charging with a knife or other blunt weapon. Any closer and his momentum would reach you.

Yet, interesting it was my fellow Auxiliary Police Officers who belittled me and called me a coward for not shooting. My attitude was I would have if I needed too. So we are both alive and he may be helped.

I went to property control the following week and they gave me the combat knife he attacked me with. I still have it as a somber reminder of how close we all can be to death even in such a benign sunny morning at the oceanfront.

Sargent Fox in his speech to the VBPD, at my retirement ceremony after 28 years as a volunteer with the VBPD made a very good comment about this incident, and stressing the diverse reaction from the regular officers and my fellow Auxiliary.

Naturally I never rode with Biltown again.

So were the issues ever resolved with your mother.?

"Well not until our last Thanksgiving, and then died the following April. "

"How so?"

LAST THANKSGIVING

"Well I had just gotten home from college for the break, and was heading to my girlfriends Sue's house for dinner. I assumed my parents were going to my mother's sisters house as they did every year, but they weren't because their immediate family had grown so large to include them. Well, I wasn't going to let the two of them sit alone, so even at the anger of Sue, I joined them just the three of us. During dinner my mother started to cry, and said that of all of her children, it was the Black sheep of the family who was here for her." Danny said with eyes tearing.

"Well I'm glad you got that closer. "

"Yes, who would have known it would be her last Thanksgiving. She died the following April. So live and love them, because you never know if it will be your last. That reminds me of a story I read about a hospital worker treating a terminal person. A young one at that."

"Go on."

It's called a good goodbye

A GOOD, GOODBYE

I remember in my early days in the lab an incident that brought home to me the importance of making a good, good bye. I was just about at the end of a long double shift, when I got a call for some stat blood gases in the CCU and since I was the only one on duty trained to do arterial punctures, I had to go, exhausted as I was.

I reluctantly grabbed my collection tray and grumbling, I proceeded to go to the critical Care Unit on the third floor, unaware of the lesson I was about to learn. I was directed by the charge nurse pass beds with the frail and the dying, a cacophony of hissing respirators and beeping life support machines. I was told the patient was an accident victim, and his young wife was on her way to the hospital. He had been rushed here from a construction site, a victim of a generator that had fallen from one story above and had caught him on the back of his head and cracked open his skull. I thought I was ready for the worse, but I wasn't prepared for what I saw, a young kid, late teens at most, whose skull was gone from the back of his head and I could see the pulsating grey matter of his brain. I wondered why he had not been taken to surgery, but I guessed they needed to assess his acid/base status first.

After sterilizing the arm, I talked to him during the procedure in the faint hope he might still be able to hear me, and inserted the needle straight down into the arm after barely being able to detect the pulse in his brachial artery. The crimson fluid, far darker than it should have as it began a slow pulsing up into the hub of my vacutainer. I then pressed on the first of three heparin tubes, and watched the tube slowly fill. I then removed it and pressed on the second tube which also began to slowly fill. After filling for only about one third, the blood flow stopped. Perhaps I had gone through the artery and so I withdrew it a little, but still no blood, and none even after pressing it in a little deeper. I started to get a fresh tube when I felt tap on my shoulder by a unit nurse who just shook her head and said "you can't stop now," as she began to un-hook his IV's and the rest of his life support.

I remember an overwhelming sadness mixed with my fatigue as I wiped the sweat from my brow. I had seen death before. In the old and in the very young, but there was something else here that that held my thoughts. Like a bothersome fly, I couldn't shake the vision of this youth saying good bye that morning to his young wife. How was that goodbye? Was it a good one, or had they quarreled that morning and maybe he had gone off mad, or she had ignored him thinking so what, we'll make up later. I wondered what a different goodbye it would have been if they both had known it was to be their last. Would they have taken the time for a real thank you, or voiced appreciation, a longer hug, or a more lingering kiss?

I thought of my goodbyes, and wondered if they were ever really good enough to last an eternity.

SISTER JEMA

The nuns themselves seemed to take delight in tormenting him. During penmanship class, he was holding his ink pen wrong and a nun smacked his hand with a metal ruler, yelling, "" Don't you know holding your hand like that is bad for your hand?" Cowering like a whipped dog, he whispered, "So is hitting it with a ruler", inviting even more abuse.

During recess, when the other kids were sent out to play, Danny had to write long punish lessons on the boards with nonsense phrases like, "I will not talk back to Sister Jema." Over and over again. I wasn't always a good kid. When small we had an aunt living with us who was an invalid in a wheel chair, and I loved to torment.

THE DOLL IN THE ATTIC

She was so easy to torment, a catatonic invalid, and I was so young. I took an insidious delight in taunting her, to try to invoke a response. I would wear masks, make exaggerated faces, and laugh at her, pointing with my finger, and bouncing up and down like a psychotic mime.

I hated her, as her unblinking eyes bore through me, and feared the retribution I would someday certainly receive. I had nightmares since the night they carried her out. We young kids were asked to go into the dining room, while they carried her out. I snuck a peek since I wanted to be sure she was really going. Aunt Mazzola was completely wrapped in a sheet, as they carried her out. But didn't anyone notice that her one scabbed and emaciated arm was dangling free, and waving loose…I chilled since I was certain it was beckoning to me.

That night my sister and I would not go to our beds, but Mom and Dad allowed us to crawl in beside them. I was in the middle, protected on both sides by them, just in case she returned.

She and her husband, Gaetano, had come from Italy to live with us. I never knew of her condition, but she was wheelchair bound and had a roughed painted face, wide eyed, and expressionless like the ceramic wide eyed doll that sat upright in a chair in my parents' bedroom. It wore a pale blue dress that fanned out around it, and with exposed arms hanging down, thin as twigs and with painted nails.

On the night they carried her out, I begged my father to take the doll upstairs into the attic, where I would never go again. I even had him pull a bench in front of the door, leading to the stairwell.

Years passed, I moved on, married and had kids. On the death of both of my parents, I became trustee of my old house and had to return to pack up all of their belongings and ready it for sale. It was not without a great deal of trepidation that I had to return there, since I had never gone back to that house since the night of her death.

As much as I feared going up there, I had to empty what was in the attic, and at least it was daylight. I reluctantly slid the bench away from the door and slowly ascended the stairs lit by the bright morning sun from two windows at the top.

Once upstairs, I quietly walked down the hall to the low slanted entrance. Dust motes swirled in the vapid air that reeked of cedar. I hesitated and then coughed, as much as to gain courage, as to clean my lungs of the musty air. I half bent down, avoiding the slant-ed wooden beamed roof and entered. The attic had always been our repository of aged artifacts like 78 rpm records, worn cloth-ing, dusty military uniforms, boxes of outgrown toys, chests of our school projects that mom refused to part with, threadbare stuffed animals, ancient first edition books now worth a lot, cracked crock ware, outdated kitchen items, and on a shelf old Kodak cameras, some movie and some stilled with large flashbulb attachments, and of course my old View Master with its circular slides. There was the old black cast iron Underwood typewriter, which I used at the age of three to bang out my first story. It was about a choo choo train I was engineering that saved a bunch of kids from a huge tidal wave, just in time. I was determined that someday I would be a great writer, but life got in the way.

With a smile I saw the old RCA Victrola with the large megaphone and sharp stylus that teased the scratchy sounds from my father's 78 rpm Italian opera records. I thought of the nights we'd all sit around and listen, since we never could afford the new black and white TV's. There were old piano rolls which we could thread into our upright Lauder piano, that my grandfather built and pushed on the pedals to pump out songs.

Then there was the chest of the dead. It was filled with old faded amber and black macabre photos of past relatives from Italy and Newark, who no one even knew. What disturbed me the most was they were photographed after their death, since photography had not been available when they lived. Well dressed and supported upright, they stared with wide clouded eyes, some propped up standing behind their seated dead wives bejeweled and garbed in frilly frock and lace. Cadavers totally oblivious to the cordite flash of a bending cloaked photographer. Why was the preservation of their corpse so important for future generations? Was this just a testimony that they had indeed lived? Did they think their generations of future offspring would really care? Why did only Italians do this?

Lit only by a stained window shade half hanging from the one clouded window, my eyes adjusted to the dark corner, then I saw it. The ridged upright straw weaved back of her old wheelchair, knowing full well what was sitting on it. She had never left, but was still there, as I spun the chair around there she was, her spirit embodied in the face of that terrible ceramic doll, still wide eyed and staring again through me. I fell backwards to the floor, tipping the wheelchair on its back. On my stomach I crawled my way back out away from her. It was then that I noticed a faded envelope laying on the floor which must have been sitting on the chair. I grabbed it and ran stumbling downstairs nearly tripping in my wild flight into the kitchen for some water and heavy breathing.

I looked back up the stairs. Had she followed me? The familiar fear I felt the night she was carried out was tympanic pounding in my chest. Looking back over my shoulder, I ran from the house. How would I ever explain to my kids that their Dad was afraid of a ceramic doll in the attic? They would have to go in to finish the packing themselves

Days passed, the house was packed and once the movers left, the house, which I knew would always be haunted by her evil spirit, was placed on the market. We all then left for home. I vowed never to return.

Days later when home, while I was gathering my clothes for the laundry, I ruffled thorough the work clothes I wore that day. I had forgotten and felt the letter in one pocket that fell from the wheelchair. Though stained and fragile, I needed to see what it portended. I was alone in my bedroom and pressing it flat on my desk, I very carefully took a knife to slit it open

It must have been drafted by her husband, Uncle Mazzola, who returned to Italy immediately after her death, and since she had no voice, she must have mimed to him what she wanted to say. It read:

"Caminuch you no blacka sheep as Mama say. No, you gooda, gooda boy. You always like me cause stay near me alla time. No you brother, sister, mama or pa, and never my Gaetano, that strunza. Eah say grazia tante to thanka you, you only one who care, and takea time to maka me inside laugh."

Stunned by this revelation, how could I have been so wrong about her for so many years. I vowed to someday find that doll, bring her home, and give it to my kids. Then I wept.

COUSIN RICHARD

During religion class, he was so scared by a catechism teacher for failing to memorize a prayer he was supposed to know, that he feigned polio, the scourge of the 50's, and was sent to the hospital. Then thought of his cousin Richard who didn't feign it. He lived upstairs in the same three story house, and was just a year older than him. Stricken before the Salk vaccine had been developed, he lived most of his early life on his back in an iron lung pumping air into his deflated lungs. Then after several spinal surgeries into a wheel chair, and lived in a convalescent hospital in Port Jervis, New York, and again with no visitors except his mother Marie and Danny. His father Frank had died years earlier. A man who started working in a candy shop, as a youth and worked there all of his life. Not much for higher aspirations.

There were two things that always bothered Danny, one that he had dared fake polio, and second why had he not contracted it instead of Richard? He suffered from survivor's remorse, and never knew why he had been spared. So much so that he visited Richard often after his cousin moved to Weehawken, New Jersey, when all of the other many cousins avoided him as much as possible. They voiced that he was tainted possible contagious. What's worse is that their parents agreed.

Then one day he received a terrible call from his mother Maria that Richard had tried to commit suicide. Danny, mow only 16, went immediately to the hospital and saw his cousin sitting in a wheel chair with bandaged wrists. His mother weeping but glad someone had arrived, since all of the other cousins forsake poor Richard because of his affliction which was contagious at that time.

Danny sat with his cousin and asked why. Richard told him that when he told a priest in confession, that he had looked at a book of naked women, when in fact it was just a National Geographic, showing bare chested women tending to gardens in the yard, and some breast feeding infants.

The priest said God may never forgive him for that. Despondent when he went home and slashed his wrists. Danny told him it was not wrong to desire females and their bodies, but held back the thought that this poor soul trapped forever in a crippled body would forever be denied the love and physical contact of a woman. So once again Danny thought why had he not been so cursed instead of him.

THE CATHOLIC YEARS

Excited at the age of seven to finally receive his first communion, during practice a bird flew into the cathedral of Our lady of Sorrows Church. He stood, pointed and screamed, "It's the Holy Ghost!" The bird flew in circles and then right smack into a pillar, broke it neck, and fluttered to the granite floor. He screamed, "The Holy Ghost is Dead! "And the rest of the kids joined in. Sister Jema did not take too lightly to this, and dragged him by the arm out into the vestibule, smacking his sad face soundly.

After his first communion, Danny tried out for altar boy, but tripped over his long tunic and knocked over all of the candles he was supposed to be lighting, and set fire to the altar shrouds.

Then as the custom of Italians, if anyone died during the year, Christmas was not celebrated and all the women wore black for a year. This was to show mourning and respect for the dead, but it played hell on us little guys for that Christmas. I offer you this poem, "Christmas in Newark."

It's almost Christmas and no one's died this year. That means we can decorate and get presents and celebrate the day. But hurry for uncle has taken ill.

Let's drag out the old paper and wire tree. City children don't know of scented pine and real twigs. Don't all trees smell like moth balls?

See it's already decorated and lit. How bright the lights shine? Perhaps just a little too bright.

Let's sing carols! But not so loud because uncle grows weaker.

Let's wrap presents! I've got a vase I made out of a fruit jar for mom and dad. I made a paper train for sis that I know she'll like. I've got a picture book of animals for brother, which he gave me last Christmas. I hope they can't guess what they are getting. Sure I believe in Santa, but maybe he needs just a little help.

I heard them talk about a priest. Why should a priest be here on Christmas Eve? Maybe he's here to help us build the manger. Tomorrow is Jesus's birthday. I'm really glad he was born on Christmas. Good night Jesus, and hurry Santa.

But when morning came there were tears instead of tinsel, black instead of rainbow. The tree was gone and without those colored lights an old picture book can't look new, a paper train doesn't really go, and a pretty vase is only a painted jar.

"Now I lay me down to sleep,
I pray the Lord my soul to keep.
Please God, if you really can hear,
don't let anyone die next year."

FIRST EXPOSURE TO THE HOLOCAUST

The real treat in Catholic School was the Friday afternoon movie. Unfortunately, there was one film about the Nazi which told of someone they had severed the right arm and the left leg off someone in Norway. He was so horrified he ran out of the movie and all the way home. Also traumatized by what he heard of the concentration camps by his Uncle Tony, who had liberated Dachau, he remained strangely connected to that era. Nightly visions and dreams haunted him, but not as a victim, but as a perpetrator. Maybe in trying to gain control as those victims of genocide tried, he devoted his life to police work and kept his amour sound with continual training in martial arts and weights. Yet try as he might, he could not escape the demon diagnosis of Diabetes, which made him blind. Thus he asked his friend and Endocrinologist Dr. Ryan, who told him he would not survive the distance of another While traumas at school with the nuns were bad enough, he often bullied on the walk home by his classmates. One day they picked him up and threw him head first into a barrel of raw meat outside a butcher shop.

NYC marathon. He showed him his EKG strips, but Danny said he knew that, and wanted only to end it in a manner of his choosing. Reluctantly Ryan agreed to lead him into his LAST LAP.

FIRST CLASS

Danny stood up from his desk as the door opened and the first of his students sauntered in. "Take your seats and we will get to know each other." Only five, so this should be easy he hoped regardless of the bizarre look and dress of some of the females, but that was the trend these days.

There was Bobbi with the buzz cut, tattoos and piercings, slouching in her chair picking at her nails and looking bored.

Then Tonya Hispanic and at least looking interested as she opened up a pad to take notes.

Becka was black and could have an attitude as she whispered to Bobbi and snickered and pointing to me.

Only two males. Cameron with thick glasses with an intelligent look sitting straight up and ready to take notes.

The other male was Booker whose reputation preceded him as the star quarterback of their team. His coach had talked to me concerning the need for him to obtain more than a passing grade in order to keep scouting agents who will watch his progress this fall to recruit him.

Clearing his throat," Good Morning class. I'm Danny Giordano and will be teaching you History this semester. I'm handing out some cards and please put your name and contact information on them."

Immediately Becka jumped up chin forward, "Hey dude I didn't know we was gonna have no quiz, I didn't even study for it!"

Cameron just looked and shook his head in disbelief.

"Becka sit your you know what in that chair and do as I just said or you will go see the man down the hall. And the name is not Dude, but Mister Giordano and don't you ever forget it."

Becka sat down and crossed her arms over her chest.

"Now why do you think this history class is a requirement?"

"To give you a job?" Bobbi offered.

"Cute Bobbi, but no. This is why, Vas Wir Vergessen Durfun. "

"Well God bless you." Becka said.

"No it means that we dare not forget the past. The philosopher Georges Santayana said, those who forget the past are condemned to repeat it."

"I agree with that," Cameron offered.

"Of course you would you brown noser ", sneered Bobbi.

"Well I guess since we are stuck together for the next semester we might as well get along. Booker you've be rather quiet through all of this. Any comments?"

"Hey I do whatever it takes to get me a good grade. I need to show progress half way through for those scouts coming to my games."

"Yes I've already been told by your coach and even your father, but you will still have to produce. Agreed?"

"Yes I said I would do whatever it takes. "

"It's interesting how students of mine talk about their final grades. They say I got an A or I got a B, but they say He gave me a C or a D. You see putting the blame for failure on someone else. We will see the dire effect of this attitude as the prevailing justification of Hitler against the Jews."

Tonya finally spoke up, "Yes as a Hispanic and you Becka a Jew we both know how we can be discriminated against. Certainly not as bad as what the Jews endured, but certainly some sense of isolation as a result of it, and restricted to what some have told me to remain with my own kind."

"Well class then this will be a real lesson in tolerance for all, because as Elie Wiesel said, evil doesn't need our assistance, just our indifference."

"Until next time, class …."

"Wait," interrupted Tonya," Can you tell us a little about yourself?"

"Sure if you have a few hours." All laughed.

"Well I have a unique opportunity to have obtain a scholarship to work in Germany. And the history of World War two fascinated me. I had the opportunity to visit and talk to individuals who were still alive and who had experienced that war first hand. While I worked teaching English to German students, on weekends I toured many other countries. Norway, Denmark, Sweden, England, France, Italy where my parents were born, and even Moscow." He smiled over the remembrance of when he too Italian in High school because his grandmother was Italian, so she could do his translations. He remembered waiting until the last minute the morning of his class to give her the Italian lesson he had to translate. She looked at it and made a strange jester, when the awful realization hit him, that sure she could read Italian, but she couldn't speak English.

"It was a both a fantastic and very sobering experience to hear firsthand how the war had impacted so many lives. Both from the standpoint of the victims and the perpetrators. But we don't have time now, so eventually."

Bobbi sitting up, "Well this may not be such a boring class after all."

"Let's hope not. I promise to make it interesting, thought provoking and ask you to consider parallels in today's society and take an active role in changing the world you will inherit long after I am long gone." Danny thinking for just a second of his demon diagnosis.

Tonya standing says, "That philosopher, I forgot his name, said if we forget the past we are condemned to relive it. "

"Exactly, now start reading your assignments and we'll pick it up next time. Dismissed."

DACHAU AT CHRISTMAS

Danny turned the book to the next lesson in his history class to his students. "Class today we continue with what we've already learned about world war two, and now we need to learn about the discovery of the concentration camps. The ugliest discovery the allies made of the millions who had died there."

"Dachau was the first concentration camp and established is 1933, to first house criminals, agitators and Jehovah Witnesses, but not Jews."

Loren, "Jehovah Witnesses? Are these the annoying shits who knock on your doors at the most inconvenient of times, like when you're on the toilet?" All laughed. "But why them, were they also Jews?

"Of course not, they were pure Aryan Germans, but would not sign a declaration professing an allegiance to Hitler."

"Why not?"

"Because their only allegiance was to their God and no earth bound leader."

"So were they gassed?"

"No, those few that were executed were beheaded with an ax, since later Hitler said that gassing was only for Jews, and the ax for true, but misguided Aryans. So at Dachau they wore a Purple Triangle as their insignia. In fact, later years when the Jews were sent to Dachau, the Jehovah Witnesses expressed concern as to why their race was sent there. Since they knew they were considered as traitors, but what had the Jews Done? "

One student slouching said, "Do we really have to go into that gruesome time?"

"Yes we do."

"Why, we already know all about it...."

"No you don't and I visited one of the camps at Dachau while visiting friends in Munich during Christmas."

Another student both hands on his face, "What a really great way to spend Christmas." The rest of the class laughed.

"Was Wer Nicht Vergessen Durfun," What we dare not forget. Those were the word of Georges Santiago written on the wall of Dachau. You see you most lazy brats, if we forget the past, then we are condemned to relive it."

"Ok." Said one student, "The rest you your just shut up and let him tell us about this firsthand experience so we can leave after the bell, as long as he makes it short."

One student raised his hand, "Do we need to know this?"

"What is that supposed to mean?"

'I mean like is it going to be on a test or something?

Danny just shook his head, realizing the banality of the students he has to teach with no interest in history, but only in gossip about who was dating who.

"Yes you will see this on your next exam if that is what it is going to take to get you to listen. And you better make notes."

"Dachau was liberated by the American Army, but the first liberated was Auschwitz by the Russians. Most were in Poland, but many discovered and even a camp just for women at Ravensbruck in Germany."

One chubby girl in the back row slide forward raising her hand, "Why just a camp for girls?"

"I'll get back to that later, but let me continue."

The lad who asked whether he needed to know this, waved a nonchalant hand as generously indicting me to go on.

"Well a friend of mine, Reiner Wohl, was a medical student on a visa to our country. He was surprised as well as embarrassed by my interest in the holocaust and what transpired at Dachau during the war since his parents lived a mere seven miles from the camp. He could not phantom why I had this determination to see Dachau if ever I came to Germany.

Whether by fortune or perhaps misfortune, I was accepted into a United Nations Student Exchange Program, and thus ended up in Munich on a snowy Christmas Eve.

I met his parents for dinner and we had a tree lite with real candles. They sang Christmas carols, as so many other German families did on that eve so long ago, warm and well fed, ignoring the frozen hunger and horror of what others were experiencing, a mere seven miles down the road years ago."

"So then what? Hurry class is almost over."

"Then I shall be as brief as possible, but no one can leave until I say so. Understand?"

"But what about our lunch?" The aggravating one complained.

"When you hear about what little the inmates had to eat, you'll be grateful to be getting the juke food you all love so well." Some laughed.

"Well when morning came Reiner, without even asking, knew what I wanted to do on this Christmas day. He first avoided my wish by saying the site probably wasn't opened, but I told him to check and it was.

Upon arrival by bus, we were the only ones who disembarked at that site.

Trudging through the snow, I was haunted with images of freezing emaciated Jews standing in the predawn Appell, (roll call), lasting for hours in thin paper-thin garb and wooden clogs. Then only those males and females who survived faced hours of cold and hunger while toiling under the constant threat of the truncheon."

"What's a Truncheon?" asked one, and another how do you spell that roll call?"

Danny explained and now even a little impressed that it seemed he had sparked some interest in these kids.

"We eventually entered the only surviving barracks still standing. Surprised at our arrival, the one woman on duty, asked "Warum" (why) this day, then shrugged punched our tickets and beckoned us to pass.

Since Reiner was now a physician, we went to the medical experimentation ward. No corpses now, but horrid photos of what those victims had to endure in the name of science. The hollow faces of subjects staring right into the camera, while submerged up to their necks in ice water baths. Doctors standing by with stopwatches timing their moment of death."

"Ugh, can we stop now? I'm already losing my appetite."

"Not yet! There were photos of those subjected to high altitude compression and then instant decompression to mimic what a Luftwaffe pilot would experience if having to bail out at high altitudes. These photos showed victims hanging in a parachute harnesses, dead and bleeding from ruptured eyes.

Then the photos of the lethal injections, experimental surgeries, X-ray castration of females, all carefully documented in the Nazi's TOTENBUCH, (death registry). So many names, not of people, but victims dehumanized to an inscribed tattoo number on a wrist. At Ravensbruck the women were called Rabbits."

"Why rabbits?" The girl at the back asked?

"Just to dehumanize them as animal subjects for experimentation."

"Like what experiments?"

"I'll get to Ravensbruck eventually, but let me continue. Hardly a word passed between us the entire time. Upon leaving Reiner said this place stands as an insult to the German people and should be razed to the ground. I pointed to a plaque on the wall by the poet George Santana, "Those who forget the past are condemned to relive it,"

We came back that night to a somber family. Reiner immediately lashed out at his parents for not taking action to stop this when they knew what was going on. His father responded that yes, they knew what was going on at Dachau. They witnessed emaciated inmates under guard through their windows repairing streets or clearing snow and ice. He went on to say they feared intervention and would not protest to protect the lives of Reiner and his young sister. Plus, neither parent were members of the Nazi party, which also placed them in a compromising position.

Reiner lashed out that he would have intervened no matter the consequences and not been the cowards his parents were. I interrupted that maybe if he were in a similar situation, you would have done the same thing. Survival of oneself and family at all costs is a common trait of human nature."

"So then what?

"Well the next day I left Munich in trauma of the photos of

those victims. What I had only heard about, but never experienced until that Christmas morning. I today still remain traumatized by the wanton slaughter of so many innocents, and yet remember an image of the tall black modern metal motif outside of the camp, all showing twisted joined bodies of the seven nationals who died there. Phantom images' crying to be remembered, longing to be told. Emblazoned in black the German words: Nie Weider (never again.)"

"So now you know of my consuming passion to teach this. I want to let this what I teach to stand as a fitting eulogy for all those who died there and were denied one. And I hope all of you will develop a fierce attitude to intervene so such things never happen again. Agreed?"

The class some even teared eye all nodded in agreement. Remember Ellie Weisel, the great Nazi hunter said, evil doesn't need our agreement, but just our indifference. Class dismissed."

They all shuffled out much less arrogant, and one girl asked, "that was really interesting. Will we get to hear about Ravensbruck?"

"Thank you for your compliment. Teachers never get accolades. Students will brag about receiving and A or B, but if a C or lower, they say he gave me a C or lower. They always fail to take responsibility for their grades."

The girl nodded and laughed, and I said, "Yes tomorrow we will see how in just one night of terror started the Nazi pogom against the Jews. That night will always be remembered as Kristallnacht.

KRISTALLNACHT

KRISTALLNACHT

Danny's students shuffled in and sat down. "So now we will hear of the tipping point against the Jews, when no more subtle actions against them erupted into a night of terror and death.

On the night of November 9ᵗʰ, 1938 two days earlier a Polish Jew living in Paris shot and killed a member of the German embassy, Ernst Vom Rath, in retaliation of the way his parents were being treated by the Nazi.

When this Storm troopers, the SS, Gestapo, and the Hitlerjugend, youth corps, beat and murdered men, women and children. Hundreds of Jews were murdered, and 7,500 Jewish shops had they their windows smashed. Thousands of Jews were sent to the concentration camps at Dachau and Ravensbruck. Thus the name marking the event, "The Night of the Broken Glass."

In addition, 267 synagogues were looted and burned. Thirty thousand Jews were rounded up and sent to concentration camps.

A more vivid account is given in the book, "Wunderland" by Jennifer Cody Epstein . In her graphic account, she notes the German Police, Polizi, just standing by and watching, and the firemen doing nothing to quell the flames in the synagogues, but directing their water to cover the non- Jewish buildings. Even the non- Jewish civilians were caught up in the frenzy and participated in the destruction. The German Storm troopers were seen throwing Jews out of two and three story balconies to the ground, and setting others on fire.

It was happening all over Germany. Prime Minister Goebbels said." We will no longer tolerate a situation where thousands of Jews in our territory control entire streets of shops, pack places of public transportation, pocket the wealth of Jewish land lords, and while their Jewish brothers shoot down German officials."

He went on to profess the belief that matzo was made from the blood of gentiles and that Jews were sex predators, and that they emitted a foul smell that could be detected when they approached.

The main character Renate, a Mischling, German for mongrel or half breed, is tainted with Jewish blood because her father had some Jewish blood in him through an intermarriage with a Catholic many years ago. She is a very attractive girl, and pursued by many, but is condemned and ostracized from many schools, shops, friends, and isolated because of this rare Jewish Taint which the Gestapo discovered and stamped her ID card with a large "J". This was in 1938 before the Jews were required to wear the yellow star.

Even her first lover Rudi, abandons her after he discovers her Jewish impurity, and commits acts of violence and derision towards her.

In the beginning, as the only Mischling in a class of full Aryans, she is asked to come to the head of the class where the Professor shamefully measures her statue and features with calipers and points out her subtle Jewish features that could fool anyone. This is done much to the derision of the class. He then further belittles her by handing her a wet cloth and telling her to wipe down her chair at the back of the room to clean it of her Jewish smell.

On the day of Kristallnacht she escapes from school and boards a tram heading home. Here she witnesses all the horror of the event. She watches in horror of a naked old Jewish man being held up by two youths from the Jugend Corps and being slightly jabbed with the DJ knives they were given upon graduation, not to kill, but to torture. Blood ran from his head and his chest and arms from the small punctures. These youths were mere boys, younger than her, and former classmates.

So she mostly avoids school and just sits in her room reading and playing her with her dog Sigi, until the worse happens. Due to the shortage of food, her mother says it's time to put the dog down. Renate screams against this idea, but the mother reminds her is more humane than what happened to a neighbor's cat next store. It was found dead with a large "J" carved into its abdomen.

So her mother gives Sigi a last meal of cheese and blood sausage laced with poison. The family doctor gives him an injection to allow him to sleep through his own death. He was then buried outside in the garden.

Days later Renate still feels the bark less silence when she enters the house. She still shifts her feet at night seeking his warm furry weight that graced the bottom of her bed. She still reaches out in the morning for a quick pat and his rough tongued kiss. And sobs when she only feels empty silent air.

So now you see how the subtle intolerance went to the overt fueled by Gobbels, and Nazi Storm troopers, Gestapo, SS, and even the Hitler Jugend, both male and female, as well as the non-Jewish citizens.

"Wow ", Bobbi said. "I just realized that I may be a Mischling and my ancestors may have lived during that time."

"Possibly", Danny offered.

"But you mentioned thousands of Jews were sent to concentration camps at Dachau and Ravensbruck. You mentioned Dachau, but can you tell us more about Ravensbruck?

"Yes, but that is an entire new class and with more slides to see next time. Class dismissed."

FACTUAL HISTORY OF RAVENSBRUCK

HIMMLER'S GOALS

Ravensbruck was a Nazi concentration camp restricted to just women. It was built at Furstenberg on the edge of the Schwedtsee Sea, 50 miles north of Berlin. It was established by Reichstfurher Heinrich Himmler in May 1939, and funded by Siemens Electric to make parts needed for the V-1 and V-2 rockets. It also served as a training center for female guards in other camps, but also served a more insidious function. It was a center for experimental surgery on those so chosen as rabbits, the term designated for those selected for experimental surgery.

SS Max Koegel was commandant from its beginning until July of 1942, when he was replaced by SS Fritz Suhren until its liberation.

THE INMATES

Inmates were not all Jews, but of the 132,000, 48,500 were polish women the largest national group imprisoned. Those that were Jewish, just 20%, numbering only 26, 4000, but suffered the greatest torment and death of at 15,000.

As to others, there were 28,000 from the Soviet Union, 24,000 from Germany and Austria, nearly 8,000 French women interned as resistance fighters, thousands from other countries, and even a few British and American women. It also included political prisoners, resistance fighters, Soviet prisoners of war, Jehovah Witnesses, and those deemed as asocial such as gypsies, thieves, prostitutes, and lesbians.

They were all tattooed, and wore distinctly colored coded triangles by offense. Red triangles by political prisoners, such as the Soviet prisoners of war, and those French women, captured during the resistance. Jehovah Witnesses, also called Bible students. The latter all pure German Aryans whose only crime was in refusing to sign a pledge to serve Hitler, worn the purple triangle. The asocial wore Black, common criminals convicted of violating the Nazi imposed laws. Those convicted of shoplifting, cheating and minor disturbances wore green. Lesbians and those accused as such wore pink triangles. All Jewish women wore the yellow triangle of the Star of David. Within each triangle was a letter indicating the person's nationality. All were given short blue and white short stripped tops that bared the bottom half of the buttocks, wooden clogs, but no underwear to allow easy access for the lash when needed. Lack of modesty and complete submissiveness was the norm.

INDUCTION and SELECTION

Upon arrival, all, regardless of age, all were stripped naked and paraded past SS doctors and female guards. The old, obese, lame, and senile were isolated and immediately sent for the gas chambers. All others, except the very shapely and attractive were assigned to hard labor outside the camp. The latter were assigned, regardless of age, for brothel service.

SCREENING JEWS FOR CONTRABAND

Upon Himmler's command, all attractive Jews were assigned for brothel service and told if they participated, they would be freed within 6 months. Since no German was allowed regular intercourse, with the risk of pregnancy, only anal intercourse was allowed. Most of the women favored this since when they were released they could return to their husbands with them not knowing how they were serviced. Not only women but very young girls were recruited into brothel service, even against their wills. Some subjected to this painful degradation even in front of their mothers and female siblings.

THE RATIONALE FOR A
CAMP ONLY OF WOMEN

Ravensbruck focused on the gender and biological issues specific to women. It was not built outright as a death camp, but a place to provide slave labor for the industrial firm, Siemens Electric Company who funded the camp, to make components for the V-1 and V-2 rockets.

MEDICAL EXPERIMENTS

However, it was also established, as an insidious camp to provide a female population needed for specialized medical experimentation on polish Jews. This first included sterilizations testing by Professor Hohlfelder, chief of the SS X-Ray battalion. Subjects were beamed for different lengths of time with a piercing focused X-ray beam until the ovaries were scorched. This technique most often caused major burns, and even in some cases death.

In July of 1943, Dr. Carl Clauberg, tested a single injection of a chemical irritants into the uterus, administered under the pretense of a routine gynecological exam. On some, the extremely painful injections penetrated to the end of the ovarian duct, and even into the abdominal cavity. He proved that with several trained physicians and assistants, several hundred a day could be sterilized.

In addition to sterilizations, other experiments included, bone removal surgeries, aseptic introduction of virulent microorganisms to test anti-biotics. These victims were labeled lapins or "rabbits" to further dehumanize them, and treat them as mere experimental animals. After such treatment, most were not allowed to survive, but were gassed, in the only gas chamber on German soil and then cremated. Others were given lethal injections, and transported to the crematorium. These medical studies were under the direction of Dr. Karl Gebhardt, who led male and even female physicians such as the notorious Dr. Herta Oberheuser who performed medical experimentation from 1940 until 1943. These experiments included muscle and bone removal, and then the sites infected with microorganisms, glass and metal to reflect what downed pilots would encounter. Many died or were executed, but 63 did survive the end of the war, one as young as 16.

I refer you to the book, "Lilac Girls" by Martha Hall Kelly, 2016, and although classified as fiction, the accounts of the medical experiments at Ravensbruck are well documented as fact.

In addition, any pregnancy was punished by death through or forced abortion. No infant delivered in secret was ever allowed to live. Pregnant Jewish women entering Ravensbruck were immediately shipped to Bergen-Belsen, and placed in an outdoor barbed wired area, labelled the "recreation area" where they were whipped, raped or locked in tight boxes and starved to death.

The polish Jews fared the worse. Referred to as "Rabbits" they were transferred to Block 32 as subjects for medical experimentation. These experiments under the command of Commandant Fritz Suhren involved forced surgical sterilizations made without anesthesia. Those pregnant would have caesarean sections and the fetuses burned. Other surgeries included septic and anti-septic bone operations, removal of bones and muscle for transfer to severely wounded Wehrmacht casualties, open wounds made and then infected with virulent microorganisms to test the effect of certain antibiotics, near drownings to test the effect of resuscitation on downed pilots, injections with gas gangrene, phenol, and acids.

Polish rabbit, Maria Kusmierczuk, was one injected with gas gangrene to test the effect of sulfa drugs on open wounds inflicted on her prior. She did not survive. Another was polish rabbit, Izabella Rek, whose leg was mutilated with bone removal did survive and testified at the Hamburg trials. In fact, prior to liberation, she smuggled out a photo of her standing tilted on her bent and permanently disabled leg.

Once used, no rabbit, if not already dead as a result of the experimentations, few were allowed to survive. When finished, they were first locked in a separate block, given lethal injections, and transferred naked on a lorry that carried them to the crematorium. Or some were allowed the "Beauty walk" to die in some dignity which they whey were denied. We will cover that later.

In an article by Martha Hall, entitled "Channeling History" in the Oct/Nov 2018 issue of the AARP, she tells that of the many women subjected to such mutilation, 63 survived, the youngest only 16, who entered the camp at the age of 9.

No babies born were allowed to survive. Once delivered, the infant was taken outside the ward, and drowned in a barrel of water. Only one is reported to have survived. A girl named Miriam who was rescued by a nurse, whose mother Frieda died on Valentine's day February 14th 1945 from typhus, but Miriam's story of her mother and father, was immortalized in a book, entitled "The

Rabbit Girls" by Anna Ellory.

OTHER TORMENTS

The "Zellenbau, a dark cellar used for interrogations employed all medieval instruments of torture, was under the direction of SS Herr Ramdohr.

There were also punishment starvation cells, and frequent attacks by the SS dogs just to amuse the SS.

Selection for Brothel service at Ravensbruck

In the summer of 1943, Reichsfuhrer Heinrich Himmler's "Reich Directive", designated special buildings to house the more attractive Jewish inmates for brothel service for those serving in the camp.

Upon arrival, all Polish Jews herded in were commanded by SS Lagerfuhrer Herr Leutener, the SS officer in charge of discipline, to line up and undress. He proclaimed that those chosen for brothel service would not have to work outside with the rest. They will be well fed, and liberated in 6 months. They would only be required to provide anal intercourse, so there was no fear of pregnancy or anyway their husbands or lovers would know what they did upon their release.

Some believing this lie, bent over, spread their cheeks wide, relaxed and thrust their bottoms out. Then deliberately presenting a wide gapping entry to show their size and willingness to accommodate any German entry.

All were then told to strip naked and stand in a line facing a wall.

While all of the regular physician monitoring of blood pressure, height, weight, oral and vaginal exams, there was one additional exam only performed on those whose bottoms were selected, those having specially shaped full bottoms.

The SS doctors would make note of those whose bottoms were perfectly shaped for a special duty. Those chosen were ordered to step back and bend over and ordered to pull their bottom cheeks apart. Then only those with perfect unflawed anuses were selected for rectal temperatures, one at a time, using the same thermometer. Photographs of face, breast and spread bottoms were taken and cataloged.

Next came the final act of humiliation and degradation, the deep digital exam. With a gloved hand, and an eager assistant taking notes, the ones selected were ordered to bend over with hands, pulling their cheeks apart, then using first one, then two to three fingers were inserted and she was told to push out to ease the entry. After testing the woman's ability to expand her anus, the doctor would then continue to push deep to track the direction up into the woman's rectum, to insure that the victim would allow the deepest penetration, regardless of the girth and length of the intruder. Then the SR (Schone Rucken) tattoo for "beautiful bottom" was engraved on the end of their original wrist tattoo.

THE YOUNG NOT SPARED ON THE STRETCHING MACHINE

Selections were only made on the basis of anal entry, not looks, or even sadly age. Girls as young as 10 and younger, whose anal width had not yet matured enough for anal or object penetration, were plugged with inflatable dildos, held down on their stomachs, legs spread and pumped to expand their rectums. This was done in the presence of their mothers and older siblings in wanton disregard of their screams or bleeding. These children were assigned to special SS who favored such.

Another technique was the stretching machine. Here the young girl was strapped bent over a bench, ankles and legs strapped to the sides. Her cheeks were spread apart, and a large and long penis shaped dildo was inserted into the poor girl's rectum. This was attached to a rotating battery driven engine, which would drive the dildo in and out at a regulated speed depending on the whim of the tormentor. Some girls would have to endure this painful object penetration for hours often in the presence of the SS officers who quipped that this would well prepare the little girls for hours in the service of the men to whom they would be assigned.

Those SR's so marked for use in anal intercourse by the SS, visiting Officers, and wounded Wehrmacht did not work the fields, nor be involved in any outside heavy labor, but sole function was to service the SS, by providing rectal access whenever demanded, and often by many, during the course of a night or day.

In exchange, they were given ample food and drink to maintain their plump bottoms. The other inmates not so selected labeled them in disgust as collaborators.

After selection, those SR's were marched into a room, still naked, and sat in a line on a wooden bench. They were then told what their special selection would involve. The SS Medical Officer, surrounded by Nazi guards, addressed the purpose of their special selection." You were so marked with the SR since you will be used for strictly for anal intercourse by the SS."

There were some nodes' by the SR's at this remark.

"This is the only type of release our officers, and even the lower ranked Wehrmacht are allowed. Regular intercourse with a Jew is disallowed by Himmler, and those officers breaching this order will be sent to the Eastern front. Thus your sole role will be to provide immediate access, whenever demanded, often and by many, during the course of any day or night.

Each of you will be assigned shifts and when you are on duty, you will be transported to the Torment Hall. Why so labeled? My men are told that your holes are not to be only used for their release, but also a form of punishment for being lowly Jew bitches that have been spared the work in the fields and the gas chambers. The rest of your female parts are open to any form of torment they wish. So hurt you they may usually with medieval torture instruments used on women during the inquisition. As written in the Malcifcant Magnum, the Hammer of Witches by a good Catholic Pope. Such treats may include bloody whippings on your chest, lower legs, and upper back, and your breasts and nipples tormented in clamps.

Your filthy cunts may be penetrated and twisted with abrasive dowels. But your ass will never be tortured in any manner since your filth hole is needed for other uses.

If you fail in any of your duties, you may be branded, but your filth hole not excused from duty. You are to accept all that is done to you in silence, or you will be gagged, so as not to frighten the other Jewish whores. "

Haupsturmfuhrer Leutener went on to say, "Despite the pain and humiliation, the news isn't all bad. In exchange for your service, you will not be required to work the fields, nor stand for hours in the freezing cold for the pre-dawn head count we call the Appell.

"And now it's time for some good news. You all will be generously given ample food and drink, which is also in our best interests, in order to maintain your plump and ample bottoms."

He and the other standing guards laughed at this contention.

"However I must add that every time prior to your assignment, you will be given a deep high volume enema by one of our female guards." Pointing to the back of the room, "To insure you are all clean of your Jewish filth."

If ever the need for punishment arises you females will never be whipped so as to not mare the beauty of your needed backside, but will be taken to the punishment tub, and your heads immersed until blackout, then revived, and the process repeated several more times.

Other non- marking options will have included the use of electroshock. Such females needing retraining in obedience will be strapped bent over the Goat, your buttocks spread, and one electrode probe with a flared end, to prevent expulsion, will be inserted high up into your rectum. The other electrode will be attached to a metal jaw device, which will lock your mouth open, your tongue secured with a metal pin through your tongue and your jaw thrust forward. An electrode will be stapled to your tongue. When the current is triggered, the electricity would travel the entire length of the alimentary canal causing intense painful violent spasms, from your Jewish filth holes to your salivating mouths. You will not be able to spit, but just drool because of the nail through your tongue. The current can be timed to stop and begin again at regular timed intervals, or the current can be put on automatic increase at every cycle. If you grow unconscious, a bucket of ice water will be thrown over you, only increasing the conductivity of the current.

How long you will have to endure this, will be determined by the nature of the offense, such violations are all documented along with the treatments required for each offense. We will enter your name and number every time you are punished in either way. As with the dipping tub, neither leave any visible marks.

After multiple interrogations if you still are showing no sign of improvement, you will be sealed in a tight metal chamber, where you can neither sit nor stand, and be slowly starved to death. On the other hand, we have known a faster demise when a blowtorch is applied to the metal box, or it is thrown into the ovens in the crematorium while you are still alive.

THE TERRIBLE GOAT

While mostly under the command of female guards, a few SS officers maintained security. However only the female guards, or fellow inmates given special rations, inflicted the punishments to inmates in the Strafblok (punishment block). Himmler ordered whippings, which began in April 1942. The victim would be stripped naked, bent and strapped over a wooden bench referred as the "Goat". Then their naked bottoms would be visited in a rhythmic fashion by the studded strap, stout birch, or cane. The SS officers would be allowed to watch, and a camp doctor had to be present to insure and document that the punishment had been carried out and effective enough.

The number of strokes was arbitrary and left up to the discretion of the guard, and was not dictated by the grievance of the charge, but based mostly on the visible effects of the thrashing slowly inflicted on the girls naked globes allowing ample time between stokes for the pain to crest and then subside. If not gagged, the victim would have to count, thank them and ask for another. The thrashed bottom would at first reddened, and then turn crimson and into a deep blue/black hue which covered the entire expanse of the proffered mounds. Then tiny pearls of blood would appear. The whipping would stop when the girl's bottom presented swollen bleeding wheals, but not always. If the prisoner fainted, she was revived with a pail of ice-cold water.

No age limit was ever taken in consideration. So not even the very young were spared. Upon the arrival of new inmates and after assigned to their barracks, a guard would arbitrarily choose one, usually favoring the very youngest, often just a child, to give 25 strokes on her naked backside on the Goat in front of the others Just to set an example, regardless of the innocence or age of the girl, and always with her mother present. This was repeated each day for the next two days in succession on the same girl. Often the whipping rack was carried outside during role call when a public whipping was deemed necessary.

There were also terminal whippings. These were reserved for female criminals, resistance fighters, some Jews, Gypsies, and Lesbians. The victim would be tied over a bench, and a thick heavily knotted wooden birch swung with a two handed full swing would be driven up into the bottom and the pelvic area. The purpose was not only to cause extreme pain, but also the fracture the bones in the pelvic area. Twenty-five blows were administered at a time, often with others present, and with a SS Doctor present who would monitor her vital signs. She would be kept conscious with buckets of ice water. Should she still be alive after the twenty-five, she was carried back to her chamber and the process renewed the next day.

Few ever survived, due to massive internal bleeding more than one or two days. If not, then the daily routine would continue until death was assured.

To really get a vivid idea of what this involved, I would like to refer you to two books, the first is "Lilac Girls" by Martha Hall Kelly. Her character Caroline Ferriday a socialite and actress in France, was captured by the Gestapo for passing out resistance literature and sent to Ravensbruck. She gives a vivid account of the medical experiments and whippings she witnessed.

LAST LAP

The other book, "Rose Under Fire" by Elizabeth Wein is even more interesting because this was a true story of an American pilot Rose Justice, who is forced down by Nazi fighters over Germany, but not fired upon. Once down, she is treated with respect and all the Nazi want to do was to inspect her plane. She is cared for and fed well as a similar combatant by them. When they learn she is to be transported to a special camp just for women at Ravensbruck, they even give her papers attesting to the fact that she should be treated well and respected as a prisoner of war. However, once at there, she is strapped over the GOAT and almost beaten to death for some minor infarction. She survives the beaten and the war and endures many weeks of recuperation afterwards in Paris. What's interesting is that when she is interrogated by members of the War Crimes Tribunal, she can't remember the beatings or even if it happened although her brutal scars prove otherwise. Truly a case of Post-Traumatic Stress Disorder (PTSD), where the brain forgets past horrors as an act of preservation in order to survive.

TREATMENT OF LESBIANS

Some of the worse torments were meted out on those discovered of Lesbianism. They were then sent to the Zellenbau for torture, each forced to view the other, or sentenced to a terminal whipping until death.

LESBIANS FORCED TO FLAIL EACH OTHER

An interesting modification of this, was that each female was forced to whip each other, with promise that the victor would be granted freedom. So in turn each would take a turn strapped over the goat, given the heavy birch and, with a two handed grip, swing it into the naked bottom of the other. Each limited to just 5 at a time, then the other taking her turn.

The SS witnessing this were amused that even though the lesbians cried during the thrashings, it did not diminish their relish to survive over the other.

MODIFICATION IF ONE LESBIAN WAS A VERY YOUNG GIRL

Recognizing that a very young girl, some even at the age of seven or younger, may have been the victim of intimidation into Lesbian acts by older women, she was allowed to administer a terminal whipping on such an abuser.

Since the youth was often too small as to deliver the required impact and force of the blows, she would be assisted in the delivery by a SS who helped her grasp the stout birch. In these cases, there was no stopping at 25, but continued until the pelvic was broken and shattered, and death declared by the visiting physician.

Though guaranteed special favors for agreeing to do this, the Reich felt that once a girl, regardless of age, would forever be tainted and intrigued into this lifestyle. Thus, she would be sent and executed in a timely, but in a painless manner by the garrote.

THE GASSINGS

In the winter and spring of 1942, those incapable of work and Jewish prisoners were gassed at a euthanasia center up in the psychiatric center in Bernberg. Ravensbruck had its own gas chamber, referred to by the code word, "Mittwerda", and the first prisoners were gassed in January 1945. They were mostly Hungarian, Jewish, polish, and Russian women prisoners. The number of those gassed is estimated to be 5,000 to 6,000, and then burned in its crematorium.

COUNTESS KAROLINA IANCORONSKA

Prisoner # 16076, the French Countess Karolina Lancoronska, was held in "Protected Custody" due to some implication with her and the French resistance. She was a recognized scholar or art, history and the ancient classics, and well respected by the Nazi. She taught several classes in the arts to the French prisoners, who were respected and treated much better and had much more freedom. Much of what is known about the victims of Ravensbruck is referenced in her book, "Michelangelo in Ravensbruck." She was assigned an upper room in the main building, where she heard the screams of those being raped and tortured throughout the night. On one forbidden nocturnal sojourn, she toured the downstairs and thorough an open door she documented what she saw and the cause of the screams.

In the first room, there stood a wooden horse, known as the "Goat" used for floggings. It was rounded with wooden slats with a leather pad on one end to elevate the buttocks. It was fitted with straps crosswise so the victim would forcibly be restrained. From upstairs, she often heard the rhythmic strokes and groans of the women. She also noted hanging on a wall mouth gags and a metal facial devise used to lock the jaw and tongue to impede breathing and to stifle the cries.

In another room, under the direction of SS officer Zellenbau, she saw a medieval instrument of torture called the "Coffin." which when pulled close had metal teeth that would penetrate the woman's body. It had ventilation holes and wolf claws, metal teeth that penetrated a woman's body but not in areas to cause death, just bleeding and pain, and the victim left to endure the closure for hours at a time.

THE DREADED APPELL

During the Appell, or roll call, all inmates were called outside for a head count to insure that none had escaped, were hiding, and those who had been gassed or killed had been checked off of the list. Exceptions were those assigned to the brothels and those privileged few such as countess Lancoronska, and others so deemed to be in" Protective Custody."

The daily role call would start at 4 Am and could last up to 5-6 hours. It was called so early, so as not to interfere with the inmate's work duties. Even corpses of those that had died during the night had to be carried and braced upright by two inmates on each side. Anyone collapsing was immediately shot behind the head, lifted and braced upright by two inmates.

This head count occurred in all types of weather, rain, wind and snow added to the abuse. Sometimes during days of subfreezing weather, they were all stripped naked, and since the sick and weak died, this was considered a type of natural selection for only the strong could prevail.

THE AUSSENS

The "Aussens", females who worked outside, were used like work like animals, with 12-14 across pulling huge rollers to pave the streets. They would till these roads in all types of weather, wearing only a short, see through chemise, that came to just the half bottom curve of their asses, and without any underwear. This allowed the female guards to easy access to whip the bottoms of those who needed it.

If one was deemed lazy, then the girl was asked to bend over and hold on to her knees, then the skiff was raised baring her proffered naked globes while being lashed with a thick studded strap or battered blue with a heavy truncheon. The other slaves were not allowed to watch, but required to continue to work, despite the scream and pleas of the poor victim. Then once finished, she was required to return to her tilling with bruised and battered nether globes, but having learned her lesson.

Fluid Most tilling the fields, preferred a stern whipping to this embarrassing treatment by the Watermen, in view of everyone, and restricted only to those young ones, with very inviting behinds, regardless of age. Especially those marked with the capitals SR who were excused from the brothels due to monthly menses.

THE WATERMEN

These were not female guards, but SS who delighted in one of the most humiliating, but not painful methods of human degradation. They would randomly select two females, and remember all in short skirts barely covering their bare bottoms, and have one first bend, and take a deep enema with a syringe and bucket of water they carried. Once the woman or even young girl was full, she had to bend and release it into the mouth of the other girl. And then the subjects would reverse and do it to the other. Much to the mirth of the SS, and in full view of all the other women working the fields. Some women so chosen would beg to be whipped instead of having to endure this.

RUSSIAN ADVANCE

With news of the Russian advance, the captors followed Der Fuhrer's mandate that no prisoner was to fall into enemy's hands, and they must kill them all. The SS screamed "Raus, Raus, Schnell, Schnell" beating on the shelters to get them out. Since it was impossible to kill them all and burn the bodies, on Saturday April 27th, a forced evacuation of the camp and a forced march toward Malchow and toward the British and American lines began.

Hans Pflaum used dogs to flush out those hiding in the blocks. He found one French woman hiding under a bed, pulled her out and beat her to death with a hammer. He continued to motorcycle around the camp and shot those too weak to join the march.

Herr Suhren ordered the SS and the female guards to gather up all of the records, of the Appell, the logs of the medical experiments, brothel records, punishment logs, torture, interrogation, execution and gassing records and brought them to the crematorium. They were told that they could not burn paper since they were still burning bodies. Sixteen thin ones and four fat ones at a time. Inmate Odette Sanson reported that live prisoners were indeed burned alive in open pits. Other inmates were put into the gassing vans with Zyklon B pellets dropped in.

SS Commandant Fritz Suhren led the rapid exodus of those who could still walk. Those that could not keep up, or fell, were shot. Interesting that some of the SS and female guards dropped their uniforms along the way and changed into civilian clothing given by compliant households.

LIBERATION:

At 11:30 AM, on April 30th, the first of the Russian tanks came crashing over the barbed wire. Of the 132,000 imprisoned, only 3000 were still barely alive in the camp. A red banner was hung over the gate and megaphones announced that they were free. One Russian liberator is quoted as saying to a survivor, "My God where have you been? Have you come from a grave?"

AFTERMATH:

Built in May 1939 and under the command of Commandant Max Koegal until July 1942 when it was then run by Commandant Fritz Suhren until its liberation in April 30th, 1945. Out of the 132, 000 women and children, from 23 different countries, were imprisoned from between 1939 and 1945, 117,000 did not survive.

WAR TRIALS IN HAMBURG:

The Ravensbruck trials were held by the British in Hamburg.

Dorthea Binz, the brutal overseer of the camp from August 1943 until its liberation, received the death sentence and was hanged on May 2nd, 1947.

Since Ravensbruck was also a training facility for SS female guards, the most famous graduate was Irma Grese, who was sent to Auschwitz. She was sentenced to death and hanged in 1945.

Hermine Braunsteiner Ryan a guard at Ravensbruck, fled to the United States and was extradited to Germany in 1981 and tried there.

Dr. Herta Oberheuser, the only female doctor who participated in the medical experiments was sentenced August 20 1947 to 20 years in prison but not death. She died January 24th, 1978 at the age of 66.

Nurses, Oberschwesters, who assisted with the medical experiments: Margarete Mewes, Grete Bosel, Vera Salvequart, Eugenia von Skene, and Elisabeth Marschall were all sentenced at the Hamburg trial.

Sentenced to death at Nuremberg in 1947, Dr. LePorz, Block 10 doctor. Dr. Karl Gebhardt, in charge of the brutal medical experiments, was also executed.

Commandant Fritz Suhren made it to the American lines, was captured, but escaped, and was recaptured in 1949 and was executed along with the notorious Hans Pflaum.

MEMORIAL TODAY:

There are several statues, "Tragedy", "The Mother Group", "The Group of Women", "She Who Carries", all erected to honor those female victims who were used as slaves, tortured and died as tools of the Third Reich. Especially young visitors can learn firsthand the violence that discrimination can affect upon their lives even today.

And yet the simplest sign on a poll driven into the ground, says it all: "Ihr Seid nicht zu Vergessen". You are not forgotten.

(DER LETZTE APPELL)
THE LAST APPELL

OLGA BENARIO PRESTES

A member of the communist youth organization, she was arrested and interned in the Barnimstrasse women's prison. In 1939 she was transferred to Ravensbruck where she secretly organized teaching activities. She was gassed at the Bernberg euthanasia center in the winter of 1942.

GRASYNA CHROSTOWSKA

A Polish Jew, after caught distributing the illegal newspaper, "Poland Lives", she was arrested and sent to Ravensbruck on September 12th of 1941. The following April, she and eleven other young Polish women were shot by a Nazi firing squad.

ROSI FORSBERG

Her family was deported to Auschwitz in 1943, and she transported to Ravensbruck. She was placed in a punishment bunker, where those selected as rabbits for medical experimentation, were isolated. At the end of 1944, she was forcibly sterillzed and underwent the horrid bone and sepsis trials the rabbits had to endure and all without anesthesia. She did survive and required ten years of over 30 surgical operations to correct her malformations.

MILENE JENSENSKA

Though not Jewish, she was married to a Jew, yet arrested by the Gestapo and sent to Ravensbruck for "re-education". In 1943 she underwent experimental kidney surgery and died in May of the following year from an infection in the other kidney.

ROSA JOCHMANN

Worked as a member of the resistance, and arrested by the Gestapo and sent to Ravensbruck in 1940. In 1943, she was placed in the punishment bunker for stealing food to give to others. She survived until the liberation by the Russians died in January of 1994.

KATHIE LEICHTER

She was a graduate with a Doctorate from the University of Heidelberg. She and participated in the resistance until 1940, until an informant told the Gestapo. She was deported to Ravensbruck in January 1940, and was among 1500 Jewish women selected for transfer to the Bernburg euthanasia to be gassed. Her loyal friend, Rosa Jochman a rabbit, described her transport: "I was allowed to accompany her. We went hand in hand, and after she boarded the truck in the bitter cold, she looked at me and waved a last goodbye."

CHARLOTTE MULLER

Neither a Jew, Gypsy, or a Communist, but a pure German Aryan and a member of the Jehovah's Witnesses. She was arrested by the Gestapo for distributing religious literature. Since she refused to sign a declarations professing her allegiance to Hitler, she was transported to Ravensbruck in May 1939. The Jehovah's Witnesses, or Bibelforscher, all wore purple triangles. Nearly 1800 of the Jehovah Witness men were beheaded, but and not gassed, because Hitler felt only Jews and other vermin should be gassed and never pure Aryan Germans.

Charlotte, after liberation, in 1950 was arrested by the Communist Government and imprisoned. So after being incarcerated for seven years by the Nazi, she spent another six additional years imprisoned by the communists.

LISETTA ROSE

A Gypsy, arrested by the Gestapo and sent to Ravensbruck in early 1944. She and her daughter were gassed shortly after.

VIOLETTE SZABO

A Catholic born in Paris, Violette joined a British Paratrooper unit and was arrested by the SS and brought to Ravensbruck in August 1944. In January 1945 she was executed by a firing squad along with other British agents, just months before its liberation.

SISTER ELISE RIVET

A Catholic nun of the order of Notre Dame, was a Mother Superior at her convent. She was falsely accused of hiding weapons by the Gestapo, and was transported to Ravensbruck in July 1944. To meet their death quotas, the Nazi selected 1500 Jewish, and gypsy females to be transported to the gas chambers at Uckermark. As a Catholic, Sister Rivet was not included in the selection.

Yet, she volunteered to take the place of a Jewish mother and her child. Sister Rivet was gassed on March 30, 1945. Ironically this date was also Good Friday, the day of her Lords crucifixion.

THE BEAUTY WALK

When those Rabbits, as the female experimental surgical subjects were called at Ravensbruck Concentration Camp were beyond further experimentation they were to be hanged. Given in mock deference they were granted a Beauty Walk by the female Nazi surgeons. This was to allow them, at the request of the Rabbits, to die in a more dignified manner.

All the other surviving rabbits would gather up the prettiest dresses, heels and hose recovered from those who had previously made the walk, and gowned the next condemned in the finest raiment. They would fix the hair and apply a red rouge sequestered from others. Some even asked for crunched up paper in order to add breasts to their cavernous chests.

All the friends who could limp, hobble or crawl would accompany their friend up to the top of a hill where the gallows looking like and inverted L beckoned the victim. The Rabbits went, not in tears, but smiles knowing their friend would soon be free of the horrid torments they would still endure.

After held under both arms the Rabbit was lifted by the female guards up the stairs, then the noose was tightened around her throat.

Though offered, they would all refuse the black hood, wanting their last view to be the smiling faces of her friends, and hear sound of their songs of the homes they once knew, until the blackness fell.

PHOSGENE

"So you ask about the Zyclon B gas used in the extermination camps? Well long before that was another gas called Phosgene used by the Germans during World War 1."

"That long ago?"

"Yes well even in ancient times the Greeks would light fires in the bow of their ships and allow the wind to carry it into the ships of the Persians blinding them on their approach. It was called Greek fire, but let's get back to phosgene and its very interesting history. Both the Germans and our allies used chlorine gas on each other during the brutal trench warfare, but chlorine was light and often just scattered in all directions.

So a German chemist, and a Jew at that, Fritz Haber invented Phosgene and it was perfect for trench warfare for two reasons."

"How so?"

"Well first it was heavier than air so after discharged, it would roll into the allies' trenches, and second and second it wasn't abrasive to smell since it had the order of new mown hay."

Going to the board Danny wrote the formula of phosgene as carbonyl chloride. "This is what it is chemically, but when combined with the moisture in the lungs it produces Hydrochloric acid which burns the lungs. The lungs alveoli, the tiny sacs, respond by producing fluid to try to dilute the acid, so in essence the victim drowns in his own body fluids."

"Was it painful? Since once it was diluted shouldn't that stop the pain?"

"Well let's try something. We can mimic the effect. I want everyone to take a deep breath and hold it in for as long as you can. Do anything you want, like pounding on the desk or stamping your feet, but don't let it out. Go ahead."

The class held it for as long as some could then gasp for air. "Painful no! but a horrid way to die. Trying to breath, but cannot transpire any air. It was first used on April 22, 1915 at the Battle of Ypres in Belgium in World War 1. On just that single day, 5,000 were killed and another 10,000 totally incapacitated. Even the mules pulling the ammo carriages."

"Poor animals. No gas masks to the allies?"

"Not all had them at that time. Those that did were also incapacitated. And remember the gas had a sweet smell, so many were caught off guard. Eventually though it lost its effectiveness for a very strange reason. "

"How so?"

"We some survived without their gas masks by urinating into a handkerchief and holding it to their nose. Since this converted the phosgene to just carbon dioxide and water."

All laughed, "Why would anyone ever think of that?"

Comically, "Well really, if you saw all your comrades thrashing around and gagging and choking, some would just piss their pants and huddle in a fetal position and cover their noses."

"So did that end it for Phosgene?"

"Yes, so Fritz developed a nerve gas, which had one benefit besides killing."

"Like what?"

"It was used as the very first chemotherapeutic agent on the son of John Donne who had brain cancer, who eventually died. You can read the account in Donne's Book, 'Death Be Not Proud', which I recommend to everyone."

"So was this Fritz ever caught and punished?"

"No just the opposite. Would you believe in 1918 he won the Nobel prize in Chemistry for something as innocuous as experiments in producing fertilizers from nitrogen and hydrogen gas. But, as a Jew, and seeing the rising anti-Semitic fervor in Germany, he fled to Switzerland and died in 1934. But no before developing a gas to use for the extermination of rats, Zyclon A. Since rats can't vomit upon ingestion they would die of internal bleeding. "

"Is that what they used in the death camps against the Jews?"

"No something far worse, Zyclon B, but I'll do into that next time."

"Interesting, but can we go now?"

"Yes, but with just this one caveat. I want each of you to go home, seal yourselves in the bathroom, and mix chlorine bleach and ammonia and breathe deeply. This will generate phosgene gas. Urine saturated Handkerchiefs optional.

See you all next time. Maybe."

BORSTEL

"So after Dachau and Munich where did you go next?", the girl in the front row asked.

"Well to better explain the next phase of my journey, let's look at a map." Danny pulled down the large European map that hung in front of the class.

Pointing to a tiny spot on the North of Germany, "I was on a student exchange visa to teach German and American history to students in a place called Borstel, a few miles north of Hamburg. Years later, in 1966, it was learned to have been a concentration camp that had been interned and without any trace of what had occurred there."

"Yes, but before I get to my time spent there I had to unique opportunity to travel all over Europe to see the effect the war had on other countries. First I went to London and spoke to survivors of the Blitzkrieg by the V2 rockets and heavy German bombers and aircraft. The V2 was built by an SS officer and aerospace engineer, Wernher Von Braun. Ironically he came to our country after the war and helped to build our space program at Cape Canaveral.

Hitler had decided that to bomb and burn London, would be the easiest way to get England to surrender. This was sad for two

reasons. First it was not a military target, and second heavily popu-
lated with innocent civilians."

"Did it work?"

"No in fact it had the opposite effect. While the could not stop
the V2's, the British Spitfires would fly around the clock sorties
against the German Bombers, the Junkers JU 88 and the Dorniers
217. Then against the fighters Messerschmitts, and Focke-Wulf
109's. All it did was unite the will of the country and lead to the
election of Winston Churchill to replace Neville Chamberlain who
gave away so much of the Balkans to Hitler without even a protest.

What's so interesting is the fact, that we were not at war with
Germany until Pearl Harbor, several of our own pilots fought with
the British against the Blitzkrieg."

"Then where? Back to Germany?"

"No, I actually decided to visit my relatives in Italy. Relatives
who lived under the Dictatorship of Benito Mussolini. I first went
to the Vatican in Rome and was devastated by the wealth in gold
coffins and the catacombs of the Popes, yet saw kids begging for
food and coins on the Vatican steps. And there was the preserved
corpse of Pope Pious Xll, as you recall, Hitler's Pope.

Then to Naples where my father was born, and more poverty.
From there just a short trip to Pompeii where the great volcano
Vesuvius erupted in 79AD and killed many in their sleep from the
lava flow. The tour guide showed many preserved bodies in grey
pumice. Some corpses still in the act of love making unaware of
when it hit."

Bobbi offered," You sure they were caught in the act, or just
knowing what was about to happen, give it one more shot.?" All
laughed.

"Maybe Bobbi, but I did get to climb Mount Vesuvius and got

to look down into the crater. Just a dark very deep hole very large abroad. What's interesting is the fact as you see in this next slide in the forefront is Vesuvius, but to the right is another volcano, Mount Somma, named after my step father's last name. "

Cameron, "But it has never erupted, and never showed any sign of activity according to Wikipedia."

"True, but when it does, look out!", all laughed.

"I went by Eurail pass up to Paris and visited the grave sites of the victims of the D Day Normandy invasion. Grave marker as far as the eyes can see. What the biggest outrage was when Paris was liberated, DeGaul who sat out the war in England, upon his return praised the French people for the courage they showed in defeating the Nazi. When, in fact, it wasn't a single French civilian that freed Paris, but the allied troops. In fact, the French Police during the war took an active part in rounding up the Jews mostly the females, and all of them French citizens, and turned them over to the Nazi's. Of the thousands, only two females survived the concentration camps alive after the war.

Then onto the northern Scandinavian countries. But it's interesting to note the order of Hitler's invasion of Europe. "

Showing grainy black and white photos. "Well as I said before, Austria and Czechoslovakia were taken without a shot thanks to England's Prime Minister, Neville Chamberlain." Clicking the next slide, next came the actual start of WW2 in Europe with the invasion of Poland on September 1st, 1939. Luftwaffe Commander Hermann Goering fitted the Stuka dive bombers with a siren that would wail like a banshee in their decent toward the earth. The scream of which sent terror into all the enemy and civilians. These Dive bombers were relentless in their slaughter of innocents. Poland was defeated in one month and 5 days, but it did bring France and

Germany into the war."

"Not us?"

"No Bobbi. We were an isolationist country thanks to Charles Lindbergh, and didn't want to get involved in another war. What was going on over there didn't matter to us, and we never dreamed we'd be drawn in."

"So not until Pearl Harbor." Cameron added.

"Correct. Now let's look at the order in which Europe fell after Poland.

First Denmark and Luxemburg in in about one day.

The Netherlands after the bombing of Rotterdam, in 5 days.

Yugoslavia in 11 days first invaded by the Italians, Germans and Hungarians.

Norway in just 2 months.

Belgium in 18 days.

Greece in 24 days. First by the Italians, but Germany had to help at the last minute.

France in just 46 days.

And then on to Russia. Hitler's stupidity in attempting a two front war, but his hatred of the communists, a stated in his book, Mein Kampf, equaled his hatred for the Jews.

Now that we've taken a complete tour of the world, let's get back to Hamburg.

Nancy, "Isn't Hamburg the city where the war trials of the criminals of Ravensbruck were held?"

"Yes very good, I'm glad you are remembering this. As a student of history this was a great opportunity for me to learn firsthand from those still alive from the war, since it had ended only 60 years before. Upon arrival, I was greeted by a Dr. Seydel, in charge of the hospital there."

"Hospital? What kind of hospital? "

"Well it was a hospital for studying pulmonary diseases for those...."

"Those survivors who were gassed?"

"Well I'm not sure, who they were treating, but let me continue. Toward the end of the war, Seydel was only 16 and put into a foxhole with three others manning a bazooka to fire at the Russian tanks entering Berlin. Before he could fire, his foxhole was hit by a Russian tank that killed all the others, but left him severely injured. He was captured and sent to a hospital and work camp in Russia. One night he escaped, and made it all the way back to Germany on foot."

Robert this time, "Sounds like the Russians were just as bad as the Germans."

"Not quite. I will relate what I learned when I went to Moscow, but the Germans in their advance into Russia, locked innocent civilians into a church, men women and children, sealed it shut and burned it to the ground. They even took one women, tied her to a stake, and burned her alive. This poster of her", pointing to one of the slides, "became a rallying cry for the Russians." Showing the next slide, "Close your eyes if you don't want to see this. Many blame only the SS and not the regular Wehrmacht infantry of the atrocities. You see here a very young woman hanging by her throat and a nurse's cap on her head. And notice the German soldiers all pointing and laughing at the woman they all just raped and hung to die."

"Germans, Russians, they all sound terrible in what they did."

Danny said, "Not just them, but us also."

"How do you mean."

Showing another slide, "Here is a picture of Frau Wempe, who

I also got to know at Borstel. A gentle woman who as the Russians were advancing, at the age of 16, put all of her belongings and into a baby carriage, and with her younger sister of 12 headed to the west in the hope of finding safety with the American Army who was advancing toward them. When she did find them, her relief turned to horror, as she and her sister were ganged raped, and her sister didn't survive.

Nancy said, "This is just too much to absorb, especially before lunch," All laughed. "Can we just go now even though it is not time yet?"

"Not until I tell you about the artifacts I brought in." Pointing to the table. "The first is a German typewriter. Do you notice anything different about the typewriter keys? Come up closer and look."

They all crowded around, "Just the one key near the bottom that has the SS on it."

"Correct, SS for Schutzstaffel this key was used to stamp all official documents and lists by the SS. Lists that may have included number of victims transported, those selected for labor and the rest, the children, and the infirmed sent to the gas chambers."

"And this book? What does this mean in German?"

Pointing to the cover and then Flipping through the pages. This book is titled, 'Pimp Hort Zu,' or youth listen to this. It is a text book to train the Nazi youth in their indoctrination against the Jews."

"Where did you get it?"

"It was from someone I met at the institute who was a member of the Nazi Youth Corp who had and extensive collection of German books left to him by his deceased father, a member of the SS. He offered me any one book that I wished to take. At first I refused since those books were a part of history and belonged left in Germany, but he insisted so that's why I chose that one."

"Did you ever read it?"

"No because it's written in the old German script, and even I can't translate it, but just look at the pictures of Nazi youth beating old Jewish laborers. "

After I shook his hand, he asked," So in America, what are you doing about your Jewish problem? I answered, What problem."

"What will you do with this book?"

"Well after eventually I will donate it to the Holocaust Museum in Richmond Virginia."

"Why Richmond?"

"That's my next story, and you will learn how the Nazi learned from us about discrimination, racial purification and slave labor, but you will have to wait until our next class. So class dismissed"

"Wait Mr. Giordano". One student thumbing through a German Guide book, "Here on page 196 is a place in Hamburg known as the Reeper Bahn," grinning, "Also known as the Red Light district. Was it called that because rape occurred there?"

"No, Reeper in German means rope, and near a street where the ships were tied to the wharves. So a perfect for place for sailors looking for fun. The streets were lined with women in windows where one could look and shop for whatever you wanted."

"Did you ever partake of the goodies? Come on fess up sir"

"Well I'm not answering that on the basis it may incriminate me."

"Come on, we won't tell."

"As I said, class dismissed. And tear that page out of your guide book." All laughing.

Class dismissed!"

RICHMOND VIRGINIA,
Nazis come to learn from us.

All filed into class and take their seats.

Cameron, "It boggles the mind how this all could have happened. So the idea of the Nazi persecution of Jews began with Mein Kampf."

Danny turning from the board, "No actually it began with us."

"No way, what do you mean?"

Shaking his head, "No we were the experts on segregation and persecution long before Hitler came into power. They sent emissaries here in the mid 20's to learn of our rules on how we subjugated the black race. Let's look at some recent slides I have from the Virginia Holocaust Museum in Richmond, Virginia."

Danny closed the blinds and turned on his slide projector. "First as you see when you first enter the museum you see a bench from a train station and note the sign, 'Whites Only', then you see separate drinking fountains, and rest room facilities. On the wall are edicts placed all over our State Capital with rules and regulations warning the blacks where they can and not go. Even how they were to travel by bus, and confined to just certain living areas. Inbreeding with whites was punished by public hangings. And God forbid if a black was accused of raping white women, whether true or not, he was castrated and burned alive while hanging by his arms from a tree.

An even more horrid thing happened in Valdosta Georgia, in 1918, when a white mob lynched an innocent man, named Haynes Turner, also accused of just looking at a white woman. What's worse is what they did to his pregnant white mate, Mary. She was turned over to a mob, which included not only men, but also white women and children, all who beheld the following spectacle."

"You mean that even children were allow to watch?"

"Yes, this was one method of indoctrinating them all as future racists. Mary was stripped naked, hung upside down from a tree limb by her ankles, doused in gasoline and slowly roasted. But before her death a white man opened her swollen belly with a hunting knife, and after her infant fell to the ground, stomped it into the ground."

"Horrid beyond belief. So then the Klu Klux Clan did this?"

"Yes to protect their identities they often wore the white garb and covered pointed masks."

"Sort of like the SS but without the pointed head gear?"

"SS?, What is the SS?"

"It stands for Schutzstaffel. Hitler's first body guards, but later they would follow the Wehrmacht into Actions or the slaughter of innocents in the conquered lands. And never having to face a single shot themselves, unlike the regular foot soldiers."

"Yes, they had their red arm bands with the twisted cross. And their attack dogs instead."

"Yes they learned very well from us and later, after the war started even from the Japanese."

"Even the Japanese?"

"Yes in 1937 after a string of victories, the Japanese Army on December 13th invaded Nanking. Over just a three-week period they slaughtered over 300,000 innocent Men, Women and Children who were only civilians and not even combatants, who most had fled before the invasion. All this was documented in the book by Iris Chang, 'The Rape of Nanking'. Her book is also at the Holocaust museum in Richmond. I will spare you the photos from her book. But the real horror was what occurred at the Japanese human experimentation camp at Pingfan in Manchuria. Here although mostly Chinese victims but all nationalities were subject to live vivisections, flame thrower testing, freezing and worse. When the Nazi came home with the idea of human experimentation was necessary in order to insure the wellbeing of the Master race. Thus we know of Mengele's experiments of on young twins and the horrid Oberthauser on her surgical victims referred to as Rabbits at Ravensbruck"

"Why didn't we stop any of this?"

"Well, until Pearl harbor, we were an isolationist country and refused to get into any conflict in Europe. This was due to, none other than, Charles Lindberg whose flight of the St. Louis brought him not only fame, but a real voice for a separatist nation. He argued what went on over there should not be our concern or it would only bring death to more our innocent youth as the first world war had done. We would not even risk helping Britain and France from the invading German Army."

But getting back to my point. The Nazi learned from us to first isolate and then to eliminate in order to purify the Aryan race from Jews as we had done the blacks. So they started in early 1933, under an interesting pretense"

"Like what?"

"They met and, and like us, drafted rules to first segregate and then eliminate those deemed genetically inferior. Their rationale was that they were doing them a favor in preventing them from reproducing and proliferating more of their kind.

"Just Jews?"

"Oh no. Dwarfs, gypsies, the mentally feeble, the retarded, those with Down's syndrome, the crippled, the deformed, gays, lesbians, and all others deemed as undesirables, regardless of gender or age."

"So were they gassed?"

"Yes, but under the pretense of being surgically sterilized, so as not to panic those so chosen and who could understand."

"What about their parents? Them too?"

"No, sometimes only one or two children in a family were effected, and they were spared, as long as they were party members.

Before the advent of the Zyklon B gas they used at the death camps during the war, they simply used carbon monoxide."

"You mean from a cars exhaust? How?"

Changing to the next slide, "Here you see such a van. They were crammed into this van, and told they were going to be driven to a place for a picnic. The door was hermetically sealed shut, and you will see here the corrugated hose attached from the exhaust pipe and entering an outlet into the interior of the van. Then the driver would head to an isolated area after a long drive to insure the suffocation of the inhabitants. Then the bodies would be burned in open pits."

"We've all been warned about carbon monoxide, like don't run your car in a garage. but how does it kill?"

"Well it binds irreversibly with the hemoglobin in our red blood cells so we can't accept oxygen, and we basically fall asleep."

"Is it painful?"

"No some people commit suicide that way sitting in a locked garage with the engine running."

"Well it doesn't sound like a painful way to go for those poor victims in Germany."

"I guess that depend on which end of the hose you are on.", some laughed.

"Is that what they used in the concentration camps?"

"No they used something far worse and extremely painful, the Zyklon B, which was hydrogen cyanide."

"Did the Germans always use gas to kills their victims?"

"Actually not. In the camps were the Jehovah Witnesses, who wore a Purple triangle, and were pure Aryan Germans, and their only crime was their refusal to sign a statement declaring their allegiance to Hitler. Those that refused, because their religion disallows any allegiance to any human or country, but total allegiance just to God some were beheaded. "

"Why!"

"Because Hitler felt only vermin like Jews, gypsies, homosexuals, traitors and many other on his list should be gassed, but not Aryans. The Zyklon B killed slowly and painfully, but beheading was quick, but not done with a guillotine but with an Ax in the true Prussian manner."

"My how thoughtful. Hitler wasn't so bad after all. At least to his own kind. So how did the Zyclon B gas come about?"

"Well you remember the gassing of enemies by the Germans was started much earlier in World War one with a gas called Phosgene, developed by Fritz Haber. The Zyclon B was developed during the second World War. But more on that later. First Let's see the reaction of two ships, before the war bearing Jews trying to escape, the

M.S. Saint Lewis and the Quanza, and the difference in the reactions to these refugees by our people."

"So next time we will start with The Ship of the Damned. Class dismissed", clicking off the projector and opening the blinds.

M.S. St. Lewis
(Ship of the Damned)

Flicking through some slides Danny said, "The M.S. Saint Lewis, a ship so named after our own City in Missouri, was owned by the Hamburg American Line and operated out of Hamburg, Germany. It had a sad and desperate history."

"How so?"

"So sad as to the entire worlds total disregard of the plight of the Jews fleeing Nazi persecution, it was later referred to as 'The Ship of the Damned'. In 1939 it was carrying 937 Jewish passengers, men, women and children intending to escape the growing Nazi persecution in Germany."

"Was this before the Nazi invaded Poland and started World War two?"

"Yes that wasn't until September first, this was May 27th when they sailed into a port in Cuba."

"Why Cuba?"

"Had something to do with their acceptance provided they paid the Governor there, a huge amount of money per person, but he fearing the anti-Semitic uproar from his people, denied entry. The

Captain, Gustav Schroder…"

"A German?"

"Yes, they weren't all bad. This one had a conscious. So let me go on. He tried many other ports, but all with the same response, so he figured surely our country would take them in, especially since we had a large Jewish population here."

"So we took them?"

"Unfortunately no."

"Why?"

"Cordell Hull, our Secretary of State at the time, advised Roosevelt, not to take them in as it would hurt our relations with Germany. When Schroder was told of our refusal, he tried to pull and interesting ploy."

"How so."

He went to the Florida coast and attempted to run aground his ship allowing the refuges to escape, but acting on Hull's instructions, the U.S. Coast Guard stopped him from doing this."

"So what happened to those poor people?"

Clicking on the next slide, "After returning to Hamburg, and you see here them disembarking down the gang plank from the ship, most were eventually murdered in the killing centers of Auschwitz and Sobibor."

"That's horrible, such a black mark on the world and especially us. Was the Captain arrested?"

"No, since he was an American, but reprimanded by his company for his attempt to ground their ship. In 1993 he was awarded posthumously The Righteous Among the Nations at the Holocaust memorial in Israel. There is also, at our Holocaust Museum in Washington not only a display, but you can watch the film, 'Ship of the Damned' with the actual footage taken by the Captain and its passengers. And one of the best displays is at our Holocaust Museum in Richmond."

"Next time we will learn of another ship carrying Jews, the Quanza but ending up here in Norfolk and with a different outcome."

"Now?"

"No not now."

"Damn!"

"No Ship of the Damned."

THE S.S. QUANZA:
The Killing of their own kind

D anny entered the classroom and drew S.S. Quanza on the board.

Cameron sitting down along with the rest, "Isn't that an African holiday like our Christmas or Hanukah?"

"No this is the name of a ship, like the M.S. Saint Lewis we talked about last time."

"Oh I remember, The Ship of the Damned. Is this another sorry tale of sure death among the passengers?"

"Well it could have been, but had an interesting twist. On September 11, 1940 it docked at the coal pier at Sewell's point in Norfolk. Virginia to refuel."

Booker offered, "Practically in our own backyard. Then what happened?"

"Well they had already been banned in Vera Cruz, Mexico and other ports, so this was their last stop before heading back to a certain death in Nazi Germany, as had the Passengers on the St. Lewis."

Cameron, "But why not just allow entry for only so few?"

"Well anti-Semitism had reached a peak in our country after Germany invaded Poland in 1939. This was due to the isolationism preached by Charles Lindberg, the candidate running for President against Roosevelt. He preached that we must not send our sons to their deaths in a war that was not ours. This fervor was responded by a rally in Madison Square Garden of 20,000 Nazi Americans.

"But even worse our own American Jews fought the entry of these 81."

Tonya aghast, "They even wanted to reject and eventually condemn their own Kind? But why?"

"Well from a direct quote from a Rabbi leading a demonstration in Madison Square Garden filled with Jewish supporters, "We feel that in your zealousness to the aid our stricken brethren overseas, you have misplaced too strong an emphasis upon our own needs. Let these unwanted parasites on our society return to Germany and face whatever happens. They are not our concern. They are not like us. We did well in this country by our own initiatives, so let them do the same... but not here."

"If you'll excuse the expressing", Bobbie said, "Fuckin unbelievable."

"Well throughout the war, there were Jews that willingly did the work of the Nazi against their own kind. In the ghettos, during the selections, and camps they were referred to as JUDANRATS, by their own kind. Even the Sonderkommando's at the gas chambers would tell those selected that they should undress and hang their clothes on a numbered hook in order to remember where they had placed it after their shower. To survive at the risk of others dying was the norm."

"So even their own kind", Bobbi shaking her head and slouching.

Danny signed" Yes there is a book called "The Painted Bird" by

Jerzy Kosinski, that bring this point out. It tells of a fiendish farmer who amuses himself by snaring birds of all the same species and showing this to a young lad. These birds, when let lose, all flock and fly away in typical patterns together. But then he shows the boy another snare of birds of the same species, but he paints one a different color. Just one. Now when he lets them lose, instead of their flying to freedom, they all converge and on the painted bird and tear it to pieces."

Cameron raised his hand, "Along that same line I have another example of mothers even sacrificing their own kind. I read an experiment where a monkey that was put into cage with her baby and the bottom of the cage was electrified and heated. Eventually the mother stood on her baby and allowed it to die rather than getting herself burned."

"Then what about the psychological experiment where subjects were asked to submit increasing electrical shocks to pretend victims they couldn't see at the command of an authoritarian figure. And despite the increasing fake screams of the victims they continued to increase the electrical shock."

"And why do you think they did that?", Danny interjected. "I'll tell you why. They were just following orders. The sick excuse at the war trials.

So regardless of what is demanded of you always have a choice."

"I beg to differ." Said Cameron. "Sophie didn't"

"Oh you are talking about the novel Sophie's Choice by William Syron where an SS officer tells a Jewish woman in the death camps to make a choice as to which one of her two children will be gassed. He gives her a time limit, and she chooses one. She survives, and ends up in Brooklyn, and has an affair with an aggressive abusive lover. No doubt to punish herself for that terrible choice, and eventually commits suicide."

"Then in The Storyteller by Jodi Picoult, she tells of a Judenrat who is asked to provide a certain number of children to be gassed and tell the mothers to pick the youngest because they won't know what's happening."

Some already teary eyed in the class when Tonya says," It looks like I have a lot of books to read, but getting back to those 81, were they forced to go back to Germany? "

"No despite the contentions of the Jewish committee, somehow word of this potential disaster reached the ears of Eleanor Roosevelt still disturbed by our countries failure to save those on the St. Louis. She Implored her husband to act, and to act quickly as the ship after refueling was to disembark. He appointed a Patrick Malin to come to Norfolk to see if these refugees would qualify for reentry and not violate any of our strict immigration laws. Malin, much to the anger of the local Jewish community, certified all qualified for entry, ignoring our immigration laws, and thus allowed all 81 of the men, women, and children to disembark. Some cried, some laughed, and some kissed the ground. For these refuges and their descendants, this was the gift of life.

"You mentioned Sunder something?

"Sonderkommandos's. But even the worse of these had their limit, and revolted to save the one small girl who survived the gas chamber. But that remains the topic of our next class. Keep up your reading. Looks like you all are developing some heart and I'm glad. Keep questioning everything and take a stand and support all those in need. Until next time. Class dismissed."

B: THE CO LEAD UP

Danny set up his screen and slide projector as his students entered the classroom and took their seats.

"So the Nazi's invented Zyclon B to gas the Jews.", Robin reiterated rather casually.

Danny turned and dismissively said, "Not exactly."

"Then do tell."

"Well an SS Lieutenant and a chemist, Kurt Gerstein, converted the A to the B actually to disinfect soldiers drinking water. When he discovered it was being used to gas prisoners, and in fact the first were not Jews, but 20 Russian prisoners at Auschwitz one night."

"Why Russian and not Jews?"

"Because the Final Solution against the Jews had not been established as yet, and the Russians were their first enemy, and Hitler's invasion, against the advice of his superiors proved to be the eventual downfall of the Third Reich.

Gerstein actually went to the Pope in Rome, Pope Pious XII, to intervene but the Pope would not because he had signed the Pact Romano which guaranteed his freedom, but not for the Jews in Italy. They were later rounded up and gassed before the allies invaded Rome. As an interesting aside, when the allies were about to liberate Rome, Pope Pious asked that black soldiers not be allowed to enter the invasion force, and so the Generals complied."

"Wow how very Pious", Robin shaking her head.

Robin again, "Why would Hitler even listen to the Pope? Was he a good Catholic?", laughing.

"No arrogant one, he was not, but many of the Nazi and men of the Wehrmacht were. On their belt buckles were the words, Gott mitt uns. "God is with us."

Early on in the 1930's Hitler instituted the use of gassing individuals considered to have genetic defects in order to prevent their reproducing. "

"Genetic Defects? How so?"

"Well the deformed, dwarfs, the insane, hunchbacks, the diseased, the feeble, the promiscuous, Lesbians, homosexuals, the blind, those with the shakes, the deaf and the dumb, Gypsies and any that did not conform to the very specific mathematical facial and statue measurements of the pure Aryan race. Collectively labelled as Undesirables"

"So the B gas was used even that early?"

"No it had not been developed that soon. Instead these so labelled were forced into airtight vans, and then a hose was hooked up to the exhaust which led into the van. Then driven around until the gas took effect. Then the bodies were removed and burned in a remote field."

"How did the exhaust kill? Should I be careful driving my car?", all laughed.

"Only if you park it in your garage, with the engine running and the garage door shut and your car windows open. "

"Does it hurt, and how does it kill?"

"No the fumes smell bad but no pain, you just fall into a sleep you never wake up from."

"Why"

"Well if you ever remember anything from your Biology class, we breath in Oxygen, and the alveoli in our lungs take it in and exchanges it for the carbon dioxide which we breathe out. However, when we absorb to Carbon Monoxide, the exchange with O2 doesn't occur so we suffocate and die. It's interesting from a chemical standpoint that the two gases differ by only one carbon atom. A body that has succumbed from CO poisoning takes on a crimson hue, that's why first responders can immediately guess the cause of death."

"Well that is interesting."

"Well I guess it's interesting unless you're sitting in your garage with the engine running.", Danny said, all laughed.

Monica said, "Since we are now on the subject of Chemistry and no longer History, I have an interesting topic. Do any of you know what an empirical formula is?"

"No due tell, Monica."

"Well it's a compound that has the same number of atoms, but when they are organized differently, they make two different compounds that are totally different. "

"Like how Monica, due tell?"

"Well if I may?", going to the board she draws two separate compounds each having 2 carbons, 1 Oxygen, and 6 hydrogens. "You will note if the carbons are placed together and the OH on the end we have Ethyl Alcohol.

"The good stuff," quipped Fred.

"You Bet. But if you just place the oxygen in the center and the carbons on each side, what do you get?"

"Cock!"

"No shithead, you get Ether. Both put you out but in different ways, and if you drink one you get high, drink the other and you die."

"Well excuse me," Fred Sarcastically "You have really really made my day. Remind me never to take a drink from you on a date."

"Date you! You dick less wonder…"

Danny interrupted, "Okay Stop it! this has gone on far enough. Class dismissed."

"But what about the Zyclon B?"

"Next time."

ZYCLON B

Danny set up his screen and slide projector as his students entered the classroom and took their seats.

"So the Nazi's invented Zyclon B to gas the Jews.", Robin reiterated rather casually.

Danny turned and dismissively said, "Not exactly."

"Then do tell."

"Well and SS Lieutenant and a chemist, Kurt Gerstein, converted the A to the B actually to disinfect soldiers drinking water. When he discovered it was being used to gas prisoners, and in fact the first were not Jews, but 20 Russian prisoners at Auschwitz, in the basement of Block 11 one night in late August of 1941.

"Why Russian and not Jews?"

"Because the Final Solution against the Jews had not been established as yet, and the Russians were their first enemy, and Hitler's invasion, against the advice of his superiors, proved to be the eventual downfall of the Third Reich.

Gerstein actually went to the Pope in Rome, Pious XII, to intervene but the Pope would not because he had signed the Pact Romano with Hitler which guaranteed his freedom, but not for the Jews in Italy, which were later rounded up and gassed. As an interesting aside, when the allies were about to liberate Rome, Pope Pious asked that black soldiers not be allowed to enter the invasion force, and so the Generals complied."

"Wow how Pious", Robin shaking her head.

Robin again, "Why would Hitler even listen to the Pope? Was he a good Catholic?", laughing.

"No arrogant one, he was not, but many of the Nazi and men of the Wehrmacht were. On their belt buckles were the words, Gott mitt uns. "God is with us."

"So what actually was this new gas and how did it work?"

"It was Hydrogen Cyanide, manufactured by IG Farben still in business today making paints. "Writing on the board HCN" Similar to the Sarin used by Assaid in Syria who claimed it was never used."

"Oh but it did I was those newsreels with the people and even children screaming and blistering and not being able to breath. Just awful."

Nodding Danny continued, "Yes the Jews, men women and children, were told to strip and naked and told to hang their clothes on hooks and to remember their numbers so they could claim them after their so called shower. Then pressed in as tight as possible to one another the door was sealed, and through a tiny glass window portal a spectator could witness the procedure. In fact, Himmler himself witnessed one such gassing and was said to vomit and never went to any gassing again. Then the pellets were poured into an opening at the top a hitting the interior began to immediately sublimate. Since the gassings continued around the clock a huge pallor of burning fat pervaded the entire area not fooling some of the victims. Now I will call upon my resident Chemist to define that."

"Sublimate! Means to pass directly from a solid into a gas without going through a liquid phase, so it dispersed quickly."

"Exactly! As the pellets went into a vapor the Somderkommando's said they could hear what sounded like a wind, but was the rising screams of the victims clawing and tearing at the walls and their blistering faces."

Clicking to a slide, "Here is the interior of an actual preserved photo at Auschwitz. Notice the bluish interior of the walls and the claw marks on the walls. A very painful way to go, and not quick. We know this to be true because the HCN gas was last used in this country in 1983 on the convicted child rapist, Jimmy Lee Grey. Witnesses said he screamed for 18 minutes before death."

"Mentioned a word, Sunder…"

"Sonderkommando's. These were the clean-up guys." Clicking to the next slide. "Here you see them dragging the corpses with ice hooks and piling them on carts into the ovens four to five bodies at a time. But not before they extracted with pliers the gold from any victim's teeth. Then they would hose down the chamber before the next group was brought in."

"I assume these guys were Jews so how could they do something like that to their own kind?"

"Well they weren't the first. There were several in the ghettos working to keep their fellow Jews in line, called JudenRats, by their own kind. But those who worked the chambers, worked around the clock shifts, and were given many benefits for what they did. They were given lavish meals and strong drink to help them forget. And they knew that they too would be gassed and a new group brought in."

Shaking her head, "So sad. Impossible to imagine facing what was to be certain death for sure. "

"Well no, there was one known survivor."

"Who and how?"

"Her name was Gena Turgel. She was sixteen when taken from her home in Krakow, Poland. She even survived testing by the infamous Dr. Mengele, then at the age of 21 was led into the Gas chamber, but somehow survived and along with others was marched to Belster where she met Anne Frank before Anne's death. Upon liberation by the Soviets she met and married a handsome officer, Turgel. Thus her last name. What's interesting is her story is told in a movie entitled The Grey Zone, where after an unsuccessful attempt to blow up the chambers, she and all the rest are systematically shot behind the neck while lying on the ground. She is shot in the back as she attempts to run off."

"The concentration camps were first discovered July 23, 1944 by the Soviets at Majdanek, and many more after that by us and the British and all of the allies. I visited only Dachau as I've told you, but due to saboteurs it never had a working gas chamber, but it was a center for those horrid medical experiments I mentioned earlier."

"There is an interesting story of a Jew who assisted in the medical experiments at Dachau under the SS Officer in charge, Dr. Rascher. This Jew did for a totally different reason, so let me read it to you."

The Phlebotomist
FROM: the collection of short stories entitled "REQUIEM"

BY: DR. C. THOMAS SOMMA

Vengeance is a thing of patience, and Neville was a patient man. No one could really judge his motives as being anything but humanitarian when, at the age of 65, he volunteered his services at Graydon Community Hospital. Not even Eloise Mackenholm, the aged director of the hospital auxiliary, could see anything but an altruistic, old, retired man looking to do some good with his remaining years. She didn't know him, but definitely knew of him.

Yes, Neville Rosenthal, the meekest, tired man before her, had quite a reputation—even if it was only for misfortune. He had come to Graydon, Texas in 1947. He appeared old even then. A survivor of Dachau concentration camp, he looked well beyond his then 30 years. He had come here alone; and people only guessed at the outcome of any family he may have had. He befriended no one and took a job as a tailor's assistant in Menken's shop. Neville was an oddity. He was small and frail in a town inhabited by robust, bullying giants. He feared aggression and confrontation in an area known for its vigilante law. He was a Jew, a strange sect among God-fearing Christians. Aside from the obvious differences between Neville and the inhabitants of Graydon, the major reason for his ostracism, though never admitted, was that he was regarded as tainted. It was nothing that was openly expressed or even generally acknowledged, but the residents regarded him much in the same way as they would a survivor of Hiroshima. A diametric combination of sympathy and revulsion. After all, he had come from a living hell and who really knew what diseases or psychotic tendencies he carried. His right wrist bore a cruel scar that pulled his hand slightly toward his forearm. Some speculated that this was where he had once born the cruel numbered stamp of a Dachau inmate. He half shuffled and half limped in a rapid, uncoordinated fashion, bent forward slightly at the waist, a skeleton twisted and broken by the twin ravages of starvation and the rubber baton. His occasional wide-toothed smile was, in itself, perplexing—a cross between an animal in pain and a Jack-O-Lantern.

Initial attempts to befriend him by self-serving church groups were only met with courteous refusals on Neville's part. On those certain Jewish days, he could be heard in the little room above the shop chanting in some strange dialect to the God of his ancestors, while an eight-pronged candelabra burned in both windows.

It was only because of old man Menken that Neville was even allowed to stay in Graydon. Henry Menken, a former Mayor and councilman, had continually defended his employee and boarder. Menken warned others that he be left alone for he had been through enough, and the town respected the highly decorated former Mayor who had served in both wars. He proudly displayed a citation from General Patton on the peeling walls of his aging shop. Most related his benevolence toward Neville from the fact that Menken had served in the armored division that, under Patton, had liberated most of the death camps in Southern Germany. In any event, the town was willing to live and let live at least for the time being.

Things soon changed for Neville when Menken died. Menken's wife, anxious to sell the place and move back East with her sister, sold the house and business to Neville for what was considered in those days to be a rather tidy sum for a tailor's assistant only a few years into the trade. Rumors were kindled that Neville had paid the widow with gold extracted from the teeth of the corpses of Dachau.

The persecution came in waves. It wasn't the whole town, of course; but those who felt sorry for him were unfortunately the reticent type and, as occurred in Germany, they chose to ignore the towns torment of the man. Still, this group did support his business which, in those days, was a chance in itself.

Jason Renker, the town's most gifted lawyer and Mayor, tried legal means to uproot Neville. He tried everything from having the property condemned, to having the land rezoned for only residential dwellings. Neville fought it in the courts and finally won, but only at a great financial expense which he could ill afford.

Next Larry Wright, the noted councilman and suspected Klansman, tried to have him extradited back to Germany on trumped up charges that he had survived the war only by collaborating with the Nazis. The town would never learn how true this assumption was. Without direct evidence, Wright's case was dismissed, still the local paper presented the case in such details to incite actions of vandals. Their nocturnal assaults on his shop brought back bitter memories of Kristallnacht. James Denton, the local sheriff, would deliberately delay in answering Neville's frantic phone calls for help. In the morning the shop's contents were either broken or missing, and black painted swastikas embellished the walls and sidewalks.

The most insidious attack of all though, came from a man of God, the Reverend Roger Lucas. In his Sunday sermons, the Reverend made his followers feel that Judaism was akin to Satanism. After all, hadn't the Jews caused the death of Christ? Were not the concentration camps just recompense for what they had done? Although he never mentioned Neville by name, his parishioners knew who he meant by the "infidel within our midst who escaped judgment in Germany and whose ancestors crucified their Christ." Even disastrous acts of nature were attributed to God's revenge on Graydon for harboring, "That Jew and his strange powers."

Still Neville hung on, determined never to be displaced again by fear. He would make Graydon his last stand. He well knew that there was no other place to run to that would be any different. And so the years went by, only causing Neville to dig in deeper and fight. It was here he was to finally enact his terrible plan.

That plan was not readily discernable by Eloise Mackenholm from across her desk. She saw no bitterness, only a gentle resignation, in the rumpled figure sitting there.

"Well, now then, Mr. Rosenthal, just why do you want to work here?"

Leaning forward, he touched her desk with his withered hand, never making eye contact and said, "Well, Mrs. Mackenholm, if you please," a phrase with which he prefaced everything, "I want to keep busy and do something a little valuable with my final years. As you know, I am now retired and have no family, and perhaps not too much time because of…" looking over his twisted frame then back to her. This he emphasized with a meekest little wink.

Eloise drew back in her chair, then wondered why she felt a slight sense of revulsion. The old man seemed both sincere and genuine as well as surprisingly eloquent. She almost wished she could have met him sooner as she began to lose credulity in those terrible tales about him. Yes, a deep sorrow overcame her as she looked at this benign figure whose tilted, balding and imploring head cowered like a beaten dog. A vision of that man in a wrinkled grey and black-striped coat, with a yellow star on an armband, head shaven and pleading through barbed-wire startled her. She caught herself shaking the vision off like a bothersome fly. No doubt, partly out of guilt, she decided she would give him the chance.

"I think we might be able to use your services. As you know, it is a voluntary job; but you'll be entitled to some benefits.
He never changed his position, but nodded, still bent forward and always averting her glance, looking just to the left of her desk.

"Those benefits, combined with your pension, should tide you over.", she continued. "If you want, you can start next Tuesday in our gift shop."

Those last two words caused him to flinch as though struck from behind by the dreaded Kapos. He momentarily caught Eloise's eyes, then remembering his place, he once again averting her gaze continued, "Mrs. Mackenholm, if you please, I would like to work not in the gift shop but perhaps as a phlebotomist." At first the very word conjured up visions of some blood-letting ancient barber draining the crimson fluid from severed veins in the arm of a listless patient.

"Oh, you mean a blood collector, like they use in the lab to draw blood samples?" she responded after she had caught herself. "Well, that takes special training and I doubt if . . ."

She was cut off by a different man. The man before her now was not the humble Neville, but the determined one. She now saw the tenacity that allowed him to survive the horrors of Dachau as well as the torments of Graydon.

He now sat upright, hands on both knees, staring her right in the eye. "Mrs. Mackenholm, if you please, as you know I was once a tailor. My hands are very good and age has not affected them." He held them up, fingers outstretched and rock steady. "You see," he said almost defiantly. "They are good. My mind is good. I can learn quickly and also; I don't need to be trained. I used to work in a hospital dur. . .," "he caught himself, "before the war came. I would draw the blood and give the injection. I have not forgotten. I am still good. You will see."

Reluctance gripped Eloise. She thought, to sell gifts is one thing; but to deal with our patients is another issue altogether. Well, why she thought? Was she also falling prey to the notion that he was tainted? She swallowed hard and now secretly wished he had never come. She really did feel a mounting revulsion to that living relic of Nazi horror. She didn't want to be near the vile thing he represented. How dare he survive and remind us of that time. We can't change it...I'm sorry it happened...don't blame us...we weren't responsible...how could we have known... what could we have done anyway...we would have tried to stop it...only the Germans could have done this...leave us alone...stop reminding us...we need to forget...stop blaming us...It wasn't us, please die and let us bury you so that we can all forget. But it was us all of us, and she knew it.

Eloise, fighting a well-spring of tears, ran to the door, wild entreaty's rebounding inside her head. She hoped Neville wouldn't follow. He didn't. In fact, not even his eyes followed her to the door.

Out in the hall, leaning against the cool corridor, she sucked in the antiseptic air and slowly regained her composure. She dried her eyes and tried to ponder what had happened to her a few minutes ago. Then she realized what had seized her. It was the realization that she and the people of Graydon were no different that the SS Nazi monsters of the 30's and 40's. Yes, over the years they had all turned Graydon into another Dachau for that poor old man. They did it for no other reason than the fact that he was different. Yes, different, different that's all. Neville was as different here as he was in Germany. Those different will always be the victims. She caught sight of the bleeding statue of the crucified Christ hanging in the corridor. The similarity startled her.

Yet she was determined to help change that. He deserved a chance for some peace and recognition in his remaining years. She would help him, but it was going to take some work. She controlled the gift shop, but the laboratory was something else.

She took a deep breath, regained her composure and then walked back into her office and sat at her desk. Neville, less defiant and not as determined, sat bent in the chair, undisturbed by what had happened.

She offered no explanation for her behavior but said, "Well, Mr. Rosenthal, since you do have some experience in that field, I'll see what I can do for you. Call me on Monday."

He called her on Monday and started on Tuesday as a blood collector for the lab.

He hadn't exaggerated in the least to Eloise about his abilities. He was very adept at blood drawing. Although he wasn't readily accepted by his peers at first due to his age and odd appearance, they soon, not only accepted him, but even depended on him. He displayed a unique knack of being able to penetrated the finest and most elusive vein and tap the red fluid within. Although the Lab Director was skeptical at first, he soon became as much a believer as the others had realizing that this man was a very valuable asset to his staff. Soon he was allowed to perform the most difficult deep-seated arterial punctures for the pulmonary studies. As his reputation spread, the nurses would often call upon him to start the I.V. solutions in patients whose paper-thin veins defied even the most skilled of nurses.

All of this praise in no way phased Neville. He was good before; so, he knew he would be good again. Besides, he was very busy these days planning his real purpose there. Daily, he would check the surgery schedule and the list of admissions for those names he had carefully chronologed in his own "Totenbuch", as the death registers in the camps were called. His notebook, which he kept with him always, listed all those in Graydon who had done him harm over the years. The letters of their names were in Hebrew and in a special code he devised while at Dachau. Eventually one-by-one all of them would come to the only hospital within a hundred-mile radius of this town.

Soon the lamb would become the lion for it was his hatred, not his fear of the Germans that had sustained him through those years of torment at Dachau. Now it would be his hatred of those in Graydon that would keep him alive until his terrible work was done.

When the War had first ended, Neville tried through legal means to prosecute his captors, but the foreign laws only protected those criminals, as it did here. Friendly countries hid and defended them. Frustrated, he had come to America, settling in the Midwest in order to forget and to avoid any people of European culture and the terrible memories of that continent. But forgive, he couldn't. And forget, he dared not. *"Was wir nicht vergessen durfen."* "What we dare not forget." Those were the words inscribed in German on the cover of his Totenbuch.

Yes, Neville was a very patient man; and he knew that eventually each of those on his list would eventually pass his way. Sooner or later they would be helpless patients in Graydon Community Hospital, and there, under the humanitarian guise he perpetuated, he would deliver his personal brand of death, as he had done so long ago in Germany.

He knew all the techniques since he had been expertly trained by them. A five-cc injection of chloroform was quick, but could be traced by a good toxicologist on autopsy. An injection of pure water caused the red blood cells to swell and rupture. Their contents, in turn, would plug the kidneys and thereby poison the body. It was slow and painful, as he remembered, but required multiple injections and he couldn't risk that. They knew he was good and multiple needle tracks would only arouse suspicion. An injection of potassium chloride would cause cardiac arrhythmias and was impossible to trace; but he couldn't risk getting caught with it on his collection tray. Plus, it was too fast. He could doctor normal saline with extra salt and inject it, causing the red blood cells to shrivel and clump, thereby plugging their pulmonary alveoli. This would initiate a painful thrombosis that caused victims to clutch at their throats desperately trying to find air. Yet these methods were no more effective than ordinary air injected in a 35-cc dose which would, upon entering the heart, prevent blood flow. Painful, and not too quick, but impossible to trace. This tried and true technique, perfected during that time, would now provide him with his long-awaited vindication.

It took nearly eight months for the first of his tormentors to appear on the surgery list. Reverend Roger Lucas had been admitted over the past week-end for massive internal bleeding caused by a peptic ulcer. He was scheduled for emergency surgery early that morning, but that night Neville was to assure that he would never make it. His condition was listed as serious, but stable, and the routine evening pre-op blood tests had been ordered. Neville went out of his way to obtain the order slip for that patient. Then with his tray in hand he took the elevator to the second floor Critical Care Unit.

Mindless of the blended cacophony of patient moans, hissing respirators, and sucking aspirator bottles, he searched for his prey in a room filled with the dying. A nurse was kind enough to point in the direction where his victim lay. There, at the far end of the long subdued green corridor was a poor feeble creature, his wrists and feet bound to the bedrails, struggling like a trapped fly in a Black Widow's web.

Neville slowed his gait as he passed long rows of incoherent sounds and thrashing legs. Like a hungry spider he descended upon the Reverend carrying his own special brand of venom.

Reverend Lucas hardly seemed the same person as Neville looked down on him. What had reduced this white-collared hell and damnation proponent to this frail fear filled creature? My, just how the specter of death reduces all to the same level. Kings, saints and slaves all equal before the reaper. He went ahead and checked his armband just to confirm that this poor creature, intubated through the nose with plastic tubing that sucked the frothy, brown mixture of blood and bile from his stomach, and infiltrated with vinyl veins dripping dextrose and electrolytes, was indeed he. Hardly the pulpit pounding evangelist now. Now only a wasted shell with rolling eyes as if warily searching for the phantom who would come and claim him soon.

Neville put his tray down on the bed stand and smartly pulled the curtain around the bed. Then, like a tape recorder, Neville began the speech he was trained to say, "Good evening, Rev. Lucas. I'm from the laboratory and I need to draw a blood specimen for a test your doctor ordered." How trite, he thought to himself. How many times had he parroted that phrase into frightened, imploring eyes?

He could tell that the Reverend was mindless of his words, so he dropped the rest of his prepared speech and went to his tray for his tools. As he prepared to fit a sterile needle atop a large 35 cc syringe, he thought that the wasted figure before him wouldn't probably even last the night, even if he didn't intervene. But still he must die at Neville's hands just to make things right. He had waited too many years for this chance. He almost smiled as he reached for the cotton dipped in alcohol. Yes, we must be careful to sterilize the puncture area in order not to expose the patient to the risk of infection. How hypocritical, he thought, that they always took these very same sterile precautions at Dachau on those branded for extermination by injection.

He was perspiring now as he turned with his tools in his hand. For this to be right, the Reverend must be made to know how and by whom his end was to come.

"Reverend? Reverend Lucas, if you please, it is me, Neville," he said with a vulpine grin. The holy man's head turned toward the voice and his chest heaved as the aspiration tube sucked brown foam through his nose deep from within the recesses of his cadaverous body. His mouth opened but emitted no sound save a frothy gurgle. His tongue lolled to one side but only vomited air as a fetid belch filled the bedside.

Neville could still tell from those bulging eyes laced with capillaries oozing agony that Lucas didn't recognize him. So he continued, bending till he was but a foot from his prey and whispered, "Mr. Reverend, sir, if you please, it is me, Neville. Neville Rosenthal. The poor soul you tormented and threatened and bullied and nearly broke. But you didn't, sir. I hung on and now it is my turn." The near-corpse now knew and twisted and pulled at his fetters. The pale cheek muscles and neck pulled taunt as he arched his back and helplessly tugged at his restraints. He now understood every word Neville had spoken and now recognized his innocently armed assailant.

"Yes, it is my turn and that is only just, isn't it?" Neville hissed. "An eye for an eye; a tooth for a tooth. Isn't that what you preached, Reverend, sir? Isn't that the passage you preached that when they painted those swastikas on my place and hung the pig entrails over my front door?"

The dying man's arms gave a pull that belied such a weak man and rattled the bed against the wall. Neville suddenly stood erect, fearing the continued noise would arouse suspicion, but became relieved when the stricken figure sank back into a calm resignation.

"Yes, Reverend sir, how fitting it is for you to die by your own dogma." He then turned to his collection tray with the tired eyes of his victim at his back. The Reverend's brain was now mindless of the pulsating pain within his abdomen and only trying to unscramble the sounds of Neville's preparation...alcohol swab tearing open...syringe plunger popping out and in... needle snapping from its sterile cap.

When Neville was ready, he turned and became the efficient lab robot he was trained to be. "First I'm going to put this tourniquet on your arm and we'll just take a look at those veins, okay?" With a tailor's skill, he had knotted the inch-wide rubber band just above the paper Mache elbow causing the large antecubital vein, to pillow out, soft and faintly blue.

"There now. You certainly do have good veins, I wish all my patients did and were as co-operative as you," remembering back then. The recording continued. "This won't hurt a bit." The Reverend's eyes glanced down at his scaly right arm now held firmly by Neville as he scrubbed the area with alcohol and then dried it with a sterile swab.

"First we put alcohol on to kill the bacteria," he instructed. "Then we wipe it off so it won't sting when the needle goes in." He reached for the syringe, strangely noting that the Reverend was behaving more like a curious student than the eyes of an animal in a butcher corral. The man's breathing seemed shallow both calm and measured. His eyes, relaxed and resigned, never left the antiseptic site of execution.

"Please make a fist if you can...this won't hurt a bit...You'll only feel a tiny pinch," Neville said instinctively without emotion, as though the person in the bed were a complete stranger. Then, with the bevel of the needle pointing up, he approached the site. Many times, he had rehearsed how this scene would play out in his mind. In order to insure only a single puncture site, he would just draw the required amount of blood necessary for the tests. Then with the needle still in, he would release the tourniquet and slowly dislodge the barrel of the syringe from the needle. With just the needle tip in and the tourniquet off, little blood would flow out. Next he would empty the contents of the syringe barrel into the various colored stoppered tubes on his tray for the required tests. With the empty syringe in his hand, he drew it full hilt to the 35 cc mark filling the barrel with a mixture of slightly red frothy air. He carefully twisted it back onto the needle, still in the arm, and slowly, very slowly, would introduce the deadly percolating airstream into his system. The air would cause the blood within the vein to form clots that would soon obstruct the blood flow and cause a form of internal strangulation within minutes. He had witnessed many such deaths before. Depending upon where the clot finally lodged, death would come immediately with a dignified calm or in a thrashing screaming agony.

Avoiding his victim's eyes, as he had always been careful to do in the past. He was about to exact his long awaited revenge when he made that one terrible error of judgment—the one he had always avoided in the camps, by looking into the Reverend's eyes.

The visage he beheld was no longer Reverend Lucas, but the face of Emmanuel Steinman dying from multiple tetanus injections in a urine stained bunk at Dachau. Then evolved the bloated featureless face of Miriam Rubin who had daily been the recipient of injections of gas gangrene and whose limbs were now bilious and blackened with the deadly festering organisms. One by one they all came back to Neville: one face after the other evolving into the next. There they were, all his long dead victims. The old, the young, the males the females, the children, a kaleidoscope of hell.

There the jaundiced faces of the unwilling recipients of injections of typhus, tetanus, botulism, gasoline, animal blood, formic acid, snake and spider venoms. There were the victims of experimental surgery, aseptic sterilization techniques, limb and bone grafts, from humans and animals. Next, those tortured by freezing and high-pressure rapid decompression experiments and those in tetany from live rabies injections. The 'Totenbuch' filled with their names as the nights swelled with their deafening screams.

The memories, those terrible memories of all of his victims seared his brain. He was going back there again. He realized that he had never left, and could never as long as his guilt remained.

Neville Rosenthal, son of a Jewish tailor, was a diminutive

third year medical student in Warsaw before the bombs came. He survived seven years at Dachau, not by strength, but through weakness as a special medical assistant to SS Schutzstaffel Commandant Dr. Rascher, medical butcher of the camp. They had early recognized this Jew's surgical skill in the captive infirmary beneath St. Christine's Church in Warsaw. With tailor-like skill, he sutured the wounds of his countrymen caused by the screaming Stuka dive bombers. Recruited by Rascher, the director in charge of human experimentation, Neville would follow him by day like a faithful dog in his deadly rounds, the willing tool of the medical horror.

Yet, by night, not as an angel of death, but one of mercy he would try to undo what the wanton beast, Rascher, had done by bringing death, hopefully swift, but always certain. Under the pretense of checking survival rates, he would make his nocturnal rounds, delegating death to those suffering the most. In time he developed a keen sense as to just when to end a victim, for to kill one too soon would only arouse his master's suspicion. Nightly, the emaciated faces would call from their beds for freedom from their torment. He would comply only with those whom he dared. Those who had been marked by enough time. To others he would offer a gentle touch, a simple Talmud prayer, and a reassuring, "Soon my friend, be patient just another day and it will be your time to be with your God."

With children he found it hardest to resist. They, nor their parents, could understand his sometime refusal. Long after the horror ended, his nights would fill with all their endless cries. Yet Dr. Rascher sometimes could not understand why, "These pigs die too soon."

It was on the night he chose to take Emmanuel's life as well as his own that he realized why he must survive. Emmanuel Steinman was a rabbi. His body was in almost complete tetany, with his back bent back like a bow and skeletal face stretched taut, as a result of the Clostridium injections and the microorganism's deadly toxin. His breathing, was barely discernable as a result of the paralysis spreading to his diaphragm. He knew his time was to be that night. Neville sought him out in barracks #12. In the bottom bunk in the flickering candlelight, he looked upon his Rabbi's tormented features. Neville had come to recognize the final stages of lockjaw, where the back bends like a bow and the mouth can barely move, stretched back by the tightening facial muscles into a skeletal grin. Even in that twisted state, Neville beheld a saintly countenance he remembered on the Christian icons in St. Christine's. He begged forgiveness from the dying man before he would end it for them both.

"It is not for me to forgive, Neville, but only God," the dying rabbi rasped through cracked lips. "Remember Neville, that only God gives life and, therefore only He is justified in taking it. Yet, although I regard your nightly rounds as unholy, they are necessary. Yes, necessary, Neville. For you see, while God gives life, I also believe he has chosen you to prevent the pain of these poor souls. You must help in the return of all His children that you now see being systematically and senselessly slaughtered. Yes, Neville, you must live to continue your rounds. Those that are here now and those still to be marked, need you. And when this horror has ended, you must live to serve as living testimony of what happened here. Your 'Totenbuch' will be their memorial and Eulogy. Only you can prevent their memory from ending here."

Neville squatted on the dirty floor watching his tears pool in the sawdust and candle wax. "Now Neville, you must understand this. With me I wish God to have His way in His own time. If I am to suffer, it is because I must. So just stay with me and let us pray together for both the victims and the tormentors alike. There are no answers in all this, only questions. And who can question God? So spare me, Neville. There is no need to intervene for I shall not see another dawn. Now take my hand and pray with me."

And so throughout that night they prayed the faith of their ancestors, and right before dawn the candle burned out as Neville felt the hand he held curl and turn cold. And so Neville continued his deadly nocturnal rounds until liberation, a liberation without any sense of justice or retribution.

There was to be no justice from a world that wanted to forget what their own species had done. Still, he needed to punish someone, if only himself.

He was back now and those once steady hands now shook as he released the tourniquet and withdrew the needle tip from its fleshy bed, the syringe barrel still holding the deadly air. He quickly applied a sterile cotton wad to the tiny pearl of blood rising at the puncture site. He backed away and then saw the Reverend's face swell, magnified by his own tears that ran into the crevasses of a face carved by time and pain. He stepped forward and pressed the Reverend's hand and whispered, "I forgive you—all of you—and perhaps someday even myself." The Reverend never heard Neville's words as he had fallen into a deep, relaxed sleep from which he would never wake.

Neville left the room with the realization of how the arrogant, the greedy, the cruel, the evil and even the brave are all eventually reduced to the same level of fear and uncertainty when confronted by death. How the deathbed, like a scale of justice, reduces all humans to poor, frightened creatures. In the end, the executioner and the victim are forever bonded. All those who had escaped their justice in Germany would eventually face this same reality on their own deathbeds. Some might regret, some not, but all would remember and die with the uncertainty of how their actions would impact or follow them into what lay beyond. And maybe a final realization that nothing now would ever undo what they had done.

Neville left the lab that night never to return. He left with the realization that as an angel of mercy he had to function, but as an instrument of hate he could not. Not even the combined nightmares of Graydon or Dachau could ever change that.

He had fulfilled his role, and now could no longer find the hate that had sustained him through those terrible years and beyond. He had long cheated his fate, so it was time for him to go, fittingly as they had, by the gas and the fire. In his upstairs room with doors now sealed, he opened the jets on the kitchen stove whose gas sought and soon enveloped the seven lighted Menorah on a table, where sat a tired old man in a black yarmulke calmly reading the ancient scriptures of his ancestors until the darkness fell.

"So Neville goes the same way as the other victims,"

Tonya asks, "I knew what Somma wrote were facts of what that monster Rascher did, but did Neville really exist?"

"Well I'm sure for just that night when he came to the author who wrote his story and eulogy."

"So you mentioned there was an attempt to blow up the chambers?"

"Yes, in fact it was a long process involving many, first by women worked in Canada the name of the place where the luggage and belongings of those were dumped before gassing. But that will be topic for next time. Class dismissed."

SONDERKOMMANDO
REVOLT

Danny went to the board pulled down the screen and put a cassette of slides into the projector as the class filtered in.

Turning "I hope you haven't eaten yet because this class will upset your stomachs." No response. "This will prove the extremes one will go through when death is all but a certainty and unlike the stories of offering others to die in their place, this will tell of payback and not to go down without a fight. This is a perfect example of Hate driving out Fear since the two emotions cannot exist simultaneously." He faintly recalled the incident with his own mother when he threatened her with the sword. His fear of her no longer but replaced with hate.

"You mean like the Jewish resistance in the Warsaw Ghetto?" Cameron asked.

"Somewhat, but this idea was fomented by Russian prisoners first."

"You remember the Sonderkommando's were special units of Jewish prisoners who had the tasks of guiding new arrivals into the gas chambers, then removing the bodies afterwards, shaving their hair, removing their teeth with gold fillings, stacking the bodies four to six at a time into the ovens, shoveled the ashes into carts, and then hosing the chamber down to ready for the next group. The Nazi referred to them as stokers. They worked in shifts all around the clock seven days a week."

Shaking his head, Cameron said. "Their own kind, why?"

"Yes we've talked about this before, but not with such an example as this. They did it for self-preservation, but also for the generous food and drink, especially the alcohol drink, no doubt to help them forget. So while they worked under hellish conditions, they knew they would be replaced and gassed in two to four months themselves, because the Nazi knew dead men tell no tales."

"By the end of June 1944 nineteen Soviet prisoners from Majdanek incited them to revolt. They made contact with Jewish girls who worked in the munitions factory near the main camp, and they smuggled small quantities of explosives in the false bottom of food trays. On October 7, 1944 the resistance heard that the SS were going to liquidate the camp and all in it, due to the reverse of the war against the Russians, in the East.

At an Appell, the prisoners first lined up, but then hurled themselves upon the guards, with hammers and axes, and even threw three SS into the ovens alive and then using explosives and handmade grenades blew up the crematorium."

"Well as you can guess, retaliation was swift and brutal. Well the SS drove up in trucks and shot 250 prisoners and 12 had escaped, but were captured and their dead bodies brought back and hung upside down.

Then the next day, October 10th, five of the women employed in the munitions camp were arrested and tortured, and then hung. Two in the morning Appell and two in the evening Appell, so every shift could see."

"So it was all for nothing."

"Not really because it showed that even the SS were not invulnerable to the hate they caused. Several SS were killed and many wounded. These final slides show the crematorium, next the burning of the corpses, a list of the Sonderkommando's, and finally a photo of Roza Robota, one of the four hanged."

"So we never knew about the camps?", Bobbi asked.

"Of course we did…" cut off.

"Well why the fuck, if you will excuse my English, didn't we do something about it? "

"While the British Lancaster's flew by day and we at night in our Flying Foresters, in our daily bombing raids over Germany, we flew right over the camps and took photos sending them back to Secretary of State Simpson asking what to do?

Simpson felt it was too dangerous to fly so low and risk being shot down, and added that the best way to help the victims was to continue to bomb Germany and end the war as soon as possible. Even Theodore Roosevelt asked if they could at least bomb the railroad tracks leading into the camps, and got the same answer. "

"The asshole was obviously not a Jew."

"You said it Bobbie. Now any of you ready for lunch?"

"Not a Chance."

MOSCOW STILL REMEMBERS

"Where to now?", Booker asked as the rest came in and sat down.

"I had to unique opportunity to join a group of the colleagues I had met at Borstel and to join them on a trip to Moscow."

"Was the Berlin wall up then?"

"Yes it was, but while Americans had to go through Checkpoint Charlie, I had to go through the German checkpoint. From there at night we boarded a prop plane on Aeroflot and soon the plane was roaring down the runway in a terrible blizzard. They passed out hard candy to suck on to pop our ears, since the pane wasn't pressurized. It seemed as though the plane was never going to take off, and the person next to me said, are we there yet?" All laughed.

"Well we finally did land and in early dawn since we were flying into the light. As we crossed the street there was a ruddy faced Russian policeman directing traffic. He came up to me and said something in Russian which I didn't understand. I just shook my head and then he said in broken English, "Friend?" I nodded yes. Then he took off his gloves and hugged me. Then I went on with the rest of the group. I asked them why just me, and not anyone else? Someone from my group said it was probably the way I was dressed in Army fatigues, and not in the fine garb they traveled in. He went on to say they still remember the Americans who risked and lost their lives fighting us Germans."

"Wow so they still remembered."

"Yes, and many more of the same reactions against the Germans. Like the night some of went to see the Bolshoi Ballet, and got lost on the way back. One of my friends stopped a woman and asked her if she spoke German. She responded yes, but she won't. Then turned to me and in perfect English said, we have many memories of what the Germans did to us."

"But they never invaded Moscow, did they?"

"No but they sieged and bombed Leningrad for 900 days and brought immense death to the civilian population. As this slide shows. There were even incidents of them eating dead horses, and human corpses. There was one woman standing in a graveyard holding up a bag of dead babies for sale."

"So much snow and destruction."

"Yes the siege, referred to as the 900 days started on September 8th, 1941 and ended on January 27th, 1944. Over one million died by starvation, exposure or by the bombardment. Hitler wanted to destroy it because it was the birthplace of the Russian revolution."

"Well besides all of the sow and destruction, did you do anything for fun besides the ballet?", Becka asked.

"Yes I actually got to take a sleigh ride drawn by several horses, but that bought back a strange memory of a book I had read."

"Which?"

"Well it was called Giants in the Middle of the Earth, and about a newlywed couple pulled by a sled at night in the snow. Then all of a sudden they were chased by a pack of hungry wolves. Despite the drivers whipping the horses to go faster, the wolves were catching up, so in order to lighten the load, the drivers threw the couple out of the sled and escaped."

"So that was a fun thing? What next?"

"I took a subway to one of their museums. Every station was decorated in fine art and not the graffiti we encounter here. The tour guide took us through the and showed us the many pieces of art, including some of us showing the lynching and burning of blacks by our Klan and others, but not as bad as the ones of the Germans."

"How so?"

"Well there was one of a German with a whip in his hand point to a ruddy faced woman to board the cattle car. The look of indignant resolve on her face with her two children behind her truly represented the represented the resolve that would eventually bring down the Reich.

Then there were the others I had shown you of the lynching of Masha Bruskina on October 26th 1941. She was a Russian nurse accused of treason after being betrayed by her close friend for treating a Jew.

This slide shows her being marched down the street toward the gallows, accompanied ironically by a friend, Volodia Shcherbatsevich, who betrayed her thinking he would get some reward for turning her in. He did, and was hanged immediately after she was.

She wrote in her last letter to her mother who opposed her activities in caring for the sick, "I am tormented by the thought that I have caused you great worry. Don't worry, nothing bad will happen to me, and you will have no further unpleasantness because of me.

Please send me my dress, green blouse and white socks. I want to be dressed decently when I leave here."

"After being marched to the gallows and made to stand upon a stool with hands and feet tied together, they turned her facing the crowd of spectators. Yet defiant to the end, she refused to face the crowd. Only after forcibly turning her did they kick out the stool from under her as you see in this slide."

"And then here is to the one of the nurse hanging by her throat with a fur hat on her head with the Russian Star, after she had been ganged raped. Notice the Wehrmacht standing by and laughing and pointing. This proves it wasn't only the SS but the regular German army that participated in the genocide.

But the worse incident I viewed, and one that actually reinforced the Soviets retaliation against the Nazi, was this one of a poster circulated among their troops, reflecting the incident. This was a young girl, Nastya, caught by the Germans while leaving her village not far from Moscow. Unlike typical public executions like shootings or hangings, for some reason she was tied to a stake and burned alive. Some 30,000 of these posters were printed and distributed among the Soviet troops."

"How awful" wept Tonya.

'Yes and as the Russian poet Vladimir Mayakovski said:
And only God, omnipotent indeed,
Knew they were animals,
Of a different breed."

Bobbi asked, "Did any of these monsters ever have a conscious."

"Actually there are several incidents of human consciousness finally taking over ones psych. At Ravensbruck physicians no longer will to partake in the horrid disfiguring experiments on the rabbits, and then sent to fight on the Eastern front against the Russians, a certain death.

Then, after the Japanese Slaughter of 300,000 innocent men, women and children at Nanking in 1937. During that time their victims were subjected to beheadings, burned alive in large open pits, tied together and drowned, castrated, torn apart by dogs and would you believe, even crucified. Then three weeks, these soldiers began to show bizarre symptoms of tears, anxiety and depression. Some refusing to bare their arms and fight anymore.

Also, remember that the final solution of the Jews in the gas chambers was because the mass shootings and burials were having a negative effect on the SS executioners. In the book by Jodi Picoult, the Story Teller, she tells of this effect upon one of the major members of the Einsatzgruppen where every night he drinks himself into to a stupor and his dreams are haunted by the images of those he killed. He is even haunted by a song. In the pits of the dead and those still alive crawling alive bleeding but not dead yet. There was a mother in the pits still alive and singing a melody to her child to keep her calm. He was so moved that he could not shoot them. Then came up a superior officer who shot them both, and told him to aim better.

"What is Einsats…."

"Einsatzgruppen were the paramilitary death squads of the SS. Translated it means one sentence for all those they dealt with, meaning death. Even after the Battle of the Bulge, the SS executed 200 of our Americans captured, and earlier had set fire to a church with hundreds of men, women and children trapped inside. All were burned alive. You see the arms of some reaching out from under the locked door."

"So these were the brave ones who never had to face a bullet themselves."

"Yes, but not until the Soviets got to them. Before we go I would like to give you another example of the subconscious of the guilty. This is from the book The Plume Tree by Ellen Marie Wiseman, where the Director of a Concentration camp talks to his Jewish housemaid in the final days of the war."

(If something happens to me, will you promise to remember my name? Will you let everyone know I tried to stop it... It will be later, when this war has ended, when we go home, when we sit at the dinner table in our comfortable houses, after we kiss our wife good night, it will be then we will dread the night. We will know the visions that will rise from the depths of our guilty minds. It will haunt us until the end of our days, and we will surely be spending eternity at Hitler's side in hell.)

"Why you ask? This question has plagued mankind for centuries, and so perfectly summed up in the Book of Malachi, Chapter 2:10, "Is it not one father that we all have? Is it not one God that created us all? Why is it then that we deal so treacherously with each other?"

MOSCOW LAST MEMORIES

"Well finally my last night arrived on New Year's eve. There was much drinking of Vodka and I passed out John F. Kennedy half dollars and ball point pens, the latter were a scarcity there. In exchange I was given several medals to put on my new furry Russian hat. The big red star was my favorite. What was ironic was because of the time zone differences, the Germans and the US would hit the magic hour at different times. So the Russian were first, and we all stood and toasted the New Years in. Hours later the Germans stood and I toasted it with them, but few Russians stood. Then later, finally the US New Years', and they all stood and toasted."

"And now cheers to you." The class stood and toasted in an imaginary way.

"What are those books you have up on your desk? ", Becka asked.

"Well you can all come up and take a look. The first is a book on weight lifting written to demonstrate the moves and training of which the Olympic lifter Vaselef Alexev who held would record in the press, clean and Jerk and the most dangerous of all the snatch where to weight goes from the floor directly overhead in one motion."

"What about the military press, the squat and the dead lift?" queried Booker.

"That not Olympic lifting, but Power lifting, mostly a form found here and not in international competition, nor the Olympics."

"Can you hit it and demonstrate?", all laughed.

"I would but the book as you can see I written in Russian so I couldn't read it. But moving on. This next is one called CAUTION ZIONISM, so you can see even the Russians, at the time of the revolution, hated the Jews."

"Why?"

"Because the Jews were always the convenient scapegoat for every wrong a nation faced."

Tonya intervened, "Not to mention a binding point uniting the opposite class."

"Very true as written in Mein Kampf. "

"And the next?"

"This one is called, A SOLDIERS DUTY written by K. Rokossovsky. He was the Field Marshall of the Soviet Union. You will note the photos of the German atrocities that we talked about earlier. Her is on one hanging after both breasts had been cut off. "

"How could anyone ever do that? "

"As Dieter said in Jodi Picoult's book, THE STORY TELLER, when you do it often enough it gets easier."

"Yes, but you said the guilt never fads."

"True subconsciously we all know right from wrong. Did you know that the SS were first respected men in their community? Doctors, lawyers, professors, and professionals from all walks of life, yet soon wanting the power and control that Hitler allowed them to need and believe."

"But getting back to the Rokossovsky book, he tells of a pilot Victor Talalinkhin, who rammed an enemy bomber on the night of August 7, 1941 to his certain death." PHOTO

"What could incite such bravery?"

"Not bravery, but sheer hate after learning as you see in this photo in the square of Volokolamsk. Eight partisans hanged by the Germans December 20, 1941 in front of a crowd of Russian Civilians. Among the spectators was the mother of one of the victims, a young school girl, Zoya Kosmodemyanskaya."

"In exchange for those gifts I gave out ball point pens, a rare commodity and Kennedy half dollars."

"And so that morning I flew back from Moscow to Berlin on Aeroflot, and then boarded a British Jet home taking with me the mixed feelings of sadness, yet hope on the determination the Russians showed at Leningrad and Moscow. "

"I thought of a poem on the way home, that seems appropriate at this time. It's called Homecoming

It seemed all too soon, when death came to lead me,

taking that one step beyond infinity.

I came before him, and at once I could see,

though try as he might, he didn't know me.

He asked what I knew, before I came his way,

I looked into his eyes, then started to say,

I knew the summer, spring, winter and fall,

I knew of life, no matter how small,

I knew the stars, the wind and the sea,

I knew of love, and how it should be.

Yet I'd sit in silence, awaiting your call,

but where was your hand, when I'd stumble and fall?

The people you created, became beasts of prey,

terrorizing our world, both night and day.
You allowed them Auschwitz, Hiroshima, Mai-Lai,
couldn't you stop them, why so many to die?
We all were your children, I'm sorry to say,
Was this your intent, I often would pray?
You never did answer, as how we could cope,
in a world gone to madness, you offered no hope.
So I never found you, and soon didn't bother,
For you were the stranger, though you were my father?

Students shaking their heads. "Yes but adequately summed up my years of searching for some meaning of the holocaust, among both the victims and the perpetrators, but never found it.

"Well speaking of flights, the next class we will talk about the NACHT HEXEN...."

"The what?"

"The Night Witches."

LL2 THE NIGHT WITCHES (DIE NACHT HEXEN)

B obbi asked, "So who were these Night Witches You Mentioned last time. Sounds scary."

"Yes they were scary, but only to the Germans who called them the Night Witches. It's the true story of valiant Russian female pilots who terrorized the Nazi soldiers at night, keeping them from sleeping by bombs and strafing. First documented by Bruce Myers in his book, (Night Witches: The amazing story of Russian pilots in WWll.) While they were belittled by the male pilots, they flew many missions, some several at a time every night. They would land, refuel and take to the air again. And they did this, as you see, in the old double winged, two seated Polikarpov PO-2, nothing more than thin fabric stapled over wooden struts"

"One pilot to each plane?"

"No the pilot sat in the back seat while up front sat the navigator. What's worse, they were not given parachutes because of there weren't enough, and can you imagine what the bitter cold felt like during the winter of the Nazi invasion of Russia."

"Any lost?"

"Yes several some by flak and ground fire and some actual shot down by the superior German fighter planes, the Focke Wulf's. Some crashed and burned after hitting the ground, but those were the lucky ones."

"How do you mean?"

"Any survivors were captured by the Nazi, raped and then killed. This was discovered by the Russian soldiers as advanced against the Nazi in the latter part of the war."

To get a vivid account, although fictional, read (The Huntress by Kate Quinn). She tells of a fictional character, Nina Markova, who flying with several female pilots and navigators completes over 130 missions. One story when a bomb refused to dislodge from the bomb bay and would make landing impossible, she climbs out of the cockpit, hangs onto the wing, and kicks it lose. In the book she and the other survivors were awarded the Red Star badge by Stalin himself."

"So I assume that Stalin himself acknowledged what they had done."

"More than that, even at the resistance of the General Chiefs of the Aviation Staff who felt they should be used to repair the planes and the air strips. For a couple of reasons. First they had more flying hours than most of the new recruits who they were losing at an alarming rate to the German Luftwaffe. And second he saw them as instructors to the new flying recruits."

"If you want to read a visual graphic novel, here is, (The Grand Duke) where the main characters Lilya and Oxana fly with the 585th flight regiment. Here you will get the feel of what this type of combat was like in that bitter winter from both sides.

Another more detailed account is the graphic novel, "The Night Witches" by Ennis, Braun, Avina, and Bowland. This one is the best, not only from the graphics but also from the conversations from both sides. But it's not good for the faint of heart. It is the best because, although it starts with the sorties against the Nazi invasion, it follows one Night witch, Anna Kharkove, right up to flying Russian Migs against our Saber Jets in the Viet Nam war."

"Since they were losing so many pilots from ground flak, they realized with was because even at night the Germans could hear them coming. So they developed two techniques. The first was to use a decoy plane to attract the flak in a different direction, while they made their drop over the target. Naturally, since the decoy planes had little chance of survival, they used the second technique. Long before approach, they would kill their engine and just glide silently toward their targets, drop their bombs and then restart and fly out of there as soon as possible."

"But now a Chemistry question which I will direct to Tonya our future Chemistry major. In order to keep awake during those long nights of many missions, they sucked on Coca Cola tablets, why Tonya?'

"Well for two reasons, first because of the caffeine and second, even back then, why was it called coke?"

Bobbie jumped up," Well since I'm the resident coke head here?", all laughed, it was because Coke contained Cocaine."

Tonya, "Correct, and it was put in there to make those who drank it addicted to it, and so definitely a great way to insure future sales."

Cameron, "Wasn't it in the 1920's that Mr. Coke, whoever he was, sold his drink?"

Danny nodded to Tonya for the answer.

"Yes he did, but not without some competition from 7up."

"How so?"

"Well someone decided to give Coke a run for its money, and developed a clear citrus drink and called it 7up and it had an upper also that led to addictions."

"What was that?"

"The only psychiatric drug at the time, Lithium. In fact, better than just an addictive substance, it also led to a great thirst insuring a lot of consummation."

"So that's why the up in 7up. It was an upper. But why the 7?"

"Allow me to impress you guys further with my Chemistry acumen if I may. "

Bekka sarcastically, "Oh yes genus girl. Do tell."

"Well if you all will look at my chart of the Periodic table of the elements. I always carry with me; you will notice that Lithium has an atomic number of 3."

"Oh yeah, then why 7?"

"Because while the atomic number is 3, the atomic weight is 7, and therefore we get 7up."

"Ok smart ass, why use the 3?"

"Well if you will all do me a favor I want all of you to in unison rapidity say 3up."

Danny watched as she led them as a band conductor in the chant of "3up, 3up, 3 up."

Then they all burst out laughing because it sounded like Throw up.

Danny, "Well Tonya, you certainly made your point. I'm sure you will go onto become a rich and famous Chemist someday."

"Yes I will, and definitely make more money than you do teaching History." All laughed.

"Well on that rather sobering, but very true comment, class dismissed.

THE WASPS

"In an era when most women didn't even have driver's licenses, the Women Airforce Service pilots (WASP) were the only unit who flew every type of military aircraft. They came from all walks of life but most already had flying experience. They trained and flew from Avenger field in Sweetwater Texas."

"Their duties were unique and dangerous, from flight testing newly built aircraft fresh off of the line, and then ferrying them to various bases in the pacific."

Cameron asked, "But did they fly any real combat missions?"

"Not in that sense, but in a somewhat more dangerous fashion."

"What do you mean? What's more dangerous than combat?"

"Well how would you like to be flying a plane towing a target called a sock with a bullseye, that ground artillery was firing anti-aircraft guns with live ammunition like needed to hit Kamikazes? While they missed a lot, they often actually hit the planes. WASP Beverly Beesemyer was one who was hit and her plane caught fire, but she safely brought it down on the dessert floor. What's interesting about her is that Bev was not a pilot, but worked in a defense plant and drove six hours each way on weekends to take flying lessons."

"Wow that is true dedication and determination. Why weren't the men used to tow the targets?"

"Would you believe they didn't want to risk losing their male pilots?"

"Typical male chauvinism even back then." Bobbie voiced.

"True and not so uncommon even during World War two. Remember the Night Witches?"

"Yes they were not even given parachutes because the men needed them." Bobbie said.

"Yes now do any of you remember who Paul Tibbetts was?"

Tonya raising her hand, "Pilot of the Enola Gay who dropped the first atomic bomb on Hiroshima on August 6th, 1945."

"Correct, and here is a photo of a B-29 Superfortress. This was the largest bomber ever built, but it had been a complete mess thus far. Its Wright engines were nicknamed "wrong engine" by pilots. Flaws in the engines caused them to repeatedly overheat and burst into flames while in midair. In fact, test pilot Edmund t. Allen crashed because of an engine fire killing him and all eight crewmen as well as hitting and killing 19 civilians on the ground.

So Tibbetts had a problem, so who did he go to for help?"

"The pussy pilots of course, who else." Bobbi offered.

"Ok, Bobbi that is enough, but actually true.

This bomber had such problems flaws in the engines, they would overheat and burst into flames while in midair that no male pilot would fly it. So what did Tibbetts do?"

"He had the women fly it?"

"Exactly. In June of 1944 he found Didi Moorman and Dora Dougherty and asked them if they would do a trial run since they had flown large bombers. What they did differently, know of the B-29's potential for fire, they managed engine temperature before take- off by avoiding the standard brake power check and instead used a rolling start to allow air flow to the engines while taking off. Nonetheless, one the engines did catch fire in mid-air, but they feathered the engine, pulled the fire extinguisher, and landed the massive bomber perfectly. Tibbetts was so impressed he Fifinella, the mascot of the WASP painted on that bomber and named it "Ladybird. "

"Good for them! Showed those dick less mother fuckers what real courage is like." Bobbi sneered.

Danny snapped, "Ok Bobbie that's enough. You know the rules."

"Sorry, yes I do. No fucking bad language allowed during class."

Danny just stared. "Well Tibbets was quoted as saying "I don't think we could have gotten our pilots to fly them until our female pilots proved them reliable. Or at least mostly reliable." Some laughter.

"But why even use those planes when we had Liberators, Flying Fortresses, and the Billy Mitchel bomber used in the Doolittle raid on Tokyo on April 18 of 1942?"

"It was because only the B-29 was built for long range bombing and with a very heavy payload. You remember the Doolittle raid was a disaster when once their carrier, the Hornet, was spotted by a Japanese patrol boat forcing them to launch much earlier and limiting their fuel in retreating to China. Some never made it, but running out of fuel, crashed into the sea. Those who did make it crashed landed and died or were killed by the Japanese. A few like Doolittle himself were rescued by Chinese patriots and made it back to the States. Material damage was small, but it had a great effect on our morale."

"Why China and not return to the Hornet?"

"No bomber had ever even been flown off a carrier let alone could land on one. The B-24's had to strip down all possible weight even guns and personnel in order to carry the bombs and be able to lift off such a short deck that only our fighter planes could do.

So after hitting their targets, despite heavy flack, most did not have enough fuel to make it to the Chinese mainland. Watch the movie Pearl Harbor, with some actual black and white footage of what the attack was like, and the rational for the raid. It was in retaliation for their attack on Pearl, on December 7th 1941. As Roosevelt refereed as our day of infamy. "

Booker asked, "Who was Billy Mitchel? I don't know of any other WWll Bombers named after a person."

"He was the first person to pilot a plane off of the deck of a ship prior to World War 2 in a double winged plane, and it ushered in the role of the Aircraft carriers in our war in the Pacific, while European countries were still building battleships."

Cameron raising his hand, "Despite the tragedy of Pearl, we were lucky for two reasons."

"So tell."

"Well first none of our carriers were at Pearl at the time, but out to sea. And it finally ended our isolationist policy by Charles Lindbergh and others who didn't want us in another foreign war. Prior to that time only England and Russia were fighting the Nazi despite many entreaties to join them."

"That's true Cameron, but now let's get back to our Superfortress.

After the successful demonstration by Didi and Dora, the B-29's soon began the nocturnal fire bombings of several cities in Japan in preparation of the invasion by our troops which seemed inevitable. While it decimated a mostly civilian population, it only served to strengthen the resolve of the Japanese soldiers, civilian men and women, and even children into fighting to the end.

Also you'll note the fanaticism and their will in to die for the Emperor, were the Kamikaze fighter pilots. Our government knew they would not quit.

So at 8:16am, on August 6th, Tibbets dropped LITTLE BOY, as it was called, over Hiroshima. The blast killed 70,000 instantly, and in five days, 70,000 more from radiation burns and poisoning. If you want to read the horror of the victims, read John Hersey's book, "Hiroshima."

"Why Hiroshima?"

"Well it wasn't really a military target, Mostly civilians and actually 200 allied prisoners of war. It was meant mostly as a demonstration to get Japan to surrender, but they refused even after a naval vessel sailed there and were devastated by what they saw.

So then on August 9th, 1945, at 11:02am a bomb called FAT MAN, on Nagasaki, killing 80,000 instantly. "

Sadly, Bekka said," I guess those were the lucky ones."

"Yes I think you are right. If you want to get an idea of the Japanese ideology read, "Midori and the 1000 Stitch Belt." A tale of a Japanese Midwife dedicated to delivering and preserving lift while her husband, in true Bushido honor destroyed life as in Nanking in 1937. While fiction, it is true to all of the historical facts that occurred."

Grabbing a pen Cameron asked, "Who wrote it."

"A Dr. C. Thomas Somma, a historian as well as a scientist."

"MIDORI AND THE THOUSAND STITCH BELT"

A NOVEL

BY

DR. C. THOMAS SOMMA

BOOK ONE
NANKING

Maelstrom atop Suribachi

Schima, alone in the vine covered bunker atop a hill on Iwo Jima, single handedly held the marine platoon from its advance with his small arms fire. Around him lay the corpses of his comrades, gone to their Gods after a baptism of shrapnel by marine grenades lobed into the dark entrance. Many of them, not much older than he, were now lifeless decaying forms cloaked in dust dislodged from the bunkers sodden roof. He knew it would not be much longer before he too would join them. Gone was the bravado he had felt earlier, replaced with a little boy's fear of the unknown and crowded now with only thoughts of his home and his mother, Midori. He could not surrender, for to do so would forever deny him his place of honor on the Thousand Stitch belt along with his father and all of his brave ancestors dating back to the fifteenth century. If he surrendered, when death finally came, his spirit would be condemned to roam forever in a desolate afterworld reserved only for cowards of the Japanese Imperial military.

The two forward point Marines sent a staccato of tracer fire into the mouth of the bunker, camouflaging the stealth like movements of a Marine Corporal with the flamethrower. Not detected by Shima, he had climbed his way on to the top of the bunker.

He crawled over the thick vines that were meant to hide the clay fortress. Careful not to betray his presence, he inched his way to the roof's small air vents. To the rest of the squad below, the two large incendiary tanks on his back gave him the appearance of a large deformed insect, waddling in its gait and seeking shelter from an unknown predator. This time he was the predator, and as he came upon the first air vent, he abruptly shoved the nozzle of the flamethrower into its rusted mouth. No longer concerned about masking his presence, he shouted an obscenity to those inside as he pulled the thick metal trigger. The first blast of flame ate the air. Shima first tasted petrol, then screamed and sucked in hot searing air into lungs that would never transpire air again. In a final act of defiance, Schima blindly charged toward the air vent to stay the dragon's fiery breath. One more trigger pull by the intruder above caught Shima centered in the full blast of a second orange ball that coated his uniform and arms with the thick petrol. Death was not instant as he had hoped, but a slow purgatory as first uniform, then flesh yielded to the fiery gel. His eyes seared, swelled and then ruptured. This last act of defiance first gave way to fear, then betrayal, and then resignation. His last living thought was neither of empire nor glory, but only a soundless plea to his mother to please come to him, and help him through the fearful uncertainty of what lay beyond.

DÉJÀ VU

Her son Shima was burning. Midori didn't have to wait for the official letter from the Japanese high command, or the stamped rice paper certificate sent to honor all who had died for the glory of Emperor Hirohito. She could sense his anguished screams of terror, as she bolted upright in the bed, her frail hands squeezing and forcing the silken sheets into her mouth, gagging on the rising bile in her throat. "Shima, Shima," she cried over and over again. "Now even you Shima, why you too." Shima, her second son, was only seventeen and too young to die in a war that had already taken her husband, the renowned General Nakura Tanoka.

Midori fell forward into her lap and cried his spirit into the sheets. She fought the dream's deadly vividness, but it would not leave, it ran in flickering ethereal images like the propaganda news-reels of the Japanese Imperial Army's sweep across China she had viewed with her husband Nakura and other high ranking military leaders, at social events in the early days of the war, the time before she received the rice paper death notice on her husband.

It was often to her Gods she turned to, and was reminded by the final letter from Shima before he was sent to a desolate atoll called Iwo Jima. Daily she looked at his photo, where tucked in the corner of the bamboo frame was the farewell letter he had written her. This was always a requirement of those who go into combat, serving as final testimony of ones written pledge, for their final sacrifice to the Emperor. Again on this darkened day she reread it, hoping his spirit was still alive, and that her dream was only the manifestation of the dread she daily felt for both of her sons, now serving in the Imperial Army. Yet she knew that her instincts were to be trusted, proven countless times in her job as a midwife. She read the hurried scrawl, written more in fear than in a sense a bravado he tried to emulate:

> "My dear and most spiritual mother, with joy I am prepared to go to the sacred place of our forefathers, and as those Samurai, I too will be brave and honor my destiny as defender of our homeland. Our sun goddess, *Amaterasu*, will light the way for me her son and yours, to this my glorious end. Please make a place for my memory on the Thousand Stitch Belt, so when the great dragon master, *Sunasee*, comes to collect all of the souls of our great warrior ancestors, I, too, shall be with them and one with my brave father who now waits for me on the other side. Please do not grieve for me, for this was why I came to be. I was born only to serve one glorious end, to die in the service of our Emperor. Good-bye my mother, hold me forever in your heart, and I thank you for the gift of life that I now willingly give back to my Emperor with eagerness and joy in the defense of our homeland."

She knew that had not been the case. Her dream of Schima's end vividly portended the opposite. In the end he died just her as her little boy again, frightened, confused and feeling betrayed by the militaristic lie they were all led to believe.

She knew it was now time to embroider Schima's name on the Thousand Stitch belt, against the wishes of her of late husband. His final wish to her was that he would serve as the last of his lineage to occupy a place on the Thousand Stitch belt, and would end with his name, General Nakura Tanoka.

Destiny at Johor

In slow silent agony Midori rose from the bed and entered the room which held the sacred *kamidana*, the household Shinto shrine dedicated to the dead. She lit the oil lights that framed each side of the altar. She was chilled by the night air, and the dream of Shima which she couldn't shake from her mind. Behind the altar hung a large flag, of Imperial Japan, brilliant white with the red rising sun extending its tentacles to each edge. Lying across the altar was the faded Thousand Stitch Belt bearing countless names in the crimson red of dark dried blood. She took it down, kneeling with it in her lap, threaded a needle with crimson filament, and sobbing, sadly weaved the name of Shima next to that of her husband's.

The belt had been passed down for generations commemorating nearly 1000 of her husband's family line dating from 1274 to the present. The first was of the brave Samurai of Tanoka's ancestors who held back the Mongol invaders, under Kublai Kahn, in 1274 and 1276, on the beaches of Kyushu. Both invasions were halted by a divine wind, *Kamikaze*, sent by the Japanese Gods that scattered and destroyed the enemy fleet isolating and stranding the Mongols on the beach, to be slaughtered by the Tanoka's Samurai ancestors.

The front of the altar displayed the photos of her entire family. There was Masako, her oldest son now seventeen, and a student of medicine serving in Manchuria in a special top secret medical unit, caring for Chinese, American, Australian and British prisoners of war. It was labeled Unit 731, a name as mysterious as the clandestine production done there. Masako deliberately withheld from her the true nature of his work with the Unit, until his first leave years later. She felt he was safe there since the wars with the Chinese had abated, no doubt in part due to the leadership of her husband, under the Imperial General Hironoka, who led the invasion of China in 1937. Her youngest, Nomuro, was only thirteen and, therefore, too young to be called to a war she felt would soon end. He was still just a student in grade school, and safe from the horrors of war that had claimed her Shima. He, when only sixteen, joined the Army wanting to follow in the tradition of his father as well as to avenge his death. He was sent to a small atoll called Iwo Jima. General Hironaka sent him there, assuring Midori that this island was of no military significance to the enemy, so Shima would be safe. Hironaka also had three sons, Yuku, Hamano and Schino all of whom ironically, she had delivered herself. His sons grew up with hers and their remained close friends, even if now separated by the war. She had felt reassured by Hironaka's promise, but no one could have predicted such an unexpected invasion would trap and claim her son. She also looked with sadness at the photo of her only daughter, Eiko, who died so young, unloved and neglected by her father. Her husband planted a cherry blossom tree at the time of each of the births of his sons, but denied one for Eiko.

Above the altar, beneath the flag, was her husband's sword: black handle and sheath, trimmed in gold, fashioned in the tradition of the Samurai, and forged in the ceremonial flame of his ancestors who bore similar weapons against the enemies of his country for generations. It was believed that if the ancestors' spirits were called upon, at the time of forging, this would allow their bravery and resolve to enter the blade, and then lend their skills and courage to the one who wielded it. It was also believed that the souls of all those killed by such a sword, are forever trapped within the burnished metal of its blade, never to be freed again. Under the sword was a large photo of her husband, Nakura, in full uniform with the Samurai sword clutched in both hands. Ironically was the very same weapon that had insured his inglorious end.

In the funeral ceremony, a month after his death, she was given his sword by his superior, General Hironaka who, during the ceremony and in front of the entire battalion, had pinned Nakura's medals on the proud chests of his three sons, Shima, Masako and young Nomuro. Hironoka then handed Midori the mementoes her husband gave him the night before his fatal death charge. He gave her the small photos of each of their sons, and a picture of his Midori. He had no photo of Eiko, because he refused one from his wife on his departure to invade the China mainland, a decision he deeply regretted. In its place he had carved her name on a tiny pressed sweetwood stick and carried it on a leather thong around his neck. He then had handed Tanoka's final letter to his wife, written the night before he chose to die.

"My dearest and loving wife, Midori,

I make this my last correspondence since in a few hours, I willingly go to my death. Please forgive me for all the abuse and my selfish neglectful ways I've been to you all of our years. Since the death of our daughter, Eiko, I was wrong in not loving you or her enough. I regret all the time and distance I allowed to come between us, and separate us all as a family, and all in the cause of mine and our countries distorted warrior mentality. I have regretfully done many terrible things and to many innocent people. My dreams are filled with their cries and images, and I can no longer sleep. The truth of what transpired and what I allowed at Nanking will someday be made known to you. I pray for your understanding, as I do their forgiveness.

I have three final wishes that I need for you to honor in remembrance of what we once had. First, at my funeral they will give you my sword for you to place at our altar. I don't want it placed there to pollute our spiritual place. I ask that you take it to the forger at *Keito* and have him melt it down as soon as possible. For in its mirrored blade, I still can see the faces of all who died by its edge, their souls still trapped within its steel. I want it melted to release the souls of all those tormented spirits. That blade was forged in flame and now it must be destroyed in flame.

Second, please add my name to the Thousand Stitch Belt as I too wish to be included on the list of my ancestors… for now I realize they were no heroes, but murderers like me, who have left countless widows and fatherless children as their only legacy. So my second wish is that, after my name is to join them, that the belt also be destroyed by fire, so it will never stand to glorify anyone for taking another's life, nor allow it to hold the names of my three sons so as not to inspire them or their offspring to such a misguided loyalty and dubious honor.

I have included a teakwood stick on which I carved Eiko's name months ago. Ashamed for having refused your offer of her photo, I made this reminder of her and hung it with lace around my neck. Please place it on our altar and, plant a cherry blossom tree, as we did for all of the boys in our garden, allowing her spirit to blossom forth each Spring with its flowers, as theirs. I regret now that I once forbade her that honor.

Finally, out of love for my three dear sons, Midori, please vow to use all of your power to protect their lives until this war ends. Don't allow them to be influenced by the twisted Bushido code that to die for the Emperor, will bring honor to them and our family. It will bring only death and disgrace, to themselves and others. There is no honor in bringing death to any human life, as you've always said. Tell them I said so.

When the horrid truth of the years of our Imperial imperative is finally brought to light, try not to judge me too harshly, I admit I was wrong and know I can never be forgiven.

Try to think upon the good times we shared as a family, and our times before the war. I will carry my memory of you into the next realm, though sadly our spirits are never to meet again. Even the God *Sunasee* cannot carry me to the protected place of our ancestors, for my dark deeds have even denied me a place in hell. No, I am condemned to roam a darkened void for all eternity, forever denied the light of *Amaterasu* and of you my dear wife, Midori.

Tanoka"

As a leader of the dreaded *Kesshitai* suicide squads, Nakura used that sword to lead his troops in one final frenzied charge across the Strait of Johar, prior to the invasion of Singapore and directly into the deadly fire of British machine guns and mortar fire. Against the wishes of General Hironaka, his superior, he led the first wave and it was over his riddled body that the secondary squads of *Kesshitai* tread on to finally drive the British from Johar and eventually the Malayan peninsula. Midori was falsely led to believe by General Hironaka that her husband, a leader in the China campaign, had died an honorable death for the homeland and his Emperor. Hironaka would not allow anything to dishonor the name of such a national hero, for his valiant death was needed as a tool to inspire other death squads. Nakura was given a full hero's military burial and fully exploited by the propaganda ministry. Unknown to Midori, Hironaka would soon contrive the death of her youngest, Nomuro, just thirteen, whose brave death would be needed to inspire the youth of the land in the defense of the homeland.

Midori could now add the name of her husband to the Thousand Stitch belt. She reluctantly took the sword, still in its scabbard, and remembered one of her husband's last wish: to have it destroyed in a melting forge, so it could never be used to kill again and to finally free the souls of all those it had killed and whose spirits were imbedded in its blade. She tried, but could find no one willing to destroy the sacred sword of the famous General Tanoka who had rid their country of the terrible threat of the Chinese hoards. It felt so heavy in her hands… heavy with the souls of the dead, and yet still foreboding of still violent future. She sensed it could never be destroyed by any means and would kill again. Still in its scabbard, it seemed to vibrate of terrible whispered horrors of a Chinese city her husband had conquered, a city called Nanking.

The Horrors of Nanking

On a humid night in July of 1937, a Japanese regiment conducting night maneuvers in the Chinese city of Tientsin near the ancient Marco Polo Bridge of Lukouchiou, claimed they were fired upon by the Chinese. During the action one Japanese soldier was found missing so the battalion marched against the Chinese fort of Wamping and demanded entrance to look for their comrade. The Chinese, not willing to allow invaders into their fort, refused. The Japanese battalion then shelled the fort. Japan used this as an excuse to start the brutal Sino-Japanese war which would claim over 900,000 Chinese troops and one half million civilians. Outside nations, including China, felt that Japan had deliberately started the incident at the Marco Polo Bridge, as an excuse to invade China and to prevent them from allying with Russia. An alliance between China and Russia would pose a great threat to Japan's mainland. Japanese Lieutenant General Kiyoshi Katsuki declared they would "chastise the outrageous Chinese," a race long believed to be inferior to their own. Japan declared war on China and Midori bide her husband, Nakura, a farewell that neither realized was to last an eternity.

Tanoka, under the direct command of General Hironaka and

overall commander Lieutenant General Iwane Matsui, swept across mainland China with little organized resistance from the Chinese army under Chiang Kai-Shek.

On July 25th a battle at a railroad station in Langfang, just twenty-four miles from Peking, quickly led to the fall of Peking. The following August brought the invasion of Shanghai, which capitulated by November. The brutality of the invading troops even shocked some of their own. With no concept of sin and no intervention by their commanders, every living human was deemed as enemy, soldier or not, was either bayoneted, clubbed, or shot to death on sight.   Suchow was invaded on November 19th and the murdering and plundering lasted for days, reducing a civilian population of 350,000 to less than 500 who managed to flee or hide. Soon followed was the fall of Chintan which ended in the same results as the Chinese army continued its retreat from the invaders more powerful artillery and armored tank divisions which the defenders could not stop.

Propelled by such quick victories against an obvious inferior enemy, the rage and wanton viciousness of the invading army peaked as they approached the capital at Nanking, bordered by the Yangtze River on two sides. The invading army was divided into three forces. Tanoka commanded the 9th division and led an amphibious assault across Lake Tai Hu on December 12.

On that same afternoon Japanese planes off the carrier "Kaga," bombed and strafed the US gunboat Panay in the Yangtze River in spite of the American flag visibly flying from its mast. The boat was shattered and sunk, two were killed instantly, while several wounded, and the few survivors swam to the shoreline and hid in the thickets. The planes circled overhead, banked, then and dove strafed the riverbank where hid the survivors.

This incident outraged the United States, and Japan eventually issued an apology in late December, stating that fog had obscured the pilot's vision and they couldn't see the American flag. Foreign correspondents who witnessed the incident refuted this excuse, saying the day was sunny and clear. The Americans accepted this accident of war and seemed more outraged by this incident than the news of what was to occur with the civilian population after the invasion of the capital.

Finally, on December 13th, 1937 the Japanese army entered the city of Nanking, after Chang Ki-Chek and his army had abandoned it just the night before. Most of the Chinese army wasn't aware that their leader had left, and they retreated in panic toward the outer wall of the city where they were helplessly encircled and trapped by the invading army. Foolishly they surrendered without a fight relying on the mercy of the Japanese, and believing in the propaganda fliers that stated, if they surrendered, they would be fed and treated with respect as prisoners of war. Not realizing that surrender was considered the ultimate act of cowardice in the Samurai Bushido, this only further infuriated the invaders, who would always choose an honorable death before surrender. When General Matsui, falling victim to TB, was replaced by Prince Yasuhiko Asaka, the Prince immediately issued orders on December 13th, to the 66th Japanese battalion that "all POW's were to be executed. Kill all captives." Those foolish enough to surrender willingly allowed themselves to be tied together in lines and led to the banks of the Yangtze where they were systematically shot, bayoneted, beheaded, or clubbed to death and then thrown into the Yangtze drowning any that were still alive. Hundreds of others were just tied together in lines, rocks tied to one end, and then thrown into the river to drown.

While some justification by the enemy might be made for the

slaughter of these soldiers as a true threat to their army, nothing within the realm of human conscious would ever justify what they did to the innocent non-combatant civilian population. In just the short span of three weeks, the atrocities that occurred defied the world's imagination who were made aware of the slaughter by letters sent by foreign nationals sheltered in the "neutral zone" of Nanking. While these nations stood by, 300,000 men, women and children fell victim to rape, torture and death. An uncontrolled rampage of genocide began where civilians, of all ages and gender, were systematically tortured and killed by burning, beheading, drowning, slow mutilation, crucifixion, castration, pushed alive from roof tops, or buried alive. The females, regardless of age, were repeatedly raped and then eviscerated. Death was never intended to be quick as hundreds had their eyes gouged out and noses and ears hacked off. Some were hung up by their tongue; some saturated in acid. At least two hundred civilians had been tied to trees and stabbed with *zhuizi*, long thin needles with wooden handles, hundreds of times along their naked bodies, including eyes, throats and genitalia. Live prisoners were buried to fill in bomb holes in order to let the caissons and tanks pass over. Some were buried with just their heads exposed above the roads in line of the tank threads. Others were tied to trees and used for live bayonet practice or slowly stripped of their flesh and fed to dogs. Tanoka and the other leaders did not condone these actions, but remained neutral, never suppressing their troops, but allowing their soldiers the full opportunity to take their retribution upon this cowardly population as a reasonable aside to any war. Tanoka felt the slaughter and mayhem would at least serve to harden his troops for future combat, as well as to provide them with the necessity of moral boosting sexual relief.

While Tanoka took little amusement in, and generally ignored the genocide, he did use this as an opportunity to give his troops real experience in live bayonet practice. Although his victims were usually men, even women and children were also tied to trees and used for bayonet practice to harden his troops to the realities of war. He assured them that these children would all too soon grow up as future enemies, and that these women would eventually breed new enemies of the State. Since death was mandated anyway on these captives, this form of execution would at least afford his troops valuable training in hand to hand combat. During combat training in the military camps at home, they only had practiced on tied bundles of straw, a poor substitute for the enemy they would someday confront.

He took this opportunity to demonstrate firsthand the proper bayoneting technique to his troops at Nanking, demonstrating to one brigade at a time. A single live victim was tied to a stake atop an elevated platform for all to see. Other victims were tied to stakes in a semi-circle at ground level, and forced to witness the fate that would soon befall them as well.

Taking a rifle with the long thin bayonet affixed to the front, he demonstrated on the hapless victim, by first driving the blade in hard just under the ribs, then thrusting it upwards and making a deep circle to scramble the organs, pulling it back out and thrusting it upwards again to puncture the heart. He pulled it out again and then repeated the process, this time disemboweling the young man. This particular prisoner was still rasping a frothy crimson breath and Tanoka decided it was not prudent to allow him the time to just bleed to death, so with a second thrust aimed at the throat, he drove the blade up through the base of the chin into the skull.

Afterwards the troops lined up for their turn to practice on those staked for that purpose. As the carnage began, some poor victims even with their internal organs shredded and intestines hanging from out of their abdomens, went on twitching and breathing for some time, affording those that followed, a chance at a live target.

One day Tanoka had related this tale and demonstrated to his three sons and to Hironoka's boys, all young at the time, the proper technique. He used a sharpened wooden stick and bound hay bales as surrogate enemies, that the boys had been jabbing at and playing war with. He also made them promise that they would never reveal this to Midori. She would never understand the importance of this work, she was more concerned with the production of life then the necessity of ending it. They all, blanched white and remained expressionless at the bayonet demonstration and their minds filled with the horrid pictures mental pictures of humans tided to stakes, screaming and bloodied. Tanoka's tale seemed to transmit both the sound of the dying as well as the grisly mental picture. Shima asked if they ever cried or screamed. Tanoka said some did, but not after the bayonet entered, then it was just more of a quiet groan of resignation. Most did scream and try to plead and kick beforehand, but some offered no resistance and seemed to welcome their release from this life. At least their passage was relatively brief, in contrast to what others were enduring in other parts of the city. He related that not all of the troops showed an enthusiasm for this type of training. Some had to be goaded and humiliated into taking that first thrust into live human flesh, for bales of hay never screamed nor silently stared at the cold steel or into their eyes. Some he noted took their turn only when they were sure the victim was already dead, and succeeded with a halfhearted attempt tempered with a false bravado. Eventually, even these slackers, were forced to develop a natural relish for the technique. Tanoka then expressed hope that all six of them would someday get their chance to serve the

Emperor in like manner.

After the demonstration, all six remained speechless at this tale. Tanoka remained puzzled by their reaction, blaming it upon the negative feminine influence of his wife in their upbringing. When Tanoka left, they all dropped their sticks having lost any desire to continue to play war against their imaginary straw enemy. Normuro, the youngest, later vomited. All six were later tormented by nightmares of the scenes they imagined on the day of Tanoka's demonstration, yet none ever revealed any of this to Midori.

Tanoka had always insisted on live practice, whenever a situation afforded his troops, to give real experience to his the infantry when confronted with an armed and dangerous enemy. He never disclosed his role as an executioner against the innocent and bound captives in Nanking to anyone, but he did achieve notoriety in demonstrating to his troops, after the fall of Nanking, the proper way to behead a prisoner by Samurai sword, which soon came to be known as the "Tanoka Technique."

THE DEMONSTRATION

He stood over the sink and once again pulled the blade across his palm after again seeing in the reflection of his sword, a face he could never forget, that of a poor innocent Chinese youth, named Chui. Chui had been caught in the sweep of households that occurred after Nanking had fallen. The soldiers took every living male as prisoner under the pretense that they were Chinese soldiers in hiding. Chui, a youth of only fourteen, could not possibly have been with the army. It was his execution, at the hands of Tanoka, that triggered the killing contest that was printed with pride in all of the Japanese newspapers, one that shocked even the staunchest civilian supporters of the Imperial Army.

The morning before his encounter with Chui, Tanoka was driven to an execution site in the woods lining Mo Chou Lake in the south west part of the city. Hundreds of prisoners and suspected collaborators had been shot, buried alive, or chained together and drowned in that lake as well as multitudes driven into and shot in the Yangtze River. Tanoka had issued a command that bullets, due to a limited supply, were no longer to be used to execute prisoners. Instead, he ordered death by beheading in the tradition of the Samurai sword. He was making routine checks to see how the processing of these prisoners was progressing, and this was his first stop.

He stepped out of his jeep and upon entering the woods, heard the screaming pleas of men about to die. He came upon the hidden execution site, and even as a warrior who had witnessed much death, he was not ready for the sight of the massive amount of raw carnage. There were headless bodies still oozing blood and severed heads everywhere. Some of the heads had been lined up in a row on a make shift shelf, with cigarettes propped between their blue lips, their clouded eyes now blind to any further horror.

He watched as the next prisoner was dragged in by two guards each pulling on a rope in opposite directions around his neck. When the prisoner emerged on to the field, and saw the sight, he knew what was about to happened. He squealed and dropped to his knees, then had to be dragged along the ground kicking and choking and pulled in front of a the bare barreled chest of the executioner, wearing a blood spattered leather apron, and holding a bright crimson stained sword. Each guard pulled on their ropes and held the head still and at an angle, with the victim with tongue hanging out and an eye cocked at the executioner standing beside him. The eye saw the blade raised high and back, then squinted shut. Instinctively as the blade descended, the prisoner pulled forward and preventing the blade from sweeping through the neck. It only severed the rear vertebrae before coming to a halt. The head hung forward listless, but still attached. The victim still breathing. It took one more swing cut though and sever the head, causing it to fly forward. The ropes came lose and the body fell to its side with the heart still pumping blood through the severed arteries in the neck. The body was dragged by the feet by two other soldiers in leather aprons and tossed onto the pile of bodies. One kicked the head like a soccer ball which bounced and then rolled joining the others.

Tanoka strode up to the heavy set executioner, whose bare Buddha belly and thick glasses were spattered in blood.

"How many today?" Tanoka asked.

The executioner recognizing his rank snapped to attention, saluted and proudly answered,

"Twenty five, Sir. And in four hours"

And when did you begin?"

"Right after breakfast, General."

Tanoka looked at his watch and said, "Terrible productivity. That's barely six per hour. It will never do, you must speed up the process."

"We've tried lining many up on their knees and going down the line, but they deliberately fall forward into the pit prior to impact or turn and catch the blade squarely across the face, a non-lethal blow. Those in the pit we just bury alive, but they are not in the least cooperative you know." He said with a laugh.

"Well perhaps what you need then is to get them to cooperate a little more."

Not knowing if he was kidding, the executioner just laughed. When he saw Tanoka's vacant eyes, he dropped his smile and asked, "Sir, how so?"

"You just need to reassure them a little. A little kindness, especially once they know they're to be killed, will go a long way to keeping them calm. Also, you need to solicit their help in this process. It doesn't take nearly as long as your way."

"Solicit their help? That's impossible Sir. Why should they agree to that?"

"Just a few words of regret for having to take their heads, and then request their cooperation, for their sake, for a clean and painless kill, in order to avoid a slower more painful end. Talk them through the process so there will be no surprises. Allow them to participate by letting them know what and when to expect it. I can assure you it will expedite the entire process. When you talk them through the process, be kind, but at the same time, never allow your resolve to waiver. Now please allow me to demonstrate, and bring me the next one. I want him brought here without any ropes around his neck to prove my point. Also, I want you to look at your watch and time me from the minute he kneels down and until his head rolls off and onto the ground."

He removed his jacket and withdrawing his engraved sword, he was soon confronted with a thin, bare chested youth with hands tied around his back and carried by his arms by two aproned men. The prisoner, barely in his teens started trembling when he saw the carnage all around him and the macabre heads of some he knew placed along on the fence post. He was thin with every rib showing in a hairless chest. He had thick black hair and an overbite with protruding teeth that gave him a comical look. The boy was too young to be a soldier, and was obviously one of the citizens of Nanking caught in the house to house sweeps by the invasion force. With the males they made no distinction between soldiers and citizens, all were to be killed without regard to age. All the females had been gathered for a special duty function in servicing the sexual needs of the invasion force. They were used for repeated rape and then afterwards to be mutilated by bayonet.

Tanoka stood with the tip of his sword pointed to the ground and in perfect Chinese asked the youth to kneel. The boy did so clumsily almost losing his balance. Tanoka looked to the executioner who looked at his watch and started the timing, after a nod from his General.

"And what is your name young man?", Tanoka asked.

With darting wide eyes directed at the sword, the boy stuttered, "Chui", he now stared at his reflection in the mirrored sword.

"That's a valiant name. Chui do you know why you are here?" The boy just trembled, shook his head no, and said nothing his eyes now darting around to the obvious. "Well you've been pronounced by our military as an enemy of the State, and I have the unfortunate task of having to execute you."

The boys eyes began to fill with tears.

"Now I can assure it's not my choice, but it must be done and will be done now. Do you have any family left?"

The boy stammered only his mother. Then, to get a little more time, mentioned that his sisters and father were taken and separated from him. The mother was left in the house along with some guards. Tanoka was sure how they had all ended up.

"Well then for the sake of your mother, father and sisters, I promise I'll see they are not harmed and are cared for if you will now cooperate with me. Do we have an agreement? "

The boy not knowing what he meant, rapidly nodded his head. The bloody Buddha held up one finger indicating that one minute had passed.

"Very good. What I want is for you to assist me in what I have to do, so that you'll feel no pain. If you do exactly as I say, I promise that what I have to do will be quick and painless. Understand?".

The boy looked up to him and trembled a nod as his breathing began to increase in rapid pants blowing cloudy vapors, like spirit souls abandoning a body, vaporizing into the cold December air.

"I want you to cooperate and count with me, and when we both say the count of three it will be over."

The boy began to scream a word over and over again which at

first Tanoka did not understand because of the vernacular, and then realized the boy was asking if he could first be allowed to defecate. The executioner and others who had gathered around to watch the spectacle all laughed. Glaring his disapproval at them Tanoka said, "No, there is no time, and it doesn't matter now. Just hold it for a little longer. Listen there is nothing to fear. We will do this together, look straight ahead at all times and don't turn your head to see the blade or you may catch it across your face which will not kill you, but make you wish it did. If that happens, then you'll have to be held upright, and since I won't be able to use my sword that near the guards, your head will have to be sawed off, a much slower and more painful process."

The Buddha now held up two fingers.

"Here is how we will do it together. On the count of one I want you to tighten your neck, and hold it real still. Now on the count of two I want you to start slowly leaning back to greet the blade, and then we will count three together. Without hesitation, Tanoka began, "Ready? One!", he shouted.

The boy didn't count, but just trembled holding his breath, tightened his neck and pulled his face into a tight grimace closing his eyes. Tanoka could see the arteries fill and bulge in the front of the neck and watching the esophagus swallow saliva for the last time.

"Two!" Tanoka shouted now leveling and arcing his sword above and well behind his head. To everyone's amazement, they all saw the boy do just as he was told, he began to lean back waiting for the next count that would take him into oblivion.

"And three!"

Chui never heard the last number as the blade swiftly passed completely through his neck severing his head in one deft blow.

Much to everyone's amazement Chui's body just relaxed but was still kneeling upright and the severed head still in place as though nothing had happened. Someone in the crowd derided, "Missed." Others snickered, "He missed."

Ignoring the remark, Tanoka looked at Chui and poked at the side of the head, and much to the amazement of the spectators, it rolled off of the youth's shoulder, blood still pulsing out from the two severed arteries in the neck. The headless corpse then fell sideways to the ground.

"Now that's the sign of a clean kill. Time please?", Tanoka called.

"Less than two and a half minutes total", the Buddha bellied soldier said.

"Exactly my point. Adding the time it takes to get one here, you can dispatch one every three minutes just by soliciting their cooperation. And remember a little kindness goes a long way, as will their heads."

Tanoka and the others all laughed. And now with more very serious import:

"Oh, and One more thing. I want all of those heads taken down, and along with the bodies, given proper burial before the next is brought out. They are our enemy, but once dead, they are to be accorded some degree of respect as having once been soldiers, even if only cowardly soldiers at best."

Tanoka wiped his sword clean, and accidentally caught in its reflection of the head of Chui lying on the ground behind him, and then the terrible stare of its glazed eyes, looking at him in the steel blue of his blade.

"Poor boy", he thought. "Just a victim of unfortunate circumstance, but surely no soldier or hardly any threat to this Imperial Army."

The news of Tanoka's radical new approach at execution spread rapidly and soon others were employing the method and with great success. In fact the Tokyo newspaper, the "Japan Advertiser," told of a contest held at Nanking between two Lieutenants, Mukai Toshiaki and Noda Takeshi, to see who could be the first to behead 100 Chinese in a day. The paper pictured the both of them standing side by side with swords extended. The caption read, "Both fighters exceed their mark, Mukai scores 106, and Noda 105 all in one day." Both had employed the "Tanoka technique", as it was now referred to, but in order to hasten the process both employed handlers to do the verbal prep to solicit cooperation before their victims were led out to their demise.

The Truth at Johor

Midori was made aware of only part of her husband's involvement in these whispered horrors. Yet in his final letter, he told of the horrible dreams that denied him any form of sleep or peace. He no longer slept in the same room as his sword, but kept it hidden. In time, some noted he would not even carry it into battle, but led his troops only with a drawn pistol. Many noticed the bloody cloths that encircled the palms of both hands, but dared not inquire as to the nature of those injuries, self-inflicted every night. Some nights his aides would awake startled at his baleful nocturnal screams.

He volunteered to lead the first wave of *Kesshitai* against what was surely to be a suicide charge. General Hironaka tried to talk him out of it, for there were others of lesser rank that could lead this charge. He was too valuable to risk and would be needed for the later invasion of the American atolls. Besides he had three sons that would soon be serving the Emperor, and he would be needed to provide them, along with all of the youth nationally, with a model to emulate.

The General wasn't sure what had changed his brave leader. Nakura was always a strong and fit man who never drank or smoked, a perfect model of a great leader. Yet now how different this man, who requested to lead the dawn charge against the British, seemed almost emaciated, drained by the festering wounds on his palms which he claimed he got from climbing the razor sharp *sakaki* tree for exercise. Deep wells, like black moon crescents, surrounded both red streaked eyes. So frail now, with his head listing and twitching like that of a bird trying to balance atop a too thin perch, Nakura had insisted on leading the charge. He appeared before the final service, given those leading the troops at dawn, strangely without his sword. He carried instead only a tiny pressed flower stick inscribed with the word of his dead daughter, Eiko. It was this, which he always wore about his neck, instead of his sword, that he consecrated and left with his personal mementoes along with his last letter to his wife, to be forwarded to her after his death.

When the service was over, his aide brought him his sword, and reluctantly he took it into his hand. Unable to shield himself any longer from the memories that emanated from its edge, he looked at the blade and into its cold burnished steel. There he could see the vacant glazed eyes of thousands of its victims whose mouths were open in a perpetual silent scream. He vowed then that his sword would kill no more.

From his field binoculars Nakura scanned the distant bank at the first light of dawn. He assembled his troops from an embankment just above the river. He then in silence motioned for his troops to first gather in a tight unit, using arm signals motioned for them to spread and deploy in a straight line along the river's edge. In the dawn silence they wadded into the dark water, attracting ebony leeches and scaly black water beetles that sought the body heat emanating from behind the cloth of their uniforms. These stewards of death, serving as nocturnal accomplices to the dark event that was about to begin.

Just as the sun first broke the horizon, Nakura's shrill battle scream echoed throughout the forest and shocked even the seasoned troops waiting in back of the first wave. He raised his sword screaming "Bonzai" and ran headlong into the knee deep black water. General Hironaka, shrouded in along a ledge high above the river, squinted through his binoculars and watched Tanoka's troops spread like a blanket of startled beetles across the embankment, and then leap into the river following their leader with the same frenzied shouts and cries. When Tanoka leading was just halfway across, the British opened fire from the opposite shore from behind camouflaged dirt mounds hidden beneath the trees. Hironaka stared at the slow advance and decimation of this first wave, but was stunned to see Nakura, when wadding halfway across in the waist deep water, fling his sword into air, raising both arms open to the sky. Tanoka looked into the rising sun, and screamed the name of his God, *Sunasee*, the god like dragon that scavenges the souls of those who die for the Emperor and carries them to the protected place of their ancestors. Even before the sword had time to hit the water, Nakura was met with a hail of red tracers appearing from the opposite bank that ripped into his body and crowded out his soul.

Hironaka, when later writing of this man's death, would not dishonor this soldier's reputation by telling anyone how this great leader chose to die, in disgrace and dishonor and without his sword. This man was a national hero and one from a proud line of Samurai dating to the 15th century. Ancestors, who back then though greatly outnumbered, bravely stopped the invasion of their homeland by the Mongol hordes, forcing their fateful destruction in the sea by the divine wind of their Gods, the Kamikaze. He would not dare to dishonor this soldier's honor, since Nakura would still serve the homeland even in death. No, this hero warrior would be given a full national burial, with plenty of media coverage, to serve as an inspiration to the present and future troops of Imperial Japan. In fact, he was going to insure that each of this man's sons would serve the nation in the same manner, each proven to die a hero's death, however contrived by him. Their youthful demise would be needed to inspire all the young males and females needed to defend the homeland, against an invasion by the United States, which few could conceive, yet he knew was inevitable.

PANTHEON OF THE GODS

Later that night, after her prayer vigil for Schima, as her tears gave way to red stricken eyes, she remembered again the wish of her husband. She took the sword from above their shrine, and purified it with the rite of *Misogi* by pouring sacred scented water over it, in a final penance to the souls it had taken. Then wrapping it in the leaves of the sacred *sakaki* tree, she performed the ritual of *Oharai* and prayed for forgiveness to those tormented and killed as an extension of her husband's hand. She had tried to follow her husband's wish that the blade be melted in a forge to release all the spirits it had claimed, but could find no one in the city willing to destroy the sword of their greatest national hero. She would have to pray to *Amaterasu* to help her find some other way to free those spirits longing for release.

She often turned to her Gods in times of distress and was reminded of the final letter she had received from Shima. Tucked into the corner of a bamboo frame holding a photo of her son as a child, was the farewell letter he had written her, a final eulogy of those who go into battle. All troops were required to write this farewell pledge to insure their ultimate sacrifice for the Emperor. On this, the day of his certain death, she regretfully reread it:

"My dear and spiritual mother, with joy I go to the sacred place of my forefathers, and as them, brave and true to my destiny as defender of the homeland. Our sun goddess, Amaterasu, will light the way for me her son and yours, to this my glorious end. Please make a place for me on the thousand stitch belt, so when the great dragon and Master Sumasee, comes to collect all of the souls of her great warriors, I too, shall be with them and united once again with my brave father who waits for me. Do not grieve for me, for this was why I was conceived and born for only this end, to die in glorious service to our God and Emperor. Farewell my mother, hold me forever in your heart, and I thank you for the gift of life that I now willingly give back to my Emperor with eagerness and joy in the defense of our homeland."

She knew that had not been the case. Her dream of Schima's end vividly portended just the opposite. In the end she was certain he died as just her little boy again, frightened, confused and feeling betrayed by the militaristic lie they were all led to believe.

Afterwards, she picked up the dried sweet wood stick in remembrance of Eiko, her only daughter, of whom she was never allowed to speak. She kissed and placed it next to the photo of her only daughter.

Behind her husband's sword hung the Japanese flag depicting the rising sun with its red tendril rays emitting from its center on a pure white background. To Midori it not only represented her Goddess, but foreboded the Imperialistic expansion of the great empire, and the high price paid in red by its fathers and sons in strange and distant lands. The sun was not a god, but ironically a goddess, *Amaterasu*. How ironic she mused, that a religion and land that worshipped a female deity would deny so few of the privileges accorded males to the females over which her Godess ruled.

Shinto myth tells of a distant time when the god *Izanagi* washed his left eye and in the tear gave birth to the great goddess of the sun, *Amaterasu*. *Susanoo*, god of the great plains frightened *Amaterasu* so that she hid in a rocky cave in heaven thrusting the world into perpetual darkness. The gods, or *Kami*, devised a plan to get her out by collecting crowing cocks who heralded the dawn, and by hanging a large mirror near the entrance to the cave. Amaterasu, curious as to the crowing crept out, and saw her brilliance reflected in the mirror and once again gave her light to all of the world. The *Kami* then forced her into the open where she was to remain for all time as the center of worship.

When the Imperial family unified the nation in the seventh century, they elevated *Amaterasu* to a national deity and the central leader of all of the Shinto gods. Declared as a direct descendant, the Emperor was treated and worshipped the same as their sun-goddess. Thus grew the fanaticism of emperor worship. In 1882, Emperor Meiji issued "The Imperial Rescript to Soldiers" which became the daily dogma of the armed forces. It outlined the duties of the soldiers and pronounced that loyalty to the Emperor was to be placed above all else, even family, and to die in his honor, was to eventually assure a permanent place with *Amaterasu*. Thus, as war and conquest was the declared mission of Imperialistic Japan, so began the strife and suffering dictated by this legacy.

Japan's ancestors conceived and revered many gods, or Kami, of nature. In addition to this worship, they also feared departed souls and sought ways to appease them. The Shinto believed that a departed soul is tainted with the pollution of death, especially if the end is not honorable. Thus the memorial rites are to purify the soul, to remove all shame and guilt so that the spirit is elevated to a position of deity. These gods of the dead would take up temporary residence in objects of worship called *Shintai*, such as trees, stones, swords and also therefore, in the memorial register of Midori's Thousand Stitch Belt. Each stitched name represented one departed warrior's soul of her husband's ancestors, awaiting purification by the benevolent fire dragon, *Sunasee*. This was the clan's guardian deity, whose fiery breath would release them from the stitched cloth *Shintai*, and all those embroidered on the belt would be united with their great ancestors for all times. Females, whose only purpose was to function as breeders preferably birthing males, were never allowed to be stitched in the *Shintai* belt. They were considered soulless, and therefore never to be memorialized on the Thousand Stitch Belt. So Midori's spirit and that of her departed daughter, Eiko, could never to be reunited with the rest of their male family.

She remembered the meetings she attended with her husband Nakura at the Great Palace of General Hironaka, where the military leaders would gather and talk of the great Imperial Empire and the early easy victories on the China mainland. She, however, would talk in small enclaves with the other women present, privileged like herself, and all equally united by a distain for war, and the so called honorable work of their husbands. Together they would exchange personal tales about the one thing that bonded all women together and elevated them above the above such men, that of children and childbirth. Bonded by their gender's sole ability to produce human life, they spoke of the fulfillment of pregnancy, the ardors of labor, of Midori's great skills as a mid-wife *Sanbas*, the miracle of childbirth, the joy of nursing and raising their children. Midori's mother had died during her delivery of Midori due to a botched attempt by an uncaring male physician, to speed up the delivery. He aggressively used forceps that ruptured her mother's placenta causing her to bleed to death but saving the infant. As she grew into womanhood, Midori chose midwifery as her profession to intervene when possible to help those avoid the same obstetric complications due to crass physician neglect her mother had fallen prey to.

Historically, the Japanese considered childbirth a dirty and desecrate event, therefore, women in labor were isolated from the other family members and delivery often took place in contaminated places such as in sheds or barns. Puerperal fever and other infectious diseases in newborns were common during those times. Midwifery was always considered disrespectful work and was relegated as a profession to the lower class. Japan's expansionist fervor during the latter part of the eighteenth century changed all that. Since more soldiers were needed for the growing Empire, childbirth took on a new prominence. The first documentation about midwifery practices appeared during the Heian Period (794-1185) where they were referred to as birth assistants. More formal documentation about midwifery practice and procedures appeared during the Tokugawa Period (1603-1868) as both the military and medical professions took a new interest in the profession. By the end of this era, midwives, or *Sanba's* as they were called, had gained recognition by the medical field with the publication of protocols about proper midwifery practice published in 1868.

In 1899, midwifery licenses were mandated in order to ensure qualified practitioners. The law defined a midwife as a woman licensed by the Minister of Health, Labor and Welfare to practice midwifery and to provide health care, not only to the women, but also expanded to include the follow up care of the newborn. As a result of this legal recognition, the profession gradually achieved an elevated social status among the health professions.

In the early 20th century, professional associations began to appear and became increasingly prominent throughout the regions. In 1927, Midori led a crusade and helped establish a national association for midwives called the Japanese Sanbas Association. Both her prestige and influence as the wife of a famous General as well as a growing need of greater importance by the military due to the escalation of the War, she became its first national leader. She was a dedicated advocate in assuring the quality of perinatal care in all homes and institutions, and in strengthening the often tenuous relationship between midwives and physicians. It was her dedication to obstetrics that influenced her oldest son Masako to commit the medical training, never realizing that his medical skills would be used in the very opposite of sound medical practice. His patients were unwilling victims in a dreadful human experimentation camp in Manchuria, under Unit 731.

Midori was trained and dedicated herself in the commitment of bringing forth new life, while the males gathered across the room lived only to sacrifice life each bound to the same blind Imperialistic ideology. Her function, elevated in this warring society, was to insure a steady supply of the males needed to maintain the hungry war machine. In birthing rooms across the land, when the war turned bad, the drop in successful male births went unnoticed as the birth of any male would only doom him to a lonely at first. Mothers knew that the tiny infant they had just produced, may eventually experience a painful death on a foreign shore. Realizing this, at the new mother's insistence, Midori and other midwives would pray over the child and then leave mother and baby to make their final bond. Those mothers would then regrettably leave their newborn male exposed to the cold for nature to claim.

Eiko was to be the fourth proud son of Nakura, but nature in direct contradiction to the proclivities of man, Midori produced a beautiful female. Nakura could not hide his disappointment and blamed Midori, whom he felt had fallen into some kind of impurity in order to have attracted a female soul. He always inferred the cause was due to her spending so much time with Father Krozier, a German physician and Catholic priest she worked with at the hospital. Nakura had encountered him only once when the priest had served as a physician in the declared Neutral Zone in Nanking, attempting to treat the few maimed and burned surviving victims of the Japanese slaughter. He knew that the priest not only treated the victims, but also hid countless females protecting them capture and from sure rape and then death. Since Krozier was a German, whose country was an ally of Japan, Nakura could not invade the neutral zone and remained hostile to the man ever since, perhaps more jealous of his Germanic good looks and stature, than of his political views. It wasn't until the death of her husband that she learned of Father Krozier work in the German Safety Zone. In providing medical services to those victims lucky enough to escape into this zone, he had first-hand knowledge of the horrors her husband had helped perpetrate. But, even often at her insistence, he had always remained reticent to relate those atrocities to Midori, not desiring to denigrate the memory of her husband in her eyes. She had been made aware of the fact that he had even drafted a letter to Adolph Hitler, begging intervention after the fall of Nanking, she thought this was a gesture just to stop the war, never realizing Krozier's real motive, the cessation of horrors perpetrated upon the innocent civilians of Nanking. Hitler never answered his letter, nor intervened, since Germany and Japan were allies.

The work of producing more female breeders, a title accorded fecund females, was the duty of others, and not the purpose of a woman of Midori's lineage. He accused her of infidelity with the Father physician and went into jealous rages with his wife, giving him even more reason to reject his tiny daughter. Not even the strength of Midori's love could bind Eiko's spirit to this violent world. She died within two weeks and was buried in an unmarked grave, in the deliberate absence of Nakura and her sons, whom he forbade to attend her funeral. Attended only by a few co-workers, the women whose deliveries she had assisted all veiled in a sheath of mourning along with her colleague and friend, Father Krozier. They accompanied her without words, but in trust and in tribute to what they all had meant to each other.

Nakura left without a good-bye to the war instigated on the Malayan peninsula against the British. Her sons, in training for the growing conflict, were sheltered in the war camps. Shima would join the army and die in a cave on an atoll called Iwo Jima. Masko, their oldest, would join the medical corps and end up in a secluded human experimentation clinic in Manchuria, the infamous Unit 731, and Nomuro, her youngest, in a foolish attempt at juvenile bravado and to impress the spirit of his father, joined the Cherry Blossom Corp, known also as Kamikazi. He figured, that at thirteen, he could assist the pilots in their preparation for battle since he was too young to be taught to fly and die, or so he thought.

Midori was left with a longing and grief for her sons and daughter, magnified by the swelling that still grew in her breasts. Her milk still flowed weeks after her baby's burial, seeping and longing for the tiny mouth of her daughter Eiko.

MEETING WITH HIRONAKA

M idori stepped off of the tram in front of her son's school and looked for him next to the gate as the others were coming out. Another mother accompanying her two daughters passed her and said,

"You must be very proud of your son of Nomuro" as she just walked past.

Midori had no idea what she meant and was puzzled as she still looked toward the entrance of the school. When no one else exited, she became worried and went in to look for him.

She walked down the dark corridor, past her son's class and, noting it empty, continued down the hallway until she came to the administrator's office where she knocked gently. She was soon invited in by the gracious Headmistress Madame Liu. She immediately asked as to the whereabouts of her son, and was met by a quizzical look on Liu's face.

"Don't you know?", she said.

When Midori didn't answer, she looked horrified saying, "Of course you don't. Oh no, how could they have done this without your consent. I just assumed you knew, and was proud of his decision to join the Cherry Blossom Squad."

Midori had heard the term before and knew it was one of the units of the new suicide squads whose goal was to sink ships by flying their planes in a final death dive directly into enemy ships all for the honor of the Emperor. The name was significant, since the cherry blossom flower blooms only once in early spring and is very short lived. What a waste, she thought, on a war already lost, made even more so by the fact that the age of these volunteers had been reduced from 18 to 15, and now they were even recruiting younger.

"But certainly not as a pilot. He is too young, only 13!" She cried.

"I guess you haven't heard. They reduced the age to 13 and many others, just like your son, volunteered to go immediately."

"What!" she screamed defiantly. "Are you mad? When did he go, and where is he!"

"I am so sorry Midori, but the Kempeitai picked him up, along with two others just this noon."

"And for what purpose? He's too young to fly any plane."

"I'm not sure, but you can inquire at the base."

"No, I'll just go see General Hironaka myself, and get him to straighten this out. By the way, who were the other two that were taken?"

"The twins Yoshie and Motoko."

Both names struck her hard, since she had delivered these twins herself.

She rushed home, bathed and dressed at dawn in a newly pressed blue Kimono, with black and gold leaf flowers, the same one she wore at her husband's funeral. She dabbed the white cream on her face and rubbed it into her swollen eye lids. Then she patted rose blush on her cheeks and with a fine brush penciled the outline of her stoic lips. Now she did look the wife of a decorated Japanese hero, a national hero, her expressionless face showing the same calm resignation she displayed the day they buried her husband. This day she would brave the unspeakable. She would talk to General Hironaka, and plead for the life of her youngest son, Nomuro.

She boarded the tram, with just a few others and found a seat near the rear. The tram lurched forward and its rusted wheels squealed in metal tracks as it turned toward the outskirts of Kyushu in the direction of the 49th Battalion Command Station. Looking from the window, she couldn't help noticing how few males were left in the city.

After she stepped off the tram, she followed a long winding path toward the Palace of the General. She noticed how beautiful the trees and flowers were just starting to bloom on this warm early March day. Another spring was coming. A rebirth as though the earth could still produce life, although she had vowed she no longer would. Yes, she had vowed she would never again assist in bringing another life into this horrid world.

She approached two guards who blocked her way with their rifles. They stopped her and asked as to the nature of her business. She noticed their tan army uniforms, bowl hats covered with netting, and their rifles fixed with long metal bayonets. She recoiled at the stories as to how they were trained to use them, at Nanking, and by her husband. She told the guards that she had a meeting with the General and presented her identification. They almost seemed apologetic upon realizing who she was. They all had heard of her husband General Tanoka, the great and brave commander, who fought across China and whose battalion drove into the city of Nanking. Later he bravely led the infamous suicide charge at Johar on the Malay Peninsula against the well-entrenched British. That brave assault quickly led to the collapse of Singapore. It was the ultimate sacrifice of such a distinguished leader and one that could have been relegated to a one of lower rank, but ignoring such requests, bravely chose to lead his troops himself. After they motioned for her to pass, she walked on through the high iron gates.

She was first shown into a waiting room with deep red oak furniture and bamboo shade lamps. Another guard stood at attention near the door eyeing her suspiciously. Probably another "comfort woman" he thought, a term used to define those unfortunate females conscripted against their will into prostitution. Those conscripted for the elite were mostly Koreans, while Chinese prisoners were offered as rewards to the ground troops in China. The Korean females, some even as young as 12, were given no option in becoming sex slaves, for to refuse would risk the option of severe punishment or even death. Death by a knife across the throat or bayonet into the womb was always the acceptable outcome for the Chinese women. This female though had the high looks, and a certain arrogance uncommon among their lot.

A buzzer rang and she heard the familiar voice of General Hironaka telling the guard to let her in. Midori stood, bowed to the guard, and then entered the room. Hironaka stood behind an oak desk littered with papers and file folders. She entered and bowed as he motioned her to a dark upholstered high backed chair in front of his desk. Behind the wall of his desk was a huge flag of the rising sun and his Samurai sword encased in an ebony and gold sheath. His office was lined with bookshelves, and on a glass table stood a replica of the battleship "Yamato" on which his oldest son currently served. It was the largest of the Japanese Imperial Navy and would soon end its history at Okinawa torpedoed on April 7th by a US submarine. It was a true suicide mission, like the Kamikaze, since it was deliberately launched without enough fuel for a return trip.

Their orders, were that that after grounding they were to use its batteries to inflict as much damage as possible on the U.S. landing craft.

"Well Midori how have you been, and to what do I owe this honor?"

She cleared her throat and looked toward the floor as females were required to do in the presence of royalty. She caught herself by habit doing this antiquated rite of honor, and refused to continue it since it was now her son's life at stake and this was no time for courtesy or decor. She boldly faced the General and said,

"Have you heard what they've done to my son?"

"Do you mean what he has done?" Hironoka interrupted.

"Well yes, I heard he joined the elite Cherry Blossom Corps. You have a right to be as proud as I was, when I heard that he and a few others from his school had bravely volunteered after my recruiting lecture to their school."

"Well I am not proud and I want him back." She said with a boldness that startled them both. "He is only thirteen. How can he possibly serve the Kamikazi Corp? He's too young to fly and..."

He cut her off and said, "Well that's for them to decide, besides he will serve our great Emperor, as will the rest of the Corp, in some manner I can assure you."

"But how could he possibly assist? In what way?"

"Please! Remain in your seat If you wish me to continue."

Midori slowly sat down and folded her arms across her chest, her lips tightened quivering in a narrow line.

"You are no doubt aware of the advance of the enemy troops toward our homeland despite the brave sacrifices of our soldiers and sailors. Your husband and your son Shima, have already given their lives to protect our land and all of you. Nightly the allied

B-29's fire bomb our capital and many other cities inflicting a tremendous loss of civilian life, innocent men, women, and even our children. They are blood thirsty heathens that, if allowed to invade our proud country, will wantonly kill, rape, and pillage beyond all imagination."

He stood and walked to a large colored map of the Pacific islands and Japan.

"I assume I have your confidence?"

"Yes, you know I was the wife of a Commander General and held to a vow of silence to any military information I might have overheard. My loyalty to my land and its people will never change, so please go on."

"Thank you Midori. I never doubted your loyalty or I never would have agreed to meet with you. Out of honor to the Samurai spirit that both your husband and Shima so perfectly typified, I will share something with you that may help you to accept the role that your son Nomuro must play in halting the enemy advance."

He stood and pointed to map of the South Pacific and to the atoll of Okinawa and said,

"The enemy has launched a great invasion force toward this island, which, if successful, will provide them with airfields far too close to our country, and allow even greater bombing opportunities than we are now experiencing. You've already seen the effects of their ruthlessness on the civilians of Tokyo and other cities. Remember they are not hitting military targets, but using incendiaries bombs to burn homes with no concern for the occupants inside. You've assisted in the treatment of mutilated and burned victims they send south to your hospital here in Kyushu."

Midori bowed her head and her eyes glistened at the memory of the burned and blistered faces of the children she helped to treat.

How they still managed a smile with a look of hope when they saw her and physician Father Krozier until the pain of the debriding of the dead skin from their torsos sent them into screams of uncertainty. Despite fearful imploring eyes, Midori could offer them no explanation as to why their young and innocent lives had to come to this. They were alone, most without parents who had not survived the infernos, abandoned to a world of pain and fear that only death would relieve. She remembered attempting a delivery on a badly burned pregnant girl whose abdomen could not be pressed upon due to blistering from the burns in order to force the infant out. Midori felt a sigh of relief that the poor girl refused to push and deliver her child into these terrible times, and both died during an attempt at a forceps delivery.

"Would you care to hear the effects of those raids?",

Without waiting for a response he struck the map's cities, each labeled with a colored pin with a numerical label using a wooden pointer.

"Tokyo, our capital, and home of our Royal Emperor, fire bombed February 25th, and then again on March 9 and 10th, over 200,000 dead. Nagoya hit on March 11th and 12th and then the 19th, 10,000 dead. Angrily jabbing with the pointer, "Osaka, March 14-15, 13,000 dead, Kobe, March 16-17th another 15,000 dead, bombed and burned alive, most in their sleep, and without any warning. Look Midori, see all the pins! Count them! A total of 53 so far in all, and yet not a single military target. Just innocent towns filled with innocent civilians. I ask you, what other nation in the history of time has ever equaled such a wanton systematic slaughter of innocents? You think this is not serious enough to spare your son, while others have gladly served and given their lives to halt this slaughter? What would your husband and Schima think of you begging for a single life while so many others so willingly give of theirs? You disgrace and dishonor not only their memory, but the memory of all those stitched on your husband's Thousand Stitch Belt."

Midori could not answer but only dabbed her eyes with her embroidered handkerchief.

"Surrender is unthinkable. Our Kamikaze are the only hope we still have to try to keep this enemy from our shores. Please let me remind you of their proud history. The first Kamikaze attack was here at the Battle of Leyte Gulf," pointing to the sea north of Mindanao, and just South of Samar in the Philippine Islands. "What a surprise it must have been to the Captain and crew of that doomed Australian cruiser, when last October 21[st,] a pilot from a single Zero from the 201st Air Group, commanded by our great leader, General Onishi, whom you and your husband both had the honor of meeting at my reception, dove into, and sunk that ship killing hundreds on deck and below, and sending it into the depths of the Leyte Gulf. And to think, Midori, that this destruction was just the work of one brave warrior and his plane, one life in exchange for hundreds. This is how we will stop the enemy, break their spirit and let them see the futility of fighting an adversary whose will and resolve they could never hope to defeat. That attack was the first time we released this new human weapon of destruction, our warriors of the wind, surprising them with a fighting spirit no other country in the history of mankind had ever, or will ever match.

At first we had set the lower age limit to serve at 18 and trained those to pilot the Mitsubishi Zero. Then as our situation worsened, we lowered the age to 15, and just last week to 13. So that's why your son was recruited. He wasn't forced to serve, but volunteered as so many other children of his age have. We should be proud we have so many youth willing to take their place in our defense."

"But why was the age made so low? They are just children who've yet to experience any real life. And what of their parents?"

"I know of no other parents who have taken such a selfish stance with their offspring who joined as you portend. Such parents are given special privileges and rewards for encouraging and support-ing their sons in our defense. But to answer as to why we are calling those younger, it's because we've lost far too many of our veteran pilots at Midway, the Coral Sea, Leyte Gulf, and 340 in just one day in the Marianas at the hands of the U.S. F6F-Hellcats. Those barbarians humiliated us by using deceitful treacherous tactics, even strafing pilots already downed in the water, and some while still fall-ing in their parachutes. What possible resistance could these poor downed pilots have offered? And for what purpose to be forced to die in such a ruthless manner? They further brought even greater dishonor to these brave flyers by demeaning that engagement as a "Turkey Shoot", an American bird with no sense that unwittingly walks into a hunter's gun.

"But just how is one so young to serve as a Kamikaze? He is too young to learn to fly, so will he serve as part of the ground crew?"

"No that will not be the case Midori. We are all now called upon to make the ultimate sacrifice to save our land and he will be no exception." He hesitated while Midori waited for his next words which, when spoken, first puzzled her, and then shocked her into a sad resignation. He said, "He will pilot, or rather steer, our newest weapon, the Ohka directly into the deck of an enemy ship."

"Ohka?" she said, softly mouthing the word.

"Yes, the Ohka gives all, regardless of age, the glorious opportu-nity to serve. It will once again level the playing field and give back to us the supremacy of the air. It is our latest weapon, and if you so much as breathe a word of this to anyone, regardless of your status, I guarantee you'll get a visit from the *Kempeitai*." Midori shuddered at the horror stories she heard rumored about the gruesome tactics employed by these secret police. "The Ohka is our latest weapon, a glider released from the belly of a bomber, like our G4M, at about a height of 27,000 feet, where warriors like Numuro will be trained to hold it in a tight glide until over the target, and then after igniting its three rockets, push it into a steep dive attaining a speed of over 620 mph, and impacting in about 30 seconds into the deck of a ship. It will deliver over 2,600 lbs. of the explosive tri-nitro aminol into their decks. The Battle to save Okinawa will be the first time we use them, and you should be proud that your son is to be a permanent part of its history."

Midori, speechless, just stared as the tears filled her eyes and ran unblotted in rivulets down her cheeks smearing her black eye liner over her white painted face. "Come now Midori, you know it is the fate of the Samurai code of Bushido to always be willing to make the ultimate sacrifice in the service of our Emperor and its people. The Bushido was written by the great General Yoritomi Minamoto after defeating the Taira in the Gempei wars of the 11th century. The line of Samurai your husband represents, and which will end with Nomuro, dates back to 1274, when the Mongols under Kublai Kahn sent a fleet of 30,000 soldiers to these very same shores here at Kyushu to conquer our land. Your husband's ancestors put up steep resistance on the beach for over a week and prevented them from moving inland. Your husband told me the tale and read the names of those brave warrior Samurai, the first to be embroidered on your Thousand Stitch Belt. When a sudden storm blew up, the invasion force felt it best to put out to sea, but once there, the storm destroyed many of the ships and thousands of the

Mongols drowned.

But the story doesn't end there. Since the Mongol Kahn would not accept defeat, he sent emissaries demanding tribute. What gall, for in response, your ancestors sent back to him the severed heads of those emissaries in the Samurai *kubibukoro* head bags. Still not having learned his lesson, he sent an even larger invasion force, this time of over 144,000 warriors. Once again the invaders were held to a narrow beachhead by the brave determination of those of your husband's line. Again our Gods sent a mighty Typhoon smashing the ships and drowning half of the invasion force. They called the typhoon Kamikaze, our divine wind, and your son has joined a group of other brave and dedicated soldiers who have adapted the same name and will achieve the same results against another invading fleet. The names of those ancient warriors are embroidered on your belt, as are all of your husband's lineage that followed throughout the centuries up to this time. Your Husband and Schima's name were the latest you stitched there, and Nomuro will soon be the last of a line of 1000 warriors over the past 664 years, forever immortalized on your Thousand Stitch Belt. Isn't it both ironical, as well as inspiring, that 664 years since that first Mongol invasion, your son will take off from the very same land that your brave ancestors, terribly outnumbered, first met, fought, and defeated the Mongol invaders? Your son will join many others in destroying the enemies navy, allowing time for our ground troops to isolate, surround and annihilate this invasion force."

She stood and said, "So all those years of nurturing and love just to produce a human bomb. Had I only known back then what it all would come to, I would have drowned him rather than live to see them take another human life."

"I know you don't mean that, but you are not the only one

that's been called upon to make a great sacrifice. You remember Yoshito Butai and her husband Tatsumaki? You met them the night of our victory celebration over the Chinese in Nanking. Both you and Your husband were one of our guests of honor that night."

"Yes, of course I do. I knew them long before that night. I delivered all three of their daughters. The last two were twins, and I'll never forget her long hours of labor and the look of joy on her face when they were born. Why do you ask?"

"Well I'm about to tell you about their sacrifice, one even greater than the one you are expected to endure. Her husband Tatsumaki had always volunteered for the Kamikaze since its first inception, but the air command would never allow a father to fly in such a unit out of deference to his children. How he grieved and repeatedly petitioned the Naval Air Board to make just one exception in his case, but they wouldn't renege. Well Yoshito, his wife, valuing his need to serve and die as a true warrior, removed all obstacles to his joining. She bravely drowned all three of her daughters, and then poisoned herself."

Midori chocked on the words and cried, "You surely can't mean that!" she cried. "Tell me it isn't true. It can't be possible. I knew them all. Surely you cannot be serious…"

"Midori I most certainly can assure you of this. Finally on March 28th, as part of the 722nd Naval Air Corp, also called the Thunder Corp, he gave his life in the way any true warrior would have, dying as a Kamikaze hero. It was unfortunate his Zero was shot down before it could hit his target, but that doesn't detract at all from his sacrifice."

"What a selfish waste of human lives. Better I had never delivered those poor children than to have their young lives end in such a senseless manner and for what purpose?"

"Midori, you'd better hold your tongue, for what you just expressed marks you as a traitor, and you know what the outcome is of all traitors against the Emperor. However, out of deference to the memory or Shima and your husband, I'll forget I heard that last comment. Now it is Nomuro's turn to follow the path of his father and brother and earn his place of honor on the Thousand Stitch Belt. I'm sorry, but I have no choice but to place national interests over personal concerns. Normuro will remain as Kamikaze in the Cherry Blossom Corps.

Midori stood, and said "I guess then our business is finished." Trying to retain her dignity and dabbing her black streaked eyes, she stood, bowed, and headed toward the door.

"Midori, wait!" She hesitated at the door hoping for a reprieve for her son, which did not come. "I might add that I may not ask this of your son if I didn't expect the same from mine. You see here a model of the battleship "Yamato?" pointing to the glass enclosed model of the grey flagship of the Imperial navy. "Did you know that my son Hamano is a junior officer on board this ship? It is expected to play a large role in the defense of Okinawa. And Yuku, my youngest, is already on the island of Okinawa helping to maintain the Kamikaze torpedo ships. You'll recall he is the same age as your son. Even my oldest, Schino, has just joined the submarine corps and will assist the repair crews."

"But none of your sons are Kamikaze, and doomed to die."

"No, but nonetheless as young Samurai, they, too, are bound to the same code of Bushido, and I can assure you each are fully prepared to make the ultimate sacrifice for the Emperor."

"Then, may our Gods protect them all from our enemies and our ourselves." , snapped Midori. Hironoka just glared speechlessly at her latest remark realizing he would need her cooperation to fulfill his plan. He would invite no interference from this woman and insure her youngest would indeed meet an honorable death in order to serve his purposes. In order to do this, he would need to enlist her cooperation in obtaining her Thousand Stitch Belt, and the sword of her late husband to serve as tangible symbols of the sacrifice needed by both the honored and the young of this Empire.

"Midori, before you leave, I have just two more requests of you." She stopped and turned to him. "After you get the rice paper notice of Nomuro's sacrifice, and after you've added his name to the belt of honor, would you bring it to me so I can place it at the Tasukuni jinja shrine in Tokyo, dedicated to these new warriors of the wind, and leave it there as a memorial to the centuries old brave line that ended with Nomuro and represents centuries of brave sacrifice on the part of your husband's lineage. His will be the last name on a belt. Secondly, I would like to request your husband's sword, to be so enshrined in like manner, and to serve as an inspirations to all who follow."

"No, they are to remain in our home shrine where the letters, photos and mementoes of Shima, Eiko, and my husband's Nakura, and..." she choked and could not say the name of her poor son Nomuro, hoping that by not admitting it, she would be able to save him.

"Midori it is not to be your decision, or I will be forced to go the War Ministry and reveal the real events about your husband's cowardly act at Johor, and the real circumstances of your husband's death."

"General what do you mean? What events?"

He stared at her and with slow intent said, "Your husband, the renowned General Tanoka, did not die as the hero everyone was made to believe. No, he died a coward's death in the face of a far inferior enemy. I was witness and can attest to his demise, which was a deliberate act of suicide with no intent of taking a single enemy soldier with him."

"Impossible", she said bitterly. "What do you mean? Documents proved he bravely led a suicide charge, which someone of his rank didn't have to. He sacrificed his life for the glory of the Emperor as well as an inspiration to his men, leaving me a widow and his sons fatherless."

"I deliberately falsified the documents of which you speak. You remember in my funeral speech when I told all of the attendees that I was up on the hill with binoculars and viewed the entire charge as he led his troops across the straits of Johar. Well it didn't quite happen as I related it. You see he did lead a suicide charge, but one that insured he would die at the hands of the British. He never once fired at the other side with his pistol hand, and when halfway across the river, I was shocked to see him deliberately throw his sword into the air and screamed to warn the British who then opened fire on him and his men. He never ducked nor made any attempt to return the fire, but threw out his arms and welcomed the metal tracers coming from the other side into his cowardly body. The rest of the troops were too caught up in the cross fire to even notice his fall into the river, as he was soon joined by his sword which was at least retrieved and given to you by me at his funeral."

Almost relieved by the revelation of her husband's action, no doubt caused by his guilt of what took place under his command at Nanking, she asked, "If that is true, then why did you lie at his funeral."

"Because, not even I could betray one who our entire nation reveled as the hero of Nanking, who dispatched over 300,000 Chinese prisoners in less than three weeks, no small task indeed, and one worthy of repeat by others so inspired by your husband's brave leadership. As to why his suicide at Johor, I could only attribute to a gradual deterioration of his mental state, most probably due to battle fatigue. After Nanking, he never stopped fighting and would never take leave, still volunteering for the most dangerous missions such as the suicide charge at Jahor. He got his death wish, but not the one of a hero, but that of a coward and traitor."

"Midori, to put it bluntly, if I don't get the belt and the sword after Nomuro's sacrifice, then your husband will be labeled a traitor and, as you know, all survivors of a traitor's family are beheaded. If you are labeled as such, by your obstinance and disobedience in obeying this order, your execution will be carried out in public. I will also see that it is carried out on the grounds of the hospital where you've worked most of your life, so your colleagues, staff members and patients will be present to view it. Your shrine and its mementoes will be burned in front of you first. But out of respect, for what your husband did at Nanking, and to you for all the male lives you've delivered for us into this world, I promise that it will be quick. I'll see that is done accurately and with the same deft skill, as did your husband countless times at Nanking. And in honor of you both, I will perform the execution using your own husband's sword. How ironic it will be, that yours will be the last neck severed by his sword, after so many countless others, by this same blade. I want both the belt and the blade brought to me by noon tomorrow or I'll send the Kenpeitai for it."

Midori shuddered, not at the scene of her beheading, but at the thoughts of what had occurred at Nanking by her husband's hand.

I feel it is better to have it here in the ministry where it will be safe from any further attempts on your part to destroy it in a forge. My secret police were well aware of your unsuccessful attempts to find a kiln operator to destroy this national relic. Several reported your attempts to destroy this national treasure to the Kenpeitai."

Midori remained motionless at this revelation and could only feel a sadness that the wish of her husband would never be fulfilled and the spirits of those killed by his sword would forever remain trapped in its tempered steel.

"If you knew of the true death of my husband, why do you want to take the belt to the shrine in Tokyo?"

"Since I am the only one that knows the secret, and with your cooperation it will remain so. With that belt, I can inspire many other of your son's age to join him as brave Ohka pilots to save our country."

Midori cried at the thought of many others sharing the fate of her Nomuro. She turned without looking back at him, and left repeating the words, "You'll get the both. I promise." With the thought of his words about her thirteen year old son, as the "brave line that ended with Nomuro" she took her leave with a burning deep in the pit of her stomach.

ARRIVAL AT AIRBASE RONOIKE

The bus carrying the first to pilot the Ohka passed through the town of Chiran on its way to Ronoike airbase. The passengers, ranging from age 17 to 13 appeared outwardly reticent and calm, but thoughts of the life they were leaving, and envisioning what their death would be like, cast a pallor over their moods. Gone was the bravado and bragging they expressed a few days ago about joining the Cherry Blossom corps to friends, who were not marked for early extinction. The town, on the southern tip of the island of Kyushu, bore little activity at this predawn hour.

Armed soldiers waved the bus through the gate at Ronike air base just as the sun was breaking the horizon. It reminded Nomuro of the flag's rising sun symbol, which he took as a positive omen that he was doing the right thing by being here. One way or the other, there was no turning back now as he had been warned. To do so would only bring a swift execution to him and his mother, dishonor his father and all of the ancient warriors whose names were embroidered on the Thousand Stitch Belt. No, the die was cast and he would honor his commitment.

After disembarking from the bus, just inside of the barbed wired gate, the trainees lined up at attention in three rows, standing one yard apart. They were greeted by a grim faced, lightly bearded soldier in full battle gear, with bayonet fixed, who barked an order to turn right, and led them at a slow run toward the supply barracks where each was issued one kaki training uniform, a sack of toilet articles, a leather helmet, white scarf and a Hachimaki, the headband worn by the medieval Samurai. Then, in a forced march, they were led to their barracks set in an area isolated from the rest of the camp. They passed in view of the veteran pilots who would deliver them to their targets, and those who would provide the needed fighter protection once aloft. These veterans, not much older, but most at least in their early twenties, starred incredulously at how young these new recruits appeared. If you were a pilot, you were already a veteran by the age of 20 since Japan had lost most of their seasoned pilots in the previous battles at Midway, Leyte, Coral Sea, and Marianas which the Americans labeled as a "Turkey Shoot" destroying 351 Japanese aircraft in a single day, while losing only 50 of theirs.

After being assigned a cot, Nomuro eyed a roommate on either side. They introduced themselves to this seemingly much younger soldier.

"Hello, my name is Motoko and this is my twin brother, Yoshie."

"Hello, I am Nomuro Tanoka, my father was General Tanoka," extending his hand to each.

"Oh you must be very proud", Yoshie said. "We've read of your father's valor in our history books and his battles against the cowardly Chinese at Nanking and then against the British in Malaya. He was a great loss to our country, but truly an inspiration for us to follow. You're from Kyushu aren't you?"

"Yes, my mother is a nurse here at Miyauchi Hospital. Where are you both from?"

"We are from Osaka and lost both of our parents and sisters in the fire-bombing of our city. All of them were burned alive in the night by those merciless incendiary raids of our enemy against a purely civilian population. That same night 13,000 others were also killed. Our city wasn't even a military target. We were a distribution center for food and medical supplies. We were targeted because our buildings and homes were of wood and would burn easily to the ground along with their occupants, like our parents and sisters. By some lucky twist of fate we were spared, since we were at the military youth training camp above the hills of our city. That night we watched in horror as their B-29's flew in low to avoid our radar. They were practically grazing the rooftops to drop their napalm incendiary bombs. Even from miles away up there, we could hear the screams of the burned and dying. Anti-aircraft units around us sent up ground fire that sent two of their planes to the ground in flames. We rushed to the wrecks, armed with flame throwers, in the hope of finding some survivors. We did and so were able to return the favor." Normuro thought of the same terrible way his brother Shima had died.

"The next morning we boarded a truck," Motoko continued, "and were taken into Osaka to help put out the fires and clean up the debris. What we saw was far worse than any nightmare. The dead were everywhere, but worse was the sight of the survivors. Men, women and little children were barely discernible as human, and to hear their cries with some even begging to be shot by us. We were almost glad none of our family survived to have to live in such torment. It was on that day we both signed up with the Cherry Blossom, to set fire to their ships, and especially their sailors. We are the new weapons of fire and death and cannot be stopped," Motoko said with a vengeful pride. "Why did you join to be with us? We are 17, but you look so much younger?" Yoshie asked.

"Well I want to do my part in killing the enemy as they did us and be a part of my family's tradition to be included on our Thousand Stitch Belt that dates back to the 12th century. And I...", Nomuro words were cut off by an officer that opened the barracks door and shouted at them all to get outside and assemble immediately.   By now the sun was reaching late morning. After they had assembled, they stood at attention and squinted in front of a wooden stage where several decorated officers were seated. One rose and walked to the lectern and announced,

"Warriors of the Sun, I present to you our Imperial Emperor's brave leader of the Cherry Blossom Corps, the most honorable General Onishi."

ONISHI'S SPEECH

General Onishi, in full formal uniform, stood and walked toward the lectern. His loud stentorian voice commanded the undivided attention of all. Tall and powerful in appearance he addressed them:

"Warriors of the Sun, I welcome you to Airbase Ronoike, your final home as we prepare you for your destiny to join those who have bravely gone before you. Your mission is no less than to die for our Emperor, a direct descendent of Amaterasu, our Goddess of the Sun, by stopping the American invasion of our proud empire. The enemy, if not stopped, will slaughter your families, rape your mothers and sisters and enslave all survivors. You are all young Samurai and are bound by the Code of Bushido, the way of the warrior. Your willingness to sacrifice your life in battle is your duty, for the way of the Samurai is death. As Samurai, you must prepare yourselves for death morning, noon and night every day until your time of honor. There is nothing to dread. The first order of the Kamikaze is to choose a death that will bring maximum destruction of the enemy.

Allow me you read to you from Senjin Kunn, the Ethics of Battle written by our Minister of War, the honorable Commander Tojo." He opened the book and read:

"Do not think of death as you use up every ounce of your strength to fulfill your duties. Make it your joy to use all of your physical and spiritual strength in what you do. Do not fear to die for the cause of every lasting justice. Do not stay alive in dishonor. Do not die in such a way as to bring shame to you and your family."

Onishi closed the book and continued, "Your training will be harsh, but it will strengthen your resolve and teach you the needed skills to fulfill your sacred mission to destroy our enemy.

Before your mission you will attend your funeral, and you may invite your families and friends. May the patron of all Kamikaze, Masashige Kunsunoki, who committed seppuku in 1336 rather than surrender to the enemy, be with you. And may all of our spirits one day meet in the place of honor at the Yasukuni-Jinja shrine." He threw up his hands and shouted "Banzai" and did so two more times as his new recruits responded in unison. Nomuro felt a strange sensation in the pit of his stomach and couldn't help thinking that what he dreaded the most, a certain death now without any hope of reprieve or the glory he had imagined, was about to happen. There was no turning back. He felt a sad longing for his mother, and in remembering the only world he was really sure ever existed.

BASIC TRAINING AT AIRBASE RONOIKE

It was not even dawn when Corporal Shinto entered the barracks with two others and hit the lights screaming for them to get up, get dressed and form up outside in five minutes. Nomuro, barely awake after a sleepless night, was ushered out by his two friends who practically had to carry him out. Since most of the flights were to be at dawn, they started their physical training in the predawn hours. Nomuro hated mornings and remembered how difficult it was for his mother to get him up and ready for school. The air was chilled and came out in white vapor trails as they began their calisthenics and then started running in formation down a cindered trail. This was to be the start of a typical day, which after a light breakfast, continued with strength and vertigo training. The former was done on a metal blade with a wooden handle centered in a board. They took turns sitting in a chair in front of it, and then pulled the blade form side to side, and then backwards and forwards, mimicking the control stick of a plane. Normuro at first lacked sufficient upper body strength to control it as required, so he was forced to do many extra practice sessions on it each day.

Their days were filled with other challenges offered under the guise of games. They had to run carrying heavy concrete blocks, placing them down at one end of the course and then picking up a heavier one to carry back to their original place. This went on until they could no longer lift the next, and the one who carried the heaviest was given extra rations at dinner. Nomuro could barely make it through two rounds of the rock shuttle without collapsing.

Yet the worse for him was the vertigo conditioning which used two six foot double wheels, welded together, large enough for a person to climb between the space where a body could fit. The recruit would climb into the wheels, and holding with two hands on top, his ankles were strapped at the other end. He was then forced to roll end over end directing the wheel first in a straight line and then throwing his weight to turn it into a circle path without losing his direction, vomiting or losing consciousness. Nomuro, however, did all three nearly every time he attempted it. Most of them laughed at his uncoordinated efforts. Often he would became so nauseous afterwards he could eat nothing the entire rest of the day. He secretly hoped that they'd realize he wasn't qualified to pilot, and maybe he'd be spared. This hope was short lived when he saw his name listed, among all of the others, on the sheet announcing the candidates qualified for the last stage of training, flight instruction. Everyone in his barracks, regardless of ability, was listed. There was also rumor of a new secret plane, called the "Ohka", specially designed for young and inexperienced flyers. The thought of piloting a plane had always been a dream of his when he heard the tales of a speaker who came to his school and had been in the first wave to hit Pearl Harbor. This momentarily lifted his spirits, until he remembered it would be his first and only flight.

THE OHKA

L̲ate one afternoon after training, they were called into the smaller hanger, which they noticed was always heavily guarded even though they never saw any planes towed out of it and onto the runway. The early March afternoon was still chilly and the trainees could see their breath in the unheated metal hanger. After given the command, they sat down upon long wooden benches. In front of them was a tarpaulin covered object, too small to be a fighter plane, and Nomura and the others wondered what it might contain. Whatever it was though, he instinctively knew that his short future was somehow tied to it. A screen was set up behind the object which held some covered diagrams.

"Warriors of the Sun," General Onishi began, "I am about to reveal to you our latest weapon of destruction. One that will be unstoppable by the enemy. You, of the Cherry Blossom Corps, will be honored to be the first to fly this new weapon into the decks of our enemies' ships, giving them a true testimony of our courage and fighting resolve. They have never seen this weapon, and you will now be sworn to secrecy from this moment on until your flights. What you are about to see you must reveal to no one, not even your family. I now give you our Chief of Kamikaze Operations,

Commander Taiedo."

Commander Taiedo stood and walked to the charts. He was a diminutive man but looked more like a pilot than most of the leaders Nomuro had seen. Maybe it was his dress, wearing the khaki jumpsuit and white scarf he had seen on the escort Zero's that accompanied the bombers and Kamikaze planes to their targets.

"Corporals, if I may," addressing the two armed soldiers standing on each side of the tarpaulin. With a flourish he pulled the tarpaulin and exposed a light blue metal and wood object. All looked in awe and Nomura squinted thinking that this was not to be flown, but rather another type of bomb to be dropped. Only this one had stabilizing wings set at right angles five feet in front of the cockpit, and a tail fin that looked it had just been glued on top of its slightly tapered tail. It had no wheels, but rested upon concrete blocks placed under its fuselage. The only hint of it being something other than a bomb was the small bubble cockpit, sitting two thirds of the way back from its cigar shaped nose. It had no markings as did the other planes he had seen other than a pink cherry blossom painted on either side about one quarter of the way back from its blunt nose.

"Warriors, I present to you the Okosuka MX7-7, Model 11, Ohka. This new plane," he said going to the charts and pointing to the figures. Nomuro, along with most of the others, couldn't figure out how this thing could fly since there was no propeller or visible engine to be seen. "has a wing span of 16'5" and a length of 19'8.5". It weighs 4,719 lbs., has a maximum speed of 570 mph, and will dive at a speed of over 621 mph, more than enough to penetrate deep into the bowels of any carrier deck. It carries a warhead containing 2,645 lbs. of the explosive tri-nitro aminol. Has anyone here ever heard of this before?"

One youth at the back raised his hand, and when acknowledged, jumped to attention.

"Sir, if I may, I was told that tri-nitro aminol was first used in December of 1937 to incinerate live Chinese prisoners bound by their wrists in the pits at Nanking, and I was also told it was used in our great victory at Pearl Harbor, causing fires that were almost inextinguishable along their former so called impenetrable battleship row." This last comment was met with some laughter.

"Very good, but hold your tongue about its use at Nanking. That is just a rumor we'd rather not suggest. If I may continue, you will notice the light blue paint. This is to camouflage it with the sky, making it invisible to the ships below. It will be flown out of the Sun, a tactic you've been told the Zero's do to further hide their presence. The Cherry Blossom emblem represents the symbol of our squad, and each of you as flowers of vivid beauty, but of short duration on the branch. Warriors, we are lucky to finally have Ohka's to fly. The first were to be delivered last November aboard the carrier Shinano. Fifty were put aboard at Yokosuka, but the carrier was torpedoed by a U.S. submarine while passing through Kumano-nada, and all fifty were lost. The ones we now have will more than pay back the debt we owe the Americans for their treacherous and cowardly attack. Yes, you back there, what is your question?"

A young bare headed recruit jumped to attention, "Sir, if I may, I see no propeller and no engine, so how is it to fly? I do see that it has what looks to be three rockets in its tail. Is that a new type of engine?"

"Good point, but I was just getting to that. The Ohka will not fly of itself. These rockets were not designed for flight, but only to allow a fast, well controlled and accurate dive. The Ohka will be carried by our Mitsubishi G4M bomber within its bomb bay area, which has been specially fitted to accommodate this new weapon. It will be released at a height of 27,000 feet 50 miles from its target; then you will hold it in a controlled fast glide at 219 miles per hour. Once over the target, you will ignite its three rockets of solid propellant and push it into a steep dive reaching a dive speed of 621 mph. Even from that height, with the aid of those rockets, you will impact target within 30 seconds."

There was a deadly silence as the recruit sat down. Most of those present, as did Nomuro, realized that they were not being trained to be pilots, as the others who had gone before them, but merely as human guidance systems for a winged bomb. What honor could there be in that? Why couldn't these Ohku's just be dropped over the targets without them inside. Without any engine, no pilot could take any evasive action against enemy aircraft or flak. Nomuro thought, "What pride could there be in dying like this? How could our deaths be accorded the same honor as those who piloted their planes and controlled their destiny until impact? Would my name ever deserve a place on the Thousand Stitch Belt, or will I not be honored as a warrior, but derided as a mere human sighting device, with the real honor going to those piloting the G4M's carrier planes. They didn't need real pilots for this weapon, and that's why kids as young as he were recruited. This weapon did not require any skill, but strictly blind obedience and youthful allegiance... nothing more."

Taiedo called for questions but was answered with only a grim silence. Onishi then called them to attention and told them that training would commence tomorrow at 0700 hours.

OHKA TRAINING

Feeling angry and betrayed by yesterday's revelation, Nomuro ignored the last call to rise and form up outside. A Corporal came in and hit him a couple of times in the ribs with the butt of his rifle and screamed at him to get up and get out or he would bayonet him. Not doubting him for a minute, Nomuro jumped up, pulled on his flight suit and stumbled outside into the cold March air.

He joined in the ranks after being cuffed on the head by the platoon leader for his tardiness. They all marched to the training field, where after the usual calisthenics, they were taken to a place that held a wooden mockup of the Ohka that was suspended by ropes from two metal towers. The recruits took turns in the mock up as trainers pulled on the guide ropes causing the wooden replica to rock and gyrate. This was to mimic the buffeting by the wind the plane would receive when first released from the bomber or when evading enemy fire. Then, to simulate a dive, one trainer would jerk on his rope pulling the tail up while forcing the nose down and perpendicular to the ground. The ropes would still be jerked as the student inside tried to control the stick while falling forward. Each took their turn and emerged from the cockpit smiling after receiving confirmation of a successful controlled hit.

Nomuro, remembering how nauseated he got with the vertigo drills, kept avoiding his turn by continuing to step to the back of the line. Suddenly he was struck hard from behind and fell forward onto the ground. He felt his ribs being kicked, and then pulled up by his collar and forced to the front of the line to take his turn in the simulator. He tried to hold back his tears, but couldn't help choking and wiping his nose much to the laughter of the trainers and other recruits. He was grabbed by the back of his neck, and forced into the cockpit and the glass canopy was pushed closed. Even though this was not the real thing, it seemed as such to him. The dank smell of balsa wood and fresh paint filled his nostrils, and he felt a total sense of abandonment. All sense of choice no longer existed for him. He felt trapped and forced headlong into a tunnel where there could be no turning back. He quickly, as trained, slipped into the shoulder harness to keep himself from flying through the glass canopy during the simulated dive and put the fake oxygen mask over his face. He grabbed onto the mock control stick and soon felt the familiar bile rising in his throat as the plane began to pitch and yaw. After trying to contain the fluid rising in his throat, he heard the command,

"Dive, dive damn you. Push the fucking stick forward you idiot!" He pushed the mock stick forward which signaled the trainers to abruptly jerk the tail end straight up and perpendicular to the ground, tossing Nomuro forward against his shoulders straps and causing him to gag and vomit green gastric fluid into his mask and then onto the front of the canopy. He was fortunate to lose consciousness before he had time to reflect that that this would be the nature of his death, not of bravery and willful control, but of shame and regret.

Invasion of Okinawa

On Easter Sunday, April 1st, 1945, Rear Admiral Richmond Kelly Turner launched the United States attack on the island of Okinawa, the main island of the southern Ryuku archipelago, against the Japanese Imperial forces of Mitsusu Ushijima. The island of Okinawa, only 350 miles from the Japanese mainland, would serve as airbases to allow for more extensive aerial raids on Japan, as well as provide a staging area for the final assault on the homeland. An allied task force consisting of over 1,600 ships, 12,000 aircraft, and 545,000 U.S. troops, the Pacific theatres largest amphibious operation of the war, bore down on the tiny island. Few in the force were ever made aware of the suicidal tendency of the enemy they would soon face. This battle would continue for two and a half months, ending on June 17th and claiming the lives of 5,000 American sailors, the heaviest loss by the US Navy in any single battle in our history. U.S. ground forces would lose another 12,000. The US fleet would be subjected to over 1,500 suicide attacks by air, sinking 34 ships, and damaging 358. All this due to the actions of just 1,035 Kamikaze pilots, some like Nomuro, as young as 13.

The Japanese, in turn, would lose over 100,000 troops, some

by enemy action, some in the Kamikaze attacks, but all preferring an honorable death by suicide, rather than surrender or be captured. Many, as on Iwo Jima, threw themselves over hills, falling onto granite rocks to their deaths. The battle between both forces also claimed one third of Okinawa's entire civilian population.

Less successful were the Japanese single manned human mini submarines, the Hai's. Like the Ohka, released from a mother ship, these human torpedoes would steer into the side of an allied ship, killing its pilot by the blast. They were used by the Japanese as early as Pearl Harbor, but without success. Most often the occupant would die by asphyxiation from the battery gas before reaching target or slowly drown permanently trapped by nets strung up in the harbors, or accidentally explode upon release from the carrier sub prior to impact. Unlike the Kamikaze pilots, most of these suicide bent warriors died before reaching a target. The one notable exception was the destruction of the heavy cruiser, "Indianapolis", on the night of July 29th with its cargo, the third U.S. Atomic bomb of the war.

The first suicide attacks at Okinawa did not come from manned subs or aerial Kamikaze, but from Shinya, small fishing vessels outfitted with a torpedo mounted in its bow. Since they rode low in the water, they were difficult targets for a ship's heavier guns. Under the cover of night, the solitary navigator was to drive it directly into the side beams of the invading ships.

After repeated aerial attacks and heavy artillery fire from shore batteries, the Japanese guns fell strangely silent just as 172,000 troops of the U.S. Tenth Army scrambled over the sides of the transport ships into landing barges set to approach Hagushi beach on the night of March 31st.

SHINYA SUICIDE

A full moon reflected off the black swells challenging the progress of the US troop carrying LST's as they approached the shore of Hagushi beach. Enemy shelling had suddenly ceased, casting a pallor of impending doom among the U.S. soldiers squatting on the rolling decks, their helmeted heads below the metal wall surrounding the flat rectangular ships that rose and fell, crashing with each swell.

The river Bisha Giwa fed slowly past the piers into the estuary feeding the channel leading to Hagushi beach. Fifty Shinya (torpedo) ships of the 32nd Japanese Army silently drifted in the prevailing current sailing out to meet the invaders. As they exited the bay, their engines were started and they pressed forward with the deadly TNT armament in their prows. Due to the darkness, and their small size and stealth, the US transports barely recognized what had happened, nor what this small flotilla of wooden fishing boats signified, until it was too late. The first of three struck incoming barges and ignited them in a bright orange conflagration casting the dismembered sailors into the flaming oil slick sea. Yuka heard the enemies' screams and then a call to arms by the shrill of syncopated sirens on the American ships. He then shoved the throttle full forward to top speed. His Shinya only belched black smoke and continued its slow crawl toward the American fleet. As the tiny armada was greeted by a barrage of incendiary shells, they fanned out to take evasive action, but still progressing forward toward their intended targets. Those in the front ranks were hit prior to any ship impact, and exploded in balls of orange flames as enemy shells ignited the TNT explosive in their bow. Other vessels were swamped by the rise of the huge swells caused by the wake of near-by exploding shells and turned upside down in the water. Yuka could see these ships still afloat, but belly up, and wondered about the agony of drowning of these trapped unfortunate crewmates.

Yuka gripped the steering wheel even tighter as his tiny boat was rocked by the increasing swells. Holding his angle fixed on a troop carrier that was floundering due to a failed engine, it was the perfect target if he could get to it fast enough. All around him, the other Shinya, held many of those friends he had trained with for just this final action. His boat pressed on through the wooden debris of shattered Shinya that had taken the lead. The water was littered with bobbing listless floating corpses, lit by the oil burning on the surface of the night sea. He could see the reflection of the entire battle painted in strokes of orange fire as a deadly mural on the canvass of the dark sea.

His breathing came in short gasps, a mixture of both terror and excitement, as he grew closer to the stranded target he had selected, wondering if he would be quickly extinguished by a sudden explosion before he could reach the American ship. Oddly, his only wish right now was that his father, General Hironaka, could witness this brave act as he drew within 50 yards of his target. His father had sent him to Okinawa to work on the docks and repair shops, deliberately isolating him from the realities of war. Yuka had never told his father of the Shinya or of his joining as a ship's pilot, but he hoped that somehow his sacrifice would get back to his father, ever proud of this, his final act. He must make the kill to insure his father would be notified of such in the documents of battle. Only then would his name be listed among the Shinya for all eternity.

He could now see the soldiers on the stranded LST barge screaming and running for cover. Some already returned small arms fire to try to halt his progress, but to no avail. Some jumped overboard into the oil slick, rather than be rammed, only to be turned into human lanterns when covered by the black tar. Bullets splintered the bow and shattered the glass on the bridge forcing him to duck below its edge, but there were no direct hits on the torpedo head. He courageously maintained his course now smiling as he grew closer and closer to the listing barge with its frenzied human cargo.

After he closed to within 30 yards, the bow rose and slapped down hard on the surface of the water, and he seemed to be picking up speed due to swells shoving him from behind. Suddenly his bridge was caught in the beam of several bright searchlights, in front, from the sides and from behind. Now blinded, he could only hope he was still on target. As he squinted through the blinding light and smoky haze, he never saw the cause of the rear swells, a fast enemy PT boat approaching from behind. It rammed his stern driving up into the rear engine, splintering the entire stern, engine and steering mechanism, and crashing on into the bridge before stopping. The impact threw Yuka forward through the broken glass impaling him on its jagged edges. He hung there suspended like a string less marionette, flailing the air with both his arms and legs, but unable to free himself off of the razored glass that entered his abdominal cavity severing liver and lungs. Blood poured from his mouth and his only hope was to live long enough to feel the impact of his boat against the side of the enemy barge. The impact never came, as he felt hands gripping him, and painfully lifting him off of the glass. He tried to scream, but heard no sound but the hiss of air exiting punctured lungs. He soon felt a grateful paralysis overtake him as he looked pleadingly into the eyes of two American sailors, young like him, each with gentle reassuring smiles. They carried him to the ships rail, and tossed him into the coal black sea.

THE YAMATO

The battleship Yamato, the largest the world had ever seen and pride of the Imperial Japanese Navy, sat in anchorage at Mitajiri near the Kyo channel awaiting orders to disembark and stop the American invasion of Okinawa that had begun this day, the morning of April first. A veteran of the battles of Midway, the Philippines and Leyte Gulf, it took on board its newest junior officer, Hamano Hironoka, son of the General of the commanding forces in Kyusha, and leader in the victory at Singapore, as well as the capture of the Philippines. Hamano saluted and was welcomed on board not knowing that the fate of this iron clad behemoth, and its sailors, had already been sealed. With the agreement of the Gozen Kaigi Imperial War Council, this ship, and its men, were to be sacrificed in one of the last grand Kamikaze gestures of the war. Only a few of the officers were privy to this fact.

Hamano followed an adjunct assigned to him who carried his duffle bag and led him to his quarters. The adjunct informed him that he and the other officers would be convening at 0900 hours to be given orders. Hamano was excited by the prospect of finally getting to see some action in this war, as his father and school mates, Midori's son already had. He had heard of Schima's death at

Iwo Jima and knew his own brothers were also serving somewhere. Security kept their location a secret, but he knew that Yuka was in training with a torpedo fleet, and that Schino was in submarine school. But only he, because of his age, had made the rank of Officer a fact that he knew his father would be especially proud. He opened his bag and set out photos of his parents and then one of him with his two brothers. He had another photo with his brothers and General Tanoka's three sons, Shima, Nomuro and Masako. How he wished they all could see him now, in his Officer's uniform and on this, the largest and most magnificent of the Japanese vessels. How proud he felt that he was the only one qualified to make officer of all his friends and family.

In a freshly pressed uniform, he joined the other officers in the elegant conference room below deck. After a round of formal introductions, most of whom Hamano had heard about, Commanding Officer, Kusaku Ariga, addressed the men.

"Fellow Officers, at 0406 hours this morning U.S. Naval forces under Rear Admiral Richmond Turner launched an attack on our forces in Okinawa. Under the command of Mitsisu Ushijima our forces are countering the invasion with stiff resistance. I've received reports that they have already suffered heavy losses inflicted by a Shinyo force of over 50 torpedo ships."

Hamano flinched, annoyed that his younger brother Yuka was no doubt part of that fleet, and had gotten into action before him. He gave no regard as to the outcome of his brother's action as he knew that sacrificial suicide was the only result. He was determined not to die this way, in a foolish ritual sacrifice as so many others had been taught to do. No, he would be victorious and return home one day as a hero to tell his war tales to his fiancé Yokuna and, someday, to their children. Yes, life and not death was his goal, just as his father Hironaka had taught him. There was no glory in death, but a valiant life to be lived without shame was the only true victory. His father never accepted this concept of suicide for the Emperor and the land, but for obvious reasons never related that to anyone. Even at Johor, he safely hid behind the lines with a heavy guard allowing Tanoka and the likes of him to lead the suicide attacks across the straits, and then claiming victory as the leader of that campaign. He would insure the future generations of his proud line, not by sacrificing himself or his sons, but allowing others to make that sacrifice in their place. He had insured this by first seeing that his youngest son, Yuku, had been assigned to maintenance and upkeep at the naval port in Okinawa to service the small ships that guarded the port. He heard of the Shinya, but knew that these were piloted only by volunteers who accepted suicide as their only fate in this war.

Since Hamano, his oldest, was old enough for a commission, he saw that he was placed on the largest and, therefore, he thought, the safest of all of the Imperial Navy ships, the "Yamato." A battleship this large would only sail with a large number of sacrificial support vessels, like destroyers, heavy cruisers, and the carriers.

Even Schino was carefully placed in submarine school where his father knew there were so few vessels left, and the training so long, that the war would long be over before he could be assigned.

Commander Kusaka Ariga continued, "The Yamato is proud to now join in the defense of our Okinawa and will lead a naval attack upon the American fleet and its transports that are already there." Kusaka continued. "We will operate under the code name Operation Ten-Ichi and be accompanied by the heavy cruiser Yahagi along with eight destroyers as escort. We are to set sail at 1500 hours with all supplies and ordinance loaded immediately. The men will be briefed beforehand according to what I am now telling you.

Our flagship and its escorts are to act as bait to attract enemy air-craft away from the air routes that our Kamikaze pilots will use, thus leaving their vessels as easy targets. We have more than enough firepower to down the enemy Hellcats, which we draw to us. The Yamato will set a course through the Bungo Strait, rounding the south coast of Kyushu, past the Osumi islands and then out into the open sea toward Okinawa." Kusaka sat down, took a shot of Sake, clasped his hands and leaning forward said, "What I am now about to tell you must remain top secret to everyone outside of this room. Do I make myself clear?" There was no response, only just a few nods. This vessel's fuel capacity is 6,300 tons, but we will only be carrying less than 600 tons." There were a few inquisitive looks and one of equal concern from Hamano. "We are to engage the enemy and after inflicting maximum damage, this proud ship will be beached and its main batteries used as additional artillery to defend our island forces. With no fuel or hope for a return, our men will be expected to die and fight to the last in our islands defense, along with each of us sitting here."

Hamano choked at the thought. How could he possibly be caught in this suicide madness which he had so long hoped to avoid? Could his father not have prevented this? Chances were, however, that the orders had been decided only this morning by those above, welcoming death, at least for others, while not risking it themselves. Armament and maneuverability were a ship's only defense, along with the resolve of its sailors. A beached ship wasn't a weapon; it was a target. He vowed that he would not remain on board once beached, but desert the ship and take his chances on the island, even if that meant the unheard of… surrender to the enemy.

Kusaka stood and shouted, "Let the Yamato strike the enemy like true Kamikaze," he then threw up his hands and shouted

"Banzai!" three times as his adjuncts, including Hamano shouted in return. Hamano's thoughts were not of brave confrontation with the enemy, but how to plan his escape from this doomed ship. Since he was in command of the rear batteries, he remembered there was a rope ladder near the life raft. Perhaps during confusion by the enemy shelling, he could make his way over the side, swim to the beach, and then lose himself in the jungle until he could surrender to the enemy that he was certain could no longer be stopped.

CONVOY RESCUE

On the morning of April 7th, the Yamato and its convoy were spotted fifteen miles south of Fukashima Island at the mouth of the Bungo Strait by a single patrolling USN Mariner flying boat. They radioed to US Task Force 58 the ships coordinates and direction of the convoy. Immediately, US Naval carrier command at Okinawa released a squadron of Grumman F6F Hellcats and radioed attack force submarines in the East China Sea to intercept. At 1215 hours the Japanese convoy fell under heavy attack by the hellcat dive bombers. The entire crew of the Yamato was at their battle stations, with Hamano commanding the rear artillery bridge. He thought to himself that this was the real thing. He could be killed now or drown with no beach to escape to. The order from the bridge was to fire at will and he passed the order onto his squad to commence firing. He figured that the attackers would forego the lighter ships and go for the last great vessel of the Imperial Japanese Navy on which he now regrettably found himself.

The 50 mm cannons fired at the attacking blue Hellcats that seemed to be coming from all directions. The sky filled with tracers and flak detonations from their barrels. One of the planes was hit by his battery fire, lost a wing, and exploded in flames cartwheeling into the sea. Cheers of "Bonsai" erupted from his crew; but the planes, like pesky mosquitoes, kept on coming in wave after wave. Hamano ducked as the Hellcat shells hit his bridge with a sharp ping of metal and sparks following each impact. He had seen films of navy combat during training but was never prepared for the horrid sound of battle, the ear shattering detonations and the screams of mutilated and dying men. Hamano feigned a wound and staggered toward the stairs to get below deck. His last sight was of their destroyer escort, Asashino, exploding amidships and listing in flames. He didn't realize that her destruction was due not to the dive bombers, but to torpedoes from American submarines who had just joined in the fray.

Hamano made it to his quarters and locked his door, crawled under the protective cover of his bunk, and determined to await out his fate in this room rather than in the conflagration going on topside. He pressed a blanket to his ears to try to mute the sounds of destruction and battle but could not quell the shattering vibrations as his ship was struck time and again by the armor piercing bombs. These ripped through the deck and bridges and detonated the ship's magazines below. The fire alert was sounded and he now knew he was going to die. He cried and prayed that he would survive and screamed as to how he had even come to this. Where was the glory and pride of battle his father so reveled in? He was going to die and for what? He envisioned all sorts of endings, being blown apart or crushed to death in his cabin when the steel beams fell, or worse being trapped and burning to death, or slowly drowning in the dark rising water.

At 1400 hours more US submarines intercepted the convoy and went directly for the flagship. Twelve torpedoes struck hitting port aft and amidships. AT 1417 two more struck her at starboard and amidships. She began to list and, due to damaged steering, could only circle as the Grumman's repeatedly kept up their relentless strafing of the helpless vessel.

With relief, Hamano heard the syncopated wail of the sirens signaling for them to abandon ship and headed for the stairs, choking on the heat and black smoke from below. He would take his chances in a lifeboat and surrender, without shame, since so many others would be doing the same.

What he confronted when he reached the tilted deck sickened him. He saw his entire battery of eight men now all charred corpses still at their stations, leathery and black. Their lipless faces were frozen in a perpetual grin. He crawled and climbed over debris, the wounded, and the dying and made it to the rope ladder swinging out over the listing side. He scampered down it and dropped into the sea. He swam toward the nearest lifeboat filled with wounded and desperate men. He said, "I'm wounded. I'm a wounded officer. Get me on board, I order you! get me on board!" They pulled him on board, but not before throwing one near conscious sailor overboard in order to make room for the Officer. They looked to see where he had been wounded, but Hamano merely held his gut, feigning a stomach wound. The life boat was rowed as fast possible from the sinking ship, when at 1423 hours the Imperial Yamato sank into the East China Sea some 130 miles west-south-west of Kagoshima, entombing within her bowels 3,063 sailors who never made it topside to the deck, including her commanding officer Ariga.

The tiny lifeboat rolled in the late afternoon swells awaiting rescue by the Americans. The Hellcats had left and the sea rolled with just the haze of battle and the cries from the burned and wounded bobbing in life jackets and those in the flotilla of other lifeboats. The quiet amplified the sharp ringing in his ears caused by the events the past hour. Cold, thirsty, and scared, but at least he was alive.

Hours passed with no sign of an American rescue ship. Then he turned, hearing the slice of a conning tower cutting through the water. They all turned with a sense of relief as the bridge, and then the deck, lifted out of the water. First just one and then two others. The first came to a slow rolling stop just 100 yards from the flotilla that Hamano was in. The other two made off toward the flotilla of survivors from the other Japanese escort vessels and they also rolled to a slow stop. Hamano could make out the letters "USN Piranha" painted on the side of its bow. He and others stood up in the boat and waved and shouted for pick up. One even waved a confiscated American flag. Then they saw the hatch on the bridge open and armed sailors in life jackets emerged taking positions at the two cannons fore and aft. Merely a precaution, Hamano thought as he and the some others continued to wave their white scarves. They abruptly turned at the sound of cannon fire and noticed, to their horror, that the two other subs had opened fire on the other lifeboats. Before they could even grasp what was happening, salvos from the Piranha opened fire on them. The first shell hit the water between two of the lifeboats and the swell immediately capsized them. The second shell hit two boats directly sending up a fiery mass of wood and human debris. Men in the boats began to jump overboard and tried to take cover on the other side of their boats as machine gun fire from the bridge of the sub now added to the roar of the canons. The sea turned red with the viscera and blood of the mutilated men. Others were bobbing helplessly in the water supported by their life vests, making them easy targets as the hail of machine gun and cannon fire continued. They screamed and threw up their arms pleading for the mercy that would not come.

Hamano never suspected that their enemy was capable of such inhuman and wanton slaughter against an unarmed and helpless foe who had already surrendered. He knew he had to get off the boat fast since it too would soon be targeted, but to jump into the water with his life jacket would only make him a an easy target as it had the others. He knew he was a strong swimmer and would take his chances underneath the water. He tore off his life jacket and plunged headfirst into the chilled water. He swam as fast as he could away from the sprays of machine gun fire hitting the water and the others, and then took a deep breath and dove straight down into the silence of the dark sea. Underneath he swam perpendicular to the last line of fire he remembered, and as far away from the hulls of the remaining lifeboats. He looked up and could see bloodied corpses floating down past him, and the kicking legs of those still alive in the water above. He surfaced occasionally to get air but kept swimming further from the maelstrom on the surface. After 15 minutes he heard the whine of engines and saw the "USS Piranha" diving and passing by him. It trailed a white stream of bubbles as it gradually slipped out of sight into the dark water beyond. With his lungs now screaming for air, he kicked to the surface and gasped in huge gulps of air and water. He treaded water in a circle to check out what was happening and noted that all three submarines were now gone. All that was left was burning smoking debris, a mass of floating dead still in the life jackets that had made them easy targets, and a few survivors. He swam toward a group that had clustered around the capsized hull of one of the boats and clung helplessly to its side along with the others. Some were wounded, some crying, some praying aloud, but most coughing up blood and water.

Night fell and some succumbed to their wounds, dehydration, or the chill of the water, lost their grip and were carried away by the current. Only Hamano and a few others had the strength to crawl up onto the inverted hull and were momentarily spared an immediate death.

At 2100 hours, attracted by the bloody chum of the mutilated sailors, sharks appeared and began a feeding frenzy among those still stranded in the water. Hamano and others on top of the inverted lifeboat kicked at those seeking the safety of the hull. "It's them or us," shouted Hamano. "If they get on board, we'll capsize and, then we'll all be eaten." An hour later the water was again quiet as the sharks having had their fill suddenly left, leaving only small morsels of human parts for the smaller denizens. Even in the dark, the survivors could see the upper torsos of the dead, heads under water, with the grizzly sight of their bottom halves missing.

Hamano felt a hopeless dread now knowing there would be no rescue and that he would soon fall asleep, lose his grip, and slide into a watery grave with the others, and never be found. How sad never to have wed, borne children, and lived a long life as a hero with great tales to tell. He would only be listed as "missing in action," his memory to be passed on by his father. How sad that in years to come, he'll have no legacy and not one thing representing his life would remain. He thought only of his girlfriend, whom he would never see again and remorse over the life they would never have. Could it have been for this end that Midori had delivered him?

Part dreaming and part delirium, he was startled by a bright light. The light was scanning the water and after clearing his eyes he saw a ship, and as it drew near, noted the insignia USN AH-6 COMFORT inscribed on its side. His first reaction was to slip off the hull and dive again before its guns erupted, but he knew his fatigue and dehydration would only take him to a slower death by drowning. He welcomed a quick metallic death to the slow asphyxiation by drowning or being eaten by sharks. He stood staggering on the rolling hull, occasionally slipping and falling to his knees and then standing up again waving his arms, welcoming the hail of bullets.   As the ship rolled past, he saw a familiar sign half way down its hull. It was a sign he had seen on his friends' mother, Midori. She wore it on her uniform and on the front of her hat. It was a large red cross, a sign that meant help and care in any language. This was the hospital ship, USS Comfort. He heard some calls from their deck and then saw life preservers being thrown into the sea attached to ropes, and the crank of lifeboats being lowered into the water. He felt a strange mixture of both joy and yet bitterness over those whose decisions had brought him to this, and left him wondering who the enemy really was?

Schino Submariner

Hironaka's oldest son, Schino, had just received a letter giving the news of the loss of his first and only child during childbirth. The letter had come from his family's friend, Midori, with little detail, except that the baby was lost due to unforeseen circumstances.

The letter was quite formal from someone who herself had actually brought him into this world.

Days later the ominous letter from his wife, Swansi, arrived.

> "My dearest husband Schino, It is not with great regret that we are no longer to be parents. You know it was my wish never to bring another life into the world in this time and place, so I chose to abort our child. My work at the orphanage treating the victims of the nighttime incendiary bombings, seeing children burned, suffering, abandoned and scarred for life, has fostered this resolve. I know you are disappointed in me for not giving you the son that was to be the first of the Hironoka clan. No, you will not have an heir to grow up and leave a wife for a senseless war as you have done to me. I've heard the

tales of rape and murder by our soldiers and will never produce any person to do the same. As to any involvement you may have shared in this national disgrace, I can never forgive. Your admission of the frequent use of the "comfort women", supposed Korean and Chinese volunteers, made available to service our Army, I will never forgive. Midori, who treated several of these poor females, some as young as 12 and 13, informed me that they were never given a choice. It was either submit or be raped anyway, then face torture and be bayoneted to death. Her tales of what she saw during the examinations of these girls, and their horrible stories were enough to sicken all of us. Since I no longer desire to have you as my husband, I will seek a dissolution of our marriage. I pray that you will remain safe during the remaining days of this war, and that you and all those that participated in this outrage against innocent females will someday be brought to justice and seek forgiveness for your selfish wanton acts."

Schino fell into a state of deep depression, and no longer wished for the safe haven of the submarine repair yards. How he resented most of all, not being allowed to go home to be with his wife Swansi during her time, and over the guilt he felt in having made the frequent use of "comfort women" since he had left her. They had married and lived at Niigata in a home overlooking the Shinano river, a home worthy of a General's son; but he wondered if it was his nocturnal excursions with other women that had angered the Gods and influenced her to offer his unborn son as punishment. He was certain that this was the case, and he had caused the death of his unborn son and the loss of his wife. He now had no right to live.

Thus when the call for volunteers was posted to train and operate the Kyukoko Heiki, the national salvation weapon, he now met all of the criteria for recruitment in the Sensei Butai, the submarine force. There was no doubt in any of the volunteers' minds that their mission would be one way and suicidal by choice.

They were to be trained in a single manned torpedo called a "Kaiten," the literal translation meaning "Heaven Shaker." The sub was 54 feet long, had a range of 14 to 48 miles, depending on its speed, and carried a charge of 3,500 pounds of TNT. Once launched, it was propelled by engines running on hydrogen peroxide. In place of the torpedo's normal directional equipment, a small conning tower was erected with a short periscope. The occupant would lay on his stomach on a sled suspended on springs, and look straight ahead into a mirror that reflected up into the view from the periscope. A mother sub, the Kaidai ClassI-54, could carry 4 to 6 of them and launch them as they would any torpedo. They had even been used at Pearl Harbor but were trapped in the harbor nets drowning their occupants.

Schino was sent for training to the Kaiten submarine depot at Otusushima, an island off the coast of Yamaguchi, southwest of Honshu, which was now part of the IJN 6th Fleet Submarine Force (Sensei Butai). The training consisted first of dry runs in a simulator; then submerged dives while suspended from lines attached from an anchored vessel; and then finally actual dummy runs launched from a submarine, but without the warheads.

The inside of the Kaiten was cramped even for a small person. There was a box of emergency rations and a small bottle of Saki just below the sled. To the right was a small crank lever to raise and lower the periscope. Directly above the occupant's head was a valve to regulate the oxygen flow to the motor, which was located directly behind him. Overhead and to the left was a lever connected to the sub's diving planes, which controlled the rate of descent or elevation underwater. Below this level was a valve for letting in sea water to maintain the vessel's stability as the oxygen was used up. In addition, there was a gyro-compass, a clock, and depth and fuel gauges. The main controls in his hands were the rudder controls, that allowed the sub to steer right or left. Since this was the last adjustment the pilots would just before striking their target, it was sarcastically referred to as the "dead man's handle." Any rapid change in movement brought immediate painful contact with these controls. The heat, humidity, and cramped conditions prior to launch, tested the claustrophobic limits of even the bravest.

There were more deaths logged in training than in combat. Several drowned when their subs were grounded on the bottom, others suffocated from the fumes of the battery acids, still other subs disintegrated upon launch, or their charges ignited without cause.

When his training was complete, he graduated and was given a shirt with a green chrysanthemum blossom on its sleeve, the emblem of the Kaiten attack crews. As the time passed before their assignment, they were given extra rations, and on the last night before the mission, the use of "comfort women" which Schino refused. Instead he went out into the balmy night and composed his funeral letter to his father. Still not knowing the fate of his brothers, his father was his only living relative.

> "My dearest father, I sit now under the night sky and see all of the constellations you taught us as a child. On the right the Great Bear, on the left the Southern Cross which points to my city Niigata by the Shinano River,

where my lost love lives and where my unborn never had a chance to be. Just above me lays the Milky Way stretching like a wispy spider gauze across the universe. Father, let me assure you that there is no use in assuming an air of bravado when faced with death. I have become detached and must continually work at this detachment. I realize that my life has been nothing but vanity, infidelity, and cowardice. This month of reflection has marked a turning point in my life and allowed me to see myself as I really was. No brave progeny of a great and fearless leader, no, just a scared little boy whose life has done no good for a single person. Does that shock you father? In just a few hours I will go to my death. Though you tried to protect me from this fate, I willingly chose it for myself. I have no reason to live, and while no reason to deny others that right, I will do my duty so as not to shame your name. My entire life is now permeated by the scent of death. The greatest gift our Gods give us is not to know the hour of our death. Why have some of us even been denied this? Could it be that I am just a child of a weaker God. The consolation, encouragement, and noisy manners of the Army, and all of its patriotic songs make me angry. How I wish for the days of long ago when we all lived in peace. For what end did we chose to bring such senseless death and destruction upon ourselves and others? In the past few weeks I've tried to draw up a balance sheet for my life, but can no longer find any meaning in it. My heart has become cold, and it lives in dismal isolation, devoid of all honor and hope. Is this what they call cowardice? When the decisive moment comes, I shall no doubt be afraid, but no matter, for in my desperate attempts to discover myself these past few weeks, the one thing that I am most certain of is that I no longer exist. In remembrance of better times,"

Your son,

Schino

Later that night he joined the others who would board their Kaiten that night, for their ritualistic funeral service. Each pilot placed the Hachimaki around their heads with the name of their Kaiten group and slogan, donned their jackets, and drank their ceremonial Saki and stood to attention for the singing of the Kimigayo.

Afterwards they marched to the docks in the humid night and Schino boarded his carrier submarine I-58, and after launch, he was lowered belly down and face forward into his Kaiten. The springs holding him creaked as he adjusted to the cramped quarters. His instruments were clouded from the humidity and he could hear the welding arch above permanently sealing him in the chamber that was to be his final tomb. He then heard the crank of chains as his sub was pulled forward into one of the torpedo tubes, and suspending him in total darkness.

He awoke several hours later and wasn't sure if he was still alive, until he heard the Captain through his radio telling him to prepare for launch since a target had been sighted.

On the night of July 29th, the heavy cruiser "Indianapolis" under Captain Charles Butter McVay III was proceeding without escort from Guam to Leyte Gulf. In a choppy sea, she came in contact with Shosa Hashsimoto's submarine I-58. Neither radar, nor lookout officers aboard the "Indianapolis" picked up the sub's presence. At 2332 hours Shosa ordered the Kaiten fired.

LAST LAP

Schino heard the orders through his radio and prepared himself for the launch, grateful to be able to see something again. He felt the rush of water and his sled pushed back and then rolled forward when it entered the water. He immediately cranked up his periscope and turned the valve giving hydrogen peroxide to his engine. He adjusted the diving planes to allow the periscope to break water. Then in the blackness he saw the red orange glow of a ship's smoke stacks as he was bearing straight ahead toward the starboard side, now no more than a few hundred yards ahead. He felt no need to kill this enemy, just himself. He increased his speed and trimmed his bow, with no feeling except for a brief final thought of his wife, Swansi. Within 85 seconds from launch, he struck the starboard side, just under the number 1 turret, and exploded in a ball of flame.

The Indianapolis took a second hit under the wardroom causing her to lose all communication. She began to list and an SOS was sent; but without any working communication, no message was received. She sank a few minutes before midnight. Her surviving crew of 1,119 drifted for 5 days before being spotted by a Catalina sub patrol plane. During those five days, 883 died from hunger, wounds, dehydration, and shark attacks.

Schino never knew the ultimate impact of his act, for the Indianapolis was steaming under complete secrecy because she was carrying the third atomic bomb to Tinian island. This third bomb was to be dropped on the city of Niigata, a port on the Sea of Japan, at the mouth of the Shinano River. Without realizing, his final act saved his wife and thousands of others.

INVITATION TO A
FUNERAL

Nomuro and his roommates knew the time of their training had come to an end as they each were instructed to pack their belongings and move into the special barracks for those soon ready to fly. Nomuro had hoped that the war would end before his call to duty came. He packed with a certain hesitancy, hoping to delay the inevitable.

The new barracks were much cleaner and each had more room. On the walls were the many faces, with a fierce determination, of all those now dead. Nomuro was uncertain he could even try to emulate the same bravado when his time came for his funeral photo. After each squadron's move to these barracks, they were instructed to prepare for their funeral rites and then be ready to go at an instant into the air when the call came.   Nomuro had already sent an invitation to his mother, who he knew would come tomorrow with the pictures of his father, brothers, and sister Eiko, and some of the mementoes from their family altar for him to see one last time.

The next morning he prayed, then bathed and shaved and neatly laid out his flight suit, jacket, scarf and head band. He then wrote his farewell letter to his mother which would be opened and read by her upon formal notification of his death. When finished, he sealed the letter and then laid down on his bed trying to imagine when, and just how, his end would come. Others in the room were not quite as somber, laughing, playing cards and passing suggestive photos of the young females they would never get to know. He saw Yoshie and Motoko throwing dice in the corner and gambling with the others. What if they did win? To what avail would it be to them? How could they all take what was about to happen to them so nonchalantly? He turned over and tried to sleep hoping to awake into what was only a bad dream.

Midori dressed in the same funeral robe she wore for Tanoka and Shima. She gathered the relics from the altar that Nomuro had requested and put them in a bag. Then with great calm she kneeled and prayed to Amaterasu that her youngest son would have a pain-less end. while waiting for Father Krozier to arrive. He would not let her face this last meeting with her son alone, despite any con-descending remarks over a Catholic priest attending a ceremony that worshipped a different God. In her prayers she bewailed the madness of men who beguile such youths into choosing suicide as a right of honor instead of life.

When he arrived, he gave her a hug, and without any words they left for the base. Once on board, they sat in silence. When Midori's eyes began to weep, he handed her his white handkerchief. She dabbed her eyes and looked out the window of the bus notic-ing the dark heavy clouds and leafless trees, all barren except for a few cherry blossoms that were beginning to blossom in this early spring. She remembered being told that the cherry blossom is short lived because it tries to blossom before its time, and is not prepared to weather the early spring's cold and frost. So much just like her Nomuro in trying to grow before his time to prove his worth to his dead father and brother. How could he abandon his mother who needed him so much and the future she had always imagined for him?

Father Krozier remained silent but read in whispers from his Bible. The bus arrived and was passed on through the guarded gate. They both stepped off along with other parents and friends who were here for the same reason. They all seemed less somber and talkative, even with a sense of pride in what their sons were about to do.

Parents of Kamikaze were given special privileges and considerations. They all carried bags with their sons mementoes and were led through a curtain into an outdoor courtyard. At the front was a long wooden altar where they formed a line, walked past it and found the section showing their son's photo. They then laid out each of the photos and mementoes they brought. They continued in a line and were directed to fill the empty rows of wooden benches. Midori continued to dab her eyes as she looked at Nomuro's smiling photo on the altar taken just days before. How noble her little man looked in his flight cap and Samurai Hachimaki head band with the red rising sun wrapped around his forehead. His fuzzy short black hair extending just above it. He had his leather flight jacket on with the collar pulled up and a white battalion scarf around his neck. The jacket was far too big for him and obscured his neck giving him the appearance of a little frightened turtle trying to pull back into his shell. She looked up when she heard the young pilots, each called by name to take positions beside each of their photos. How tiny and frail her son looked to her now. He caught her eyes and smiled for the first time in days. He and the others all stood at attention as General Onishi was introduced and walked to the middle of the altar.

"Family and friends of our great warriors of the Sun, I welcome all of you here today for this time honored ceremony."

Behind the audience, stood General Hironoka, feeling a sense of relief at seeing Midori's son in funeral garb and seated on the stage. With a smile he also saw Midori seated near the front. All was going well and soon he'd have his little hero's name on the belt to assist him in his recruiting efforts.

Onishi cleared his throat and addressed the audience.

"Our country now lies in great danger. A ruthless enemy is already fire-bombing our cities and killing thousands of innocent citizens and children in their wanton nightly raids. If they are not stopped at our island of Okinawa, then our home shores will be next. If we don't defeat them now, then every man in our homeland will be slaughtered. Our wives and sisters raped and then used as slaves. This has been their method of conquest to date." Onishi turned to face the pilots at his back.

"Spirit warriors, look at those before you. Do you want them to suffer so?"

Midori shifted in her seat and Krozier just shook his head, she remembering the tales of Nanking, and he having lived it. This was actually Japan's method of conquest.

"Their fate is in your hands. The salvation of our country is now beyond the powers of the Ministers of State, the General Staff, and lowly commanders like myself. It can come only from brave spirit warriors such as you. Only you can free our country from the desperate situation in which she finds herself. Thus, on behalf of your hundred million countrymen, your relatives, mothers, fathers, sisters and brothers, I ask you this sacrifice and we all pray for your success. You are already Gods, without earthly desires. You are our new Divine Wind that will again turn back the invaders of our land. Do not think of death as you bravely carry out your duty. Make it your joy to use up every last bit of your physical and spiritual strength in what you are about to do. Do not be afraid to die for the cause of everlasting justice. Do not live in dishonor, nor die in such a way as to bring shame upon those you leave behind. Your crash dive will not be in vain, for we shall note your efforts and report your deeds to the throne. Your spirits will all meet again at the Yasukuni Shrine. All we ask is for you to be brave and never falter in your duty to all for never has so much depended upon your bravery and determination. Now allow me to toast all of you." He picked up his glass of Saki as the pilots also did in unison. Holding it up to them he recited the traditional haiku.

"Fall my warriors,

Like our cherry blossoms,

Be proud to fall,

Just as I will fall

In the service of our Gods."

With that he emptied his glass as did the others and then led a chorus of three "Bonsai's" to seal their vow.

After the ceremony Nomuro joined his mother who tried to hold back her tears as General Hironoka slipped away without notice. Nomuro had retrieved the mementoes of his family from the altar, and after holding and looking at them for the last time, handed them back to his mother. Krozier shook the lad's hand and, without a word, left the two to make their last goodbye.

"I will be brave mother. I promise. I would never do anything to blemish our family's name and its proud history. You'll know that to be true after it's over. I will make you proud of me."

Midori choked on these words and the tears rolled down her cheeks.

"I will go now for I know this is hard for you. I promise to write you before I fly, so be brave now, and pray for me."

They hugged for the last time and Krozier came back to hold Midori as she reached out for her son who was now departing, daring not to look back despite her calls to him, as he joined his squadron in marching back to their barracks.

FIRST OHKA RAID

Yoshie was the first called. Nomuro and Motoko stood, on the morning of March 21ˢᵗ, at the edge of the airfield and watched Yoshie climb into his light blue Ohka. It hung from the underbelly of a Mitsubishi Model 22 type 1 bomber, numbered 49 and was the color of the sky. He was lifted into the cockpit and strapped into place by the ground crew. He gave a final farewell wave to his bother and new friend. Then the cockpit bubble was slid forward and locked in place. In an attempt to look brave to the onlookers, he took control of the stick and checked the ailerons, elevators and rudder. Then with a final thumbs up to the ground crew, the Mitsubishi bomber with its human cargo in its nose, rolled to join seventeen others in lining up on the runway. Heat vectors, from the engines, made a rippled surreal vision to those bound for death. Nomuro thought that there could now be no turning back for poor Yoshie.

Strategy called for the experienced pilots, survivors of the wars earlier aerial campaigns to act as hiutsuji-kai (sheperds) in carrying wave after wave of mure (herds) as the inexperienced Ohka pilots were referred to in secret.

At 1145 hours Yoshie's bomber, the last in line, lifted from the field, climbed and made a slow circle toward the sea following the others before it. Yoshie saw the land gradually recede and waved to his companions below, just in case they could still see him.

Unbeknownst to this attack force, consisting of eighteen bombers, sixteen carrying Ohka's, and thirty Zero escorts, they were inadvertently doomed from the start. U.S Carrier task force 96, leading the attack force to Okinawa, spotted a Japanese FIM2 reconnaissance float plane 320 miles southeast of Kyushu. In response, the carriers launched a total of 150 fighter planes to sweep the area. At 1430 the US Grumman F6F Hellcats intercepted the task force heading for their carriers and began their attack on the outnumbered foe . The Zero escorts, heavily outnumbered, proved no match for the American fighters. Their planes were hit, disintegrated, burned and went down in trails of flame and black smoke. Some of the Zeros tried to abandon the bombers but were chased, and 15 of the escorts were downed while others that were damaged crashed on the return flight.

Without escorts, the Ohka carrying bombers became easy targets. Answering only with their anti-aircraft guns, on top and to the rear, they had a hard time tracking the more maneuverable dark blue U.S. Fighters, which came at them from all directions. The Grumman leader called for strikes to the underbelly of these bombers, since there were no defending guns in sight, since these guns had to be removed in order to accommodate their Ohka. One by one the Hellcats attacked from below tearing into the underbelly of the bombers, erupting gas tanks or separating the fuselages into flaming parts. Those of the crew attempting to escape by parachute were quickly dispatched midair by a hail of tracers. It was accepted practice, in this late phase of the war, after the atrocities of the Bataan Death March, Nanking and the island wars became known, to actually fire on the parachutes and not the crewman, in order to allow their prey a long and slow death plunge.

"Give the Jap bastards time to consider what they've done to us. Let's send them back to their Gods, but let's make their journey slow." This was a familiar quote papered to the wall of the briefing and locker rooms.

Lieutenant Brighten, flying Hellcat 26, followed Bomber 49. He dove underneath it to avoid the top fire, circled below at 300 feet, then pulled back on the stick and gave a full throttled climb toward the underbelly of Bomber 49. He had been briefed on the design of this plane and knew where the vulnerable gas tanks were. This was going to be easy work for a plane with no undercarriage armament. As he closed in on his target, he saw the strange blue cigar shaped object hanging from the belly near the front of the nose. No doubt a bomb of some kind, but he took particular interest in the fact that it had wings, and that the ailerons seemed to be moving. He thought that it must be some type of radio controlled bomb set to be launched and began to fire syncopated bursts into its wooden blue undercarriage.

Yoshie witnessed the destruction of some of the other bombers ahead, but so far his had not been hit and still proceeded toward the carriers. He thought what a shame that these Ohka pilots would have no tales of victory to relate to fellow spirits at the Yasukuni Shrine. The ride was now getting very rough as his bomber tried to take evasive action from the fighters. He was sure the carriers were near and decided to test his controls. He pushed the stick forward and noted the elevators to the rear rise and fall. Then right and left and noted the rudder respond as expected. With his feet he tested the ailerons pushing each down and up in turn, and looked to the wings noting their alternate rise and fall. He was confident and ready when suddenly his kneecaps exploded separating his calves from his thighs and splashing the cockpit with blood and fragments of bone. Brighten's Hellcat shells had penetrated the front of the seated figure from below. The shells not able to penetrate the hard metal seat designed to protect the vital organs of the pilot, leaving only the legs vulnerable from below. Yoshie was warned of this possibility, but not of the pain. All he could do was scream and grab at his bleeding stumps. He then frantically beat the cockpits bubble with his fists screaming to for his pilots to drop him now to his death regardless of the presence of any target, but to no avail since both pilot and co-pilot lay slumped in the cockpit each having already caught deadly shells from Brightens Hellcat.

Lieutenant Brighten called off the other fighters and said he needed to check this one again to get a better look at this new weapon. The bomber, now defenseless seemed to be gliding on auto pilot. The rest of the crew had already taken their ill-fated chances by parachuting to their deaths. Brighten pulled up alongside of the light blue cigar shaped object, and to his shock he saw a human in the cockpit beating his fists into blood toward him. He turned the channel of his radio and could now hear Yoshie's screams in Japanese, "kill me, kill me."

He falsely assumed that this was a prisoner put in this device by the Japanese to keep American fighters from firing on an innocent victim. It was obvious this young prisoner was suffering terribly. So, after shooting photos of the winged bomb for analysis later, he decided to end this kids suffering. Others of the squadron joined him and offered help, but he radioed that the target no longer presented any danger to him, and he didn't want anyone to witness this act of mercy killing. Brighten banked and circled once more, and then bore down directly at the Ohka again. When close, he fired first at the elongated nose then trailed the tracers to the cockpit. Since the sides of the cockpit were also protected by thick layers of steel, the shells did not penetrate and kill Yoshie but did penetrate the tank of trinitro-anisol. Brighten pushed his Hellcat into a steep dive as fast as possible from the bright orange flame that started to spew from the nose of his target. Rather than exploding, the trinitro-anisol began a slow sizzling flame that burned backwards toward the cockpit to the shattered and screaming occupant.

Brighten took more photos from below as he saw the entire cigar shaped object engulfed in bright orange flames, and then spread to the nose of the G4M. His only thought now was not on the object, but rather a sad regret that its mysterious cargo had been denied a quick death. He must have slowly burned to death as the G4M disintegrated and plunged toward the sea.

He radioed back to fleet command that the enemy was now using a special bomb that had live prisoners strapped inside in order to persuade them from strafing the bombers, and he asked what should they do. Command just radioed back that he was probably mistaken and had misjudged what he had seen, since no one could possibly subject any human being to such a death, not even a prisoner of war.

SECOND OHKA RAID

News of the first Ohka raid was broadcast as a great victory against the allies, when in fact all were lost without even having sighted the enemy ships. Nomuro's squadron was assembled and they were given the false news of the success of several carrier and cruiser hits by the Ohka's piloted by their comrades. Most listening knew better since none of the G4M bombers had returned.

Nomuro was saddened by the loss of his friend, but the effect on his brother Motoko was unnerving. Motoko began to rant and rave more and more each day, angry and begging for the chance to redeem his brother. His chance came just three weeks later on the morning of April 12th. The invasion of Okinawa had started just 12 days before and it was imperative that the supply ships and air cover provided by the carriers to the U.S. forces on Okinawa had to be stopped.

Motoko's ride was much more turbulent due to foul weather conditions, but his pilot radioed to tell him that the clouds were a good sign for they would provide good cover for the attack. Motoko remembered hugging Nomuro before he boarded and told him to be brave because his country and Emperor depended upon him. Nomuro just nodded and watched his last friend strapped and sealed into the cockpit. His carrier plane was a A6M Zero-sen; and as it lifted to join the ones already in the air, Motoko saluted to his young friend below. Motoko"s rage settled into a calm resignation of what needed to be done, and he was glad to be a part of it. The fire bombings had killed his parents and sister and with his brother now gone, life to him didn't really matter. What was important was to die while taking as many of the enemy with him. Destroy their lives as they had his. Due to so many earlier losses, the Japanese decided to change their tactics. While carriers were still the main targets, they would now attack isolated support ships on the perimeter, as this would reduce incoming fire power and increase their chances of a kill. They needed more confirmed sinkings, regardless of the size of the vessel, in order to keep up the morale of those yet to fly.

At 1310, they spotted the US Navy 2,200-ton destroyer, "Manner L. Abele," in full steam attempting to rejoin the rest of its convoy. Since it was isolated from the rest of the pack and the carriers and their heavy fighter protection, the "Abele" sailed isolated and vulnerable.

Motoko heard the pilot above him radio the rest of the force informing them that he would be the first to go in. Motoko knew it would be only minutes before he faced the greatest challenge of his short life. He kept his mind focused on the memory of the charred bodies of his parents and sisters to keep his anger flowing and extinguishing the fear and self-doubts of his mortality. Motoko moved the stick and pedals to check the function of the rudder, elevators and ailerons and noted all were functioning smoothly. He reviewed his altimeter which showed a steady 27,210 feet, and the speedometer showing an increasing air speed now at 520 mph. As the engines of the bomber increased in power he felt his Ohka begin to buffet severely. He hung on tight to the stick and knew this increase in speed signaled his drop was coming soon. Due to the low level clouds, he could not see any target as yet. Then through a small cloud break, he spotted black smoke from the stacks of the destroyer. His excitement grew, for as yet there was no anti-aircraft fire nor any fighters in sight, as they closed in on their kill.

USN radar man Culbert, aboard the "Abele", spotted a several incoming blips on his screen, and immediately reported to the bridge,

"Possible enemy aircraft spotted bearing 260 degrees, 20,000 feet, range 30 miles."

Lieutenant Commander Parker immediately sounded the call to battle stations, and his men scrambled to man their guns.

"Target in sight?", called Motoko's pilot.

"Target spotted, ready for release", Motoko said.

"Good" the pilot replied. "After we release you, glide through that cloud on the right for cover. When in it, break hard left and angle your dive at 40 degrees after you emerge. Then you ignite your rockets and hold your angle of incidence steady. Lower it only when you are within sight of the bridge, and then head directly for it. Steer directly for the bridge, that's where their officers are. Go get them. Those behind you will follow you up on your kill. Be proud that you are to lead the attack. We all wish you a good kill, and we'll all meet again at the Yasakuni shrine."

With these words, Motoko felt a sudden weightlessness as the Ohka was released. His stick wobbled furiously until he steadied it with a harder grip. The training simulator was not at all like this. This felt very nose heavy and much more difficult to control. Still, as commanded, he maneuvered and entered the thick white covering veil of the cloud.

Even before the "Abele" was able to visualize any target, on board guns fired into the coordinates given by the radar. For a brief moment they saw a shadow within the cloud and directed their fire toward it.

Motoko's Ohka bucked as the first of the shells tore into it. As he emerged from the clouds he could see his target in the closing distance. He then flipped the toggle switches as each rocket ignited in unison, and pushed the stick forward into his dive. With the increasing surge of speed, he gained more control. He was now gliding into a hail of incendiary tracers as pieces of the Ohka began to spark and splinter off to the rear. He was close enough to see sailors scatter and hit the deck. Only the gunners kept up their relentless strafing, but without much effect since his angle was straight on and presented very little target. He noticed that his fuel was nearly spent so he angled the nose down a little to give him greater glide speed, and more range should his rockets flame out. His excitement grew as he knew he was so close that nothing could stop him. The thought of his death, and how it would feel, could not over shadow the sight of those sailors lying flat on the decks and the officers scattering on the bridge. In his last seconds of life he thought of his family, and dedicated this final act of retribution to them. Now trailing a banner of flame from his left wing and angling left, the Ohka crossed over the railing and crashed through the glass and metal bridge igniting the 2,600 pounds of tri-nitroaminol and throwing the greater part of the bridge some two hundred feet into the air. It burned alive 79 American sailors, in the same way his parents and sisters had died in the night bombings. He would never know that his Ohka was the first to assist in the sinking of an American ship, and the first Ohka ever seen in action by US Naval forces.

As fire hoses were directed toward the deck, the sailors noticed the blackened remains of the pilot among the smoldering wreckage. His skeletal face still held the grimace of hate he held upon impact. His teeth bared and grinning through a lipless mouth. His eyes had melted, yet some of his uniform still remained. A portion of his blackened leg lay some 50 feet away, and one sailor took it to central stores where the bone would be carved into souvenirs of rings, necklaces and earrings for their loved ones at home as a testament of their survival. This was to become a common practice among those ships that survived Kamikaze hits. But the "Abele" was not to be among those as it began to sink, listing on its side. Ignoring this, those nearest the corpse were preoccupied with casting dice to see who would be lucky enough to receive the buttons off his blackened tunic. Buttons, though burnished by the heat, still showing the stamped insignia of a cherry blossom with its three petals.

Nomuro's Fate is Sealed

Later, back in the commander's office, they were discussing the problem with this young kid Nomuro. The great General Hironoka presided over a special meeting of the group flight leaders. After hearing about the problems Nomuro encountered during his training by Captain Uma, The General merely raised his eyebrows and leaned forward clasping his hands with a determined look and commanded,

"He will be allowed to have a mission, and I want that mission no later than tomorrow. Is that clear? It is only fair that we do this in order to allow him a means to honor his father and ancestors."

"But what if he loses control and fails to hit his target because he cannot contain his stomach, or passes out as he has during his training," Captain Uma responded.

"Then I suggest we give him an easy target and have the bomber release him directly over the target so all he will have to do is push the stick forward. In fact this is to be his target." Hironoka rolled out a map and photos of a ship that made them all murmur and look at each other. "As I said gentlemen, an easy target. One leaving Okinawa without escort or fighter cover."

"With all due respects General," Uma interrupted, "if he's unconscious, then I doubt we could trust him to even do that much."

"Then I say we don't even allow him that option. His Ohka could be rigged so it dives immediately after release, taking the possibility of any control out of his hands entirely. Captain, can I make myself any clearer?"

"Then why bother using him at all? Why not just drop the Ohka without a pilot?"

"Well let's just say that it's vital to the war effort to have him die as a hero and thereby insure his place on the Thousand Stitch Belt, marking him as the last of a proud line that dates back to over 600 years. We need a willing or, if necessary, an unwilling sacrifice on the part of this warrior to prove to others how even a thirteen year old was willing to die for our country and our Emperor. His death and funeral will serve as an inspiration to all of our youth to do the same. We will give him a funeral of national prominence, as a true hero, to encourage not only the males of our land, but also all the females, in fact every young girl and boy, who may someday have to defend our homeland on its shores and in its cities, if an invasion of our mainland should occur. Now gentleman, we've all had to make sacrifices to prevent this, and now it is Tanoka's son who is to serve us by his death tomorrow. Any other remarks or can we begin?"

"As you command. I will call out attack Squadron "C" early next morning and I will personally fly Nomuro and his Ohka to his rightful eternal place on the Thousand Stitch Belt. Of this you can be assured."

"Well put Captain. And now I toast you and all who accompany you on your mission for a successful flight, and the hope of a safe return, but without the Ohka in your planes belly, or you will take the Seppuku blade in yours. Understand?" Captain Uma grimly just nodded in agreement.

Hironoka smiled, then stood and shouted Bonsai!" and toasted the men who repeated the shout as they all drained the ritual Saki down their throats.

BOMBER PILOT BRIEFING

The occupants of barracks "C" were roused from their sleep by the headmaster. It was only 3am, and they all knew what this meant, the final briefing before takeoff. Nomuro awoke with the grim realization that last night was the last sleep he would ever awake from again. The war and this madness had not ended in time as he had hoped, and now his destiny was certain.

Neither tears nor sickness would relieve him of his final obligation, so he arose and dressed with a calm resolve, distracting the phantoms of fear and the preview of what death would be like hitting a deck at 900 KPH. What final thoughts would he feel, sense and hear as the Ohka descended closer and closer until impact. Returning to base not an option, as some piloting the Zero's had done, under the pretense that no targets had been sighted. This was already destined to be a one way trip since the enemy had been sighted, and was steaming with a full naval flotilla including troop carriers toward Okinawa. Even if he decided to choose life with his mother and friends instead of the unknowns of death, once dropped there would be no way to pilot it away to some isolated island, far from this war to await its end. The rocket fuel would only last seconds and be just enough to minimize the short time needed to reach impact speed. How sad, that at only thirteen, he had no more time, when others his age had a whole lifetime ahead to look forward to. "I must be brave", he thought to himself, "for my country, my father's and Schima's memory, and for my right to be immortalized forever on the Thousand Stitch Belt. After those of "C" squadron had assembled in the pre-dawn chill of the far west hanger, they took their seats and a pilot dressed in fatigues, skull cap, and headband embroidered with the emblem of the Rising Sun approached the lectern. He was introduced as Captain Uma, leader of the Ohka bomber carriers. He walked with a limp on boots that even a recent shine could not cover their age, and his brown leather flight jacket looked as old and lined as his face. He had wide bulging eyes and an overbite that set his chin in a permanent scowl, and even gave him a comical look.

"Spirit Warriors", he said, "your hour has come. Enemy targets have just been sighted and we will take you to your target. We will commence coordinated take-offs in just four hours beginning at 0700 hours and expect all thirteen bombers to be aloft no later than 0715 hours. We expect to intercept the enemy ships, mainly cruisers and destroyers, by 0745. Good news for us is that our spotters have sighted our main prize, their carrier the "Bunker Hill".

By 0800 hours the release over targets will begin. I will follow the others and lead the last Ohka to target no later than 0815 hours. By that time your brave spirits will all meet at the Yasukuni Shrine. We no longer have the advantage of fighter escort, so we go in alone. We will maneuver and approach our targets with the sun to our backs, and will have the added benefit of low hanging cloud coverage. We hope the concealment will confuse them; and by the time your Ohka's have broken through, it will be too late for them to fire at you and thereby ignite your tri-nitroaminol before impact."

"We will be detected well in advance by their radar, and heavy anti-aircraft fire is to be expected. The early Ohka raids forced a change in their tactics. Command tells us that they now fire with more concentrated, but less accurate fire. Sometimes they will even fire only in the general area of a suspected attack showing on and off their radar screens. While such fire stopped the first valiant Ohka raid last March 21st, we feel that the added concealment of cloud coverage will allow us the victory our homeland needs.

They have also resorted to exploding shells around their vessels to create water spouts in order to hide their outlines, but you will strike them from above where they will least expect it. We are told that their carriers no longer carry dive bombers, but more Hellcat fighters used as interceptors. In fact, they now have fighters continually in the air above their ships for protective cover. But don't worry for we will have unarmed bombers preceding us to act as decoys, to draw them away from us while we slip through their defenses. But please rest assured that your attack may not be easy nor without incident. You always face the possibility of a fighter attack. If it occurs, there is nothing for you to do but wait and be patient. Your bomber pilots will return fire, but not engage. They will go into a series of evasive maneuvers that may feel unnerving, but will eventually bring you in proximity of your target."

"Your pilot will be in constant radio contact with you, and you him. After drop, they will immediately return, but without you of course," he said with a wide toothy grin met with only a few forced laughs, "for another pick-up and return to your drop zone. That means your squadron will be sent into maybe three separate strikes, so be patient if you're not in the first wave. The enemy has already gained a foothold on our island of Okinawa, and we must destroy their ships and isolate their ground forces to allow our troops time to annihilate the invaders. We will be another type of "divine wind", but one, as in centuries ago, will also stop these invaders."

"Incidentally, the enemy has renamed our proud Ohka as Baku, which translates as "fool" which they think we are to make this sacrifice. It was reported that the American Admirals Nimitz and Halsey so fear the news of our Ohka's, that they, along with the British, have declared a complete news blackout in order to prevent panic among their troops. Even by their most modest estimates, they still have to admit that one in four of our planes are striking their ships, and one in thirty-three of those attacks are sinking a ship. And to think, they call us the fools?" he laughed. "We are showing them, and will continue to show them who the real fools are, especially when we jam today's Ohka's down their throats."

His fiery diatribe trailed as he calmly said, "There is no need to return to your bunks. You just have time enough to finish your letters, eat, pray and prepare. All must be on the airfield by 0630 hours for your bomber assignments and embankments. As Samurai of the new order, wear your Hachimaki headbands with pride. At 0600 we will assemble for our ritual farewell of tai-I seki in the same manner as Samurai of old. Each of you will be given your mizu (water and Saki) by our venerable Commander, General Onishi himself. Any questions?"

There were none. Just a lot of blanched expressionless faces, far too young for this or any war.

"Then let us now stand and sing the song of the Cherry Blossom Squad and make it loud enough for those who will oppose us this day to hear."

Nomuro rose, his body tired and stomach queasy, as hesitantly joined in:

LAST LAP

"We are born aloft as Samurai of the skies.
Our eyes ever-searching for the signs of battle,
See how our outstretched arms carry us forward
Like divine wings.
We are comrades of the Sacred Land of the Rising Sun!
Enemy ships are sounded, loud alerts are sounded.
Let us drive them beneath the waves!

Men of the Cherry Blossom Squadrons – rally to the charge!
As we look down at our base spread below us,
Through the flow of tears that fills up our hearts,
We can see a fading glimpse of hands waving farewell!
Now is the time for our final, plunging blow.
We're ready to spill our blood, oh so red.
See how we dive toward the ships in the Seas of the South!
The cool waves will console our departed spirits
And someday we'll be reborn as cherry blossoms
In the garden of the Yasunkuni-jinja."

Nomuro thought of the beautiful cherry blossom trees in his family's garden, each child having his own special tree assigned by his mother, Midori. Under each of theirs, she would read to them, teach, and pray with them. Not even the three loud shouts of "Banzai" could quell the fear and the foreboding Nomuro felt at this hour. Strange how he longed just for his mother to be here to accompany him to his Ohka and assist him into the cockpit, just to be able to see her one more time.

He never once thought of his father, his Emperor, nor of any of the spirits of his brave ancestors, immortalized on the Thousand Stitch Belt. He knew that if she assisted him into his Ohka, then he was surely doing the right thing for his mother would never lead him into wrong. But mother Midori was not here and was not going to come to him again to hold him and give words of reassurance, as she often did in the middle of those nights when he felt fear and longing for his father and brother at war. He was going to die and he would be facing it all alone. At least both his father and brother had other soldiers with them, but once dropped, he would have to face both his demons and dread in total solitude. He hoped it would be quick and that he would not have to suffer much from any early enemy hits that might shatter his legs.

The Demon Calls

A black demon crept into the chasm of his mind, threatening and coming ever closer. In its jaw a human infant bitten through. It opened it bloody maw and the infant fell and tumbled in separate pieces into a black pit below. The beast then snarled and through a fetid breath and gnarled teeth emitted a baleful howl.

Nomuro bolted from his restless sleep and into the howl of the duty alarm. He rubbed his face trying to erase the memory of his dream. He returned to this time and place and realized that his nightmare was never going away. The nightmare of his certain death, this day now heralded by the noisome call to arms. The speakers shouted to get ready for flight in one hour. The barrack was a flurry of youths running about to dress and prepare. Some had already started writing their farewell letters, others were quickly dressing in their flight suits, and a few were even praying to the Gods they would see on this day.

Nomuro watching all of this frantic activity through glazed eyes and pressing need to urinate, stumbled into the bathroom. Two of his roommates were vomiting into the toilets, but none this day saw any need to crowd the sinks to shave or bathe. Nomuro relieved himself into one of the sinks and thought, "when will I do this simple act for the last time? What If I need to go after I've been strapped in or in fight? This seemingly simple everyday act that he had always taken for granted now had taken on critical importance and added to his rising anxiety.

How he now regretted volunteering for this death mission in his typical childlike show of bravado. He did it more to impress his friends, rather than in any real commitment or willingness to die, nor even any expectation that it ever would happen. After all, wasn't he the son of a national hero? Surely his life was more important than others; and besides he knew he was too young to actually learn to fly a plane, so maybe he would be assigned assist duties like fueling and maintenance. But he never could have conceived of anything like the Ohka, nothing more than a death coffin for the young. When he realized that there could be no turning back the clock, nor any way to change the outcome of his choices, he cried in fear and regret. Not until finally accepting the outcome of his actions, did he leave the bathroom and walked to his bureau to dress.

He ignored the call to breakfast for he had no appetite, and was afraid of embarrassing himself by vomiting in the cockpit as he had done many times in training. He took a parchment of rice paper, and with a sigh, finalized his last letter to his mother. He filtered each phrase to insure there would be no indication of his cowardice this hour, nor reveal any of the regret or dread he now felt filling his mind, spirit and soul. He carefully folded it, and then sealed it in wax with the imprint of the Cherry Blossom Corp.

He left the barracks for the last time after taking a few of the photos his mother had given him of the family he had been a part of and now longed for more than ever. He shoved them inside his jacket. The morning air was crisp and cool and he sucked it in deeply joining the others coming from the breakfast hall on their way to the line assembly. Strangely he thought he saw General Hironaka in the distance but was not sure.

Hironaka strode to the maintenance hangar where today's Ohka's were being tested for readiness. He walked over to the one numbered 19 and approached Flight Commander Uma.

"I assume all is taken care of?"

"Yes General it is," Uma answered. "His control elevators and rudders are welded in place. Once dropped, he will not be able to alter or change his dive position."

"Why not the ailerons also?"

Those are controlled by the foot pedals and will have no effect on his dive. If he tries to use them, it will only place him in a spin, but having no effect upon his vertical position or dive angle and he will impact all the same, spinning or not."

"I see. And I assume you will be carrying him in the plane that you pilot."

"As we agreed, and it will be my honor to fulfill your wishes as you command."

"And the target? Do you have accurate bearings on the target? Only that one will do and none other."

"Yes, we have excellent co-ordinates and have amphibious planes tailing it now to update its position to me as we approach. The rest of the squadron will head to our left and draw off any fighters that may not have followed our earlier decoy planes, and they will engage the carrier. Since our target has little armament, we should have no trouble in our approach. That ship is doomed and so is your Nomuro"

"How come you insisted on no fighter escort?"

"My experience has been that escorts seem to create more signals on their radar and only serve to invite their interceptors. Plus with the quality of the junior pilots we have in our Zero's today, we can't depend upon them for any real protection anyway. It is safer for me to go in alone. Drop my bomb and head home."

"Very good. I'll wait for your radio signal immediately after drop and your news of a confirmed hit with Ohka number 19, I believe?"

"Yes, he will be in number 19, the one we've specially modified just for him."

"Excellent, I can hardly wait for your word."

"You'll get more than my word, but something even more useful to you, a complete camera film of the entire incident to use in your national memorial funeral and for recruiting purposes."

"Well done Captain, you've covered it all and are to be commended. Have a safe trip. Bring them all home except the one who will now serve our cause in more ways than he could ever expect."

Nomuro's flight into oblivion

As each of their names was called, the Ohka pilots took positions behind their designated bomber carriers. Nomuro's Ohku, number 19, was now just being wheeled out and getting ready to be suspended in the open Bombay of the dull grey G4M. The Ohka's powder blue, toy like appearance, betrayed its deadly intent.

Captain Uma strode to his plane as number 19 was being lifted up into the open Bombay. He walked over to Nomuro and, putting a hand on his shoulder, he reassured him."

"How proud you must be at this your hour of triumph knowing that your father and brother are looking down upon you, and so grateful for your having the same courage as they. Now it's time to climb on board. Men prepare our little pilot for his flight."

"Captain sir, I have to pee." Quivered Nomuro.

Uma and the crew all laughed out loud. Patting him on the back, he told him to go behind the cherry blossom tree next to the runway, but also to hurry. When he returned, Nomuro took one last look around to see if his mother had come and then, with a shaken sadness, allowed them to lift him into the cockpit and strap him into place. Uma did not board until he saw the cockpit pulled close and welded into place. He nodded toward the hanger to Hironaka who was standing there and nodding back his approval. Hironaka was also pleased to see the boarding of a cameraman, three assistants and a lot of equipment. He could hardly wait to receive and release this newsreel to the public. He crushed out his cigarette and strode to the tower to watch the take offs.

After the rest of the squadron was airborne, Uma pushed forward the throttle and the bomber lurched forward throwing Nomuro back against his seat. The Ohka bounced over ruts and holes as it rolled down the runway. Nomuro held onto the sides of his seat and prayed the flight would be smoother than what he was now feeling. He felt the familiar rise of gastric fluid in his throat even with nothing in his stomach. The bomber's speed picked up and gradually lifted from the field. Nomuro felt its slight drop and the impact of the wheels lifting into its fuselage. As the plane hit some turbulence in its climb, Nomuro looked behind for one last look at the land and people he loved. He even waved a goodbye to his mother who might have arrived late and may be waving somewhere below. He coughed up the sour fluid that now burned his throat. How he wished he had requested a canteen of water to carry with him to quell this awful burn.

All he now saw nothing but ocean far below. Only an occasional wisp of a cloud vapor partially obscured the clear sea reflecting the bright late morning sun back into his eyes. In front he saw the faint vapor trails of the bombers leading the task force, but not the planes themselves. Except for the deafening roar of the engines, the silence was disturbing especially after so many hours in close contact with the other recruits during their time of training. He desperately needed some human contact as well as some urinary relief, which he feared might never happen. Unable to contain it any longer he pressed the intercom and called to Uma,

"Sir, are you there?"

"What is it?", Uma answered.

"Sir, I need to go."

"Go where?", Uma laughed.

"Sir, I need to pee bad, real bad."

"Just try to hold it, we are almost near target."

"Sir, I need to go right now."

"Well you'll just have to hold it, or go in your pants. No one will know or care." Nomuro heard the co-pilot laughing in the background. "Just concentrate on your controls and look around to take your mind off of it. You know we can't make a stop for you."

"Okay, I'll try."

"Good lad, it won't be much longer."

Uma radioed and listened to the new co-ordinates given by the amphibious plane tracking their target and then banked the bomber hard left in pursuit of the ship. Nomuro felt the G forces of the hard bank, and was pressed hard to the right of his seat. In front were gone the vapor trails that once were ahead, instead they were to his far right. Wondering why they were leaving the rest of the squadron, he radioed Uma,

"Sir why aren't we following the rest of the squadron?"

"Because our target is straight ahead. Just keep quiet and trust us. You'll get your turn to fly soon enough. We are lucky to have a single target and since we have no escorts, the incoming flak should be light. Consider yourself lucky to have a target that won't kill you ahead of time. Your other friends won't be so lucky. Just sit tight and hang on, Okay?"

"How much longer do you think it will be?"

"We already have a visual straight ahead. You'll be over target in less than five."

Now since they had spotted a target, Nomuro knew his fate was sealed. There would be no excuse to turn around as others had when no target was located. He had just about 5 more minutes to live. His breathing increased and he felt unable to get enough air through his mask, so he tore it off. He sucked in heavily the thin air and he could no longer control his hysterical reaction, as his breaths began to cloud his cockpit. He was getting too light headed to think, so he jammed the mask back over his face and sucked deeply until his head cleared. Training was nothing like this. He cried for his mother to somehow rescue him from this untimely end. Perhaps she would intercede in time, and the plane would be ordered back. He then lost all control and urinated in his pants.

"We are nearly over target. Nomuro get ready."

Instinctively Normuro grabbed the stick, and when he tried to test the controls, the stick was locked in place and only the ailerons at his feet showed any movement.

"Sir, my controls are not working," hoping for a reprieve due to system failure.

Uma looked at his co-pilot and smiled speaking into the intercom.

"That's to be expected pre-drop. They will work after you're dropped and gain more air speed. Just keep calm you're doing fine."

Nomuro had never been told of this in training, in fact he was told just the opposite, all Ohka pilots were to insure that every control of the stick was operational just prior to drop. He didn't have time to relate this to the pilot as Uma cut in.

"Fifteen seconds to drop. They'll be no glide to target needed nor firing of you rockets, just stick down, and be a brave warrior so we'll see you at Yasukuni."

Nomuro had no time to see the target as he felt the sudden drop and then his vision went from sky to sea in the predicted fast dive as the nose dipped down and the Ohka dove to the target below. Barely able to take a breath from the increasing speed of the fall, he sighted the lone ship below growing larger in his bomb sight. He was pressed back hard into his seat and screamed at the shear sensation of falling as he plummeted directly down toward the vessel. Suddenly he realized why this vessel had not fired back when he saw the same symbol on her decks that he had seen so many times on his mother's uniform, that of a red cross.

These were the wounded and maimed Americans of the Okinawa campaign. These were people no different than those his mother had worked all of her life to help. He suddenly became determined that he was not going to make any more victims in this war. He pulled and pulled hard on the stick to avert the ship, but to no avail. In desperation he pushed the ailerons, but this only sent him into a corkscrew spin even faster down toward his target.

He was dizzy, choking, and beginning to black out as he saw the red cross growing in size and little figures scattering on the deck. Seconds before impact, he cried not to his Gods, ancestors, Emperor or father, but only to his mother the words, "Forgive me" as Ohka #19 crashed through the deck, crushing out his life when his straps ruptured flinging him against and then through the glass cockpit, but not exploding until crashing through three decks below into the bowels of the ship.

Hamano, Hironoka's son, rescued from the Yamato, and posing as a Chinese prisoner of war was aboard the "USS Comfort" hospital ship that morning. He was assisting with the injured and changing IV bottles, when suddenly he heard the ships terrible shrill siren call to arms. Seconds later he heard the crash through the upper decks, and then saw the blue bomb tearing down through the ceiling in a cloud of debris and soot. In the few seconds before explosion, he had just enough time to recognize the tiny shattered pilot hanging from the cockpit by his straps as Nomuro, the friend of his youth.

Uma, on returning to Kyushu, radioed Hironoka, "Target hit, you'll have your films in less than an hour."

Hironoka didn't respond, but just smiled, not realizing he had just unknowingly engineered the death of his own son.

UNDER THE CHERRY BLOSSOM TREE

On that same morning, Midori knelt under the cherry blossom tree planted for Nomuro. She carefully opened the last letter from her son. With tear filled eyes she read the his final testimony:

"My dearest mother: This is my last letter to you for I shall soon join my honorable father and brother, and all of those of our proud line that came before me, in this my final hour.

I want to thank you for all of the kindness you've shown me in our brief years together. I will carry those memories of us on this my final day. I am no longer your little boy, but now a man and eager to fulfill my destiny to die as a hero for our Emperor and land. I hope that this final act of bravery will, in some small way, pay you for all of the love and devotion you've given me. Please don't cry for me for I will die bravely and smiling. I attack in two hours, and I shall soon fall like a blossom from the radiant cherry tree where you once read to me, and where we played under. As I will soon be going to the land of our ancestors, please pay tribute to my memory and add my name to the Thousand Stitch Belt."

  Your very grateful son,

Love in all eternity

Nomuro

 As she read these last lines, a single blossom left the tree, and tumbling in the breeze, fell gently into her lap.

UNIT 731
Home from Manchuria

The train hissed steam and bellowed black smoke from its chimney as it rounded the final turn, entering the glass covered station in Kyusko. It braked and squealed to a stop with a final sigh of steam from oiled drivers. Frantic activity ensued as conductors lowered steps and passengers began to disembark. Midori looked down at the long line of passenger cars for her son Masako, who was coming home on leave from a prisoner hospital and biological water treatment center in Pingfan, Manchuria. He was flown to Tokyo and then took the long train ride to his home in Kyusho.

Masako, her oldest and last surviving son, served as a student at the Army Medical College in Tokyo where he was training to be a physician. He had been ordered to an isolated area of China in Manchuria, under the false pretense of assisting prisoners infected with various diseases. These prisoners were mostly Chinese, but also included Australian, British and American survivors from the Bataan Death March, as it was known after the fall of the Philippines. Even ordinary Chinese civilians, including woman and their children, accused of subversive actions, were sent there for special treatment.

Midori looked down the long line of passenger cars and walked down the platform, buffeted by people disembarking and going in the opposite direction. Eventually, in the distance she saw her son, walking toward her in full uniform and carrying a black duffel bag over his shoulder. When he got closer, she could hardly recognize him. His tall stature was slightly bent and his face looked haggard, eyes deep set with dark ageing rings and much older than his 20 years. She tried to hide her shock and ran up and hugged him.

"Mother, I am so glad to be home."

"It is so good to see you my son." She said as they walked arm in arm down the platform. "How long do you have?"

"Just two weeks and then I'm supposed to go back." The words "supposed to" sounded strange to her.

"Is there a chance you won't have to return and stay here with me?"

"I'm not sure yet, but let's not worry about it. Let's just enjoy the time we now have together."

"Have they been feeding you enough? You look so thin and frail."

"Yes, they do, but it's just that I'm kept so busy that sometimes I just have no time and, other times I'm just not hungry."

"When we get home you must tell me all about what you do. Helping all those poor sick prisoners, you make me very proud and I want to hear all about it. It will be nice to know there is still some good going on in this world." Masako said nothing, but kept his eyes straight ahead and kept walking.

Revelation in the Garden

Midori prepared a large meal of rice, fish and sautéed vegetables, but Masako just barely picked at it. He made the excuse that he had just eaten on the train. He then asked if they could adjourn to the garden and sit under his cherry blossom tree. She brewed tea and went to get him. He was standing near the altar looking at his father's sword, the photos of him, his brothers, Eiko and, of course, the Thousand Stitch Belt. She walked up next to him and said, "Someday your name will be on the belt also, right next to Nomuro's" she said choking on her dead son's name, not revealing her true intent to destroy the belt.

"Mother, no matter what happens to me, I don't ever want my name on that belt. I never want to be associated with centuries of killers. Let it end with Nomuro, who had no choice. I refuse to die for the Emperor, or for anyone for that matter. How dare anyone take glory in killing others? I read of an American poet, Longfellow, who accurately said that the paths of glory lead only to the grave. How I would like to forever unravel the last three names on that belt, Nomuro's, Schima's and that of my father, if it would bring them back to us, even for a day."

"So would I," as tears began to fill his mother's eyes. "Come

Masako, I've made tea, let's go into the garden and talk under your tree just like we did when you all belonged to just me and not the world." Together they headed out into the garden.

"I see the tree is still strong, but without any blossoms of beauty," Masako noted, thinking of how much it represented himself.

"Yes, the last of the blossoms fell just weeks after the news of Nomuro."

"What a terrible waste of such a young life. He wished only to emulate his father and brother, just so his name could be added to the belt, and for what purpose? Would he think it such an honor today if given the opportunity for life over immortal glory? What good is glory without life? Generals sons fared no better. Did you hear Yuka?"

"No, Hironoka and I had some words a week ago, and we haven't spoken since. Someday he'll come for the Thousand Stitch Belt and your father's sword, to use it as a recruiting tool to lead other youths to their deaths."

"Then mother, you must destroy it now. Let it end with Nomuro."

"I cannot since to do so would put you and I in grave danger. But what of Yuka?"

"He volunteered for the torpedo boats and according to a letter from his brother Schino, died in the harbor fighting during the invasion of Okinawa."

"So terribly young, and as I remember a very stubborn birth. Their mother never survived, and I always felt Hironoka held me responsible. Any news of Hamano?"

"No, the last letter I received from him was that he was a junior officer aboard the Yamato enroute to Okinawa."

"Yes, his father told me that."

"Well, the news was that the Yamato was torpedoed and sunk. I've never heard of his outcome. He is listed as missing in action, but I do suspect the worse."

"I delivered all three of those boys. What a terrible, terrible waste. And you say you converse with Shino? What of him?"

"He may survive until the end of this war, since he is part of a submarine maintenance crew. Far enough from the combat zones."

"His wife will be thankful for that."

"Does she still run the orphanage and heal the wounded children?"

"Oh yes, she is very dedicated to helping our young people, but you are even more honored, to think you help the enemies wounded."

He grabbed her by the shoulders and looked her straight in the eyes, "Mother, I had hoped to spare you what I am about to tell you, but it's time you learned of what we really do at Pingfan."

The Dreadful Secret of Pingfan

Tea wasn't strong enough for what Masako needed to relate, so his mother brought him a bottle of Saki. He drained two glasses very quickly and then began to speak.

"Pingfan is located four kilometers south of Harbin in Manchuria. Approximately 3,000 of us conscripted from the ranks of the Army and the medical schools are housed there. What goes on there is so secretive that aircraft are forbidden to fly over the site. The building's extensive facilities are hidden behind a high wall, moat and high voltage wires. Within those confines is a railway siding, an incinerator, an animal house, an insectarium, administration building and housing. At its center is the forbidden square shaped building known as Ro Block. Within its center are two other buildings, blocks 7 reserved for men and block 8 for women and children. Prisoners are led through a dark tunnel. For them this is the start of a journey of no return, just of agony and death. This is where I work.

I am part of a Unit called 731 to hide its real nature. We are under its commander, General Shiro Ishii, and I work directly for the Unit's pathologist, Colonel Ishikawa, as part of the Center for Bacterial Production and Disease Research."

"Production? Whatever do you mean my son?"

"Yes mother, Pingfan is not a prisoner rehabilitation center, but a human experimentation center."

"You can't truly mean that! How do you mean experimentation center?"

"We do experimentation in three areas: toxic gases such as hydrogen cyanide and mustard gas, frostbite, and disease vectors. I am part of the latter. My Unit is housed in the dreaded Ro Blocks 7 and 8, from which there is no return of prisoners condemned to us. The Kenpeitai, secret police, supply us with all of the humans we need to test our pathogens. They even refer to those so condemned as Maruta, or just logs of wood for experimentation, to further dehumanize them. Maruta's are used up at a rate of 2-3 per day. We systematically inject, or expose them to *thyphoid, anthrax, cholera, rickettsia*, and *clostridia*, which produces gas gangrene and results in multiple amputations, often on the same person. But my specialty is *Pasteurella pestis*. Do you know what that is mother?"

Shocked and unable to speak she just shook her head. "Plague mother, Bubonic plague! The pestilence of the dark ages, and we are trying to produce it again, and in even greater numbers. Producing even stronger strains and infecting our Maruta just to measure the outcome. Are you still proud of your oldest son, mother." He quaffed off another glass of Saki.

"But why kill humans in such a terrible manner? For what purpose is...."

"Just for the sake of providing our Emperor another means of killing the enemy, that of germ warfare. Allow me to present how it's done. In our animal quarters, we infect rats with the plague germ. Then we allow hundreds of fleas of the human

variety, *Pulex irritans*, to feed on the rats. One flea will ingest nearly 5,000 organisms at just one feeding from an infected rat. Its blood will contain 100 million organisms per milliliter. Once ingested, the bacteria multiply in the flea's digestive tract. A few days after it has fed on infected blood, the microorganisms rise up and clog the throat and esophagus which becomes distended. It is at this stage that the flea becomes infective with its bite. The elastic recoil of the walls of both its pharynx and gullet, when the flea stops sucking blood from its victim, regurgitates back into the wound as many as 10 to 24 thousand organisms at one bite."

"We discovered that an infective flea could live and carry its deadly bite for up to one month or longer and that a single bite was enough to cause a deadly infection. An additional plus was that this strain of human flea, was sturdy enough to resist air drag if released from a low flying plane and infect our enemy. Mother would you care to guess how many Maruta it took for us to find this out?"

Midori just shook her head in despair, and wondered to what depths could human depravity sink.

After another shot of Saki, he continued, "Have you ever witnessed the effects of bubonic plague on a person?"

"No," she forced.

"Bubonic plague is characterized by a swelling of the lymph nodes in the armpit and the groin. After 2 to 3 days they invade the lungs. The onset is abrupt, with chills, high fever and extreme weakness, but the curse is different in different people. In some the eyes become red and the head congested and their tongues coated. Some become bloated, and some emaciated, others were blistered and had rotting limbs with bones protruding through the openings. All become delirious, writhing

in agony and in pain. And, of course, all showing some degree of skin blackened by necrosis, hence the medieval term, '*black plague*.'

Forgive me mother for what I am about to relate, but I was ordered to infect a Chinese girl of nineteen with a jar of fleas held over her arm, then a day later, drew her blood at timed intervals afterwards, and injected it into the veins of girls ranging from 14 to 20. Thus I was able to prove that the transmission route didn't have to be a flea, and that a person's blood was infective within less than a half hour after a bite. I carefully recorded the predicted demise of all 15 subjects, some lasting a week, while I prayed for it to end sooner. I wasn't that lucky, and neither were they. For this practically obvious discovery, I was awarded these two weeks of furlough to come home. So due to the death of 15 innocent girls, I get to come home and celebrate. So let's celebrate," he said downing another shot of Saki.

Midori just leaned her head forward into her lap and covered her ears. "Who were these monsters, what type of dreadful barbarian could order this."

"No not monsters mother, but surgeons, pathologists, medical students and noted scientists, some visiting and some on loan from some of our greatest universities."

"But why and how could they have been brought to these inhuman acts?"

"I think we have to accredit this to the philosophy of our leader, General Shiro Ishii, who welcomed all invited newcomers to Unit 731 with the following speech." Masakto pulled out of his pocket a worn sheet of paper. "He admonished us to read it daily if ever we should weaken or hesitate from our righteous duty. If I may read it to you, you may have your question answered." He unfolded the paper and began as Midori sat:

"Our God-given mission as doctors is to challenge all varieties of disease-causing micro-organisms; to block all roads of intrusion into the human body; to annihilate all foreign matter resident in our bodies; and to devise the most expeditious treatment possible. However, the research upon which we are now about to embark is the complete opposite of these principles, and may cause us some anguish as doctors. Nevertheless, I beseech you to pursue this research based on the double medical thrill; one, a scientist to exert effort to probing for the truth in natural science and research into, and discovery of, the unknown world, and two, as a military person, to successfully build a powerful military weapon against the enemy."

"Mother, I was very shocked after I arrived and found out about the human experimentation. Very few of those so called scientists and physicians had any sense of conscience. They treated the prisoners as animals. The prisoners were the enemy and would eventually be sentenced to death anyway. They rationalized that death was at least honorable if they contributed to the progress of medical science. They held weekly seminars on their findings and even published their results in our military science journals."

I became terrified at what I saw and was asked to do, but there was no way out. To request to leave was tantamount to treason, and I would be executed."

"Since it was December when I first arrived, and subfreezing cold, my first assignments were to assist with the gas gangrene and freezing experiments. Gas gangrene is caused by wound infection with the anaerobe *clostridia*. The purpose of the experiment was to see if it was possible to infect people with gas gangrene at temperatures 20 degrees below zero, in the hope of finding a biological weapon that could be used in the winter against the Chinese. I assisted in tying ten Chinese prisoners to stakes, in subzero weather, thirty feet from a shrapnel bomb that contained the *clostridia*. The prisoners heads and torsos were protected with metal shields and thick quilted blankets, but their legs and buttocks were left unprotected. The bomb was exploded and the shrapnel, bearing the germs, wounded all the prisoners in their legs and backsides. I kept track of the progress of the disease, and within 7 days, all died in severe agony."

"Some other field tests in the cold were done with flame throwers on Marutas, to test their effectiveness in extreme cold. This was wantonly referred for as wood cutting. I glad to say I was fortunate enough to be spared from seeing these atrocities first hand. I was not so fortunate with the freezing experiments."

"Experiments in freezing were done in the coldest months of the year, from November to February. The purpose was to determine the best temperature to use to relieve frostbite. The prisoners were taken out at night at about 11 O'clock and, some naked, and their arms or legs dipped in water, and then made to stand until their limbs were frozen solid, which was tested by striking them with a stick until the sound it made was like that of striking a board. I can still hear their screams in my dreams while they were made to endure the cold. After hours, they would be taken to a room and the effected limbs placed in water and the temperature gradually increased to test the best temperature for healing frostbite. Their recovery was not without consequence. Many ended up with rotting limbs, and skin blackened by necrosis. I remember some with black hands and no fingers, or fingers that were only bones without flesh. Limbs were amputated, not for humane reasons, but only to preserve their lives for further experiments."

"One of the most horrid experiments I was involved in was to test the survival of a human at 40-50 degrees below zero, temperatures not uncommon in a Manchurian winter. I led two naked Chinese prisoners in an enclosed yard, several of the researchers had gathered to witness this, and filmed the entire process until they died. I was forced to watch in order to toughen me up for the pathology work which was to come. They suffered such agonies that they dug their nails into each other's flesh, and screamed and screamed until the cold mercifully claimed them. It took over three hours for them to die. No one regarded the "logs" as human beings, just inanimate objects to be experimented on." "During the hot summers Marutas were mummified in dehydration experiments. They were sweated to death under the heat of hot electric fans, to test the human adaptation to heat under limitations of water or salt water ingestion. At their death most would weigh only one-fifth of their normal body weights. Others were slowly boiled alive to test the extremes of temperature on survival of the human body."

"Heard enough yet mother? Well you haven't heard the worse of what I had to participate in. Let me tell you of the pathology work. Many female Marutas died in our studies on syphilis and pregnancy. They were trying to solve the venereal disease epidemics, and their effect on infant births, raging through the Japanese female population caused by soldiers on leave from their military occupations. Pregnant Marutas were deliberately infected with the disease. On one occasion, right at birth, both a woman and her baby were dissected."

Midori looked startled. "Do you mean autopsied?"

"No mother, dissected. Dissected while both were alive and fully conscious. Vivisection was the greatest horror of what went on at Pingfan. Those responsible were two teams, one headed up by DR.

Kozo Okamoto, and the other, who I worked for as a pathology squad assistant, Dr. Tachiomaru Ishikawa. Yes, Unit 731, I am so ashamed to say, did surgery on living human beings. These vivisections were announced ahead of time to our country's best medical institutions, and some of the best medical visitors from all over our country, were brought by special invitation to observe them."

"My job was to prepare the infected victims of the Bubonic plague for autopsy and to take and preserve their organs. In the tiled operating room, I would first clean the victim front and back with a scrub brush, then dry them off. Dr. Ishikawa would then use a stethoscope to make sure the victim was still alive. Then without anesthesia, the victim was held by their arms and legs, while he would quickly and methodically cut the person open and remove the organs, despite the terrible screams and prayers for death. The organs were then handed to me to be put in the formalin jars for later study. I was told that anesthesia could interfere with the later study of these organs and that they needed to be taken alive before putrefaction had time to set in."

"With this particular mother and her infant, they were curious to see how far the disease had progressed at birth. I knew her from the time she was first infected. She was a beautiful girl of no more than 18. Immediately after she gave birth, they both were strapped to a gurney and wheeled into the autopsy room which was full of medical spectators. Both were held down and Ishikawa, began to cut into and across the abdomens to assess damage to the kidneys, and ovaries, and the spinal columns in both. As the incisions were made, blood spurted all over the ceiling. Her screams and wailings were unimaginable. No anesthesia at all."

Masako joined his mother, and both began to cry uncontrollably. "I prayed for a quick death for her, and soon she fell unconscious but her limbs continued to flex and jerk as her organs were systematically removed. They were handed to me to put into formalin jars and continued to twitch even in there.

They both sobbed and sobbed, and then Masako asked, "Mother what can I do to shake these images of horror from my head? How can I ever be forgiven for my participation in these atrocities? I did it out of sheer cowardice and only to protect my life. And now all I want to do is to end mine rather than go back."

Midori wiped her eyes on a napkin and said," No amount of repentance will ever free you from this past. The only thing you can do for these poor victims is to live, live for them. You must write down everything you've told me and pass it on to the Americans, after we are invaded and occupied. I am sure the perpetrators will try to destroy all of the things that transpired at Pingfan, as they did at Nanking. We owe it to the victims to stand as their witness, and to see justice prevail against your Unit 731. What you've told me goes beyond anything imaginable by the human mind. You must not think of suicide, for then they all would have died for no purpose at all. No, don't go back. You must go and hide. You will not be safe here, since Hironoka will be coming by soon. Just hide somewhere, but don't write since it may be traced. Hide until you can wait out the final days of this war. Now rest, and I will hold you under your tree as I did when you were little, and we shall both pray for the victims and perpetrators a well." They both slept, and by morning Masako was gone.

Only a few days later, Midori sat at her altar and wondered how long it would be before the Kenpeitai and Hironoka would come for the sword and the Thousand Stitch Belt. She vowed both would never fall into his hands. She knew her world was at an end, and so were all of the memories of her family.

A harsh knocking at the door jolted her, and thinking it was already the Kenpeitai, sneaked a look cautiously through the curtained window. She was relieved to see it was only the mailman, but why such an urgent knock? Once she received the letter, she knew what it was without even having to open it. It was the same type of letter she had received three times before from the Imperial Ministry of War. It read:

"We regret to inform you that your son, Masako Tanoka, has paid the highest price for our Emperor and our country. He unfortunately contracted Bubonic Plague as a result of his dedication in treating the prisoners of Pingfan and died with dignity and peace. I had the opportunity to attend to him in his final hours. We all hold him in the same pride and honor that I'm sure you do.
Regrets,
Colonel Tachiomaru Ishikawa
Surgical Pathologist
Pingfan Prisoner Treatment Center"

She knew his death was not an accident and tried to block the visions of how his end might have been. She would not disgrace his memory by stitching his name on the belt. It had ended with Nomuro. She took the sword and wrapped the belt around it, then folded both into an embroidered sheet. She placed the photos and letters of her children and Nakura, in a carrying case, and then left for the hospital to say farewell to Father Krozier.

HIROSHIMA

She arrived at the hospital, with her package and valise in hand and inquired as to the whereabouts of Father Krozier. She was directed to the burn ward, where she found him among his patients. He could tell she needed to see him and he told her to go to his office and he would join her as soon as possible.

When he arrived, he sat down beside her and inquired as to what was happening in her life these past few days since he had not seen her. Without a word, she handed him the letter about Masako's death. He became greatly grieved and said her son should be commended for such a brave action to help the sick. No, he hadn't ever heard of a Unit 731, but yes some of the Japanese physicians here visited a hospital in Pingfan to study more effective treatments against biological agents. He also had visited the site, but refused to stay when he learned of the atrocities occurring there. He thought for sure he would be killed because of what he learned, but escaped under the cover of darkness and flew back.

Midori recounted Masako's tales and Father Krozier grew pale over this travesty of the science of healing he had dedicated his entire life to. She handed him notes that she had taken listing everything that Masako had told her, including the names and dates. She said, "It is now up to you to see justice prevail against them all."

He said he would question the physicians who went there to verify what Masako had told her, but later all names on the list would not even acknowledge the question for security reasons they said, even at Father Krozier's insistence. He asked why she didn't just reveal this information to the Americans herself. She answered she had another mission, equally important, but couldn't reveal it to him, out of concern for his safety. She just said she would be going to Hiroshima in the morning and that he wouldn't be seeing her again. He must promise to keep her whereabouts a secret to anyone who asked, especially Hironoka.

"Have you not seen the leaflets the Americans are dropping? Hiroshima may not be safe, since it may be a target for this new bomb they are talking about."

"No, please don't worry about me. I would never go anywhere where I felt I would be in danger. Trust my female instinct on this." It wasn't her instincts that were driving her to Hiroshima, but rather her dreams which were guiding her to her destiny.

"I am familiar with your female instincts, since I've seen it at work so many times with your patients in labor. You are good, no doubt about it. And just how many Caesareans have you prevented me doing by forcing me to wait just a little longer." They both laughed. "But your work is hardly finished here. I need good midwives, we all do."

"No, that work of mine is now forever finished. I will not bring any more lives into this world ever again, and you must know why."

"Considering what you've been through and seen here at this hospital, I can't really blame you. I understand."

"But before I go, I need just one more favor."

"Whatever you wish. But I already did promise you I'd pursue this Unit 731, and the outrage against those practicing my profession."

"That's not the only thing I want, but just one more favor, and it has to do with your profession also."

"Okay, I'll do it."

"Promise?"

"Yes, I promise."

"I want you to tell me everything you experienced with my husband in the Safety Zone at Nanking."

Tales of the Safety Zone

"**O**kay, I will, but it's not going make you feel any better about your husband, and of his role in the massacre at Nanking. And it's not a pretty picture."

"I'm prepared. Please go on."

"The Safety Zone was an area of two and a half square miles, that housed the University of Nanking Hospital, a seminary for women and several other small buildings. It was under the direction of a John Rabe, and supposedly safe from the Japanese, since it was a territory claimed by Germany, their allies. John Rabe saved hundreds of thousands of Chinese lives by sheltering them within the zone. He was not only a German citizen, but also the leader of the Nazi party in Nanking. At the time of the invasion, there were only twenty of us left in the zone, and only four of us were physicians. Besides myself, there was Robert Wilson, C.S. Trimmer, and Richard Brady. By the time the city fell there were over 250,000 refugees packing the buildings, lawns, open streets, trenches, and bomb dugouts. The zone was marked by flags bearing the red cross and the Nazi Swastika.

"Rabe did his best to keep the Japanese out, but they still, managed to get in mostly at night. But one day, in broad daylight, they entered the Seminary and raped several women in front of their husbands and children."

"Rabe even made several trips into the city trying to prevent the atrocities and rapes. I heard that he even bodily lifted a soldier up off of a girl, despite being threatened with bayonets. His only defense was his swastika arm band. Once four Japanese soldiers in the midst of raping and looting saw his arm band and ran away screaming, '*Deutsche! Deutsche!*' to warn others that were about to enter."

"Rabe had even set up a warning system to protect the women. Whenever Japanese soldiers were caught scaling the walls of his yards, the women would blow a whistle sending Rabe running out into the yard to chase the Japanese away."

"After a few days of what Rabe had witnessed he wrote to Adolf Hitler to request him to intercede and stop the slaughter, but Hitler ignored his request and never replied."

"Even though this area was under the protection of Germany, the Japanese made several forays into the zone, under the pretense of finding Chinese soldiers, or to abduct the women. They would examine all of the men's hands for calluses, since their logic implied that those who fired guns would have them, and took them out to be shot. This unfortunately included innocent farmers, rickshaw coolies, and manual laborers. Their bodies, some 1300 in all, were dropped into ponds or buried to fill the tank trenches the Chinese had built for the invasion. When they ran out of prisoners, they shot nearby residents or buried them alive in these trenches. These atrocities, I'm sorry to say, were ordered under the command of your husband, General Tanoka."

"The murders, though brutal enough, were no match for the thousands of rapes that occurred. There were massive gangs rapes in the streets on females aged 8 to 70. Some that we saw, eventually hemorrhaged and died, or killed themselves. I treated women who had their bellies ripped open and others raped with sticks, various other objects, and even bayonets, both vaginally and rectally. They brought us the corpses of women who been dragged over glass and lanced by bamboo shoots.

"Some of the worse things I saw was a young farmer who had his penis cut off and he bled to death before we would help him. Then there were those charred and horribly disfigured whom the Japanese tried to burn alive."

"Your stories defy the imagination. Who brought them to the hospital?" Midori asked.

"Some were carried in under the guise of nightfall, others even managed to make it on their own. I will never forget one such woman. Her head was nearly severed and was teetering from just a point on her neck. She was one of several that the Japanese had abducted to wash their clothes by day and to be raped by night. She was forced to satisfy 40 men each night. When she bled so bad, she couldn't service these men, they took her to an isolated place where they attempted to cut off her head. The muscles of the neck had been cut through, but they failed to sever her spinal cord. They threw her into a pit where she feigned death, then dragged herself to the hospital. I worked on her for hours, and managed to reattach her head and save her life."

"How horrid! The same work of my husband, taking heads with his sword."

"That's not all, Midori. I remember a twenty nine year old woman, who struggled in with four of her children. She had been shot in the right eye sending the bullet through her eye and out her neck. She had fainted in shock, but awoke the next morning lying in a pool of blood, and next to her crying children. She was too weak to carry her youngest so she had to abandon it and made it on foot with her other children to the Safety Zone. She survived my surgery, but lost her eye. She never found the baby she had abandoned."

"Did any fight back? I would have given my life, rather than be raped."

"Yes, I remember one that resisted and survived, but just barely. Her name was Li Xouying. She was eighteen and seven months pregnant. She and her father had fled to the Safety Zone and hid in the basement of the elementary school, along with others. On December 18th, Japanese soldiers entered the Safety Zone and broke into the school. They dragged the young men out of the school and executed them for no reason at all, despite protests from Rabe. Fearing what the Japanese would do to a pregnant woman, she tried to kill herself by slamming her head against the basement wall. When the Japanese returned, they thought she was dead and dragged off several of the school other females. She awoke, in a pool of blood, to the sound of heavy footsteps coming down the stairs. Two of them dragged the remaining females screaming from the room. The one remaining soldier began to kick her, but before he realized what was happening, she jumped up and grabbed his bayonet. He grabbed her wrist, but she bit it with all of her might. He screamed for help, and when they arrived, they failed to stab her effectively with their bayonets, because she had put their comrade between them using him as a shield. So they aimed at her head, slashed her face, and knocked out her teeth. Her mouth filled with blood which she spat in their faces. She told me she had no fear; her only thought was to fight and kill them. Finally one soldier plunged his bayonet into her abdomen and she collapsed into unconsciousness. The soldiers left her for dead. When her body was discovered and brought before her father, they thought she was dead and dug a pit for her grave behind the school. Fortunately someone noticed, before she was buried, bubbles of blood foaming from her mouth and that she was still breathing. They immediately rushed her to the hospital and I began surgery immediately. Although they had stabbed the whites of her eyes, she did not go blind. I counted and stitched up no less than thirty-seven bayonet wounds. It was a miracle she survived, but while under sedation, she delivered prematurely a stillborn later that evening."

"So this is what my husband caused. These were the heathens he trained for the glory of the Empire. I hope he and the rest get to pay retribution for these horrors. I thought I knew him better and refused to believe the rumors I had heard."

"This and worse Midori. I have countless tales of what we saw on a daily basis in the Safety Zone. War brings out the worst in men."

"Then I never really knew him, did I? But the war apparently brings out the good also, like you and your John Rabe."

"The choice is still up to us to define our destiny, and we live forever with the outcomes of those choices. But why are the good so seemingly outnumbered?"

"I don't know, but it is the bad spirits that have to reincarnate and learn again, not the good. Maybe that's why we're outnumbered. Father, I thank you and now I must go. It has been a real pleasure working with you all of these years, and thank you for the information. And please remember, not a word to Hironoka if he should come by looking for me. Promise?"

"I promise," Father Krozier said tearfully hugging Midori goodbye. "You know in my religion no woman was ever called upon to save mankind, at least not until now. Your mission is to save the lives of countless others and in that end my God will protect and serve you well."

"And it is my solemn wish that we will meet once again in a world that does not know of war or suffering."

"Midori, my religion doesn't accept the concept of reincarnation," they embrace tearfully once more, winking, "but just in case, I'll be sure and look for you."

Blinking back what tears she could contain, she quickly turned and fled up the stairs with her packages, not looking back and both not noticing she had dropped the Hiroshima leaflet she recovered from the American B-29's, that slid under the stone table.

Father Krozier had no idea, at the time, how brutal the Kenpeitai could be in extracting vital information from a person, even if that person was both an allied German and a priest. Hironaka was relentless in his examination of the priest wanting to know where Midori was hiding or to where she had fled. The interrogation was cut short when one of his men discovered the leaflet she had dropped, and signaling to the General that Hiroshima was her probable destination. Hironaka ordered his men, "hold the bastard down; it's time for him to meet his God. Two soldiers grabbed him by each arm and flung him face down upon the granite table. Hironaka shouted, "Now die man of God, and remember your slut Midori will soon be joining you." He raised the sword and brought it down just as Father Krozier whispered, "Father forgive his kind, and come rest with me my Midori...."

PREQUEL

All the talk in the port town of Hiroshima was of the leaflets. Like snow they fell from the skies, dropped by the daily runs of American bombers during the night. Unanswered, except by a few anti-aircraft batteries, some even manned by children no older than her Nomuro, they arrogantly assumed the skies dropping no bombs, but these paper messages forewarning of a great force that would be unleashed on the land unless Imperial Japan immediately surrendered. Most of the civilians had suffered first hand in some way in this war. They had endured the nightly raids, the fires, deadening sounds, followed by debris and the death. They watched children, the infirmed, the old, the homeless, the wounded, the hungry, the abandoned, all cringing inside shelters secretly deploring the backlash of Emperor Hirohito's dream of Imperialistic conquest. They each sensed the end was imminent when the bombers began low level raids in the daylight as well. With no longer any defense from the destroyed air command, the Liberators, and Super fortresses flew virtually unchallenged in their daily raids. Instead of bombs, there was the soft whisper of the brown paper leaflets, like leaves in a great wind, falling from the skies. They warned of a great new weapon that would burn the land, destroying all, and insisted on nothing less than the immediate surrender of Japan. Children would leap in the air trying to catch them before they hit the ground. They played to see who could retrieve the most, and then twist them into origami toys for play. Adults could only speculate on the message. They believed in the destructive capabilities of the Americans, having witnessed firsthand their relentless fire-bombing of civilian towns, but also knew of their Emperor's fierce resolve and saw it reflected in the faces of the new suicide youth corps being trained to repel the American invasion now all but imminent. Most felt resigned to the invasion, though warned of torture, rape, and starvation in American prison camps, at least the uncertainty and destruction would end. It was written that a force worse than a million gallons of gasoline would be ignited over the land, unleashing fire and a wind greater than the one of Kyushu that ended the Mongol invasion centuries ago.

Midori heard reports of the leaflets and received one in the mail from a nurse whom she had trained with at Teishin Hospital in Hiroshima and who now worked for the Shima Clinic. Could this be her Sunasee, ridden by a now vengeful Amaterasu that had dominated her dreams of late?

Memories of a Distant time

She had ridden the same tram many times to this same town center for the Matsuri religious festivals. She brought her three sons here annually to the Koinobori boys' festival held on May 5th of each year. Each with carp streamers, symbolizing strength, flown from poles, they would take their place in the march of the children past their proud parents.

At the doll festival, Hina Matsuri, which was held each March, she would sneak away and purchase the small plastic geisha dolls vendors sold to place it in memory of Eiko on the platform of dolls. With this act she felt she was honoring Eiko's spirit and uniting her with those of other children she never met in her short life here. It hurt Midori to think Eiko's spirit was forever denied the reunion granted to those embodied on the Thousand Stitch Belt. To become so isolated and doomed to solitary existence was her only regret about her daughter. She stood along with the procession of little girls lined to place their dolls on the colorful dais decorated with flowers and the scrolls of children's poems, all framed with wooden prayer plaques. Looking out of place, the children inquired as to the whereabouts of her daughter. Midori replied, "she is here," clasping her hand over her heart.

It was in this same square that they all had come one night in July for the Obon festival. It was the last day they would all get to share together before the war would take them from her life forever. Far removed from the shadows of war, in regal dignity they marched with other families carrying brightly lit paper lanterns, each a symbol of the Sun God whose nightly sojourns illuminated the way of all whose destiny found them on strange shores. The parade would end at the harbor when, one at a time, they would each cast their lanterns afloat upon the darkened sea, to guide their people or their spirits back to their home. One by one the lanterns would imbibe the sea and extinguish in a predictable fashion.

Into the Forge

She hoped to take the tram all the way to the Aioi bridge, but instincts prompted her to disembark at the Schima clinic. She always found her peace in hospitals where she had spent most of her life working. She disembarked from the tram and found the place peaceful and somewhat desolate. She thought about going into the hospital to see her friend, but sensed there wasn't time. She found a bench near a garden, sat down, and laid out the mementoes and photos from her altar. She picked flowers and placed one alongside each photo.

She suddenly became aware of the faint drone coming from the direction of the now rising sun. She rechecked and repositioned all the items in her portable shrine, her own Mikoshi, as she had during each of the feasts. She kissed each photo arranged them in line, and placed the farewell notes from Nakura, Shima, and Nomuro in between the prayer plaque of Eiko. She heard the wail of air raid sirens and above it, a motor brigade screeching to a halt in front of the hospital. She turned and saw Hironoka, along with several rifle armed soldiers, rushing down the path toward her. Now for the first time she felt a fear never allowed, not of her own demise, but that it would happen before she time to complete her destiny with the belt and the sword. With her heart pounding rapidly, she reached under the bench and pulled out the embroidered wrap, and removing the sword she then wrapped the Thousand Stitch belt around it. The steady drone of the Enola Gay grew louder in the eastern sky, a metallic harbinger that would fulfill her wish to save thousands of the Japanese youth as she was denied for her own, and to finally release the captive spirits in the sword. She then stood, rigid and tall, squinting toward the now fully risen sun. She prayed to Amaterasu to release the dragon and then, with outstretched arms, she held the sword and the Thousand Stitch Belt over her head in an offering to her God Sunasee. Just before Hironoka and his troops could reach her, the *Enola Gay* disgorged the uranium blight in its belly, and then began an anxious climb arching back toward the east and away from the falling Atomic bomb.

First came the light of a different dawn, and again as in ancient times a great wind of the Gods. And as foretold in ancient scrolls, there soon came a dragon separating sinew from her soul and carried her to an ancient land that knew not of war... but to a land where the memories never die.

Authors Epilogue

With the exception of the character names listed in the front of this book. All names and incidents are factual. While "the Demonstration" is fiction, the beheading contest is not. Nanking today is the city of Nanjing. They have a museum there that chronicles the tragic events of December 1937. Its told that Japanese business men traveling to China are first required to visit the museum before any business transactions can occur.

The author is indebted to Ms. Iris Cheng and her book, "The Rape of Nanking", for the tales of what transpired and its photos which served as documented proof of the atrocities related. She spoke with courage and passion and opened the world's eyes to these unspeakable horrors. A final victim and conscious of the horrors she documented, Ms. Chang took her own life, near her home in California, on November 9, 2004 at the age of 36.

All incidents of the Kamikaze deaths and ships damaged and destroyed, are factual except for the characters. In the absent of a target, some Kamikaze returned to base and did survive the war. Those poor youths assigned to the 'Ohka's' did not.

The author is also indebted to Raymond Lamont-Brown's book, "Kamikaze: Japan's Suicide Samurai." Takushiro Hattori's

"General History of the Battle of the Pacific" lists total strikes by the Kamikaze as follows: 13 destroyers, nine battleships, ten aircraft carriers, four cruisers, 58 destroyers, and 93 other vessels damaged. He lists the number of 'juvenile pilots', those 15 and under, killed in the Okinawa operation at 1,035.

Okinawa Kamikaze dead are commemorated at the Peace Museum in Kyushu. The complex includes a bronze statue of a Kamikaze pilot and a statue of the Goddess of Mercy, Kwannon. Every year on May third, groups gather at the museum for services to honor the Kamikaze dead.

The incidents at Unit 731 regrettably are all true, and some even more horrid, were left out of this book. The author is indebted to the Virginia Chapter of the Alliance for Preserving History of World War II in Asia (ALPHA), for providing me with the information on Unit 731. What occurred in Pingfan even exceeded the atrocities of the Nazi concentration camps, if not in numbers, then in terms of human barbarism. We hear more of the Nazi atrocities because there is a large American Jewish element that speaks for their people. The Chinese had no such advocates, because after the war, America sought to cover up the incidents, granted amnesty and prosecuted none of commanders of Unit 731 in exchange for the results of their human research. Ishii, Ishikawa, Okamoto, Kitano, and Uezono were never prosecuted and, in fact, returned to Japan to serve as University leaders, physicians, and industrialists. One even rose to prominence in Japan's pharmaceutical industry, while others went to work for the Health Ministry.

Only Yoshio Shinozuka, a Japanese medical student and former member of Unit 731, has expressed public apology for what transpired there. He often wanted to tell his stories but he was ignored by his government. He said that the Japanese prefer to think of themselves as victims in the war. In 1997, he constructed a monument in Yokaichiba, Japan to the Chinese victims of Pingfan. That same year he testified on behalf of the 180 Chinese suing Japan for compensation. The court denied them their wish. Japan has, to this day, denied reparations to the surviving victims and families of Unit 731.

Conservative estimates place the number of the unit's victims at 250,000. These were mostly Chinese, but included American, Russian, British and Canadian prisoners as well. Pingfan has now been restored as a museum and depicts many of the atrocities which occurred at that site.

Hiroshima, an industrial city, lay at the southernmost end of Japan's peninsula across from Kyushu to the south and separated by the Inland Sea. The city was spread along six channels of the Ota River delta. It was hardly a military target, having only one military garrison to the North, the Second Army Headquarters, which housed 43,000 soldiers. Its shipyard housed the Mitsubishi Heavy Industries, Machine and Tool Works. Mitsubishi, the maker of the Japanese Zero, would suffer little damage, but the two hospitals, the Teishin and the Red Cross, Hiroshima University, a Women's college, the Schima clinic, and several Normal schools would be at the center of the Hypocenter, a term used to describe those areas that were centermost and were totally burned and leveled. The civilian population numbered 280,000 Japanese with an additional 20,000 Korean laborers, along with 28 American prisoners of war. Eight thousand school girls were working at the time in the housing areas; and since most structures were made of wood, they were totally destroyed in the resulting firestorm.

The bomb was dropped and exploded 1,900 feet above ground on August 6, 1945. The time of explosion was determined by wrist watches pulled from the ashes, frozen in time and reading 8:16:02 AM. The intended bombardier target was the Aioi Bridge, but the bomb drifted southward and exploded directly over the Shima clinic.

The bomb would instantly kill 80,000. Another 60,000 would die within a year from thermal burns and radiation poisoning. Additionally, another 3,677 would never be found, and 130,000 would be physically disfigured forever. It left over 5,000 children as orphans.

Yet, I believe perhaps unnoticed among the debris; a melted sword, an incinerated cloth belt, and the scattered ashes of a valiant midwife.

"Well so much for Midori. I hope it has given you a better understanding of our war in the Pacific from both sides. As someone once said "When there is no war, the sons bury their fathers, when there are wars, the fathers bury their sons.""

Well before getting back to the final review and the legacy of the WASPS two more are worthy of note. Elizabeth MacKethan Magid and Marie Mitchell Robinson. They had the dangerous job of flying previously damaged and malfunctioning planes that had been repaired. One day, in October of 1944, while flying in separate planes side by side, and noticing the nuts and bolts were popping and flying off, they both gave a thumbs up to imply all was well. Marie was piloting a B-25 Billy Mitchell bomber which suddenly stalled and went into a flat spin and crashed killing all on board. Marie was only 20 years old.

Elizabeth was devastated. She continued flying but wrote a beautiful eulogy for her friend Marie entitled "Celestial Flight."

"She is not dead, but only flying higher,

Higher than she's flown before,
All earthly limitations , will hinder her no more.
There is no service ceiling, or any fuel range,
No anoxia or need for engine change.
Thank God that now her flight can be
To heights her eyes have scanned,
where she can race with comets
and buzz the rainbow's span.
For she is universal, like courage, love and hope
Of vast and godly scope.
And understand a pilot's fate is not the thing she fears,
But rather sadness left behind, your heartbreak and your fears.
So all you loved ones, dry your eyes
Yes it is wrong that you should grieve,
For she would love your courage more,
And she would want you to believe, she is not dead.
You should have known, that she is only flying higher,
Higher than she's ever flown before.

"But getting back on the subject of the WASPS. Their program was re disbanded In December of 1944 before the end of the war because of the opposition of the male pilots who feared they would lose their jobs to some of these women when the war ended."

"Of the 1,102 women in the WASP program, 38 died in the line of duty, and sadly since they were civilian volunteers, they were not accorded military funeral at Arlington Cemetery, and even had to take up collections to have their colleagues remains shipped home.

After the war, some took jobs as traffic controllers, waitresses stewardesses, and airplane mechanics. So these valiant women who had contributed so much of their time and even lives to the war effort were not recognized until November 23rd, 1977 when President jimmy Carter signed a public law 95-202 along with Senator Barry Goldwater giving the survivors veteran status.

And again on July 1st 2009, President Obama signed a bill to grant them the Congressional Gold Medal the highest of civilian honors awarded by the U.S. Congress."

Bobbi sneered, " so all they got was a lousy medal in recognition."

"Well not so much recognition as inspiration."

"How so?"

"Their legacy went far beyond not what they did but what they inspired. In 1976, the US Air Force accepted the first females as pilots, and in 2015, Brigadier General Jeannie Levite was the first female fighter pilot. So you may never know how the long term impact of your actions will have on someone."

Raising her eyebrows, "Even us?"

"Yes even any of you….Well maybe." All laughed.

"But lastly, before we go, I would be remiss if I didn't tell of you of the bravery of another female fighter pilot, 1st Lieutenant Heather "Lucky" Penny. Who proved not only to be brave, but really lived up to her name on our second day of infamy, the hitting of twin towers and the Pentagon on 911.

On that day 25 year old first Lieutenant Heather "Lucky" Penny. She flew with the 121st Fighter Squadron in DC. With the news of another airliner headed toward our Capital in Washington, Heather and her wingman, Colonel Marc Sasseville, scrambled their F 16s Vipers and took off to intercept it. Because of the desperate need to act fast, they there had been no time to arm their jets, and so they would be flying a kamikaze mission ramming their jets into the airliner.

Sass said, " I'm going for the cockpit", and Penny replied, "I'll take the tail." She and her wingman headed in pursuit, of United Flight 93 when they received word that the plane had been taken over by a group of courageous passengers who were willing to sacrifice themselves, as she and Marc were, and crashed into the ground. "

The class sat speechless reflecting in silence on the power and inspiration of this class.

"Well, that's it for today, only one more meeting before our semester is over. So until then, you're dismissed."

LAST CLASS

"Welcome back eager learners to our last class of the semester. I bet you will all miss me." As the class entered and took their seats.

"As like in not", Bobbi said slouching into her seat.

"Well I have some good news and some bad news."

"Tell us the bad first."

"Well as the lawyer said to the condemned criminal facing execution, the Governor has denied your reprieve and you will be executed within the next 15 minutes. But now for the bad news." All laughed.

"The bad news is that this is indeed our last class."

"That's bad? That actually the best news I've had all day. What's the good news?"

Smiling, "The good news is that you will not have to come back for a final exam."

"So do we all just get A's"

"Not exactly. If I base your grade on tardiness you get an A. If I Based it on comments like, "Do we really need to know this?" You get a D. "On comments like, "Why is this subject a required class, another D. And a D+++ on when I asked you a question on an assignment, and you didn't answer, forcing me to run to the back of the class raise my hand and give the answer. I other words, my having to do both parts."

Bobbie laughed saying, "You know when I pray or need sex, I often have to do both parts." The class howled, but Danny didn't.

"And Bobbie, based on your typical foul language you get an F."

"You mean whenever I said Fuck!" The rest looked at Bobbie.

"Exactly Bobbie."

"Well I only said it, I didn't do it.", all laughed.

"Ok Bobbie, I will let that pass. Now if I base your grade on your interest and emotional response to all the topics, you all get an A++."

"Thank you. Can we go now?"

"Not quite. Not until we've gone over every subject and reviewed the major topics."

"Ugh, so even more bad news."

"Yes but even more. It's not me who will summarize the salient points, but you all and in the order your learned them.

To summarize:

Dachau

Kristallnacht

Ravensbruck

The Beauty Walk

Phosgene

Borstel

M.S. Saint Lewis

Richmond

Prelude to Zyclon B

Zyclon B

Crematorium Blow-up

Quanza
Moscow Still Remembers
Moscow Memories
Night Witches
WASPS
Only fifteen in all."
"Only? And from rote memory?"
"No you may use your notes."
"So let's start with Dachau. We will go around the room and each of you, one at a time make a statement from what your remember or from your notes. Ready start."

DACHAU

First concentration camp in 1933, Munich Germany.
First inmates were criminals and Jehovah Witnesses, not Jews
Jehovah Witnesses wore Purple triangles and some beheaded
The daily predawn Appel for 4 hours in freezing weather.
You visited there on Christmas Day with you friend Reiner
One block still there and learned of the medical experiments on Russians
Freezing experiments and high altitude decompressing
Reiner blamed his parents for not intervening
They lived only 7 miles away and saw victims shoveling snow.
Their parents response who were not members of the Nazi party.

LAST LAP

"Excellent review and comments. Now on to Kristallnacht

KRISTALLNACHT

Night of the broken glass
Thousands of Jewish shops destroyed
All Synagogues burned
Many Jews killed and sent to concentration camps
Mischlings, half Jews, included
A great book "Wunderland" makes it personal

RAVENSBRUCK

Only camp for Women
Made parts for V1 and V2 rockets
Those subjected to horrid medical experiments were called Rabbits
SR tattoo on those selected for brothel service
The GOAT whipping block
Medieval torture on some
The humiliation of some by the Watermen
Liberated by the Russians April 30th 1945
War trials in Hamburg, Germany
Some were hanged, but not Herta Oberheuser
Sister Rivet, Catholic nun took the place of a Jewish woman to be gassed
She was gassed on March 30th, 1945 on a Good Friday
Same day as the crucifixion of her Lord

"Good that highlights the salient points of Ravensbruck, now the last topic of Ravensbruck, the Beauty Walk by those rabbits no longer useful for further experimentation. Yes, I know this was rough on all of you, but this allowed them a modicum of dignity in facing their end. Much as you remember Mariska, the Russian nurse who refused to face the crowd before she was hanged. So let's start with the Beauty Walk. Who can describe what it was?"

THE BEAUTY WALK

> The final walk of a condemned Rabbit up a hill to be hanged
> Rabbits would dress her in dresses and heels from previous victims
> Fixed hair and applied rouge
> Used crunched up paper to add breasts to cadaverous chests
> Limped or crawled with victim up the hill to the gallows
> Victim refused a hood so she could see the faces of her friends
> Other Rabbits sang songs from the homes they once knew
> Until the darkness fell

PHOSGENE

> Invented by a German Jew, Fritz Haber during World War 1.
> First used at the Battle of Ypres, April 22, 1915
> Heavier than air, so it rolled into the trenches killing 5,000 that day
> Replaced Chlorine gas with its astringent smell
> It had the sweet smell of hay

Converts to Hydrochloric Acid in the lungs causing pulmonary edema
Can be neutralized by breathing through a urine stained handkerchief
Haber wins Nobel Prize in 1918 for work on fertilizer
Haber flees to Switzerland in fearing the rise of the Nazi.
Never mix Ammonia and Chlorine bleach, generates Phosgene

BORSTEL

Sent to Germany to work at Borstel, near Hamburg
Went to London where the V2 rockets bombed
SS Wernher Von Braun built them
After the war he comes to US to build our space program
World War ll begins when Germans invade Poland September 1, 1939
Nazi's take most of Europe and then invade Russia
Nazi atrocities against Russian civilians
Leningrad surrounded for one year, but hold out
Russia advances and liberates the first concentration camp
France and the site of the D-Day invasion
Allied troops liberate concentration camps
To Rome where Pope pious XII allows Jews to be deported
Pope denies Negros access into Rome during liberation by allies
Your artifacts, Pimp Hort Zu, Nazi armband, Russian books on the war

RICHMOND

Nazi come to Richmond Virginia in the early 30's to learn from us
They learn of our facial and segregation laws against the blacks
Separate benches, drinking fountains and rest rooms.
Restricted to the back of the bus, and confined to certain areas to live
Nazi learn of the isolation of Jews into ghettoes areas from this
A black man even looking at a white woman could be hanged
Inbreeding with the white woman Mary was punished by his death
She was burned alive and the Klan gutted her to see the fetus drop
From the image of the Klan, the SS developed the skull and cross bones
Hitler doesn't intervene in the Japanese slaughter at Nanking
300,000 slaughtered in a three week period
The Japanese human experimentation camp at Pingfan, Manchuria
From all of this, the Nazi learn of human experimentation
Mengele at Auschwitz and Oberhauser at Ravensbruck
Early ethic cleansings on anyone randomly deemed as undesirables

First gassing were done in Carbon monoxide vans

Even Jehovah Witnesses, although pure German Aryans,

were killed

M.S SAINT LEWIS

American liner based in Hamburg named after the capital of Missouri
Under the command of Capt. Schroder left Hamburg in summer of 1939
Carried 937 Jewish passengers fleeing persecution by the Nazi
First to Cuba and denied and then to many other ports with the same result
Attempted to enter the US port in New York , but was denied.
The Captain headed to the Florida Coast and tried to run it aground
Coast Guard stopped this, so ship headed back to Hamburg
Passengers disembarked and were sent to Concentration Camps
Movie was made appropriately entitled, "Ship of the Damned."

THE QUANZA

September 11, 1940 the ship Quanza docks a t a coal pier in Norfolk, VA
Eighty-one Jewish passengers last stop before heading back to Germany
They had already been banned by many other countries

Our own Jews didn't want them, fearing our own un-
limited resources
Our Jews referred to them as Unwanted Parasites
Judenrats, another example of Jews sacrificing their own
kind
Painted Bird, Monkey in Cage, experiments how others
will kill their own
Book Sophie's choice she must decide between one child
or both shot.
Judenrats tell mothers to pick youngest child since they
won't understand
President Roosevelt send rep to Norfolk to assist Quanza
passengers
Against all immigration laws, the Rep allows the entry
of all passengers

SONDERKOMMANDO REVOLT

Special units of Jewish prisoners guiding arrivals into
the gas chambers
Assisted with the removal of gold teeth, and burned the
dead
Worked in shifts around the clock seven days a week
Given generous amounts of food and drink
Knew they would also be gassed and replaced within a
month
Women smuggled gun powder in from munitions plant
October 7, 1944 they revolt killing some guards
SS retaliate killing over 250 they captured upon escape
October 10th two of the woman were hung at the morn-

ing Appell
That evening, two more were hung
The movie, The Grey Zone, tells true story of one girl
gassed who survived

ZYCLON B: THE CO LEAD UP

SS Lt. Gerstein asks Pope to intervene in CO gassing of
undesirables
Pope refuses and allows Jew to be selected from Rome
In early 1930's Hitler institutes the gassing of those
with genetic defects
Victims were sealed in an airtight truck with hose
hooked up the exhaust
Driven and then corpses were burned in a field

ZYCLON B

First tested on 20 Russian prisoners at Auschwitz early
1942
All victims, men, women and children stripped naked
Hydrogen Cyanide pellets Poured into the top of the
gas chamber
Pellets sublimate, going immediately from solid into a
gas
Excruciating Death takes over 18 minutes
Gene Turgel , at age of 21 only known survivor

MOSCOW STILL REMEMBERS

MEIN KAMPF written by Hitler in 1920 while imprisoned in jail

Nazi siege and bomb Leningrad for 900 days 9 /1941 to 1/27/1944

Victims eating dead horses and human corpses

German atrocities by SS and the regular Wehrmacht against the Russians

One woman burned alive at the stake

Russians liberate first concentration camp Auschwitz, January 1945

MOSCOW MEMORIES

Last night in Moscow, three separate New Year's Eves

Germans don't toast the Russians on the time of their New Years

And vice versa, but all toast me the only American

Brought back several books

One sowing Russian pilot ramming an enemy bomber in August 1941

Passed out several ball point pens and Kennedy half dollars

Flew from Moscow to Berlin then back to Borstel

NIGHT WITCHES (NACHT HEXEN)

Female Russian pilots bombing the Nazi at night

Given that name by the Nazi ground troops bombed at night

Knew they were female after capturing one survivor of a crash

Flew a flimsy biplane made of wood frame and silk stretched over it

Carried a pilot in back and a navigator in the rear cockpit

Not allowed Parachutes wince thee were reserved for the male pilots

Lessened noise of being heard, by killing engines and gliding to targets

Stalin awards medals to them for stopping German advance to Moscow

Anna Kharkove survivor of most missions

WASPS

The Women Airforce Service Pilots who flew during WWll

Duties including testing newly built planes, towing targets, and ferrying

No males would fly the newly built B-29 Superfortress due to fires

It was need for long range bombing to Japan

Paul Tibbetts asked two WASPS to fly one to prove it can be trusted

They tried a trick that worked and safely landed

Tibbetts was so impressed, he named that B-29 "ladybird"

Thirty Eight WASPS died in the line of duty

Maria Robinson, only 20, crashed and died test flying a repaired B-29

Her partner, Elizabeth Magid, wrote " Celestial Flight", a Eulogy to her

Since the WASPS were civilians they were not accorded
military rights

B-24 bomber flew off the carrier Hornet and bombed
Tokyo April 1942

August 6th, 1945, Tibbetts drops Atomic Bomb over
Hiroshima

August 9th , 1945 bomb dropped over Nagasaki

1976 US Sir Force accepts first female pilots

2015 Brigadier General Lievite first female fighter pilot
Lucky Penny and her wingman fly to find third plane
after morning of 911

Their F-16 Vipers had not been armed

They agreed to fly a one way Kamikaze mission

Her wingman would ram the front and she would ram
the tail

Both were spared death when Flight United 93 was
down

DEMON DIAGNOSIS

Closing his notes , Danny asked ,"Great job on the oral exam and review. Any final comments?"

Becka offered, "Just one, well frankly I skeptical at first over why we needed a History course, since current events really mattered the most, but I was impressed by what you said that philosopher Santa something said."

"Santayana."

"Yes, that those who forget the past are condemned to relive it. And I really learned a lot, and will tell all of my upcoming classmates to try and get you as their teacher. "

"Well I appreciate that, but that won't be necessary."

A quizzical expression on her face, "Why not?"

"Because I'm not coming back."

"What! Why not?, You really were the most interesting teacher I've ever had." The rest of the class nodding in agreement. "You not only taught us, but inspired us, and seemed to care about our future."

"I appreciate that, but I'm falling prey to my demon diagnosis, of insulin dependent diabetes."

"How so?"

"Well you may remember from your Biology class that the Pancreas makes a hormone called insulin. In my type of diabetes, type one or insulin dependent, I don't make insulin so I need to inject it."

"Why do we need insulin?"

"Insulin is necessary for the carbohydrates we consume to enter our cells for the energy we need for our muscles to work."

Booker says, "That's why we consume Gatorade before practice and our games."

"Exactly, to give you the energy for your sport and your body reacts by releasing insulin, to pump the sugar into your muscles. "

"Over time this continuous high blood sugar wreaks havoc with our kidneys, nerves, blood vessels, and heart, which I've kept somewhat in control because of my running. But it's the impact on my vision that I'm losing control over. High glucose enters the eye and at first causes blurriness, then bleeding, and then blindness. So I'm leaving teaching to pursue just one more goal, since I don't want to end up in a hospital blind and on life support."

Booker. "What is that?"

"To run the New York City Marathon again before the darkness falls."

Tonya interjecting, "But you mentioned not only issues with your eyes, but also with your heart. Can your heart last all of the 26.2 miles to the finish line?"

"I hope not."

"What's the point of the book then?"

LAST LAP

BLIND RUNNERS QUEST FOR RECOGNITION AND HIS FINAL FREEDOM IN CHOOSING DEATH.

LAST LAP RATIONALE

Does any book really need a rationale or justification for being written? Of course not, but I'm giving you one anyway.

1) This book serves as a tribute to the common man. The underdog who achieves dignity and purpose on sheer guts and determination, and not inborn talents.

2) To give insight into the challenges one faces an ongoing basis with Type 1 Diabetes (insulin dependent) juggling diet and exercise and trying to avoid the dread of severe hypoglycemia which could lead to coma and death. And to give insight to the slow deteriorating effect it has like a ticking clock on one's cardiovascular, circulatory, vision, nerve, hearing, and kidneys.

3) To serve as an admonishment to those who can, but don't, and a tribute to those who can't, yet do.

4) To acknowledge the back of the pack runners (as I define the plow horses versus the gifted Gazelles) and the

challenges the latter face in their training.

5) To share the extraordinary physiological adaptation a body must make in order to train and to finish a run that for most can take over 6 hours.

6) To note that neither man or woman, unlike any other animal, were not made for distance running, ever since evolving into an upright position.

7) Maybe to just give some incentive to those who only served as armchair spectators, the encouragement to give it a try. Even if their Last Lap.

8) Finally, to learn why marathon runners write names of certain people on the back of their runner numbers, and who they are running for in remembrance.

"THE WOODS ARE LOVELY, DARK, AND DEEP
BUT I HAVE PROMISES TO KEEP
AND MILES TO GO BEFORE I SLEEP. - ROBERT
FROST (1923)

" LET US RUN WITH PATIENCE
THE RACE THAT IS SET BEFORE US. – Hebrews
12:1

" ...THEY SHALL MOUNT UP WITH WINGS
AS EAGLES; THEY SHALL RUN, AND NOT BE

WEARY..." – Isaiah 40:31

"...THE RACE IS NOT TO THE SWIFT, NOR THE BATTLE TO THE STRONG"
NOR THE BATTLE TO THE STRONG" –Ecclesiastes 9:11

MARS AT MIDNIGHT

Tonight was just ours, and we both knew.
As once before your burnished beacon, from light years away,
touched a primordial synapse within, lending memory
of waning strength blended with fearful resolve.

Roman God of war, how many times have you forged your
will upon this frail anvil of time?
How many midnight warriors did your orange light guide?
Warriors in search of food, shelter, or kidnapped mates.
Warriors in search of fortune, glory or youth.
Warriors searching for something higher than themselves.

Your light so steady and sure,
unlike the syncopate of such tired steps,
a heart bruised by the memory of loss,
legs worn by the rhythm of time.

How many countless warriors did you lead,?
tracing your great ecliptic across the night sky,
guiding them through midnight sands across frozen
tundra,
straight into the abyss of fearful conviction.
Always giving glow, when moon and Aurora,
dare not shed light on midnight stealth.

And how many times, across eons of space,
did you lend your light, to this too tired warrior,?
still in search of stolen dreams.
Dreams scoured clean...by dawns rising beams.

HISTORY OF THE NEW YORK MARATHON

Each year, the first Sunday in November the New York City Marathon event takes place that tests the hopes and fulfills the dreams of over 100,000 runners, and inspires millions more who line the 26.2 mile route, and those who watch through satellite transmission sent around the world.

The race with the international elite from all over the world, is not just for them, but for everyone. There are those who run on wheels. Those who run for charities for those who cannot. And those who run to defeat their diagnosis. As many different stories as there are runner.

The race transverses the five boroughs of New York City: Staten Island, Brooklyn, Queens, Manhattan, and the Bronx. First conceived by Fred Lebow, a Holocaust survivor form Romania. The first race was held in Central Park in 1969 with just 127 runners and only one woman among them. By 1975 it grew to 534 and there was talk of expanding it to all five boroughs in time for the

Nations bicentennial. So on that Sunday morning, October 24, 1976, 2,090 runners lined up in Staten Island to start the race by running over the Verrazano-Narrows Bridge.

The race has gone on every year regardless of weather, or even terror because just seven weeks after 911, runners started the race with a banner, "United We Run."

So the fast, slow, old or young, healthy and infirmed, beginners and pros, as well as the volunteers and spectators all bond together for just this day.

So how did the concept of such a long distance run begin? The theory is that Pheidippides , an Athenian warrior, ran 150 miles from in two days from the plains of Marathon to Athens in 460 B.C.to announce the Greek victory over the Persians. After he announced, "We have won!" he dropped dead. Speculation is that he actually an only 18 miles and died from dehydration.

It wasn't until the first modern Olympics in Athens in 1896 re-created his run at 18 miles, not at the current distance. It was lengthen to 26.2 miles, not for the convenience of the runners, but for the British Monarchy. At the London Olympics in 1908, the British Queen wanted not to be inconvenienced by traveling to the Olympic stadium, but insisted the race start in front of Buckingham Palace. And so it stands today.

LAST LAP PROLOGUE

Danny was born a loser. At birth born with club feet, and confined to wear thick boots to turn his feet inward, gave him the gait of a ruptured duck. His awkward waddling invited the scorn of both genders of his classmates and isolated him from everyone except the all too eager bullies.

His mother bordered on bi polar mood swings, that went to obsessive control to outright brutality. She was the only figure in the household, neglected by a husband who claimed to bowl every night until the wee hours of morning. She took her vengeance for him out on Danny.

Danny grew thin and malnourished with lunches packed with salami and butter on white bread. During school breaks at St. Antonineis, when everyone could buy chocolate milk and cookies, he could only watch.

The nuns themselves seemed to take delight in tormenting him. During penmanship class, he was holding his ink pen wrong and a nun smacked his hand with a metal ruler, yelling, "" Don't you know holding your hand like that is bad for your hand?" Cowering like a whipped dog, he whispered, "So is hitting it with a ruler", inviting even more abuse.

During recess, when the other kids were sent out to play, Danny had to write long punish lessons on the boards with nonsense phrases like, "I will not talk back to Sister Jema." Over and over again.

During religion class, he was so scared by a catechism teacher for failing to memorize a prayer he was supposed to know, that he feigned polio, the scourge of the 50's, and was sent to the hospital.

Excited at the age of seven to finally receive his first communion, during practice a bird flew into the cathedral of Our lady of Sorrows Church. He stood, pointed and screamed, "It's the Holy Ghost!" The bird flew in circles and then right smack into a pillar, broke it neck, and fluttered to the granite floor. He screamed, "The Holy Ghost is Dead! "And the rest of the kids joined in. Sister Jema did not take too lightly to this, and dragged him by the arm out into the vestibule, smacking his sad face soundly.

After his first communion, Danny tried out for altar boy, but tripped over his long tunic and knocked over all of the candles he was supposed to be lighting, and set fire to the altar shrouds.

The real treat in Catholic School was the Friday afternoon movie. Unfortunately, there was one film about the Nazi which told of someone they had severed the right arm and the left leg off someone in Norway. He was so horrified he ran out of the movie and all the way home. Also traumatized by what he heard of the concentration camps by his Uncle Tony, who had liberated Dachau, he remained strangely connected to that era. Nightly visions and dreams haunted him, but not as a victim, but as a perpetrator. Maybe in trying to gain control as they did over his life.

While traumas at school with the nuns were bad enough, he often bullied on the walk home by his classmates. One day they picked him up and threw him head first into a barrel of raw meat outside a butcher shop.

Always weak and frail, dinners at home were particularly traumatic because his mother would hit him with a wooden spoon if he failed to eat or didn't eat fast enough.

He and his sister used to bath together, and one day he asked how come she was different down there? She told him she once was, but she cut it off because she was bad, and now she was nice and clean down there. From then on Danny always slept on his side with a protective hand between his legs.

She would never allow him to even talk to girls, and caught him talking to two twins up the street, grabbing him by the hand, calling them whores, she dragged him home.

He was so afraid of his mother, that when home from school he would just lock himself in the bathroom until his father would come home late at the night.

Was he always destined to a life of fear? No, one day he discovered it antidote, and quite by accident. His mother had a bad habit of unscrewing fuses to turn the entire house into blackness, or even worse, to let out blood curdling screams. One day she was chasing him up the stairs swinging a wooden spoon, Danny ran into the closet, and found an old sword from an uncle who fought in the Spanish American War. He grabbed it, pointed it at her, and warned it she dared come any further he would run it right through her. She stopped, and crying ran back down the stairs.

This was now the most defining moment of his entire life. He realized that both fear and hate could not coexist in the same person at the same time. And hate was just so much more desirable. He embraced it as a mantle of amour and started training with weights, and went after all bullies as a champion of all underdogs.

Thus he devoted his life to police work and kept his amour sound with continual training in martial arts. Yet try as he might, he could not escape the demon diagnosis of Diabetes, which made him blind. Thus he asked his friend and Endocrinologist Dr. Ryan, who told him he would not survive the distance of the NYC marathon. He showed him his EKG strips, but Danny said he knew that, and wanted only to end it in a manner of his choosing. Reluctantly he agreed to lead him in his last lap.

Signature of the Reaper

"It would be suicide"

"Exactly"

This simple exchange between physician and friend formalized what would be their final run together.

An hour earlier the pen of the EKG monitor leaped like a frightened flea across the scrolling paper as the aging athlete kept a rhythmic pace on the inclined treadmill. Entangled, like a trapped fly in a web of wires, the electric monitors probed the cells and synapses of this failing machine, sending the grim message they both suspected. His forced breaths were captured by a tube that ran form his mouth attached to a bellows designed to measure breathing rate, volume as well as his oxygen uptake.

After twenty minutes of sustained effort, he was almost glad when Dr. Ryan Matthews, his closest friend of twenty years, slowed the treadmill to a rapid walk and then to a stop and retook his blood pressure.

"Why are we stopping, I haven't hit my maximum rate yet?", but Danny knew why.

"We found out what we needed to know. You were right I'm sad to say, it was what you expected", said Ryan averting Danny's glance.

Toweling his sweating body gingerly feeling his way off the treadmill, Danny felt for the chair and sat down daring not to question any further.

As his breathing resumed to normal, Danny asked, "Well doc, how bad is it?"

"The pattern shows that the irregularity begins as you near your anaerobic threshold. In other words, even at a slow walking pace you could go into cardiac arrhythmia. Your other vital signs look great due to your running, but as you know, your diabetes has taken its toll." Then hesitantly, "You're going to have to give it up, if you want to live." Ryan mentally measured the impact of those words on the figure before him.

"Damn doc, you know that's all I have left. Can't you rewrite this prescription?"

"I wish I could", putting a reassuring hand on his friend. "I only wish I could"

Danny winced, "But this is all I have left"

It was all he had left.

DECISION IN DEATH (THE WAY OF FIXX)

Yes, it really was all that Danny had left. Running was his final and only source of pride in a body that betrayed him daily. His vision gone, and extremities that grew more uncoordinated and numb daily. Diabetes had even robbed him of his manhood, when the nerve damage it wreaked, left him impotent.

His world of darkness and betrayal was only relieved in his daily runs with Ryan, with a hand on his shoulder, Tim would lead him in those excursions into a world he could no longer see but remember through his senses. Danny knew that Ryan was one of those naturally gifted runners, lean, genetically efficient, he quipped referring to as one of the gazelles. While he represented the back of the pack breed that just slug it out to the finish, running not on skill, but just on heart and hope. Those he called the plow horses. In the six marathons they ran together, Ryan easily finished in under three hours, while Danny's best was just barely under six.

Danny once met the great marathoner, Bill Rodgers at a sports conference. Bill Rodgers whose marathon times average about two and a quarter hours. When he asked Danny what his marathon time was, Rodgers was astonished and commented, "You mean you can actually run for six hours? I couldn't"

The marathon, and all that it represented, was all that Danny had left. In what other athletic event do world class competitors and compete at the exact same time? It defined his being and set him apart from others in his age group of 60 and over. Only a tiny fraction of a percent of individuals nationally, in that age group, can complete the 26 mile 385 yards, an event that some compared to child birth and to death in measured doses. It was this, that finally gave Danny his claim to individual athletic fame, not because of his time, but in just being able to finish the demanding distance, giving him a distinction above other men. That distinction was a direct testimony to his tenacity and to his courage. He had even surpassed the gazelles of his youth, many whom were now overweight sloths who long ago forsaken their genetic gifts from God.

"Ryan, buddy we need to do it one more time"

"Do what?", Ryan pretending not to know.

"We need to do one last marathon together", Danny standing and grabbing Ryan's shoulders to emphasize his intent.

"Why, so you can kill yourself?"

"No, but to allow me to die with dignity. I have that right!"

"What are you saying man, I won't allow you to kill yourself. I won't allow you to end your life."

"What life, Ryan? You call this life? My wife abandoned me when I lost my manhood, lunatics slaughtered my dog silver for no reason at all. I live in a world without color and form, and a now you tell me I can no longer run. What life Ryan?"

"Listen you are a good teacher, and your students..."

Danny cut him off, "Listen Ryan, my work here is done. I've already told my students goodbye and why I won't be coming back. I'm ready to go on to a place where I can see again, run without someone leading, and maybe even feel loved again. What do I really have to look forward to? Ending up in a hospital with vinyl tubes in my arms, and machines substituting for my lungs. Everyday my body becomes more and more a prison to my spirit. Let's free it with one more run."

Ryan didn't answer because he knew that if it was him, he would make the same choice. I don't know Danny; I just don't know"

"You know Ryan I won't be the first to end it this way."

"What do you mean?"

"You remember the running guru of the sixties, Jim Fixx?"

"Yeah, he did die running, but it was due to an undiagnosed cardiac problem. He didn't go running just to deliberately kill himself."

"Oh I think he did.", Danny continued, "Before he found running he was an overweight smoker with a family history of heart disease. Running freed him from the prognosis that he would end up as his father had, an early death from coronary disease."

"So what, it didn't even help him the long run. In fact, it started a public outcry against the running movement and all he had tried to accomplish."

"That's because the public felt that his death was accidental."

Danny responded.

"Are you trying to tell me it wasn't just an accident?"

"No I really don't believe it was accidental. You see after his books brought him fame and made him a hero, he paid for that acclaim in time. Time for endorsements, time for travel, time for sequels. He eventually gave up running and reverted back to his former destructive life style, smoking, drugs and booze. The same habits that killed his father. I went to a book signing of his in Connecticut the year before he died, and was astonished to see him overweight and smoking. You know I think?"

"What?"

"I think that one day he was sitting at his desk and felt the familiar tightness in his chest and maybe a pain radiating down his arm, and then thought of how his father had to spend his last days laying in a hospital bed tied to monitors, peeing through a tube stuck in his cock, infiltrated with tubes pumping him full of unknown fluids.

He decided that he wouldn't go this way, not while he still had a choice. He, like me had nothing to lose. His kids were grown and would inherit his fortune, his wife had left him, and he probably felt that he could no longer represent the ideal he expounded and evangelized about in his books. The gazelles were laughing at him.

So he put on his shoes for that one last run, that one last tribute to the life style that had granted him a new life of hope, fortune and dignity. It granted him the control over his destiny wanting to go with dignity."

"Ryan, I want that same choice, just to go with Dignity."

"Then why don't you just go out and run and get killed by yourself?", angrily, "Why the hell do you need me?"

"Because I need you Ryan. Jim Fixx wasn't blind; I am. You've always been my sole support and running partner, and I think you understand. It would be no different than your disconnecting a life support machine from one of your terminally ill patients. Would it?"

Ryan didn't answer. He knew Danny was right because he would expect the same of him. He knew in time Danny's diabetes would eventually destroy his kidneys, forcing him on daily renal dialysis to purify his blood of its metabolic toxins. He had witnessed the slow decay of others as the soul screams to leave the body. And yes, he been asked to disconnect the life support machines by these individuals with advanced directives. It would be hard for him, because of their long friendship and the fact that he was Danny's only true next of kin. He had no one else. He couldn't abandon him to the slow torture of the reaper. Together they would race with it and deprive it of its force and fear.

"O.K., I'll do it. When?"

"New York, that's when."

THE QUEST FOR THE BLUE GRAIL

Danny never felt he deserved a friend like Ryan. Danny had known him since the third grade, when Ryan moved into the neighborhood from Chicago. Ryan was everything that Danny was not and everything he wanted to be. Ryan was good looking, outgoing, and a natural athlete. Danny was just the opposite. The girls adored Ryan; they ridiculed Danny. What was unbelievable to Danny, was the fact that Ryan would even want to be his friend. But he was a friend to all, and his willingness to associate with the clumsy overweight, nerdy Danny caused others to begin to accept him also. So it was that Ryan was not only a real friend, but in a sense his confidence crutch.

It was Ryan who gave him the confidence to try out for sports in grammar school and then in high school. First Baseball, then track, football, and wrestling, all failures for Danny who was just too uncoordinated and lacked endurance. While Danny shouldered the embarrassment, Ryan championed in all he attempted. Despite these differences, Ryan was still a friend and consoled him each time.

Danny realized that part of his problem, besides his mesomorph build, was that high school heroes, like Ryan, had been schooled in those sports at a very early age. Mentored by self-serving fathers or older brothers. This was the case with Ryan, whose father saw in his son an extension of his youth and former glory. Unlike Danny grew up as an only child, raised by his mother and abandoned by his father.

With his high school years now in its last semester, in the spring of his senior year, he decided to make one last try for the holy blue grail. He wanted, above all else, to letter in at least one sport. He needed to receive his badge of courage in the form of the letter "C" from Columbia High School. His yearbook would always show him as captain of the Chess Club, member of the astronomy society, and Year book committee. Everyone knew these things didn't really count. It didn't count with college recruiters, the wife he hoped to meet, and a father long gone. He needed to prove himself to Ryan and all of his classmates, especially the girls who avoided him in the sports arena.

A notice had been posted on the gym door by Coach Monty, nicknamed because he resembled the British field marshal, that try-outs for the Spring track team would begin at 3:30 that day. Since he knew he wasn't fast, he decided to try out for the field events such as the javelin and the shot put. Due to his weak upper body, he failed that first day to meet the minimum distances and so decided to try some of the track events.

When you made the team, you were issued your blue sweats with the black panther on them. After that first day, only Ryan and a few others had received theirs. By the week's end over half were warming up in the new blue sweats by the start of the second week, those still in grey took the hint and quit, but not Danny. The word was that Monty had never cut anyone from the team who just stuck it out. He just had others ways to make them quit.

If Danny could only stick it out. Even if he never got to compete for the school, if he could just make the team. As a graduating senior he would be guaranteed the cloth accolade awarded at that ceremony and finally receive the recognition he so desired.

With only one week left until the first meet with Chatham, Danny was the only one still showing up for practice in the grey sweats. By now the Gazelles were beginning to smirk and laugh among each other.

He even went to the assistants and asked if he could get his sweats, but they told him not until Monty said so. Still he hung in until two days before the meet when it was obvious that Monty didn't want him and planned to shame into quitting. He was convinced that if he could prove to Monty that he wasn't a quitter, Monty would at least keep him on the team.

The last qualification was for the 100 yard hurdles. Danny knew this was his last chance, for he would never be a senior again.

Totally out of place in the only grey sweats among the blue, he dared to show up at the 100-yard team placement trials. On that gloomy humid Thursday afternoon, the blue gazelles not only outpaced him by at least 50 yards, but Tony managed to knock down every hurdle along the way and clumsily careened over the last one skidding to the ground into the biting black cinders. The sharpness of the cinders did not hurt as much as the laughter of the gazelles.

Monty then called him over. "Listen son, you sure tried hard and gave it your best all these weeks, but frankly I don't think you're made for running. You are wasting my time and yours. Your legs are too heavy; you're built like a plow horse. You will never be runner.

Danny pleaded, "But I just need a little more time. You've never cut anyone. I don't need to compete, but just want to be on the team. ..."

"Son, you're already a senior, you have no more time. You're too old to improve. It all downhill from here on."

"But please just..."

"I said you are wasting your time and mine. And yes I'm cutting you. You should at least proud as being the very first to cut someone." Laughing.

"Now please leave and let me get back to the team. Take it from me kid try something else, you'll never be a runner."

In shocked silence he headed alone to the locker room. Monty's words reverberated in his head, "you'll never be a runner", burned into his soul again and again. But even worse was the thought that he had been the first ever to be cut by Monty. This would soon get out and circulate among all of his classmates.

THE LAUGHTER OF THE GAZELLES

"You'll never be a runner". In the locker room, by himself, those words burned into his soul, again and again. Someday he would show Monty; he would show them all.

He showered and changed quickly in the hope of avoiding the gazelles in their return from practice, but no such luck. The locker room door banged open with raucous shouts and the sounds of spikes meeting the concrete floor. Most avoided looking at him, since Danny represented all their greatest fears, that of not being good enough for what you tried to do. Not to be a part of and belong. not to fulfill the expectations of others, not to let them down. To continue in a self-confident belief system that was programmed into you by your parents, trainers and teammates. Just to be caught in a web into which you were programmed by society to excel, to succeed, to not end up as a Danny. How dare he even occupy the same locker room as the victors? This vanquished phantom that by his very presence insulted what they were, what they stood for, and what they most feared to be.

Ryan approached him just before Danny attempted to leave unnoticed. "What happened?", Ryan asked blocking his move to the door. "You're not quitting are you"?

Blinking back the tears, "I have no choice. I was cut".

"Why Monty would never cut anyone, He never has...", Ryan stopped when he realized by the tears in Danny's eyes it indeed had happened.

"Well at least I just set one new school record for being the first. Gotta go, see you", Danny turned and walked toward the door.

Ryan followed, "Danny, believe me, there are more important things in life than making this damn team. They'll be other races for you, take my word for it. Wait for me and we'll go get a soda." But Danny was through the doors and gone. He had even left the grey sweats laying on the floor that symbolized his failure.

"Cut by Monty. Nobody is ever cut by Monty", laughed Darin the number one sprinter. Everyone else joined in the laughter, except Ryan who confronted him. "You assholes are just lucky. I wonder which of you would have had the guts to stick it out as long as he had to. Which of you could have tolerated that amount of humiliation from that cunt Monty?" He picked up Danny's grey sweats and threw them at Darin. "Wear these and see how they make you feel, you stupid insensitive shit."

Darin threw them back at him, "What the fucks gotten into you man?"

Ryan grabbed the sweats and his bag and stormed out of the locker room. Outside he looked for his friend but Danny was gone.

Can one's entire self-esteem and dignity be controlled by the actions of one coach? Can it be so simply interwoven in the felt letter "C" awarded to the champions of Columbia High? If so then was it that part of the explanation why the victors with the "C" guaranteed them access to the best universities, professional schools, jobs and mates.

Ryan never found Danny again who would not answer his calls. Danny heard that Ryan won a track scholarship and went away to one of the best Universities in the East. Then later on to medical school. Then married a woman who was a former stripper.

Danny graduated high school and went to work in the local Ballantine Ale beer bottling factory in Newark New Jersey. He attended night school and eight years later, like the proverbial whipped dog that returns to his master, he took a job teaching history at his alma mater, Columbia High School.

While Monty was gone, the memories weren't. He was reminded in the fall, as he drove past the football field and heard the drumming of helmets and pads against the sled, in winter the staccato of the basketballs on the polished gym floor, and of course the spring time firing of the starting gun as the gazelles left their puncture marks on the cinder track.

Yes, he was indeed an underdog for all seasons.

The Dream Shop

Danny pushed open the door and swung his white tipped cane in rapid semi-circles, like an insect probing the recesses of it's dark dank world for any hint of danger while in search of food. He was greeted by the tinkle of a bell overhead and the heavy scent of lycra and polyester. A familiar smell that once greeted him with the blaze of rainbow racks lined with shorts and singlets, and the color-ful array of shoes stacked up along the walls like colorful butterflies impaled on a velvet mat. First hearing footsteps cushioned by run-ning shoes making their nearly soundless imprint.

"Hi, can I help you with something?", the salesman said. The voice was young, and Danny figured him to be in his late teens or early twenties.

Danny extended his hand and said, "Hi, I'm Danny. I teach at Columbia High School and I'd like to buy a pair of running shoes". The youth shook his hand and introduced himself as Jason. Danny could tell that the person on the other end of this hand was not only a salesman, but also an athlete, maybe a runner. The hand was lean, the grip strong, and he surmised that Jason was perhaps no more than 5% body fat at most. A Gazelle.

"Sure, I'd be glad to help you. What size shoe does the person take"?

Taken slightly aback, Danny shrugged looking down said, "Well actually there're for me."

"Oh", humbly, "I'm sorry, I didn't mean to imply..."

"No need to apologize. I guess you don't get too many blind runners".

"Well no we don't, but I sure have to admire you", Jason stated a little guiltily. "What did you have in mind? We're having a sale on all our models of walking shoes?"

Danny decided to ignore the last insult. "I want to see the Evanar 5000, do you have it in a size ten?"

Jason hid his surprise and figured this person wasn't acquainted with the price of this top of the line running shoe. It would be a waste on anyone but the most elite of runners, and certainly overkill for someone on just a walking program. "We do, but it's $145 plus tax, but I can show you some excellent alternatives that are made specifically for walking and there're a heck of a lot cheaper."

"No, it must be the Evanar. It's for a very special event, the New York Marathon." I'm running it this year, so I want the very best you see."

"I'm sorry, I just didn't realize", Jason said. "Is this your first?"

"No, actually my twelve, but my first without my sight. I've got this close friend who is going to lead me. I'll keep one hand on his shoulder and he'll get me there.

Jason thought how could this blind man have trained the countless hours and miles to complete the entire 26.2 miles. He well he knew of the endless hours on the road in all kinds of weather and at all hours of the night running through fatigue, sickness and hell to log the miles necessary to even complete that distance.

He knew the toll that distance takes first physiologically, then mentally at the dreaded wall, when at about 18 miles, the body is depleted of all glucose and glycogen and begins to burn fat as its only fuel. This produces ketoacidosis in the blood, a condition that alters the bloods tight acid base balance to near lethal levels. Coupled with dehydration and mineral loss, causes the legs to cramp and to slow as muscle synapse fail to trigger.

At 20 miles the will starts to go, and if the training has been sufficient, then like a horse heading back to the barn, the body continues on pure instinct alone. Instinct tempered by those countless hours and miles of preparation.

Those who, must wonder why does any human need to cover 26 miles 385 yards on foot? Why? Because of all sporting events, the marathon is unique.

Nothing irritates a marathoner more than when non-runners ask, "just how long of a marathon was it?" A marathon is not just another long run, but an Olympic event of 40 Km or 26.2 miles. All marathons are that exact same distance regardless when or where they are run.

This accounts for the second unique aspect of the marathon, the fact that it is nearly unequalled in its physiological and psychological demands. There are longer runs and even triathlons where a marathon is added after a 2.4-mile swim and a 122-mile bike ride, but these events are not for the plow horses, but for those genetically endowed. With the exception of others like the Boston marathon which has a qualifying time to even compete, the New York City Marathon is one of very few worldwide where the plow horses and the disabled can compete in the exact same event as world class runners.

The Gazelles finish in just a little over 2 hours, while the Danny's are still running five hours and longer. It is the plow horses and the physically challenged, such as those of the Achilles club, that have to pull from something deeper, because they have no chance at prize money, rewards or ranking. They run with just the pride of knowing that they went ran the same course and went the distance as their heroes who finished hours before. And despite their physical limitations, they have accomplished a feat that less than 1% of a healthier and more youthful population could not do. They do with tools denied gifts to those who don't even have the will to try.

Finally, the marathon transcends the passage of those miles, and transforms their very lives before and after. Marathoners carry with them the same courage and determination in all the challenges that life throws at them, a will tempered and honed by that 26.2-mile odyssey.

Danny tried on the shoes and knew they were perfect, just enough support yet light at 9 1/2 ounces. Jason put them in a bag and rang it up. "That'll be $151.52, including the tax, but let's call it even at $140," laughing, "Unless you have a corporate sponsor?"

Danny laughed, "No, at least not yet"

"Well maybe after you break the record at New York in your age group", Jason quipped.

"Thanks Jason, I really appreciate it". Then Danny counted out what he thought was seven twenty dollar bills, all that he had in his pocket. Jason noticed that two of the bills were tens, leaving him 20 dollars short of the reduced price.

Danny sensed a hesitation after he handed him the money. "Is something wrong, Bob. Isn't it all there?"

Jason looked at him and thought of the odds this poor guy faced every day of his existence from now and until forever. Yet he ran, still dared to hope, and dared to dream. Jason thought of the two work-outs he missed this week because of, what was it? the weather, fatigue, no time, too busy, too hot, too cold, too dark, too ... damn lazy. He had the gift, this man before him did not. How dare him not use it. How dare he insult and rebuke the gift that had been given him.

"No", Jason said, determined never to miss another workout or take for granted his gift of speed and endurance, "You have the exact right amount. Good luck in your race. In all your races. These shoes have that new polymer so they'll last you well beyond your marathon."

Danny half smiled, "Just getting me through the New York will be enough."

Laughing, "You already talking retirement?"

"In a way". Danny knew these shoes would be used for only this one last great event to take him as long as he could then back into the world of the light and freedom he once knew. These were his freedom shoes.

Danny nodded, "Well thank you for all your time and all you've done for me. I must get back to my training if I hope to break these in before the big day arrives."

Jason thought to himself, "And thank you for all you've done for me".

Danny turned beginning the antler-like movements of his probing cane in the direction of the front door.

When his cane abruptly reminded him of the portal, he turned to Jason and asked, "Oh, by the way, I almost forgot, just what color are the shoes?"

"I'm sorry, I should have told you. There're silver. Silver with red stripes."

A warm tearing vision momentarily stirred in the blackness of his mind of the tragic useless end of his support dog, Silver.

"Silver?", Danny mumbled, "Yes of course there're silver. They had to be silver."

"Best of luck with the shoes and with New York. They'll get you to the finish line, I promise".

Danny turned smiling, "and you said beyond?".

"And beyond", said Jason not realizing the significance of his statement, and as he watched the lone figure pass through the door, the small bell overhead echoing a lonely knell.

SILVER'S GUIDE INTO OBLIVION

It was just another hot humid day with Silver, Danny's guide dog leading him by its rubber collar. The dog's pace matched the rate that Danny ran having done so since his master qualified for such an animal. Silver was a blue eyed white huskie, genetically used to colder climes, and so often cantered with his tongue hanging out salivating in this his heat.

Silver suddenly stopped his pace and Danny felt the abrupt halt through the handle. He knew that the dog would never halt unless he sensed some sudden obstruction in the way.

"Well, well what do we have here?" A voice mocking him from the front.

Another voice, but now from behind, "Give it up freak. All of your money or we cut you good."

Silver turned trying to lead Danny away, but his master was surrounded on all sides and even by a third thug.

"But I carry no money. I have no need too." Secretly hitting an emergency 911 button on his belt that sent out a signal to the police and gave his location.

"Well then maybe we will just take your puppy then. I'll bet it's worth some bucks to someone or maybe a ransom by you even." all laughed. "Well give it here, and we'll give it a nice home."

Danny pleaded while stalling for more time, "You don't understand, these dogs are trained to run with just one master and ...." He was cut off by the wailing sound of police sirens.

"Well then since it will be useless to us anyway, lets end it now."

Danny heard a loud yelp and dropped to his knees grabbing for Silver, as he heard the rapid footsteps of the thugs running off. He felt the warm and copper smell of blood filling his hands and was at least glad that Silver had gone quickly. Danny cried at the cruel injustice of this world, and the way only the innocent seem to suffer. It was too late to obtain another animal with his last lap now approaching.

The police arrived with animal control. Danny asked if he could keep Silver's harness, which they handed to him, and after one last petting of his dog, they took him away.

One of the officers asked, "Can you please give me some description of the assailants?"

Danny just answered, "Look at me. How can I?"

BOOM BOOM BRIANA

"Have you lost your fucking mind?", Rachelle yelled jabbing her finger at her husband Ryan.

"Not since this morning, but I finally found it."

"Don't be such an asshole. Don't you know that assisted suicide is illegal in this State?

Shaking his head, "Well not with an Advanced Directive. I've pulled the plug on many at the request of their families and…."

"Oh and I'm sure Danny has a Directive. You know he can't survive and what you're planning and is nothing short of murder. That in the eyes of the law is medical malpractice making culpable. So you are risking to threaten your entire career on this death run? "

"It's not a death run. He may survive."

"Bullshit! You know he wants to end it this way. So why?"

Angrily. " Why? I'll tell you why. Because I would ask the same of him. That's why." Turning and walking away, "I can't believe I fell for someone with such a ridged mindset as you."

Smiling wickedly, "Oh it wasn't me that got ridged, but it was you and once you saw these." Shaking her corpulent breasts, then turning and wiggling her ass in a bump and grind with a head turning toward him. "Get some. Get some. Stuff those 50's into my G strap big boy."

Ryan laughed remembering the night he first saw her on stage, and even more of the private lap dance that sealed his fate and eventually marrying her.

"While in college how did you ever pull that off with your father, Boom, Boom?"

"Well you know what a tight ass he was about money. So I told him I would add to his allowance by working part time in the Library. I needed more cash for drugs and booze."

"So how did he find out?"

"He was so glad that I was making some of my own money, and it all was going great until Sanchez a friend who had seen me strip, visited him. My father was so proud of me he bragged that I had gotten a job working in the library."

"And then?"

"Sanchez says, oh you know about it and approve? My father says why not? When Sanchez tell him it is the hottest strip joint in Richmond, my father screams, a strip joint! that is a father's worse nightmare and then guess what?"

"He leaves Virginia Beach one night and drives to Richmond to pay you a visit?"

"Yes so there I was strutting my stuff to Shoo, shoot me tonight, shaking my tassels, and doing the credit card swipe with the stage pole between my cheeks. Then hanging upside down on the pole and tossing my top to the crowd I saw him."

"And then?"

"I dropped right on to my head."

Laughing, "So I assume your career ended that night?"

"Yes, and it was good we had already met. So love, this Boom Boom Briana now only dances for you."

"Well I'm glad" remembering their prior conversation, "Even if we don't always see eye to eye. "

"That's only because of your obstinate overly logical OCD mind. But maybe I can bring you to my point of view with these." Shaking a pair of her pink thongs. "Remember these?"

Shrugging, "Well of course I do. You wore those the night of our first lap dance Boom Boom. You mean you had those all this time? "

"Yes I did in case I needed to change your mind about anything."

"Well Boom Boom, that's really playing it dirty."

Running a seductive finger across her red glossed lips, "Yes love, just the way you like it." Beckoning him to follow her to the bedroom.

THE MERCI FUCK

Titty Trish was ugly enough to go out with me. I really needed to lose my virginity. Something my mother's intervention would always made sure I would never do. Trish was very popular because of her easy ways as the jocks liked to refer to her as they passed her around in the parking lots at parties. But to have her it was best to keep your eyes closed. She had an ass the width and size of a handball court, built short and stout as a football center and was nearly bald with jagged teeth looking like a Jack o Lantern.

One day I casually sauntered over to her locker which was open and I could catch the waif of salami and skunk. "Hi Trish, would you like to go to a drive in movie with me this Friday?"

She scrunched up her bilious face and said, "What the fuck for?"

"Well to see a movie of course."

"Okay but you are going to have to feed me and feed me well."

I nodded not knowing how true those words would be.

We parked and I rolled down my window part way to attach the speaker box. The movie, a Marx Brothers flick dull enough to insure many romantic couplings throughout the drive in.

It had not started but a black and white cartoon did showing a jackass running head first into a tree and as its eyes made wild gyrations in opposite directions. Titty roared in laughter pounding the dashboard, and I wondered why.

Even before the second cartoon started I was startled by a gum chewing well breasted girl on roller skates. "Take ya odder sweets?"

"Well no. I don't think we…."

Titty just chortled, "Don't be such a cheap fuck. If you spectin to get laid you better gimme that menu." Snatching it from the girl.

I just held my head as she ordered everything on the menu than told Missy roller derby to double it.

"Shu ah hon, ahs be back in a jiff."

When the food arrived, I could hear the chin ching of a cash register as I peeled off each bill. Titty Trish just didn't eat the food, but used both hands to stuff it into her mouth. More snorting than chewing, she would belch loudly and looking at me laughing.

Naturally I lost my appetite and thought just what some guys would do to get laid. And what's worse, I wasn't even attracted to this pachyderm, but only wanted the bragging rights to tell Ryan I had actually done it. Ha ha.

The movie finally started and as the lights dimmed, I did the yawning one arm slide over to her side of the seat and put my hand on her shoulder and pulled her to me.

"Just what the fuck do you think ya doing wise guy? "

"Well I thought maybe just a little finger play?"

"Ok, but make it quick. I don't want to miss this movie."

Surprisingly she lifted her flabby ass leaving a sweat spot and pulled her panties to her knees and spread her tree trunk thighs. In a crazed attempt to get an erection before the movie took back her attention to Manny, Moe and Joe slapping the shit out of each other, I asked her if she could stroke it until it got hard.

She smirked, and began a rhythmic disinterested stroking, more like churning a tub of butter.

But try as I might I could not obtain an erection to which she laughed, "What's the matter stud? You queer or just a freak? Boy you spectin to git laid you better give me the hard pool cue or else."

Pulling up my pants and totally humiliated, I pleaded, "It's because of my diabetes…"

"Dia Jes ease! What the fuck is that? You are either a fucking fag or freak and what until I tell all my friends at school I went to a drive in with a freak." Laughing, "Now take me home Mister queer freak.'"

After that night and walking the halls the next day with the murmurs and stares, the word had certainly gotten out.

Danny never tried again despite attempts by Ryan and Bianca to fix him up with friends or prostitutes.

GETHSEMANE

No one really sleeps the night before a marathon. Like Jesus in the Garden of Gethsemane the night before his crucifixion, you pray for hope from above not to have to endure what was soon to be. Yet knowing only to face it would free you both with the dawn of a new life.

Like Jesus dragging his cross on the way to Calvary, Danny boarded the bus to Staten island for the start of his own destiny.

EULOGY AT THE PALLISADES

Ryan sat on a park bench in the pouring rain in Weehawken, New Jersey, where they had taken Danny's body for an autopsy. He starred teary eyes at the Twin Towers across the river with Briana holding Danny's crumpled number in her hand. She read off the names the names Danny had written on the back of his number. First was his precious lost dog Silver, then a litany of names of those he knew, both the good and the not so good, but all those who had made and impact on his life. First his students, Cameron, Bobbi, Booker, Tonya, and Becka. Remembering the transition, they all made and how they grew under his teachings.

Then his friend Ryan who carried him through his final dream and beyond. Reading with tears, her own name Briana , then Jason who sold him his silver shoes, and even those who had humiliated him, Titty Trist, Darin, all those laughing Gazelles, and yes, even Monty. Where he was going there was no time for resentment.

Ryan said " had I done the right thing? Why did I so willing agree to end the life of the best friend I ever had? "

Brianna leaned on him rain dripping from her cornered hat,,

"Sure at first I was opposed to it, but in retrospect, if you had been in the same situation, I would have asked someone to grant you that wish also."

"But these thoughts will haunt me the rest of my days."

"Not if you think how terrible his end would have been if you hadn't helped him.

"I have an idea, come with me to his school. I have one more act to do for my lost friend. "

"What?"

Grabbing Danny's number and Silver shoes they drove to Columbia High School in Maplewood, New Jersey.

A PLACE AMONG THE
GAZELLES

In the trophy case in the gym at Columbia High School all of the retired jersey's and trophies of the greats athletes the school had ever know was now one centered in the very middle.

The engraved plaque read: "DANNY GIORDANO, FORMER TEACHER HERE AT CHS, RUNNER AND VICTOR IN THE NEW YORK CITY MARATHON." Around the plaque was his ribbon and medal commemorating the event and his sweat stained runner's number. And laying at the bottom? You guessed it. His Silver Shoes, and Silvers black harness.

THE END

www.ingramcontent.com/pod-product-compliance
Lightning Source LLC
Chambersburg PA
CBHW030932020726
47498CB00001B/218